D0958925

DARING *Their* HEARTS

A NOVEL BY SHARLENE MACLAREN

WHITAKER
HOUSE

All Scripture quotations are taken from the King James Version of the Holy Bible.

THEIR DARING HEARTS

Sharlene MacLaren
www.sharlenemaclaren.com
sharlenemaclaren@yahoo.com

ISBN: 978-1-62911-930-4
eBook ISBN: 978-1-62911-931-1
Printed in the United States of America
© 2018 by Sharlene MacLaren

Whitaker House
1030 Hunt Valley Circle
New Kensington, PA 15068
www.whitakerhouse.com

Library of Congress Cataloging-in-Publication Data
Names: MacLaren, Sharlene, 1948– author.
Title: Their daring hearts / Sharlene MacLaren.
Description: New Kensington, PA : Whitaker House, 2018. | Series: Forever
  freedom series ; 2 |
Identifiers: LCCN 2017050546 (print) | LCCN 2017053855 (ebook) | ISBN
  9781629119311 (E-book) | ISBN 9781629119304 (softcover)
Subjects: | BISAC: FICTION / Christian / Romance. | FICTION / Christian /
  Historical. | GSAFD: Christian fiction. | Love stories.
Classification: LCC PS3613.A27356 (ebook) | LCC PS3613.A27356 T455 2018
  (print) | DDC 813/.6—dc23
LC record available at https://lccn.loc.gov/2017050546

1 2 3 4 5 6 7 8 9 10 11 **ய** 25 24 23 22 21 20 19 18

Dedication

This marks my eighteenth published novel. So far, I have dedicated each specific work of fiction to someone significantly special to me—my husband, my children, my grandchildren, my family, my friends. However, I have not once dedicated any of my works to the most important person in my life: my Lord and Savior, Jesus Christ—the One who first inspired me to write; the One who, one night after I'd passed the "halfway point" of my life (age fifty-two), planted in my mind a dream that I had written a novel. Initially, I didn't acknowledge Him as having prompted the fanciful vision. In fact, I dismissed the dream the next morning, thinking it far-fetched. Me, write a novel? Surely not. The last time I'd dabbled in fiction writing was as a teenage eleventh grader. The whole notion was plain silly.

It took several more similar dreams for me to finally take note. Next thing I knew, a plot started pitching around in my head. I plopped myself in front of my computer and started plunking away at the keyboard, and, just like that, a seed of passion took root—and flourished in a way I'd never imagined possible. I was going to be a writer!

That was in the summer of 2000. Now, eighteen titles later, I'm finally dedicating a book to the One who gave me the gift of writing.

Thank You, Lord Jesus. Thank You for speaking to me—even when my ears are not fully in tune with You. Thank You for loving me—even when my heart and mind are not fully engaged with You. Thank You for accepting me—weak, damaged, imperfect. You give me strength, You make me brave, You complete my being, and You amaze me. I know that some glorious day, I will meet You face-to-face; and when I do, I shall fall on my knees in gratitude and praise.

1

July 1863 · Philadelphia

Josephine Winters! What do you think you're doing?"

The strident whisper caught Josie off guard, and she whirled at the sound. "Go back to sleep, Allison. I didn't mean to wake you."

"What are you doing?" the girl asked again.

Josie clamped shut the valise in which she'd packed the barest of necessities. "I'm doing it, Allison. I'm joining the army."

"You are not!" Josie's cousin threw off her covers and leaped out of bed, then hugged herself in the chilly air coming in the open window. The flickering flame of the bedside lamp casted a long shadow along the marred wood floor of Allison's small frame dressed in her tattered long-sleeved nightgown.

"I am, and you can't stop me."

"You can't join the army. You're a woman!"

"Shh. I'm not joining as a woman, Allie. I'm joining as a man."

"A man?" The girl shifted her weight from one bare foot to the other. "And how do you propose to do that?"

"Well, for starters, I shall cut my hair short. I'll rub my face and fingernails with dirt, and I'll dress in Andrew's clothes, including his straw hat and work boots. I'll pass just fine, and then the army will issue me a man's uniform and a new pair of boots."

7

Allison crimped her pretty brow and tilted her face. "It's going to take a lot more than that to make you look like a man."

Josie refused to let her cousin's negative words deter her. "It will work. You'll see."

The rest of the house was quiet, but soon Aunt Bessie would start shuffling around in the kitchen, and the rattle of pans and clink of dishes would rouse Josie's other four cousins. She had to get going if she was to escape unnoticed.

"You have no idea what you're getting yourself into," Allison muttered.

"Maybe not, but I'll soon find out, won't I?" Josie took a deep breath. "I can't stay here, Allie. I'm only a burden. Another mouth to feed. I see the worry in your mother's eyes when I sit across from her at the table. Sure, I'm an extra pair of hands, but Aunt Bessie needs money more than she needs my help around the house. I'm nineteen. It's time I start taking care of myself." She straightened, stretched her five-foot-three-inch frame to its tallest, and stared her fifteen-year-old cousin in the eyes. "I'll make it just fine. I'm strong and sturdy."

"But…but why the army, of all things?"

"They'll take care of me. I'll get three square meals a day, and pay on top of that."

"But it's war, Josephine—a vile and brutal one. The reports are grim. Gettysburg was terrible. What if you get caught in a battle such as that? The Union may be winning, but the Rebs aren't about to surrender. Not yet, anyway. We've already lost Andrew."

Josie's stomach knotted. *Andrew*, her only brother. She swallowed a lump of emotion. "I'll keep my head down."

"But—"

"I promise I'll write you. The name I'm using is Gordon Snipp, so be sure you address your return correspondence to him. And don't include any details that might betray me."

"Gordon Snipp? How did you come up with a name like that?"

Josie shrugged. "A childhood friend of mine was named Gordon Stipp. I took his name and altered it slightly." Josie picked up her valise and turned to go.

"Wait." Allison snagged hold of her wrist and looked at her through pleading eyes.

Josie set the suitcase down again and hugged her cousin to herself while holding tears at bay. After a quick embrace, they both straightened. "I'll leave it to you to tell your mother. I can't bear to say good-bye to her or anyone else. In fact…." She reached into her pocket, grabbed a piece of paper, and thrust it at Allison. "I wrote this letter because I didn't want to say good-bye to you, either."

"What?"

"Please, just take it. I have to go. Thank your mother for me, but please don't give her the details of where I've gone—at least not right away. I don't want her getting any notions about trying to hunt me down and bring me home. I need to do this. I should've gotten out on my own before now, and I believe in the Union's cause just as strongly as Andrew did. I want to pick up where he left off. I feel almost obligated to finish what he started, in honor of his efforts. Please tell Aunt Bessie I appreciate all she's done for me over the years. When I start making money, I'll send some back to the family."

Allison took the letter from Josie and pressed it to her chest, her face long, her eyes moist. "I don't want you to die like Andrew did. That would wipe out your whole family."

Her pointed words of truth stung Josie to the core. She and her brother had been orphaned eight years ago when their parents had caught that awful yellow Jack fever. Amazingly, neither child had caught it, probably because some kindly neighbors had taken them in on a temporary basis. After Josie's parents died, it was decided to burn the house down, leaving Josephine and Andrew homeless—until Aunt Bessie and Uncle Clarence had rescued them. Bessie had probably felt obligated to do so, since they were her sister's children. Uncle Clarence had passed into glory last year, and Andrew had joined the army, in spite of his being underaged and inexperienced. With barely any time to train, he'd marched into the Battle of Drewry's Bluff in April of '62. A week later, two Union soldiers visited Aunt Bessie's farm and informed her that he'd sacrificed his life for the good of his country. They also delivered to Josie the bloodied sack containing his few possessions. Because his body had lain for three days before someone had found him, he'd been buried with half a dozen other soldiers under the shade of an old tree.

The cousins stood only a few inches apart now.

"Where are you heading first?" Allison asked somberly.

"The recruitment center on Market Street. It's only a couple of miles' walk from here. I saw an enlistment poster tacked to a post in front of Fred's Fish Market a month ago. I'm confident they won't turn me away, given how many were lost at Gettysburg."

Allison bit her lip. "You aren't scared? Of being killed, I mean?"

"I won't let that happen," Josie stated, as if she could read the future. "Like I said, I'll keep my head down. I need to do this. I feel it's the best way to honor Andrew's memory."

"Why can't you honor his memory in a safer way, say, by volunteering as an army nurse?" Allison's face wrinkled with concern.

"I cannot make any money volunteering, Allie. Please, try to understand." She forced a smile.

A period of painful silence passed between them. She'd said all she needed to say, and time waited for no one. She leaned forward and kissed Allison's cheek. "Give everyone an extra squeeze for me, and tell them I'll miss them."

"I will." Twin tears slid down Allison's face. "I'll pray for you, Josie."

"And I for you."

Without taking even a tiny glance backward, lest she change her mind, Josie picked up her valise and slipped out the door, then tiptoed down the staircase, purpose in her step, quiet resolve in her spirit.

⌒

Levi Albright quickly reread his latest letter from Mary Foster, then carefully folded it up and tucked it inside his sack along with the dozen or so other long missives she'd sent him over the past three months.

After closing his reticule, he crossed his outstretched legs at the ankles, lowered his cap just above his eyebrows, folded his arms over his broad chest, and leaned back against the trunk of an old tree for some day-dreaming in the shade.

He liked Mary, as much as a man could like a woman he'd never met in person. She was a good Quaker, as far as he could tell, and she'd started attending services at Arch Street Meeting House, where his parents and siblings attended, shortly after he'd joined the army. Levi's sisters all said Mary was sweet and pretty, and that he'd be a fool not to come home and marry her. Of course, they would say that; they would say anything in their efforts to convince him to leave the army and return to the farm. *Now.*

Quakers were pacifists, and he'd broken his covenant by joining the army. He wasn't the only Friend who'd done so. In fact, he'd met a few fellow Friends while serving, one of whom had died in battle. But Levi had stayed at home long enough, and after much thought and hours of prayer, he'd reached the conclusion that he couldn't just read about the war. He had to join the fight. And that was what he'd done, in late summer of '61—almost two years ago to the day. His brothers were old enough to handle the farm, so it wasn't as if he'd left Papa on his own. Lord willing, Levi's squadron would be mustered out in '64—unless the Union brought the war to a victorious finish before that—and he'd go back to the farm. Perchance he'd even end up wed to Mary. He'd already built a fine clapboard house on Sunset Ridge, a mile from his parents' home, roomy enough for a wife and children.

"Sergeant Albright, you're bein' summoned," said a voice behind him.

Levi jolted to attention and lifted his gaze to his friend and fellow soldier Jim Hodgers. "By whom?"

Jim grinned. "Who do y' think, Sarge? It's Lieutenant Grimms. Prolly gonna throw another one o' his fits. I just saw Captain Bateman and a few of his men leavin' the lieutenant's tent. You know how Grimms gets after the captain pays him a visit."

Did he ever. For some reason, no doubt due to Levi's calm demeanor and levelheaded thinking, Grimms always wanted to talk to him after being visited by the captain. Levi didn't relish the man's apparent reliance on him, or that the captain had promoted him to sergeant for his role in the Battle of Fredericksburg in December of '62. When he and the small unit of soldiers he was leading encountered a Confederate squad, he'd acted on impulse—Grimms had been too far up the line to consult—and charged the intruding Rebels, forcing them to retreat to the hills from whence they'd come. His initiative had paid off, precipitating a promotion for Levi from private to sergeant. He'd not felt worthy of the commendation, saying he'd only done what any good soldier would do. But Captain Bateman and Lieutenant Grimms insisted, the captain saying that brave, smart-thinking soldiers such as Levi would one day help lead the Union to victory. Levi hadn't joined the army in search of accolades, but he did believe in preserving the Union and helping to end slavery. If his superiors wished to sew another patch on his uniform, so be it.

He leaned away from the prickly tree trunk and stood, brushed the dirt from his army pants, and hefted his sack. "Thanks, Private. I'll go see what he wants."

Jim nodded and walked away. Levi watched him join a group of four privates playing cards, and then he set off for Grimms's tent.

He found the tent flaps pulled back, the lieutenant seated at his makeshift desk, writing what appeared to be a letter. When Levi gave a knock on the tent post, the middle-aged officer turned and gave a sweep of his arm. "Come in, come in. Here, have a seat." He pointed at the old tree stump in the middle of the tent.

Levi accepted the invitation. He figured he would be there awhile. "You summoned me, sir?"

"Indeed, indeed." Grimms pulled a cigarette from his pocket and lit it, then took a few puffs, blowing the strong-scented smoke in Levi's direction.

It was all Levi could do not to wave the smoke out of his face.

"Pity you don't smoke. It's good for the nerves, you know."

"My nerves are quite fine at the moment, sir."

"Yes, well, mine are not." He took a couple of more drags before blowing the smoke out. "Captain Bateman just left, and I'm hotter than a cooked hen right now—and it's not because of this blistering heat, either." He tossed his pen on his desk, then rotated his body to face Levi, his neck peppered with blotches, his cheeks above his graying beard redder than beets.

Levi maintained his composure. "What did he have to say this time?"

"Blast it, Levi, we aren't in this war to twiddle our thumbs. These men joined up to fight."

Levi actually believed a high percentage of them were fine just playing cards and checkers, whittling, and writing letters home. Any day they didn't have to march into battle was a good day, as far as he knew.

"You hear that?" The lieutenant tilted his sun-worn face to one side.

Levi stopped to listen, then nodded. "Sure do. Fighting in the distance. Sounds like some heavy artillery and musket fire."

"And we should be there. But, no, we've got more important things to do, according to Captain Bateman—such as guarding the rear of that lousy supply train for however long he chooses. Can you believe it? What does he take us for, nincompoops?"

"No, sir. I don't believe so, sir."

"He sure seems to." Grimms fired off a slew of cuss words, and the veins in his neck looked near to popping.

Good Quaker that Levi was, he'd never been one to use foul language, but he'd certainly had to accustom himself to hearing it in the throes of war.

"When do you suppose he's going to forget that little mishap at Salem Church?"

Levi bristled but tried not to show it. "I wouldn't exactly call it a 'little mishap,' sir. Several Union soldiers died when we mistook them for Rebs. We opened fire on our own men, sir."

"It was unfortunate, for sure, but it was a foggy morning, with dust clouds everywhere. Accidents happen, even in war. It doesn't make us bad soldiers."

"And you weren't responsible, sir. Those fellows were scared. They fired out of sheer terror."

"My superiors tell me I'm responsible. I'm always to blame for whatever happens as long as B Company is under my authority, Sergeant. That's the way of it. And the captain hasn't let me forget it." Grimms blew out a breath of air, and another big cloud of smoke came with it. "He takes pleasure in reminding me every time he sees me. If he weren't my superior, I'd tell him to go bury himself."

Levi bit back a smile. "That's a trifle extreme, wouldn't you say, Lieutenant?"

"Maybe. But that doesn't change the fact that I'm mad. We even had to remain in reserve at Gettysburg."

Levi hadn't minded that one bit. "Give it some time. We'll get a worthy assignment soon."

"Humph. I hope you're right. It's downright embarrassing, if you ask me, guarding the rear of the supply train, day in, day out—as if some Reb is going to come sneaking around."

"You never can tell, sir. It's happened before."

Grimms flapped his arm in disgust. "Well, I didn't call you in here purely for the sake of listening to me rant. Captain Bateman announced we're to welcome seven new soldiers to our company today. Hear they're a bunch of greenhorns."

"Weren't we all in the beginning?"

"True enough." Grimms shrugged. "Well, I'll expect you to add them to the roster and instruct the rest of the company to treat them with respect. Private Adams will document each man's specifics. He's been doing a fine job as company recorder, don't you think?"

"He has. You'll have yourself a nice book of facts by the time this war ends."

"That's the intent. Decades from now, folks will want to know all about Company B from the Twenty-third Pennsylvania Regiment. We'll make history yet."

"Yes, sir."

"There'll be drills first thing in the morning. I'm sure the greenhorns will need some guidance."

"I'll be sure to provide it."

Grimms put down his cigarette, took off his hat, and gave his head a good scratching, then plopped the dusty headpiece back in place. "How's morale?"

"As good as it can be, I suppose."

"Good, that's good. Army's done a lot of regrouping since Gettysburg because we lost so many. I expect the fighting will subside all around when we can muster up more soldiers. The government's put out a plea for new recruits, even offering some extra incentives—higher pay and better meals and the like." Grimms scoffed. "Better meals. That'll be the day."

Levi chuckled. "One taste of hardtack and they'll beg to go back home."

"Indeed." A brief smile, then Lieutenant Grimms turned back to his desk. "Well, I've got work to do." In other words, Levi was dismissed.

"I'll see to those new recruits when they arrive, sir."

"You do that."

Out of respect, Levi saluted, and then grinned to himself and shook his head as he departed the lieutenant's tent with nary a farewell from the man.

2

Josie's stomach roiled on the bumpy ride to who-knows-where. All she was certain of was that they were joining forces with Company B of the 23rd Pennsylvania Regiment, but she had no idea of their location or how much longer their journey would take. After two days of preliminary training in Philly, they'd started out, boarding a train to Baltimore. There, they'd debarked for a brief time before boarding another train bound for Washington City. They'd spent the night, being treated to a nice meal with a few hundred other recruits and given leather sacks of supplies, including a wool blanket, writing supplies, a canteen, eating utensils, a gun and cartridge box, and some winter clothing. This morning, they'd started out early, riding on a wagon bed and stopping occasionally to stretch their legs and to relieve themselves in seclusion. The latter proved to be Josie's biggest difficulty—maintaining her privacy so as not to reveal her gender. Thankfully, no one followed her into the wooded area she selected. At noon, they stopped for a sparse lunch, each of them getting one hunk of dry meat; two apples; a sort of tough, bread-like biscuit called hardtack; a chunk of cheese; and a cup of strong, cold coffee. As they journeyed, most of them—Josie included—lay down in the straw for a nap.

Of the six other recruits jouncing along on the trail with Josie, two were talkative; the others were more reserved, probably thinking the same thoughts as she: *What have I done? Where are we going? Am I going to make it out of this alive?*

"How'd you fellows come to enlist?" The question was posed by the oldest, who'd initiated most of the intermittent conversations during their journey. He had broad shoulders and a thick, graying beard; the visible skin on his face was tanned and furrowed, she supposed, from outdoor work. Had he left behind a farm?

Josie set her gaze on the hilly terrain and then cleared her throat. "I wanted to serve my country," she said, lowering her voice and speaking with a casual drawl to give it a manlier sound.

She felt the men's stares like ants crawling across her body, and it gave her spine a tingly sensation. Would her disguise hold?

Her questioner grunted. "So, you're runnin' away from home, too, eh?"

Josie glanced back at him. The burly man, who looked to be in his forties, picked up a piece of straw from the wagon bed, stuck it in his mouth, and chewed. The absence of a front tooth caught her attention.

"I...I ain't runnin', sir. Like I said, I want t' serve my country. My brother was killed last year at the Battle of Drewry's Bluff, so I'm takin' up where he left off."

The fellow's expression sobered. "That so? Don't that scare you? I mean, you could die, too."

"I ain't afraid to die."

"Well, that's somethin'. I thought everybody was afraid to die."

"I don't have a hankerin' to die, mind you; I just take comfort knowin' that, if I do, then it'll be for a cause I believe in."

The man tilted his whiskery face at Josie and squinted. "What's your name, young fella?"

She had to think for the briefest moment. "Snipp, sir. Gordon Snipp."

"Gordon Snipp, eh? Well, Private Snipp, let's hope you live to tell your family about it. If you got one, that is. How old are you, anyway?"

It was just the sort of question Josie had wished to avoid. "Old enough, sir."

The man gave a sly grin, as if he sensed her discomfort. "Well, we all got our own secrets, I s'pose. You underage?"

"No, sir!"

"How old are y', then?"

Josie kept her eyes averted. "I don't know why it should matter to you, but I'm nineteen."

"Pfff! If you're nineteen, I'll eat a handful o' straw." He grabbed a fistful of hay from the wagon bed.

Josie lifted her eyes and stared him down. "Start eatin', then."

He chuckled and threw down the straw, then fingered his messy beard. "Y' sure don't look it, but if you wanna say you're nineteen, we'll accept that. Won't we, boys?"

"Right," the rest said in unison.

She'd known this would be a problem, having a smooth complexion with not a single whisker.

"Well, pleasure to meet you, Private. Name's Harvey Patterson. Most call me Harv." He spit out the piece of straw he'd been gnawing on, then hauled a dirty hand down his scruffy face. "My wife died six months ago. I got no kids or family, so I joined up."

Josie blew out a quiet breath after the attention had shifted away from her. "Sorry 'bout your wife," she offered.

"Miss 'er every day," Harv muttered. "Figured war would keep my mind occupied." He scrutinized the landscape, where wildflowers grew with abandon. One of the wagon's wheels squeaked with every rotation. "How 'bout the rest of you men? What's your story?"

One by one, each fellow introduced himself, then gave a brief explanation of how he'd found himself in this wagon bound for the battle lines. Their responses varied from a strong desire for independence, to patriotism, to deep convictions about the war; one man said he wished to see as much of the countryside as possible, and enlisting seemed as good a way as any to do that.

Josie did her best to memorize their names, but her mind went blank at the sight of a dead soldier—a Confederate—lying on his back in a cluster of tall grass by the side of the road, his shirtfront nothing but one big red stain. She glanced at the soldier driving the wagon, but he displayed no alarm whatever. Josie wondered how long the corpse would lie there till someone came along to bury him.

An image of Andrew flashed through her mind, and she pictured—against her will—her brother lying on the hard earth days before someone had finally come along and put him in the ground. Her heartbeat quickened, and she swallowed down a wail that wanted to escape. To distract herself, she stared at the rolling hills in the distance.

"S'pect that's just the beginnin'," said the man who'd introduced himself as Hugh Fowler. "Might be we'll shoot a few o' them Rebs ourselves."

"I ain't shootin' anybody if I can help it," Josie blurted out. So much for keeping her head down, as she'd promised Allison she would do.

Harv laughed. "You will if one of 'em charges you. It'll be your life or his, and I 'spect you'll choose yours."

Josie couldn't imagine making that type of a decision. Then again, this was war. Perhaps she would come across a Rebel soldier and have no choice but to shoot him. Would she have the courage to pull the trigger? As she pondered the question, she picked up a piece of straw and stuck it between her teeth, just as she'd seen Harv do. It was a constant effort to feign being a man; the entire male manner of moving about, talking, sitting, walking, and gesturing felt completely unnatural. Her stomach growled from hunger, and she wondered when they'd get their next meal.

Toward dusk, the driver announced that they'd reached their destination. Everyone jumped to attention. "Just beyond that knoll up ahead, you'll see Company B's camp. There's a whole slew of other companies scattered about that make up the regiment, but you'll get real accustomed to your own company 'fore y' know it."

Josie craned her neck to see. Sure enough, as their driver maneuvered the team of horses up a crest, she spotted a settlement of soldiers.

Some sat around fires; some leaned back against tree trunks to read, write, or sleep; some lay sprawled on bedrolls; and some stood around smoking and talking. Two soldiers, who appeared to be on guard duty, raised their weapons at the approaching wagon, then quickly lowered them when they seemed to recognize the driver. They nodded their heads and stepped aside to allow the wagon passage, during which they surveyed the seven new arrivals, no doubt sizing them up and mentally deeming them a sorry sight.

"Here's where you soldiers get off," said the driver after pulling his horses to a halt. "Good luck to ya."

No one, not even Harv, uttered a single word. They all gathered their measly belongings and solemnly climbed out.

⌒

While the seven newcomers may have been green behind the ears, Levi gave the men credit for the immediate line they formed, followed by a salute, proving they'd paid attention during their initial training at their enlistment station. "Welcome to Warrenton Junction," he began. "In case you weren't aware, you're in the fine state of Virginia. I'm Sergeant Albright, but feel free to call me Levi. We're fighting this war together, so although I am your overseer, I hope you'll also think of me as a friend. Now, at ease," he told them, then proceeded down the line to shake hands with each one and learn his name and place of residence.

There was middle-aged Harvey Patterson from Williamsport, Pennsylvania; Hugh Fowler from Hazelton, a town east of Williamsport; two brothers from Butler, Pennsylvania, Henry and Joseph Gower; a kid by the name of Gordon Snipp, too young to grow a beard (and someone Levi intended to watch, half suspecting him to be a runaway); Anthony Fisher, a family man who'd left his farm to his older brother to manage; and, finally, a young man named James Galloway who was engaged to be married but, to his fiancée's chagrin, had decided to put off the wedding in order to fight for his country.

"I presume you were issued the standard supplies," Levi said to the bedraggled-looking group.

"Yes, sir, in Washington, sir," said Harv. "They didn't have enough tents, though, so they said they'd send some along on the next supply train if any of us wanted to bother with one."

Levi nodded. "I think you would find the tents rather heavy to carry in your packs. Most of us sleep on bedrolls spread out on oilcloth. There are usually extra blankets in the supply wagon."

"I packed a tent, sir," said Gordon Snipp. The lad thumbed over his shoulder at the sack strapped to his back, which looked a bit too bulky for a boy his size to be hauling around. Already Snipp was leaning forward under its weight. How would he handle a 15-mile trek? Levi decided not to bring it up, though. He'd learn the answer soon enough.

"We can discuss the sleeping arrangements later," he told the group. "Right now, I'm sure you're famished, so let's scare up some food for you. The rest of the camp ate a couple of hours ago."

They all trudged off through a wooded area, the grass stamped down from heavy foot traffic. Levi's wasn't the only company that had camped here over the past couple of years. He walked in the direction of the cook's tent, the others tramping along behind, saying nothing. He knew they were tired, but he also knew there was no sympathizing with them. This was war, and the hard truth was, none of them was guaranteed to survive. Not even he himself.

Moments later, Levi noticed several soldiers engaged in a fistfight about 20 feet to the left. He immediately changed course and headed toward the altercation, his new recruits on his tail. It was a hot, clammy night, so his guess was that tempers were short, and someone had said something to set the other off. The occasional brawl wasn't unusual, but he didn't feel right ignoring it.

By the time he reached the brawlers, a circle of onlookers had formed around them. Levi broke through the bystanders. "What's going on here?" he demanded, placing a firm hand on both men's shoulders in an effort to separate them. One was Chester Woolsley, a big, strapping fellow; the other was Hiram McQuade, a boisterous brute known as the bully of Company B. Both were red in the face, likely from a combination of heat and anger. "You fellas are supposed to be saving your energy for fighting the Rebs."

"He keeps calling me 'little mama's boy,'" complained Woolsley, an unmarried man in his twenties. Word was that his father had died when Chester was a boy, and the only child had never left his mother's side until his country had called him to serve under the Northern Draft of '62.

Although Woolsley surpassed McQuade in height and size, he was about as smart as a box of blocks, so McQuade easily had the advantage. Many times Levi had suggested to Lieutenant Grimms that they send Chester back home before he accidentally shot himself.

"The baby gets a binder full o' letters from his ma every week," bellyached McQuade, also in his twenties.

"And why should that matter to you, Private McQuade?" Levi could think of a few choice words to call the brute, but his Christian witness held them in check.

"'Cause he don't get no mail," someone from the crowd piped up. Brave soul. Rarely did anyone cross McQuade for fear of retribution.

"Well, this is no time for arguing over such matters, so drop it," Levi ordered. "Now, shake hands, both of you."

McQuade and Woolsley just stared daggers at each other, McQuade's jaw twitching, Woolsley's fists loosening and tightening at his sides.

Levi scowled. "Shake hands, or you'll both run the perimeter of this encampment twenty times."

After almost a full minute, Woolsley made the first move. McQuade followed suit, a sneer on his face, and they shook hands.

Once the air had cleared, Levi looked once more at his new recruits. "See what you're in for, fellas? It doesn't take much for tempers to flare, especially in this heat." Young Gordon Snipp's eyes grew round and wide, and Levi couldn't help but chuckle. "Don't look so worried, Private Snipp. These men will treat you kindly, or else they'll answer to me." Then he turned to the bystanders and said, "We're adding seven new recruits to our company, men. See to it that you introduce yourselves and make them feel welcome. You included, McQuade."

"Sure, sure. Welcome, one and all." McQuade spread his arms wide and looked each recruit up and down. Finally, his eyes came to rest on Snipp. "You're a little whippersnapper, ain't ya? You old enough for the army, boy?"

Snipp stretched to his full height, which wasn't much. "Sure am."

McQuade sniffed, his upper lip curling back. "You don't look it, but I'll take your word for it." To the rest, he said, "You men have a good time, hear? War is one big party." Then he turned around, cackling, and headed for his camping area.

"Don't mind him," Levi said to the recruits, shaking his head. "He derives pleasure out of making life miserable for others. You'll soon get used to him."

"In the meantime, most of us in Company B are good fellows," said Charlie Clute, a soldier who'd enlisted about six months after Levi. The two had become friends after discovering their common Christian faith, and they often shared Bible verses with each other. "We welcome your willingness to come alongside us and fight for the preservation of the Union."

Several others stepped forward to shake hands with the newcomers before dispersing to return to their camping areas.

Soon a clap of distant thunder warned of an impending storm. "We'd best get over to the cook's tent and find something for you fellas to eat so you can get back and stake out your sleeping spots," Levi said. "Tomorrow will be a busy day, and you'll want at least a few good hours of sleep before you go through our drills."

As Levi led them onward, he thought it would take a great deal more than just sleep to prepare these greenhorns for the demands of army life. What in tarnation had prompted such a ragtag group of men to enlist?

3

He raced through mud and muck, his boots splashing through puddles past his ankles. It couldn't be far now, not if he'd gotten his directions straight. The other side of the bridge would be his endpoint. Water dripped like a spigot off his hat brim, splattering his face and making it difficult to keep his eyes on the dimly lit path. Dimly lit, because he'd turned down the wick on his lantern to avoid detection.

He cursed into the blackness. Lightning bolts like a dozen crooked spider legs burned across the inky sky, giving his heart a tremendous jolt, but he didn't slow down. If anything, he ran all the harder, determined to reach his destination—the other side of an ancient bridge—before anyone discovered his absence.

These missions were growing more dangerous every day. One mistake, and he might well find himself hanging by his neck from a rope. Captured spies from the North and South alike had suffered the worst of all consequences for their traitorous activities. For him, the risk of hanging was worth it, since espionage was the best method he could think of to avenge the deaths of his parents and little brother at the hands of the filthy, murderous Yanks who invaded his family's Tennessee farm in March of '62 and pilfered anything of value they could carry. He'd been shot, as well, but it ended up being no more serious than a surface wound to the shoulder. He'd feigned his own demise, though, by lying on the ground in a twisted heap beside his lifeless brother, keeping one eye open a slit to watch the murderers' movements.

He'd later found out they were a crooked faction of Union soldiers who targeted defenseless, unsuspecting Southerners without the army's sanction, but that didn't matter. They'd planted an everlasting hatred in his soul for all things Northern, and as soon as he'd recovered from his wound, he'd started planning his revenge. He'd moved to Pennsylvania and joined the Union as a spy. He wore a Union uniform, but he was every bit a Confederate at heart, and his only mission in this war was to foil the Union's cause. Confederate heads employed him, for a trifling fee, to share secrets big and small; so far, he'd managed to aid the Southern cause without arousing any apparent suspicion from his company. Even Grimms trusted him with his life.

Coming upon a fork in the road, he stopped to do some quick thinking. Left or right? He'd destroyed the instructions sent to him via a covert contact, so he'd had to rely on memory for making the trek thus far.

Right. He remembered now from the association he'd made with being right-handed. He veered right and ran along the riverbed, the rain soaking his Union garb so that it sagged and clung to his body. He muttered another curse and lowered his face. He may as well have swum to his destination.

A good quarter of an hour later, he reached a bridge he hoped was the right one. He slowed to a stop, then bent over to catch his breath, panting like a dog. Then he straightened and assessed the structure. It looked pretty dilapidated, but he hadn't come this far just to have his courage stolen by a lopsided bridge. He stepped forward, his chest pounding with exhaustion, and set his right boot on the first board. It appeared able to hold him, so he settled his weight on it, then continued forward, one board at a time, slow and steady. The slicing raindrops pinged against his face and chilled him clear to his innards, but he pressed forward till he reached the other side. Through the torrent, he spotted a figure draped in canvas and huddled under a tree, a horse tied behind him.

His heart skipped. He was aware of the risks involved with these missions. For all he knew, he could be stepping into a trap. The figure stepped forward. No rifle was visible, but the fellow had to be armed.

"Hullo," said the monotone male voice.

His stomach churned. He said nothing, just nodded his head twice.

The fellow stepped closer. "What do you have for me?"

He raised his dim lantern to illuminate the Reb's face. It didn't ease his anxiety. "Bateman's courier reported to Lieutenant Grimms that the Twenty-third is making a move day after tomorrow," he said. "I overheard him telling our lead sergeant."

"That so? They know you were listening?"

"No, 'course not. Couldn't see me outside the tent. Tell your commander we're heading to the north fork of the Rappahannock. They'll be forming pickets to hold back Rebel forces. That's all I know."

"That's all, eh?"

"I don't know nothin' more. If I did, I'd tell ya."

"Fine."

He held out his open palm, and for a second, all the Reb did was stare at it, motionless. At last, he reached into his pocket, withdrew a small pouch, and plunked it into his hand.

He closed his fist tight around it. Feeling the coins through the rough canvas, he whirled around without another word and fled back across the bridge, mindless of the rickety boards, anxious to sneak back into camp unnoticed.

Another streak of lightning flashed across the sky, and Josie shivered, from fright as well as from a chill that shot clear through her body, starting with her toes. That there should be a thunderstorm, of all things, on her first night with Company B set her nerves on edge! Although she'd found a sheltered spot beneath a tree to pitch her little tent, water droplets found their way through a hole, and now her wool blanket was damp. Sergeant Albright had noted the rip in the roof of her tent when he'd passed by that evening and had urged her to bunk up with the others under one of the supply wagons. "If you're bound and determined to have a tent," he'd told her, "you can mend it tomorrow by stitching another piece of canvas over top of the tear. But for tonight, just sleep under the wagon where you'll stay dry."

"Uh, I'll be fine, sir, but thanks for the offer," she'd answered. No way would she sleep alongside any of the soldiers, if she could help it, lest one of them happened to bump against her in the night. Although she was a slender woman with barely a curve to her name, she did have a few of which, despite the coverage of her overlarge uniform, were hard to disguise.

A wave of guilt raced through her for the lies she'd had to tell to mask her identity, and she silently vowed to be as truthful as possible in the future. "Lord, help me to be a good soldier, though I be a woman," she whispered. "Make me brave in the face of terror, and help me stay focused so that I don't bring harm upon myself or any of my fellow soldiers. May I honor Andrew's memory, but may I also honor You in my service to my country. Help me, heavenly Father…help me. Amen."

Then she lay there, trying to find a sense of calm rather than alarm in the sound of the steady rain. Allison's image came to mind, along with those of the rest of her young cousins, and her chest squeezed with pain at missing them. What had Aunt Bessie said when she'd discovered Josie's absence? Was she rattled and worried, or was she more vexed and annoyed with Josie for leaving without warning? As soon as she received her first wages, Josie would send the bulk of her pay to Aunt Bessie, along with a letter of explanation.

Besides missing her cousins, she missed her long locks of wavy hair. For years, it had reached clear down her back, although by day she usually pinned it up in a tight bun or wove it into two long braids. She'd cut them off with a pair of long shearers from Aunt Bessie's toolbox before leaving the farm, but with no mirror in the shed for her to assess the job, she'd feared it looked horrendous. So, after passing muster with her recruiting lieutenant at the station on Market Street, she'd visited a local barber and paid him a nickel for a decent cut.

She frowned now while running her hand over the short bristles atop her head. A verse from her Bible that she'd read by firelight that very night before retiring now rolled around in her frazzled brain. It came from the book of Proverbs, and the wording stuck like glue in her memory: *"For the LORD shall be thy confidence, and shall keep thy foot from being taken."* As a blast of thunder made the earth tremble beneath her, she chose to repeat the verse over and over in her mind until it finally calmed her mind and lulled her to sleep like a babe in a cradle.

The next morning, instead of thunder, she awoke to the sounds of male voices outside her tent, and the peace she'd found before drifting off to sleep now flew out the slit in the roof. Even though the sun had not yet pierced the opening, she figured it must be time to rouse. She sat up, wiped her eyes with her fists, and pushed the damp wool blanket off. On her knees now, she moved to the door of her tent and drew back the flap an inch or so to see outside. A soldier was carrying pieces of wood to a fire that someone had started, while another fellow used his hatchet to chop a downed branch into good-sized sticks. Another fellow busied himself making coffee over the fire, and the toasty aroma wafted in her direction. Her stomach rumbled, and she couldn't help but think wistfully of Aunt Bessie's hot biscuits and gravy. Something told her there'd be nothing near as good as that dish for her breakfast this morning.

A quick glance in another direction showed Sergeant Albright striding purposefully toward the fire. My, but he was a fine-looking man, tall, strapping, clean-shaven, and—what was the word?—commanding. Yes, that was it—commanding, without being forceful. When the sergeant stopped to talk with the men busying themselves around the fire, Josie closed the tent flap and went about folding her damp blanket and rolling up her oilcloth. Would they sleep here again tonight or move on? She supposed she would find out soon enough. Right now, though, nature called, and it was imperative that she scope out her surroundings for a suitable area to see to her morning ablutions. *Lord, may there be a creek nearby. Please.*

Levi sipped on hot, bitter-as-gall coffee while chatting with a few of the men around a warm fire, damp logs popping and sizzling with orange flames. Last night's rain had cooled the air, to his great relief. He doubted anyone had caught a good night's sleep due to the thunderstorm, so there'd be plenty of grumbling when Corporal Willie Speer sounded the five o'clock wake-up call with his out-of-tune bugle. Bedraggled-looking soldiers would emerge from under wagon beds, sprawling oaks, and homemade shelters of sticks and leaves, and Levi pitied the fellow who would cross any of them. The few who'd slept in their own tents would be a bit better off, but not much.

He glanced up from the fire and, in the murky darkness, made out the figure of someone emerging from the woods. With squinted eyes, he determined it to be Gordon Snipp. The young fellow hefted his pants and adjusted his belt, bent down to retie his bootlace, then stood up and continued in Levi's direction.

"Hello there, Private Snipp," Levi called to him with a wave. "You sleep well in that storm?"

"Yes, sir, just fine. Thank you for askin'."

"How'd you fare with that rip in the roof of your tent?"

"Oh, it leaked some, but I managed to move over so the rain didn't fall directly on me. I s'pose plenty of fellows got soaked clear through, so I won't complain."

Levi liked the boy already. Snipp reminded him of his younger brother Milton, except that for Milton was a fair piece taller; and, from what Levi's sisters had told him in their letters, his voice had started changing. This lad spoke in low tones at times, with a higher pitch at others. Levi had plenty of questions for him, but he'd save them for later. Clearly, Snipp had his reasons for joining before the legal age of eighteen, and Levi intended to find out what they were in due time—once the boy came to trust him.

"Come on over here, young man, and sit yourself down." Levi pointed to a thick upright log the men used as a makeshift stool. "The fire's warmth will help dry your uniform."

"Yes, sir." Snipp sat and stared at the fire as if searching deep inside it for something more to say. He probably had his own host of questions to ask, and no idea where to start.

"We'll be drilling today, moving on tomorrow," Levi told him. "I talked to Lieutenant Grimms late last night, and he said a courier came in with fresh orders for us to march toward the north fork of the Rappahannock." He paused to study the boy's expression.

Snipp raised his head. "How far is that?"

Levi chuckled. "Let's just say it's a hike." No point in telling him they were in for a long two-day tramp over hill and through gulley. He'd find that out soon enough. "There's the possibility of picket duty, but I think it's unlikely. With so many companies in the Twenty-third, we'll be one of the last chosen."

"Picket duty?"

Snipp really *was* green. "A picket is a scattered line that moves in advance of the main encampment but within supporting distance. It's particularly hazardous, because the picket bears the brunt of the enemy's attacks."

When the poor kid's eyes bulged, Levi smiled reassuringly. "Don't worry. They rotate picket duty, and, like I said, we're not apt to be chosen. Still, the lieutenant says we're ordered to move on the slim chance they need us. We'll continue guarding the back of the supply train as we make our trek. That's our main task for now, until we hear otherwise."

"I see." Snipp nodded. "Well, I ain't scared, if that's what you think."

"I wasn't thinking that at all," Levi fibbed. "I'd say you're pretty brave just enlisting, and if anybody gives you a hard time or tries to convince you otherwise, you just come to me, you hear?"

"I don't need protectin'."

He was an independent young cuss, for sure. "You want some coffee?"

Snipp straightened his slim shoulders. "That'd be real nice, sir. My stomach's been makin' noises since I got up."

"Well, I'm sorry to say you shouldn't expect much for breakfast. Sadly, the number one complaint around here is never getting enough to eat." Levi picked up a tin mug from where it lay on the ground, filled it with brew, and passed it over to Snipp.

The boy made a slight grimace as he accepted the cup. He'd have to get used to drinking and eating off unwashed utensils.

"That's for durned sure," said Private John Cridland, who dropped two fresh-chopped logs next to the fire. "Most days, I'm so hungry, I could eat a wagon wheel if I didn't think the army would miss it."

Levi laughed. "We'd probably miss you before the wagon wheel, Private. You'd die of stomach splinters, not to mention indigestion."

He glanced at Snipp and found him smiling. The kid had a pleasant face when he turned up his mouth.

"I don't mind not having much to eat, as long as I don't starve to death," Snipp remarked.

"If you show signs of perishing, I'll offer you an extra portion of hardtack," Levi assured him.

"Which ain't much of an improvement over wagon wheels," Cridland put in with a chuckle.

"I know we went to the cook's tent to scrounge some food last night, but he generally prepares meals for the officers alone," said Levi. "How are your rations holding out?"

"Oh, I've still got quite a bit in my pouch. Hardtack, jerky, an apple…."

"You can always stop by the sutler's wagon and get yourself something from there to cook—that is, if you've an idea of how to do such a thing."

"I'm a good cook," the boy offered. "Decent, anyway."

"That so?" Levi raised his eyebrows. "Well, if news spreads about that, you're likely to get some company around your fire, myself included. Where'd you learn to cook?"

"My…my aunt taught me. I ain't as good as her, of course."

Levi was about to inquire further when Willie Speer sounded his ear-splitting bugle call, ending their casual fireside chat. "Excuse me, men. I'd best get back to my quarters. Roll call will be in ten minutes, and after breakfast, drills."

"Yes, sir," said Private Snipp, raising his right hand in a salute. The others offered only weak nods.

⁓

Nothing could have prepared Josie for the drills. They were confusing, frightening, and loud. She was no tenderfoot, though—she had experience shooting guns while hunting animals and could even hit a target square in the center from a distance. The challenge would be hiding the fact that the idea of shooting at people, Rebel or not, soured her stomach. Nor would she admit that cannon fire—the blank cartridges they used in drills—scared her nearly out of her britches.

For one drill, Company B and several other companies had engaged in a mock battle, half of them pretending to be Rebs. Everywhere she turned, there was deafening noise and blinding smoke. Although the exercise wasn't dangerous, it was entirely disagreeable to her ears, and more than once she found herself lying prone behind a tree, certain she was going to die. During one particularly heavy shooting spree, Private Howard Adams crawled over to her and hissed, "You're gonna die if all you do is lie there with your head stuck to the ground, boy. This is war. Get up and start actin' like it."

She must have gawked at him for some time, because rather than say another word to her, Adams snagged her by the arm, stood, and hauled her up beside him. "There! Now, shoot some Rebs." Before she could speak, he darted behind the closest tree and resumed mock-fighting.

At the sound of a gun firing nearby, Josie whirled, raised her rifle, and fired on impulse, hitting a "Reb." The fellow gaped at her for a moment, and then his eyes rolled to the back of his head before he dropped to the ground in a heap. Josie stared at him, dumbfounded, until he sat upright and grinned. "Good job, kid. Got me square in the chest." He swiped at his filthy pants, then leaped up and ran off in the opposite direction.

No sooner did he leave than Sergeant Albright scuttled up beside her, weapon in hand.

Josie's heart skipped a ridiculous beat.

"You're doing fine, Private. You learning the maneuvers?"

"I—yes, I sure am."

"Our gun crew chief, Corporal Vonfleet, tells me you're already adept at handling a weapon based on your training session this morning. Is that another skill your aunt taught you?" She noted the hint of playful sarcasm in his voice, accompanied by a slight twinkle in his eye.

"No, sir. My uncle taught me to shoot. I had to learn quick if I wanted supper."

"I see. Your aunt and uncle raise you?"

"Yes, sir. My parents died when my brother and I were real young. We were born in Norfolk, Virginia, but we moved to Philadelphia after they passed."

"I see. Well, I'm mighty sorry to hear about your parents. Must've been tough to lose them so young. My homestead's in Philly, as well. I grew up on a farm. My brothers are helping our pa keep things running there."

Mock gunfire persisted around them, but it barely registered with Josie in the presence of the sergeant. He lived in Philadelphia, too? It was a small world, indeed.

Just then, someone hollered for Sergeant Albright. He nodded at her, told her to keep up the good work, and rushed off. Another fake Reb fired at her, and this time, she cocked her rifle yet again, aimed it at his gut, and fired. He clutched himself and went down. "Gotcha," she mumbled under her breath.

That afternoon, Lieutenant Grimms ordered his company to clean their equipment and keep watch. According to trusted sources, several units of Confederate soldiers were drawing closer; even if no conflict ensued, it was wise to keep one's equipment clean in case of last-minute orders. Besides, he'd said, they were heading for the Rappahannock at break of dawn, and you never could tell whom you'd come across.

Chest pounding, Josie cleaned her weapon with diligence. A mock battle was one thing, but could she handle a real one so soon? Corporal Vonfleet issued everyone in Company B five rounds of ammunition, which, she knew from experience, wouldn't go very far. She prayed she wouldn't need it.

Thank God she didn't. The fighting, while it went on for some time and came quite close to where Company B was stationed, ended when another unit rode in and saved the day. Their horses pounded through a clearing on the other side of the woods from where Company B stood in formation, prepared to move forward, if ordered. Josie could hear the *pop-pop* of rapid musket fire, and the smell of burnt gunpowder drifted through the trees, singeing her nose.

When the shooting tapered off, Company B remained in position for at least another hour, until Lieutenant Grimms rode into the thicket and announced that the worst was over; they could return to camp. Never had Josie been so relieved. She really didn't wish to die on her second official day of service.

4

*L*evi marched along with his comrades as they fulfilled their usual duty of guarding the rear of the supply train. It wasn't too laborious a job; just about the only things they had to worry about dodging were the droppings of horses and mules. Meanwhile, if Grimms had his wish, Company B would be on the front lines, leading the entire Army of the Potomac to victory. Levi told him to be patient—their day would come, and then he'd wish it hadn't. But Grimms insisted, "We didn't join this army to guard the rear of the supply train. My men want to fight!" It never did any good arguing with the lieutenant. In fact, Levi figured he did himself a favor by keeping his mouth clamped shut most times. Grimms was a lot of talk, and Levi didn't mind serving as his sounding board.

The ground was sodden due to the storms they'd had the night before, and the men trudged through mud and mire for the better part of the morning, until Lieutenant Grimms rode back to tell Levi it was time to stop for the noonday meal. At his orders to cease marching, the soldiers loosened their haversacks, laid down their weapons, and found a shady spot to rest their weary bodies before digging into their food rations. Captain Bateman sent word by horseback to Lieutenant

Grimms that the regiment would set up camp near a stream later that day where men could bathe, if they so desired. Levi hoped everyone would take advantage of the opportunity. Some of the men in his squadron smelled to high heaven.

As Levi rested against the trunk of a tree, Howard Adams, Company B's official recorder, came up and hunkered down next to him. Two quarreling squirrels scuttled up another tree not ten feet away, then went out on a branch, the leaves rustling as they wrestled. "Just spoke with Jim Hodgers 'bout some questions for my journal report," Adams said, looking worried. "He don't sound too good. Private Morse don't, neither. Coughin' and sweatin' like crazy. I sure hope they aren't gettin' the ague that's been goin' around. Whatever's ailin' 'em, I hope I don't catch it. Or anyone else, for that matter."

"I'll have a medic check them over when we get settled this evening," Levi assured him, concealing his own misgivings. The widespread sickness could very well cripple their unit. The journey they'd made today had been especially tiresome, scaling hills, slogging through streams and thick woods, scrabbling over rocky terrain, and stomping through mud up to their kneecaps. And they were only halfway to their destination.

Adams nodded, and both men were silent for several minutes. A light breeze tousled Levi's hair, and he swept a grimy hand through it, thinking how good it would feel to bathe in the stream tonight.

"We made good time today," Adams finally said. "In spite of the circumstances."

"That we did. I'd say we marched at least ten miles this morning, maybe more. I'll admit I was mighty glad to get word that we were stopping for sustenance."

"I'll say." Adams stood and stretched, his knees cracking.

Levi grinned. "Aren't you a mite young for having rusty joints?"

Adams chuckled. "The army'll age you like nothin' else."

"True enough." Levi's stomach rumbled, so he opened his sack to retrieve the apple he'd been carrying for two days. It had turned a bit mushy, but he didn't care. It would tide him over until his next meal.

In reaching for the fruit, he managed to grab his latest letter from Mary, which he had yet to read. He unfolded the missive as he bit into the apple, enjoying the spray of tart juice on his tongue.

"I've noticed you've been getting a good deal of mail these past weeks," Adams remarked. "You sweet on somebody?"

Levi chewed and swallowed as he pondered how to answer. "There is a young woman," he finally conceded. "I haven't actually met her in person, but my sisters gave her my address, and I feel I'm beginning to get to know her through her lengthy letters. She is a fine Christian woman, from what I can gather."

"Well, I guess that'd be important to you. Me? I'm not much for religion, but that don't mean I don't respect those who take a different view."

Levi had often wondered where Private Adams stood when it came to matters of faith. Levi's aim was always to live in such a way that he pointed to Christ so that others would take notice and perhaps have a desire to do the same. As a member of the Society of Friends, he wasn't one to flaunt his faith but rather sought a life of quiet grace and devotion.

"What's the young lady's name?" Adams asked him.

"Mary Foster. I don't know what she sees in me. My life back in Philly is anything but exciting."

"Well, if she's a Quaker, I imagine it don't take much to excite her, right?" Adams winked.

Levi chuckled. "We Quakers may be known for living plainly, if that's what you mean, but we like to have a good time as much as anybody else."

He would've liked to say more, but a whistle sounded then, indicating their break had ended. Levi refolded the missive from Mary and finished off his apple. It was time for Company B to hit the trail again.

Nothing about the afternoon march was easier than the morning trek, so Levi made sure to fall out of line several times in order to go back and speak words of encouragement to the men, hoping to boost their spirits. He was especially pleased to find his newest recruits forming relationships and developing a sense of camaraderie. Harv Patterson and

Hugh Fowler kept up a constant chatter, Patterson spinning tales that made Fowler laugh. Anthony Fisher and Jim Galloway had chummed up with John Cridland and Levi's good friend Charlie Clute as the four moved along side by side. His youngest recruit matched stride with the others but said little, no doubt struggling to keep up under the weight of that tent he insisted on carrying. The poor kid's cheeks were redder than two fresh strawberries, but when Levi suggested he consider tossing the rolled-up canvas to the side of the road, he hefted it higher on his narrow shoulders, saying he was no sissy of a soldier and could manage it fine. At his smart remark, Levi gave him a swift nod and moved on, hiding his smile. Gordon Snipp had grit, to be sure.

They marched five hours, taking only brief breaks to rest, before the orders to stop finally came down the line. Once they reached the place where they would set up camp for the night, on the crest of a hill, sighs of relief flooded the air. The men shucked off their gear, and a few even ran down the hill to the flowing stream and dived in with their uniforms on. Thankfully, the sky bore no clouds, a hopeful sign of a good night's sleep—for those who hadn't been assigned to guard duty, that is. They would have to catch their winks tomorrow on the back of a bumpy wagon.

The first thing Levi did was seek out the smoothest area of ground he could find, where he quickly unfurled his bedroll and spread it out, claiming his spot. He noted Private Snipp doing the same—staking his claim on a nearby patch of soil, then methodically erecting his small tent.

"How'd you fare today, young man?" Levi called to him.

"Just fine, sir. I'll admit I'm a bit worn out, though."

"Well, I'm glad to hear you admit that, because I'd feel mighty silly telling you I was worn out if you weren't."

His remark earned a small grin from the boy, who turned his gaze down the hill to where the men were swimming. "That water looks inviting, don't it?"

"It does, indeed. Why don't you go on down there yourself? You can always pitch your tent afterward."

"Oh, no." Snipp shook his head. "I'll go later tonight—when it's not so crowded."

The kid was still shy. "I might do the same. Maybe I'll see you down there."

Willie Speer sauntered over. "You find your spot, kid?"

"Yes, sir," Snipp replied. "Did you?"

The corporal unloaded his gear and dropped it on the ground. "Sure did. Right here, next to you."

Levi detected the frown on Snipp's face before it fully emerged. He grinned to himself as he went back to preparing his bed. If anybody could crack the kid's outer shell, it would be fun-loving Speer.

Supper that evening consisted of a hunk of bread, a portion of jerky, two apples, and a big, juicy tomato. Because so many fruits and vegetables were in season right now, the soldiers ate far better than in the fall and winter. This would be Levi's third winter serving his country, and he well remembered how desperately hungry and cold he and his comrades had gotten last year, despite the government's best efforts to provide rations and extra blankets.

He refused to waste time worrying now about what was to come. Today had its own set of cares, and God alone knew how long this war would drag on.

⌣

After downing her supper, Josie settled on the ground, cross-legged, near the cozy fire she'd helped Willie Speer to build. She hadn't really wanted company, but Willie was an easygoing guy, even amusing, and she found herself enjoying his presence. He had a smooth, entertaining wit and could maintain a straight face while telling jokes, a skill she'd never mastered. Far be it from her to even remember a joke after she'd heard one, no matter how hard she may have laughed at it.

"Here's one for you," Willie said, staring into the fire. "What's the difference between the Prince of Wales and water from a fountain?"

Josie shrugged. "Beats me."

"The one is heir to the throne, and the other is thrown to the air."

Josie laughed, still working to keep her tone as manly as possible. "That's a good one. I think you could do better, though."

"Ah. Was that a challenge?"

"If you're up for it."

"All right, then. What's the difference between your greatcoat and a baby?"

"Don't know, but I'm sure you'll clue me in."

"One you wear; the other you was."

She frowned.

"Get it?"

She gave an exaggerated sigh. "I get it."

"Mind if I join you?"

The familiar voice made Josie's heart catch.

"Not at all, Sarge," Willie Speer said, waving his arm in invitation. "Pull up a log."

Levi planted himself on a log opposite Josie and grinned at her over the fire. "Has the corporal cornered you with his pathetic jokes? He's desperate to make people laugh. You do know you'll never get away from him once he starts."

"I'm beginnin' to see that, sir."

His smile widened. It was the first time Josie had noticed his sparkling teeth. In fact, it was the first she'd dared to really study his countenance—maybe because dusk had fallen, and she could afford to be a little sneakier. He had clear-cut features, a firm chin, and a square jaw, as well as thick dark hair and attractive eyes. What an awkward thing, playing the role of a man in the presence of one to whom she was attracted.

"Did you hear this one, Sarge?" Willie said. "What's a lady's least favorite tune?"

Levi grimaced. "I'm almost afraid to ask. What is it?"

"Why, the spittoon, of course."

Josie and Levi groaned in unison, but then they humored Willie with a laugh. My, how good it felt to drop her emotional barrier for a moment.

Their lighthearted banter continued until Levi excused himself to check on several soldiers who were being evaluated by the medic, to see whether they were up to the task of making the long trek planned for the next day. Shortly after his departure, Willie rose and stretched, then announced his need to go relieve himself in the woods. At his words, Josie felt her cheeks burn red, and silently thanked the Lord for the darkness of dusk.

Somehow, she had to accustom herself to the way men behaved. She'd been doing a lot of observing since enlisting a few days ago. Men walked with long, loping, athletic strides, so she'd been attempting the same, although apparently not with much success, since one soldier she didn't know had marched past her today and muttered under his breath, "You got ants in your pants, Private? You're walkin' like you do." Men also perspired profusely, spat on the ground, and gripped the lapels of their coat with both hands while conversing, standing with feet firmly planted at least 18 inches apart. When sitting in chairs, they often folded one leg over their opposite knee and clutched their ankle. Many of them also had the revolting habit of chewing or smoking tobacco, if they had the money for it. She'd made up her mind never to partake of that disgusting practice, and if anyone asked her why, she'd just say she didn't want to waste her money—a legitimate excuse, since she had so little to her name to begin with and had spent a fair portion of it on supplies from the sutler's wagon. Soldiers also had a dreadful propensity for cussing, something else she wouldn't entertain the idea of copying, no matter that she would probably stand out more as a result. She drew the line on certain things, cussing and making a smokestack of herself among them.

After the corporal left, she cast her gaze at the inviting stream. No one appeared to be swimming right now, so she gathered a bar of soap and a towel, then headed down the hillside. How good it would be to let the refreshing waters wash over her, even if she had to do it with her clothes on. After washing, she would put on her other uniform and hang this one out to dry overnight. The crickets' chirping and bullfrogs' croaking grew louder as she neared the stream, and she smiled just imagining these creatures cheering her on.

5

*B*irds twittered their pleasant morning melodies, stirring soldiers awake even before Willie Speer had a chance to sound the wake-up call. Sporadic coughs echoed through the camp. Last night, Lieutenant Grimms had ridden out to converse with Captain Bateman and Lieutenant Colonel Hughes, who had settled a few miles north with Company D. The lieutenant, of course, had hopes for a worthier assignment from the colonel than guarding the rear of the supply train. Levi would find out soon enough whether his superior's wish had been granted when the two sat down together for a routine talk. Of particular importance to Levi was the matter of the several soldiers apparently stricken with the ague. Levi had wanted to discuss this particular issue last night, but Grimms had returned to camp too late.

Speer and Snipp had built themselves another fine little fire, and Levi had been tempted to go over and partake of a cup of coffee with them, but he had to get to Grimms's tent. After a quick chat, Levi would do the roll call, and then B Company would begin another long day of marching. Fortunately, these late summer mornings were staying cooler longer; it wouldn't be long before September came upon them, and with it quite welcome autumn weather.

Levi meandered past several more fires surrounded by soldiers sipping mugs of steaming brew. Some looked up and saluted when he walked past, while others didn't so much as glance his way. Here and there, other soldiers moved about, rolling up their beds, rambling down the hill to the stream for a morning swim, or munching on hardtack, bread, chunks of jerky. It wasn't exactly a breakfast fit for a king.

Levi found Grimms standing outside his tent with a straight-edge razor in hand, trimming his mustache and beard in front of a small round mirror propped on a stack of crates. He muttered a hasty, cheerless greeting and gave Levi the tiniest glimpse.

"Morning, sir." Out of respect, Levi saluted.

"At ease," the lieutenant said. "How'd you sleep?"

"Fair."

"Humph. Same here. Even though I got a decent cot, it's missing the soft mattress that awaits me back home in Philadelphia."

"I understand, sir. We all want this war to end."

"It can't end soon enough, far as I'm concerned. So much for Lincoln's notion that the fighting wouldn't exceed four months! What's it been, now—two years?"

"A bit longer than that, I'd say." Levi cleared his throat. "I wanted to talk to you about this cough and fever that seems to be spreading through our unit."

"It's no better, huh?"

"I'm concerned about a few of the men in regard to their ability to march today—privates Hodgers and Morse, in particular. The medic assessed them last night and determined they both have high fevers and the shakes. Sergeant Wilson suggested they ride in a wagon bed today."

"Then that's what they should do."

"I'll see to it, sir. Is there anything you wish me to address with the company today before we march? Any new orders?"

"Orders are the same. Guard the rear of the train. Captain says when we reach the Rappahannock, he may issue new orders. I'm holding him to his word. Doggone sick of guarding the rear of the train when we could be doing something far more valuable."

"Someone's got to do it, sir, which tells me it's a worthy enough assignment."

Grimms rinsed his razor in a nearby pan of water, then wiped his face with a towel. When done, he folded up the cloth, set it on a table, and dumped the dirty water on the ground. A couple of soldiers came along and began dismantling Grimms's tent. He barely acknowledged them.

A short distance away, Speer blew out the morning bugle call, albeit playing out of tune.

Grimms groaned. "Why can't that fellow learn the proper way to play that thing?"

"You can't say he doesn't do a good job of waking everyone," Levi returned with a smile.

"Including every living soul this side of the Rappahannock," Grimms muttered.

Levi chuckled. "Well, if there's nothing more, I'll be going back to my camp. Roll call in ten minutes."

"Oh, Sergeant, there is one more thing." Grimms raised his index finger and stepped closer. "Captain Bateman says the regiment's chaplain resigned. Seems Private Morris's wife has taken ill, and he felt the need to return to her. He's agreed to stay on another week or so, until the army finds a replacement. Bateman wants to offer you the job."

Levi's body jerked involuntarily. "Pardon? He wants me to fulfill the role of chaplain? But I—I'm hardly qualified."

"Sure, you are."

"The President wants chaplains to be ordained ministers, which I am not."

"The President has more important things to concern himself with than chaplain assignments. Besides, the War Department recently approved a motion to allow regiments to appoint their own chaplains. Shucks, if you want ordained, I can tell you about a couple of ordained quacks that slipped through the cracks. At least we know you're legitimate when it comes to your faith—not that either Bateman or I are experts on religion or anything. We just happen to know you have the respect of everyone who's met you."

"Well, I appreciate your vote of confidence, sir, but—"

"You'll get an increase in wages, of course. While your rank of sergeant won't change, you'll be awarded with the pay and allowances commensurate with the rank of captain."

Levi couldn't help but lift his eyebrows a notch. "Is that so? Well, I didn't join the army for the money."

"Of course, you didn't. That's why you're such a valuable soldier. You're here for the right reasons. You'll still be in Company B, although you'll have to be prepared to travel a bit. We'll assign you a horse." Grimms made it sound as if he and Captain Bateman had already sewn up the deal.

"But I don't preach. Nobody does in the Society of Friends. We just speak as the Spirit leads us." Levi paused. "You should consider Charlie Clute for the job. He's a fine Christian and a good friend."

Grimms shook his head. "I plan to promote Clute to Sergeant. He can shoulder your duties, at least for now. You're more qualified for the job of chaplain than you think. The regiment needs someone of commendable character with compassion, strong faith, and morals. That's you, Albright. I'm convinced you're a praying man, too. I can't recall the last time *I* prayed. I guess it was in Gettysburg. The captain called us out of reserve to assist for a few hours, and I uttered a few nonsensical words while crouched behind Private Rowland's corpse for protection when some Rebs came charging at me…something like, 'Lord, give me proper aim; and if I miss, give that monkey-faced Reb an aim equal to mine.'" Grimms shrugged. "As you can see, I'm still here, so I guess He heard my sorry excuse for a prayer."

Levi didn't respond, so hung up was he on the idea of having to preach a weekly sermon. At Quaker First Day meetings, men and women alike expounded on various Scripture verses as the Holy Spirit led them. Some meetings might consist of a hymn followed by an hour of total silence, as the worshippers reflected on God's Holy Word and the Spirit's divine teachings. Other times, one or two members might stand to speak if they sensed a tug from God to do so. Could Levi possibly come up with a different topic to speak on every week? Chaplain Morris was a fine orator. How was Levi supposed to fill his shoes?

"Well, what do you say?" Grimms asked.

"Do I have a choice?"

"Well, of course, you have a choice. But I should tell you, Captain Bateman is pretty clear about thinking you're the best man for the job."

Levi nodded slowly. "I can't give you a definite answer without praying about it first, Lieutenant."

"Well, all right, then. But see that you pray about it in quick fashion. With soldiers dropping like flies, we need someone to pray them into their eternal home before they breathe their last."

As he returned to his camp, Levi kept his head down, his mind swirling with all manner of thoughts. What would it be like to pray with dying soldiers, to visit the sick, to fill his days encouraging others, and to devote more time to Bible reading and prayer? If he were going to preach on Sundays, he'd need to dive deeper into the Word and seek God's wisdom and insight.

"What would You have me do, Lord?" he whispered.

⌒

Wasn't this an interesting turn of events, Albright's becoming the new chaplain? Besides learning that little tidbit, his eavesdropping hadn't resulted in anything meriting a report to the Rebs. No fresh orders coming down from the captain, either. Poor ol' Grimms had lost his dignity when his company started firing on their own men at the Battle of Salem Church back in May, and now Grimms had to regain the trust of Bateman before he got another worthy assignment. It had all been an accident, of course, or so the officials thought. No one would ever know that *he* was the one who'd actually fired the first shots and activated the so-called misfortune. The dense fog had only magnified the confusion. Soldiers were running toward their own company, soldiers that several reported they'd mistaken for Confederates. It only made sense to shoot at them, they'd said.

In the end, Captain Bateman blamed Grimms for failing to have full control of his men. What a day it had been. Satisfaction welled up in him at the mere memory, and he couldn't help the grin that blossomed on his ruddy face.

He followed Albright at a distance before veering off the path to relieve himself in the bushes.

6

*J*osie wiped the sweat dripping from her brow as she forged ahead, managing to keep pace with the rest of B Company, even maintaining a position close to the front. Three times today, Sergeant Albright had complimented her on her marching abilities; but then, he made it a point to encourage everybody, so she tried not to dwell on his praise. She wasn't in the army to garner admiration and acclaim. She had joined in order to carry on what her brother had started, as well as to gain her independence and earn enough money to begin repaying Aunt Bessie for all the years she'd taken care of her.

So far, things hadn't been so bad—unless she counted the "three square meals a day" Andrew had claimed the army provided. No doubt, he'd wanted to paint a positive picture of army life to prevent her from worrying. She hoped he hadn't also exaggerated about the monthly wages of thirteen dollars. Anything less, and she just might have to defect. Of course, she wouldn't do that. She had nowhere else to go.

She'd been hopeful, at break of dawn, that the cooler air would hang around for the day, but that afternoon, the sticky heat returned, along with a relentless sun that scorched her shoulders. She would've liked to shuck a few layers, as so many soldiers had done—namely, her army coat—but she couldn't risk revealing her feminine frame, so she walked on, thankful that today's terrain was a bit easier than that of yesterday.

"Hey there, kid. You survivin' all right without your mommy?"

She felt a tiny pinch in her chest at the sound of Hiram McQuade's heartless jab, but she managed to take a deep breath and continue marching, with even more purpose—one, two, three; one, two, three—not even bothering to glance in McQuade's direction. It was the second snide remark he'd made to her today. That morning, he'd called her a "pretty boy," causing her to worry about the effectiveness of her disguise. Ever since, she'd been more conscious of her comportment. While having lunch with six fellow soldiers, she'd laughed at a few crude jokes she didn't consider the least bit funny. It took a great deal of effort to speak in a lower tone, but she'd been improving every day.

"I've been survivin' just fine ever since my 'mommy' *and* my daddy died, when I was eleven," she finally said, realizing McQuade expected an answer. She kept her gaze pointed straight ahead.

That shut him up—for a moment. To her chagrin, he kept up with her. "So, what'd you do, raise yourself after that?"

"I lived with relatives," she stated curtly, having no desire to continue conversing with the rude and inconsiderate McQuade. Knowing the way he treated men in the camp, particularly the slow-witted Chester Woolsley, she wanted nothing to do with him.

"Oh, yeah? They make you join the army just to get you outta the house? I bet they kicked your sissy little rear end right out the door." He laughed as if he'd just told the funniest joke in history.

"No, and I can't imagine why you'd think up such a thing unless is was precisely what happened to you." This time, she did take a quick peek at him. "I'll bet your family was real anxious for you to leave. Bet nobody's pinin' after you; no, they're all pleased as punch you're gone, and it upsets you so much that you take out your bitterness on everybody else." Before she had a chance to think about them, the words gushed out of her like a sudden rainfall. Stars in heaven! Now she was going to die an untimely death before she even set foot on an actual battlefield. She could already envision his hands encircling her throat to squeeze the last breath out of her.

"You're a bold one, ain't ya, kid? Y' got some nerve, talkin' to me like that, a wee thing like you."

She stretched to her full height and marched on, deciding it best to keep her mouth shut from now on.

"You aren't pickin' on my friend, are y', McQuade?"

Willie Speer, taller than McQuade by a head, came on the scene just when Josie was about to part company with McQuade by sprinting closer to the front of the line. There was nothing light about the load she carried, but she would force herself to speed up if it would mean escaping the bully.

"Nah, I'm just funnin' with 'im. Trouble is, he can't take a little kiddin'. Somethin' ain't right with somebody who can't take a little funnin', don't y' think, Speer?"

Speer gave Josie a friendly slap on the shoulder as he slipped between her and McQuade. "There's nothin' wrong with this kid. He's downright brave, considerin' he joined just a few days ago. Look at 'im, marchin' in formation like he's been doin' this for months."

"That's 'cause he can't be more 'n twelve or thirteen. Look at 'im. He don't even got a single whisker to his name."

"I'll have you know I'm nineteen, Private McQuade," she said.

"Pfff. I'll eat your boot for supper tonight if you can prove it."

She leaned forward to see around Willie and schooled her expression to say, "Nothin' would please me more than to watch you eat my boot, but I'm afraid I need it for marchin'." So much for keeping her big yapper shut.

Willie produced a hearty laugh. "That was a good one, kid. He's a clever one, ain't he, McQuade?"

McQuade gave a cold smile in return. He seemed about to speak but then stopped dead and stared into the nearby thicket, his rifle aimed and ready.

"Who's there?" Willie hissed, stopping and pointing the tip of his own rifle toward the copse of overgrown scrubs. "Come out, or we'll shoot."

Everybody else in the vicinity halted his movement and cocked his rifle in unison, so Josie followed suit, planting her feet firmly into the ground and settling the butt of her rifle tightly in the pocket of her shoulder.

A whimpering sound issued forth, followed by a fragile-sounding female voice pleading, "D-don't shoot. Please. I ain't got no gun."

"Come out!" Willie ordered.

From the center of the thick shrubbery emerged a slender Negro woman carrying a wee child, both trembling with fear. Their dirty, tattered clothing hung on them, and the baby, big-eyed and skinnier than a fence rail, had his little legs wrapped snugly around his mother's waist, his head nestled in the curve of her scrawny shoulder. Josie slipped her rifle back into its sheath and moved forward, but McQuade blocked her with his arm. "Don't be stupid," he muttered, loudly enough for all to hear. "She might be part of a Rebel trap." Josie hadn't thought of that. "Speer, circle around that way, and you"—he pointed his gaze directly at Josie—"take the other direction. And get your blasted gun up, soldier!"

Josie's cheeks, already burning from the day's heat, now also burned from embarrassment. She raised her rifle once more.

At least seven rifles were now pointed at the poor woman's head.

"I jes' a slave woman tryin' t' escape," she murmured. "They's Confederates all around these parts. I was skeered you was some of 'em."

"Shut up!" McQuade yelled at her. Then to Josie, "Don't just stand there. Move!"

She startled, then proceeded clumsily around the dense brush, her heart thrashing in her chest. Fear threatened to overwhelm her. Was this the same sensation one got just before dying?

When she and Willie met on the other side of the thicket, Willie pushed aside the bushes for a good look, then stepped back and eyed her in silence. They both nodded.

"It's clear back here," Willie yelled.

Josie followed him back around to the group that had gathered, their rifles now lowered, their stances relaxed, as they continued to regard the Negro woman.

"Please, suhs, don't send me back to my massuh," she pleaded, her dark face drooping with fatigue. "Me an' m' baby will be done fo'. I been walkin' three days, eatin' berries and whatever else I can find. My baby, though, somethin' wrong with him. He don't eat or cry much no mo', and I don't got much of anythin' left in me t' feed 'im." Her eyes grew moist.

Josie was filled with pity for what the poor woman had endured.

"What have we here?"

Josie's heart lilted at the sound of Sergeant Albright's voice. He had evidently gotten wind of the commotion and had circled around to investigate, accompanied by several other soldiers. He came up beside Josie, and just standing next to him settled her fears.

He eyed the Negro woman with curiosity, then reached out and tenderly stroked the baby's cheek. Josie tamped down a wave of emotion.

"I found her hidin' in these bushes," said McQuade, pointing the barrel of his rifle toward the thicket.

"Speer, you and McQuade take her to the medic's wagon and stay with them until you hear otherwise," Sergeant Albright stated without a second's hesitation. "While they're treated, I'll try to make arrangements for them to travel north to Washington where they'll be safe."

"Thank you, suh," the woman whispered, her eyes wide with astonishment.

Sergeant Albright placed a hand on her shoulder, and Josie could only imagine how bony it felt. "You'll be all right, ma'am. You and your baby will be just fine. You stay strong, hear?"

She gave a slow nod, then lowered her head as a few tears dripped down her face and fell to the ground. She wiped her wet cheek with her filthy sleeve. "Ain't no white man ev' call me 'ma'am' befo'."

Silence engulfed the circle of soldiers. Even McQuade had lost his tongue.

"Well, you put that thought behind you now and concern yourself with regaining your strength," Albright instructed her. "The main thing now is getting that baby healthy again."

"Yes, suh. I thank you, suh. You is kinder than anybody I ev' knowed."

Willie and McQuade led her away, and as they did, the others resumed marching, leaving Josie and Levi alone. They set off together, and his presence pleased her. It would be nice to have him to herself, if even for a short time, just to become better acquainted.

"You never did tell us how you happened to join the army, Sergeant Albright," Josie began.

"I guess I didn't. But, please, address me as 'Levi.'"

"I'd feel mighty disrespectful, sir."

"Not at all." He jabbed her shoulder in much the same way Willie had earlier.

"Well, all right, then…Levi." Just saying his name gave her a silly shiver, and it was doggone hot out. What was wrong with her?

"As for how I came to join the army, it's a pretty long story."

Josie glanced upward, noting the position of the sun still high in the sky. "I don't see that we're short on time."

Levi chuckled. "You're right about that. Probably a few hours more of marching before we reach our destination. All right, then, I'll tell you how I came to join. First, you need to know that I'm a Quaker."

Josie couldn't help raising her eyebrows.

"I know what you're thinking. Aren't Quakers pacifists?" Levi grinned. "I thought my mother's neatly pinned prayer cap would fly right off when I announced my intention to join. Our family adamantly opposes the institution of slavery. My father, and now my sister and her husband, are heavily involved in the Underground Railroad. When President Lincoln made a plea for seventy-five thousand additional volunteers to help hold our country together and also put an end to slavery, I prayed long and hard, and finally concluded I couldn't simply sit back and do nothing.

"Mother said it was my duty to pray from home, not fight, and for the most part, I agreed with her. But then...." He cleared his throat and paused a moment before continuing. "Then a good friend of mine died in the Battle of Hoke's Run. It broke me up, and I asked myself, *How many more of my friends are going to die while I sit at home and work the farm?* I had to take action. Don't get me wrong—I'm a pacifist at heart. I hate the brutality of war. But some things are worth fighting for, and freedom is one of them." He removed his dusty hat and ran a hand through his thick, dark hair. Josie watched out of the corner of her eye, not wanting to appear interested in his every move.

She turned her attention to the ground, watching her steps as she traversed the rocky terrain. "I admire you for takin' a stand. Holdin' to your convictions."

She felt his eyes on her. "You admire me for breaking covenant with the Society?"

"Well, I'm not a Quaker, mind you, but since you prayed about your decision, I've got to believe God honors you for that—and that He's watchin' over you day by day."

"I'm glad to hear you say that, Private. I had you figured for a man of faith."

His statement warmed her heart. She hadn't been sure if God still considered her one of His own, considering all the untruths that now constituted her existence. "My parents taught me about Jesus from a very young age, and after they died of the fever, my aunt and uncle took my brother and me to church every week. I ain't perfect, o' course. I still sin plenty."

"We all do, Gordon. We're human beings in need of a Savior. Being a Christian doesn't make us perfect, but it does enable us to live in God's grace."

As they walked on, their conversation turned to lighter topics. Levi told her about his love of farming, and she disclosed how much she enjoyed reading, as well as hunting and fishing. It felt good to be able to speak the truth for once.

"Have I told you how much you remind me of my kid brother Milton?" Levi asked. "He's fifteen, but a good deal taller than you." He shook his head. "Sorry. I'm sure you get that a lot, comments about your height."

Josie grunted. "And my lack of whiskers."

"Don't let the men's remarks bother you. They're just having fun."

"I s'pose—unless you're referrin' to Hiram McQuade. That man doesn't seem to know the meaning of fun. He's downright cruel."

Levi frowned. "I've known Private McQuade for some time now, and I still haven't figured him out. You'd think he'd want a friend or two, but he doesn't seem to know how to make friends, let alone keep them."

They plodded on for the next several minutes without speaking, listening to the loud tramp of soldiers' boots and the occasional marching chant. When Levi reached into his sack for his canteen and took a big swig of water, Josie broke the silence between them. "So, you come from a big family, do you?"

Levi took another long drink, then screwed the lid back on his canteen and easily slipped the container back into his pack without missing a beat. "If you consider eight kids a big family," he said with a grin.

His was the sort of smile that lit his entire face. Even his eyes seemed to glint with sunshine. Josie had to look away, lest he detect her unusual attentiveness. She focused on her boots, watching them kick up dust with every stride, and concentrated on walking in as manly a fashion as possible. She hoped he wouldn't find her movements exaggerated.

"Eight kids sounds huge, considerin' I had only one brother. Did I tell you he died in the Battle of Drewry's Bluff?"

He stopped with a suddenness that caused the soldiers behind to ram into his back. Josie, too, stood motionless, while other soldiers around them and marched onward. "What?" she asked.

Levi gawked at her, his feet appearing to be pinned to the ground. "Drewry's Bluff. You didn't tell me your brother died there." He resumed marching.

Josie hurried to keep up. "Didn't I?"

"How much older than you was he?"

"I'm the older one."

"You? Then your brother had to have been mighty young when he joined."

She regretted now that she'd brought up the matter of Andrew's death. "He was young, yes, but…he was mature for his age."

"Hmm. Mature, you say? But he got himself promptly killed. Drewry's Bluff was one of the earliest battles."

Anger welled up within her. "You sayin' it was his age, or lack of maturity, that caused his death?" She sped up to put some distance between herself and Levi, no longer interested in hearing about his family.

Moments later, he was by her side once more. "Sorry, Gordon. That wasn't what I meant to say. At least, it didn't come out the way I wanted it to. It just surprised me to hear your younger brother joined before you. I mean, you seem young yourself, so.…"

She huffed loudly and maintained her quick pace, staring straight ahead. "I'm nineteen years old, Sergeant. Legal age for fightin'. My brother was not, but he was a true patriot."

"Don't get all worked up. I believe you," Levi assured her. "So, you must have joined because of his influence. Is that right?"

She was quiet for a moment. "I had my reasons, but that was a big influence, yes."

They marched on for several minutes without speaking. Josie grew uneasy, wishing she could escape.

"We can talk about your brother at a later time, if you like," Levi told her. "My family is my greatest influence, too."

She sniffed. "So, why don't you tell me about 'em?"

As Levi described each of his siblings, he spoke with such fondness that Josie could barely keep her eyes averted from him. They walked and talked for the next hour or so, alternately posing and answering questions of each other, and Josie decided she would love to be part of a big family. But now was hardly the time for entertaining such far-fetched dreams, when surviving the war was a big enough hope.

7

When Company B, along with nine other companies belonging to the 23rd Pennsylvania Regiment, set up camp at the north fork of the Rappahannock River, everyone that had a tent, pitched it; everyone else found a spot to settle out in the open, unless he chose to erect a crude wooden structure with a roof made from a mixture of mud and straw. Word was, they'd remain here for at least a week or two. Of course, in war, anything might happen, so no one put down stakes with any sense of permanence. Still, the notion that they might actually stay put for more than just a few days was like a fine melody to Levi's ears.

Over the past couple of days—including last night, which he'd mostly spent staring up at an inky sky and fighting off whining mosquitoes—Levi had prayed about whether to accept the position of regiment chaplain. Unable to think of any good reasons to decline, he walked to the lieutenant's tent that very morning after breakfast and told him he'd take the job, unless they found a more suitable replacement in the interim.

"That's good news, Sergeant. Good news, indeed," Grimms said, shaking Levi's hand. "Captain Bateman will be relieved to hear it. Why don't you ride over to his camp later today and let him know, yourself?

You can go down to the stable wagon and request a horse. Whichever one's allotted you will be yours for the duration of your assignment."

"I appreciate that," Levi said. "I'll see to it later, after I've checked on Hodgers and Morse. They didn't show up for roll call. The major moved them to the nearby barn where the regiment's hospital has been set up. Meanwhile, I hear the medic is examining several other men for possible cases of the ague."

Grimms frowned. "That doesn't sound good. Let me know how things progress. Captain Bateman reported early this morning that we've got orders to remain here indefinitely. That should give the men a chance to rest, maybe rid themselves of this nasty bug. Those who are healthy will resume the work already begun on the bridges, and others will build fortifications. No guarantee we'll need them, but it's best to prepare. Of course, there will be drills today."

"Of course, sir."

"That's all, Sergeant."

Levi straightened, stood at attention, and saluted. "Yes, sir."

Next, Levi headed for the camp hospital. The barn-turned-hospital held dozens of foldable cots, many of which were occupied. Medical personnel bustled about, carrying such items as bedding, medicine, and cups of water. The occasional moan arose from a soldier's mouth, and Levi's heart beat with compassion for the patients and the volunteer staff alike.

He was greeted by Major John Walden. "Better not get too close," Walden warned.

Levi didn't know Walden well, only that the doctor had enlisted at the start of the war and had worked his way up the ranks. He was enlisted with another company, so Levi didn't have much occasion to see him, unless it was to check on one of his own men. Walden was rare among medics in that he had an actual doctor certificate. Most of the medics were trainees with a special interest in medicine but no training to show for it. Unfortunately, many of these trainees were performing surgical procedures without the first clue as to how to do so. Levi hoped and prayed he would never need their services. He'd endured his share of sickness since enlisting, but he'd managed to fight off each bout without assistance. He'd also managed, by God's grace, to dodge any bullets or cannon fire.

"How are privates Hodgers and Morse?" Levi inquired.

The doctor moved to a cloth-covered table holding an array of medical instruments, primarily varying sizes of steel scalpels. It appeared the doctor had been washing them in a bowl of sudsy water, then laying them out on a clean towel to dry. He proceeded to pick up a scalpel and drop it in the water. "Morse is worse off than his comrade," he said under his breath. "I don't know that he'll make it."

Levi's head jerked to attention. "I didn't realize he was that sick," Levi stated quietly.

The doctor cleared his throat, then continued in a hushed tone. "He's developed a diarrheal condition that has weakened him significantly. There's little to do about it except to continue giving him fluids and hope the condition reverses itself. I've been trying to educate men on the importance of sanitation—washing their hands as often as possible, not drinking contaminated water, and reporting any untended wounds or infected sores—but I'm fighting an uphill battle. Either the men don't want to take the time to wash, or conditions are such that filth can't be avoided. Regardless, our circumstances are dire, and it's only going to get worse—to the point that more soldiers die from disease than from combat."

Levi grimaced. "Is there nothing else we can do for Morse?" he whispered.

Major Walden shrugged. "If you're a praying man, I'd suggest you beseech the Almighty on his behalf. Other than that, I've been doing my best to keep him comfortable. It's about all any of us can do in cases such as his. If he were in a great deal of pain, I'd give him a dose of morphine or a good shot of medicinal whiskey, but he's not. He's just weak, and his cough doesn't help any."

"May I talk to him?"

Major Walden raised his eyebrows. "You'd be risking your own health to do so."

"Isn't that what you do every day?"

"Well, I'm the doctor. I guess it's more or less expected of me."

"And I'm the newly appointed chaplain. Seems the expectation would be the same."

Major Walden lifted his graying brows even higher. "Is that so? Well then, I suppose I can't deny you access to the patients, as long as you understand the perils." He nodded over his left shoulder. "You'll find Morse about halfway down that row of beds."

Levi tipped his cap at the doctor, then stepped past him into the hospital. As he approached Walt Morse's cot, he could see that the fellow had lost a considerable amount of weight, and his complexion was as gray as a raincloud.

He reached down and touched the frail soldier's arm. "You awake, Private Morse?"

The fellow startled, then slowly opened empty eyes. Upon recognizing Levi, he gave a slow shake of his head. "I ain't doin' so well, Sarge," he murmured. Levi had to strain his ears to hear him.

"You don't need to talk, Private. I just wanted to stop by and see you."

The fellow coughed and tried to catch his breath. After a couple of attempts, he regained control.

Levi knelt beside Morse's cot. The stench of waste in the room was almost more than he could bear, but he silently prayed for strength and sensed the Lord's girding almost immediately.

"I'm scared, Sarge."

"What are you afraid of, Private?"

"I don't wanna die."

"Of course, you don't. No one does."

"What if I ain't fit to meet my Maker?"

Levi's gut clenched. *Lord, give me wisdom and discernment.* "Have you read much of the Bible, Morse?"

"Not hardly any, sir."

"Do you know that God loves you?"

"My grandma always told me that when I was a boy. I didn't pay her much mind. I wish now...."

Levi smiled gently. "You can decide right now that you want to live the rest of your days for Jesus, Morse. The gospel of John, chapter three, verse sixteen, says, *'For God so loved the world, that he gave his only begotten Son, that whosoever believeth in him should not perish, but have everlasting life.'* You have only to confess your sins, acknowledge that Jesus is the Son of God, and ask for His forgiveness. The Lord is faithful, Morse. He hears our cries and answers us, and that's a promise."

Morse gave no immediate response, but a single tear did trickle down the man's ruddy face. He heaved a labored sigh. "I...I want to... but...."

Levi leaned closer. "But what, Private?"

"I ain't...good enough."

"None of us is 'good enough,' Morse. That's the beauty of salvation. If we were good enough, Christ wouldn't have had to sacrifice Himself for us on the cross. God's not looking for perfect people, Morse. He's looking for willing ones."

Morse's eyes lit with a tiny flicker of interest. "Willing ones?"

"Yes, people who are willing to give it all up and just say, 'Lord, I come to You. Please take me as I am.'"

Morse's nod was barely discernible. "Yes," he whispered.

"Would you like me to pray with you?" Levi offered.

"Please."

Levi bowed his head. If he'd needed any kind of affirmation that he should serve as chaplain, he had it now.

On his way back to camp, an overwhelming sense of peace came over him—a sense of assurance that he'd found the place where God wanted him to serve, at least for now. After praying with Morse and then watching him drift into a deep sleep, he'd visited Hodgers and then a few other sick and wounded soldiers, offering them a word of encouragement. Several soldiers asked him to pray for them, as well; the rest just preferred to talk, his company alone seeming to provide a measure of comfort.

Back at camp, he found the troops getting into formation as they prepared for drills. He hurried his steps, ran to grab his rifle musket from its case, and quickly fell into line next to his good friend Charlie Clute. Standing on the other side of him was Private Snipp in his clean, crisp uniform, his eyes trained on the commanding officer, too focused even to notice he'd joined them.

"A little late, aren't we, Sarge?" said Clute out of the side of his mouth.

"Reporting for duty, Private Clute," Levi replied in a mocking tone, keeping his voice down. "I was visiting some patients, primarily Private Morse."

"How's he doing?"

"Not well. Major Walden fears he won't make it."

"That's too bad. The ague?"

"It's more than that, now."

"Attention!" the drill sergeant called.

All the soldiers snapped into position, facing forward without the slightest movement.

"About face!"

The entire company turned 180 degrees to the right.

"Left shoulder, arms."

They placed their rifles on their left shoulders, their left hands holding the butts of their rifles, their forearms parallel to the ground at a 90-degree angle.

"Order, arms."

They brought their rifles back down to their sides.

"Right shoulder, arms."

As he followed the command, Levi glanced to the right and gauged how Gordon was doing. Not bad. The kid impressed him.

"Forward march!"

Leading off with their left foot, the soldiers set off, their boots pounding the earth like an unusually organized herd of elephants. They marched down a gulley and halfway up another one, until the next command came—and then another—and still another. Before long, they'd covered hills, valleys, and everything in between.

The clipped commands continued for at least the next hour, and sweat rolled down Levi's face till he didn't think he had another drop of it in him. But he knew the drills were worth the struggle. The best way to prepare for battle was to drill all day long—morning, noon, and night—until nothing else echoed in your head but the loud, brisk ricochets of the drill sergeant's orders. If Levi came out of this war alive, he wondered how many years it would take for the memory of those repetitious commands to leave his mind—if ever they did. Perhaps he'd be hearing them all the way to his grave.

Between drills, soldiers spent their free time in a variety of ways—catching a quick nap, playing cards with comrades, writing letters, playing the fiddle or the harmonica, or just sitting in the shade of a tree, whittling something or jawing with others. Levi wanted to skip the afternoon drills, go pick up his horse, and ride over to G Company to seek out Private Morris, the regiment chaplain. But he figured tomorrow morning would be soon enough to do that. He needed the man's counsel regarding chaplain responsibilities. Nothing about taking over the job worried him, unless he counted the preaching aspect. Sunday services didn't last much longer than 20 or 30 minutes, lest they interfere with army duties; but, still, the idea of preaching for even 10 minutes gave him the shudders. Growing up Quaker, he'd attended First Day meetings and participated in silent worship; thus, the prospect of officiating a traditional Protestant service set his nerves on edge. He was about the last person qualified for such a position, save for God's divine intervention. He wondered how his mother, with her staunch Quaker beliefs, would react when she read in his next letter home that he had taken to delivering a weekly sermon.

After supper that evening, Levi fell into step with Gordon Snipp. That kid always managed to make him smile.

"Private Clute tells me you're takin' over as chaplain," Snipp remarked.

Levi was a full head taller than the boy, so he had to look down when conversing with him. "Indeed, I am. Did he also tell you he's moving up in rank and assuming many of my responsibilities?"

"He didn't mention that, no. I'll be missin' you, sir—er, Levi."

Levi chuckled. "That's kind of you, Gordon, but don't worry; you'll still be seeing a lot of me. I'm not leaving Company B."

"Oh?"

"I'm told I'll be traveling more, but I envision myself coming back to camp most every night."

Gordon grinned. "That's good to hear. You'll be a fine chaplain. You've got the heart for it."

"You think?"

"Sure. The heart and, hopefully, the stomach. I'm sure it can be gruesome, but I wouldn't mind helpin' out with the sick and wounded, myself."

"Is that right?" Levi briefly studied the boy's countenance. To be sure, he wasn't overly masculine; in fact, one might even call him effeminate with his small chin, rounded cheeks, and brown oval eyes. Despite his slight frame, he carried himself well and made a fine soldier. "And I suppose you have the stomach for it?"

"Sure do. I've seen my share of blood."

"Oh? And where would that have been?"

"In the barn back home. I've delivered more calves than you can count, put a few sick animals out of their misery and then buried them, and even assisted in some surgeries."

Levi grinned. He might have pointed out the vast difference between treating animals and treating human beings, but he didn't wish to stomp on Gordon's dream. "Well, if you're serious, you could always take up your case with Lieutenant Grimms. I'd first go to the hospital, though, and survey the scene. You'll know after that if you have the stomach— and the nose—for that sort of work."

"Then I think I'll do just that."

Levi smiled again and gave the young man a mild slap on the back. "You're a good soldier, Gordon. I like your grit."

The boy grinned back, his brown eyes flickering.

"How 'bout we go get some grub?"

"Sure thing. I'm hungry enough to eat a whole chicken."

Levi laughed. "Prepare yourself for some salt pork, dried beans, and corn bread, instead."

"That'll do."

8

*J*osie plunked down under a tree on a grassy mound and leaned back against the expansive trunk, every muscle in her body screaming with pain from all the marching maneuvers the drill instructor had put the soldiers through today, never mind that they'd spent the entire week walking. And to think she had to go through it all again tomorrow! In his letters home, Andrew had not mentioned how grueling army life could be. If he would have done so, she might well have rejected the idea of joining.

She blew out a tired, shaky sigh and closed her eyes for just a moment, but when she did, all she saw were soldiers in front of and beside her, marching in unison, rifles parked on their shoulders as they chanted in unison, "One, two, three, four; one, two, three, four." The soldiers also sang such marching songs as "May God Save the Union," "Battle Cry of Freedom," and even "John Brown's Body" while they trudged along. Never had she heard such an array of croaky, cracking, out-of-tune voices; but then, neither had she heard such forthright patriotism and enthusiasm for winning the war, either, and she found the men's excitement contagious.

She opened her eyes again and heaved out another long breath. Using her Bible as a sort of desk, she laid a piece of stationery atop it and thought about how to start her first letter to Allison. She knew her cousin would be wondering how she'd fared since leaving her aunt's home several days ago. Without further contemplation, she put her pen to the paper and threw herself into the act of writing.

Dear Allison,

I hope this letter finds you in good spirits. I have been ever so busy since joining the army, but I must say things are going as fine as can be expected, considering we are at war. I have not yet participated in a real battle, and I will be happy if it stays that way; but then, no war is won without a fight, so I expect to see an end to this period of calm. It is said that since the awful Battle of Gettysburg, both sides have had to reestablish their forces, but I believe the Union is growing in strength and numbers.

I have met some good soldiers, others not so good; but I will spare you any negative news. One soldier with whom I have become friends is a sergeant who is kind, supportive, and encouraging; on top of that, he's a fine Christian man.

The weather thus far has not been worth complaining over, except for one bad storm in the middle of the night that soaked everyone in camp to the point of being wetter than a fish's whiskers. Since then, we've had a few drizzly moments, but nothing as soaking as the storm I mentioned.

The food here is not very likable, but it's edible, at least. I miss your mother's cooking, but it is best that she has one less mouth to feed. Please give her my best, and assure her that when I receive my first pay, I shall send the bulk of it to her. She needs it far more than I do.

My daily schedule goes as such: rise at dawn; find a private spot to wash up; eat a bit of breakfast; march to our destination; set up camp; drill, drill, and drill some more; and then, after we've had a bit of a break, drill again. I relish the rare moments of freedom such as this that allow me to write letters. I must sign off soon, however, as it is nearing bedtime. Sleeping on the ground in my tent hasn't been as bad as I'd expected. The worst part is the mosquitoes.

Please write when you get a chance and tell me everything that is happening at home. You can send all correspondence to Gordon Snipp, Company B, 23rd Regiment, Pennsylvania Volunteers. Any correspondence will likely take a few weeks to reach me, but don't let that deter you from writing.

Love, your cousin,
Gordon Snipp

Satisfied that she hadn't included any details that might be censored, she folded the letter, addressed and sealed it, affixed a 3-cent stamp to the upper right corner, then stood and headed down a well-traveled path in the direction of the mail wagon.

On the way there, Charlie Clute fell into step beside her. "Got a letter to send, I see. Have you got a sweetheart waiting for you back home?"

The question took her by surprise, and she gave a little jolt.

"Did I embarrass you? Didn't mean to."

"No, no, not at all. I—I'm only nineteen, sir. I guess I…I…."

"Haven't thought about it? Well, you've got lots of time. I had me a girl by the time I was fifteen, but I knew she was the one for me right from the start. Married when I was twenty. That was eight years ago. God's given us two sons so far. If it hadn't been for the war, we might've had a couple of more by now. 'Course, God knows the two little whippersnappers are enough for Jenny to handle right now." He chuckled. "Jenny's faithful to write me almost daily, so I usually get about ten days' worth of letters by the time the carrier finally rolls in."

"You must look forward to mail day, then, Private Clute."

"Sure do. And call me Charlie, won't you? We're all friends around here. Well, most of us, anyway. You had any brushes with McQuade lately? I heard he was giving you a hard time the other day."

"Who told you that?"

"Levi, of course. He looks out for you, in case you hadn't noticed. Says you remind him of his little brother. He may be a nice guy, that Albright, but he doesn't miss much. The men take note of his leadership, McQuade included."

Josie recalled how quickly Levi had broken up a fight between McQuade and Woolsley. She'd immediately admired his show of authority.

"I understand you're to assume some o' his responsibilities now that he's steppin' into the role of chaplain."

"That's right. Grimms just promoted me to Sergeant this morning."

"Congratulations."

"Oh, no congratulations necessary. It's just a title, nothing more."

They reached the mail wagon, where dozens of soldiers had gathered, hoping to find a letter or, even better, a small package addressed to them. Unexpected loneliness grabbed hold of Josie, but she forced herself out of its grip and walked up to the mail carrier to hand him her missive. He took it with nary a glance in her direction, just tossed it into a slotted box labeled "Outgoing," then went back to his job of calling out the names of men who, if present, stepped forward and retrieved their mail. When Charlie's name was called, he accepted his stack with a big smile, then retreated, presumably to a remote area where he could read each note in private. Josie, seeing no reason to stay, turned on her heel and headed back toward camp.

She'd traveled only a few yards when a familiar voice called after her. "Hey, Gordon! Wait up." Levi jogged over, clutching a big wad of letters. "No mail for you, eh?"

Josie shrugged. "No, but I wasn't expecting any. I did mail a letter to my cousin, though."

"Oh? Male or female?"

"Female. Allison's her name. We've always been close."

"Ah, that's nice. Nothing like family, is there?"

"No, sir."

Josie nodded at his load. "I see you aren't wantin' for mail."

He grinned. "When you come from a family of eight kids, it's a sure bet somebody from the bunch is going to write." He sorted through the mail as they walked, and she thought she detected a glimmer in his eyes at the sight of one envelope in particular. Sure enough, he immediately tore open the seal and pulled out the contents.

"That from somebody special?" she asked.

"You could say that."

How foolish of her to allow her heart to drop to her feet. "A—a lady friend?"

Levi nodded. "Mary Foster. She's been writing me for a few months, now. My sisters rave about her beauty. Blonde hair and blue eyes, they say." He gave her one of his big, friendly smiles. "They could be exaggerating a bit, though. I'll judge for myself once I finally meet her."

Josie was intrigued. "You mean, you've never talked to her in person?"

"Not yet, but I will."

"I suppose you'll be writin' back to her today, huh?" Immediately, she wanted to slap herself for her outright nosiness.

"If I can find the time. She receives about one letter to every four that she sends me."

"Then she must be very sweet on you." Josie hated how her voice squeaked. Why couldn't she stop being so meddlesome?

"I suppose she is."

"And you feel the same?"

"Me? I'm coming to like her quite a bit."

A crazy stab of jealousy sliced straight through Josie. "That's nice. You'll probably go home and marry her after the war—or once you've mustered out, whichever comes first."

"I don't know. I might. I've been praying and asking the Lord for clarity about our relationship, but without having met her in person, it's difficult to know His leading."

"O' course."

"She and I do seem to have a lot in common, though."

Josie couldn't help it. She had to know more. "Such as?"

"Well, first, she's a fine Quaker. She loves the Lord and abides by all the tenets of the Society. She enjoys farming, riding horses, and working in the garden. She also has a strong heart for abolition."

"So, she must not mind your joinin' the Union, despite your pacifistic views."

"She's never said one way or the other. Now, my mother, on the other hand…." He shook his head with a slow grin. "She thinks I've lost my last scrap of faith. She's a stalwart Quaker, and in her mind, there is very little room for departure from the principles we adhere to. I hardly ever see her without her prayer cap, and she's careful to speak in plain pronouns at all times."

Just then, they reached the clearing where Company B had set up camp. Only a few soldiers were milling about. Most were sitting around the fires they'd built, smoking hand-rolled cigarettes, conversing with friends, playing musical instruments, or gnawing on hardtack. Several men had already curled up in their bedrolls, preparing for sleep. Looking up, Josie noted several stars already appearing in the night sky.

"You want to build a fire and sit a spell?" Levi asked.

Oh, how she would love to do just that. She longed to converse at length with him. But getting to know him too intimately could very well blow her cover, and she couldn't risk his discovering her true identity. It was hard work pretending to be a man, and even harder in the presence of a man to whom she felt such a strong attraction.

Against her deepest desires, she gave an exaggerated yawn. "If you don't mind, I think I'll just turn in. I'm about to fall over from exhaustion."

"Could've fooled me. You looked great during today's drills." With his fist, he gave her a light sock in the arm. "All right then, Private. You get a good night's sleep, and we'll see you in the morning."

She started to turn away, then stopped. "When do you start actin' as chaplain?"

"I already have. Tomorrow after breakfast, I'm riding over to meet with Private Morris, the man I'm replacing. I intended to meet with him today, but I needed to talk to Captain Bateman first, so I did that instead. He's glad I took the job, probably most of all because it meant he didn't have to go through the process of contacting church leadership to make a plea for candidates and then reading through a bunch of applications. I suppose he bent the rules a bit by selecting someone who was already enlisted, but he seems to doubt anyone will put up a fuss about it."

"Well, I hope you have a good talk with that Morris fellow. I'll be prayin' for you."

Levi looked surprised for a moment, but then he grinned. "I appreciate that more than you know. Good night, now, Gordon."

"'Night." Josie lifted the flap of her tent and slipped inside.

9

After breakfast the next morning, Levi went to the livery wagon to pick up his horse. Rosie was a "good ol' girl," according to the stable keeper—reliable, strong, and fast when she needed to be. Levi mounted the chestnut-colored mare and started up the trail, preparing himself for a five-mile ride past several other units. All told, approximately 3000 soldiers were camped at or around the Rappahannock's north fork. Brigade drills were going on in the open fields, so he avoided those areas, taking to the woods instead. After directing Rosie through tall brush and trees for a good quarter of an hour, he came to a mucky two-track and veered onto that, glad for the slightly easier trek. At least here there was a path to follow.

Up ahead, a hay wagon stuck deep in sludge caught his attention. The driver—a farmer cursing as loud as a rooster at two stubborn mules while whipping their backsides—didn't see Levi coming.

"Beating the poor beasts probably won't help much," he called to the man.

The farmer whirled around, then quickly snatched a rifle from the wagon bed, held the butt against his shoulder, and approached Levi, narrowing one of his eyes on the scope. "Don't ya come any closer t' me, Yank."

"Now, put that rifle down, mister," Levi cautioned gently. "I don't have any argument with you."

"You're a Northerner, ain't ya?"

"Put the gun down. Please. No point in starting something, not when it's plain to see you could use my help."

"I ain't needin' the help o' no filthy Yank," he grumbled, making no move to lower his gun. "This fool war has ruined me, an' nobody t' blame but the likes o' you." Levi might have reached for his own weapon, but he wasn't about to give the fellow a reason to shoot him. "My fields are trampled to ruins, the blasted Union took over my house an' chased my wife an' kids clear down to Florida, an' I'm stuck here tryin' t' hold on t' what's left."

Levi wanted to reason with him, but it was clear this man wasn't the reasoning type.

Rosie stepped forward and whinnied, which seemed to compel the two mules to end their rest break and begin moving forward. The farmer, too busy staring Levi down, didn't even notice. While his mules dragged his wagon out of the mud, the middle-aged guy launched a tirade about the senseless nature of the war, insisting that the South had the right to secede and form a separate country, and sputtering that Jefferson Davis far surpassed Abe Lincoln in principles, intelligence, and political experience.

In some ways, Levi didn't blame the man for his anger. Most folks in these parts were ordinary people just trying to make enough money to keep their families alive and safe. Unfortunately, for those living in the border states, their dreams had all but vanished, forcing many to abandon their homes for safer territory.

Someone came riding up behind Levi, and his first thought was that it was another Southerner wanting to pick a fight. He turned in his saddle and, to his relief, recognized the rider as a Union soldier, albeit not one he knew personally.

"Howdy, there," the soldier said. "Just passing through on my way to Company G. You needing any help?"

The farmer stood his ground, his feet firmly planted, his rifle aimed and now cocked. "I already tol' this here Yank I don't need no help. I can get my team outta here with no problem, so be on y'r way."

"And what team would that be, sir?" the soldier asked.

"This"—he swiveled on his heel toward where the wagon had been stuck—"hey, where...? Ya get back here, ya dumb animals!" By now, the mules had pulled the wagon a good forty feet. The farmer turned back around, scowling. He lowered his rifle but now pointed his forefinger at Levi as if it were a dagger. "Why didn't ya say somethin', ya low-life Yank?"

Levi couldn't hold back his chuckle. He shook his head. "You were too busy spouting at me, mister. Figured I'd let you blow off some steam."

Something must've spooked the mules, for they went into a sudden trot, the wagon tipping and swaying. Without another word, the farmer set off after them, holding his hat in place as he slipped and slid in the mud, still throwing cuss words into the wind. Somehow, he managed to reach the wagon and leap onboard.

"Limber fellow," Levi remarked. "Crabby as a trapped bear, though." He and the other soldier watched as the farmer clambered over several bales of hay to reach the front of the wagon, clumsily threw himself over the railing and into the seat, then grabbed the reins and regained control. He bounced along the two-track, fading from view.

"I would've paid money to watch the scene that just unfolded," the soldier said with a laugh. "Name's Captain Thomas Lucas. Battery Commanding Officer at Company G."

In the hubbub, Levi hadn't even noticed his insignia patch to identify his rank. He immediately saluted. "Sergeant Levi Albright, sir. Pleasure to make your acquaintance."

"Likewise, Sergeant. At ease."

Levi relaxed his stance. "I happen to be heading to Company G, myself," Levi said. "I'm meeting Private Byron Morris, Chaplain of the Twenty-third."

A light dawned in the captain's eye. "I thought your name was famil-iar. We're fortunate to have you. Lord knows we can use you for moral support. How about we ride together?"

"I'd like that very much."

The men nudged their horses into a trot and headed up the trail.

"Morris is an Episcopalian," Lucas pointed out as they got under way. "What denomination are you?"

"Quaker, sir."

"Quaker? I thought they were pacifists."

"Most are, you're right. I suppose I'm a bit of an insurgent; at least, that's how my mother views me. Truth be told, five years ago, I never would've pictured myself on a battlefield. But I became so passionate about the Union's cause that I had to join."

"Well, your mother should be pleased about your assuming the role of chaplain. You probably won't bear arms, then, correct? Though I sup-pose it's a personal decision on your part, since you enlisted with the intention to fight."

Levi nodded. "I realize that most of the chaplains are ordained min-isters who enter the army ranked as private. I don't know if there are any other 'sergeant-chaplains' out there."

"Well, nobody's going to strip you of your title just because you're taking a different job, and no one can force that gun out of your posses-sion, either," Lucas told him. "Never can tell when you might need it."

"Yes, sir. I've been fortunate so far, but I realize my good fortune could run out any time. I leave that matter in God's hands."

"No better place for it."

A half hour later, they rode into camp to the familiar sounds of mock warfare. Captain Lucas informed Levi that companies K and E had joined them for the day, and that they would break for lunch and then resume fighting for another couple of hours.

Levi thanked him for escorting him there.

As soon as the two dismounted, officers seemed to appear like magic, all wishing to discuss one issue or another with the captain. One soldier took both their horses, with a promise to water and brush them down. After appointing another man to take Levi to Private Morris's quarters, the captain bade Levi farewell.

They found the chaplain in his tent, packing items into a crate. His bedroll was neatly tied, a sealed knapsack next to it, as though he intended to leave that very day. "Excuse me, Private Morris, but you have a visitor," the soldier announced, then pivoted on his heel and left with nary a word.

The gray-haired fellow looked up and smiled from behind his thick beard, extending a hand to Levi. "Ah, you must be Sergeant Albright. Please come in."

Levi walked in, and the two shook hands. "It's nice to finally meet you, sir. I've attended some of your Sunday services, but there always seemed to be a throng of men gathered around you afterward, so I never had an opportunity to introduce myself."

"Well, I'm pleased we've finally met, although I'm sorry to say my time is limited. I've just been informed a driver from Richmond is coming this very morning to take me to Washington, where I'm to catch a train home to Buffalo. My wife is ill, as you may know."

"Yes, and I'm sorry to hear that, sir. I pray she recovers soon."

"The report is that she's doing better, particularly since hearing the news that I'm coming home." He winked at Levi. "I don't mean to imply that her illness may have been blown a bit out of proportion, but then again, it's a possibility. At any rate, I've served for over a year, which is longer than most chaplains can say. It's a challenging task, but a very worthwhile one. God has been gracious to me during my tenure, and I'm confident He will bless you, too, as you seek to do His service."

"Thank you, sir. Can you tell me a bit about what to expect?"

"Certainly, but I fear you may change your mind if I go into too much detail." There came that sly wink again.

"Oddly, the one thing I dread the most is speaking on Sunday mornings."

"Oh, you'll have no problem there. Simply allow the Spirit to guide you, and you can't possibly go wrong."

"You make it sound so easy."

"Not easy in your own strength, but with God's strength, you can do all things."

"Philippians four, verse thirteen."

"There, you see? You're already working on your first sermon. That's your Scripture verse. Now, all you have to do is come up with a brief reflection on it. The army frowns on long-winded sermons and lengthy services. They don't want to give the impression that the Sabbath is a day of rest—not here, anyway. To the government, it's just another day to prepare for battle." He raised his index finger. "There, I just gave you another sermon topic—preparing oneself for *spiritual* battles as well as *physical* ones."

"Would you mind sending me a list of suggested sermon topics, along with accompanying Scripture verses, once you get back to Buffalo?" Levi teased.

Morris chuckled. "We'll see about that."

While the private finished packing, he offered Levi some advice regarding his other major responsibilities, including visiting the sick and wounded in the hospital, penning letters home on behalf of illiterate soldiers, tending to soldiers' spiritual needs, holding the hands of dying soldiers on the battlefield, and distributing Bible tracts and pocket hymnals. "It can be excruciatingly exhausting," Chaplain Morris said, "but it's eternally rewarding at the same time."

The more Morris talked, the more Levi's enthusiasm grew for the task at hand. God had destined him for this, he was sure of it; and he had Captain Bateman to thank.

⌁

Josie sat with a group of fellow soldiers under the shade of a tree, downing her noon meal of caked, dehydrated vegetables, two slices of stale bread, a partially spoiled apple, and a bowl of cold rice. She could barely stomach most of it, but she forced herself to do so because she was hungry. Everyone grumbled about the meal, but not for long, because it wasn't worth one's breath. No one cared about anyone else's grievances, since everybody shared the same ones. Even those of higher rank rarely ate better than the privates, unless visited by individuals of distinction, in which case they always dined on finer fare.

"Somebody should scare up some ducks for supper one o' these nights," said Harv Patterson. "I'll cook 'em if somebody else'll shoot 'em."

Josie had been sticking somewhat close to the men with whom she'd traveled from the recruitment center and was getting to know them fairly well. Harv, in particular, was not as tough and gruff as she'd first thought, and she found herself enjoying his quick wit and talkative manner.

"I'll go," she offered. "I'm a good shot. Did a lot of huntin' as a kid."

"When you were a kid?" put in Hiram McQuade, who had just plunked himself down, uninvited, and thought nothing of butting into the conversation. "You mistakenly put that in the past tense."

She ignored his remark. "Anybody else wanna go?"

"We will," said Henry Gower, gesturing to himself and then his brother, Joseph.

Hugh Fowler set his empty tin plate on the ground beside him, took a couple of swigs of water from his mug, and then wiped his mouth with his sleeve. "I'll go, too."

"How 'bout settin' out at first light tomorrow mornin'?" Henry suggested. "We'll have to make fast work o' huntin' them down so we won't miss roll call."

"I know where there's some marshland," said Joseph. "Came across it yesterday morning while I was strolling around. Even saw some ducks swimming and thought to myself how good they'd taste."

"It's settled, then," said Hugh. "Tomorrow morning, first light."

"What's tomorrow mornin'?" asked Howard Adams, dropping down next to Josie with a pencil and a pad of paper in hand. Josie gave an inward groan at the sight of the tablet in which he kept his army journal.

"Some of us are goin' on a huntin' spree," Henry explained. "We need some real food in our stomachs. Hopin' for duck."

"Well, you've got my full support," said Howard. "You get a sweet-smellin' duck cookin' over a fire, and you're bound to get visitors. I'll be first in line."

"You come to interview somebody?" Joseph asked the recorder.

Howard nodded. "Sure did. Come to talk to Gordon Snipp, here. I figured mealtime was as good as any to catch 'im." He turned his attention on Josie. "You don't mind, do you? Lieutenant Grimms wants me to write an accurate account of every soldier in Company B. By the end of the war, all my writings'll be compiled in a big book that everybody's gonna want to read."

"Sure," sneered McQuade. "Because we are by far the most interesting company in the army."

"I'm sure that's true," said Harv. "We got *you*, don't we?"

His comment sparked a round of laughter, and even McQuade himself cracked a feeble grin.

Josie wasn't the least bit thrilled at the prospect of being interviewed, for Howard's questions would no doubt force her to tell a few more falsehoods. She finished the last of her lunch and stood up. "You want to follow me down to the river so I can clean off my dishes, Howard? You can interview me on the way."

"Sure." He stood up when she did and opened his tablet.

"You mean, we don't get to hear you fire off the questions?" asked McQuade. "Then I think I'll tag along. I'm mighty curious myself about this young man."

Josie's stomach did a little somersault. The last person she wanted listening in on her interview was Hiram McQuade.

"Sorry, but I conduct all my interviews in private," Howard informed him. "You'll just have to wait till the lieutenant publishes my account."

Josie exhaled a quiet sigh of relief.

"Pfff," McQuade sneered. "Bunch o' nonsense, if you ask me."

"Think what you want. Come on, Snipp."

They headed down the cliff, and Josie could almost feel McQuade's eyes drilling holes in her back.

10

*D*on't let McQuade get to you," Howard said when they had reached the water's edge. "He's a lot of talk."

Josie crouched down and dipped her dishes in the cold water, wishing in that instant that she could dive in and wash off all her sweat. "He doesn't bother me," she fibbed. Of all the men in Company B, McQuade made her the most leery, always giving the impression that he was trying to figure her out.

She had nothing with which to wipe her dishes, so she just set them on the ground to dry, then lowered herself on the riverbank, her legs spread wide apart, her arms propping her up from behind. Howard joined her, and together they sat there looking out at the broad expanse of river.

"Somewhere over there, the Rebs are campin' out," he said. "Probably waitin' for one of us Yanks to venture over so they can make mincemeat of us."

"Do you think they're watchin' us even now?" she asked, as a little quiver shimmied up her spine.

"They might be."

"Do they have lookin' glasses?"

"'Course they do, but they're not gonna waste their time on you and me. Just sittin' here like this, we pose no threat. Don't worry about it."

"Okay." She uprooted a long slice of grass and studied it for a moment, then tossed it aside. "I guess I have a lot to learn."

"Yep. Which brings me to my list of questions. What's your full name?"

"Gordon Snipp."

"Middle?"

"Pardon?"

"What's your middle name?"

She had to think for a second. "Oh. Paul."

He wrote it down. "Birth date?"

"June ninth, eighteen forty-four."

"Birthplace?"

"Norfolk, Virginia."

"Is that where your parents live now?"

"No, they…uh…they died of a fever about eight years ago. After their deaths, my younger brother and I moved to Philadelphia to live with our aunt and uncle."

"That so? And what're their names?"

"Why do you have to know that?"

He glanced up from his journal. "You don't have to tell me if you don't want to. I'm just tryin' to include as many details as I can. You heard me say Grimms wants to publish it after the war."

Josie nodded. "My uncle's name was Clarence, but he died a year or so back. My aunt is Bessie."

"No last name?" he asked, eyebrows raised.

She supposed it couldn't hurt to share her aunt's last name. She didn't want to give Howard reason to suspect her. "Garlow."

He nodded as he wrote. "Just a few more questions. What prompted you to enlist?"

"My little brother died at the Battle of Drewry's Bluff in the spring of sixty-two. He believed so strongly in preservin' the Union and abolishin' slavery, and I wanted to honor his name by pickin' up where he left off."

"I see. So, you allowed your little brother to go to battle without you?"

Her stomach muscles tightened of their own accord. "I tried to stop him, but he was stubborn. Bein' older, I had a certain responsibility to my aunt, but Andrew...well, he figured he could do more good if he fought for his country."

"I guess that was hard on you when he died."

"It was awful."

"I s'pose you felt partially responsible."

Josie grimaced. "It should've been me."

As Howard continued scrawling lines in his journal, a drum sounded in the distance, indicating it was time to get ready for drills. Josie picked up her dishes and stood. "Guess we'd better get back."

"Seems so." Howard pushed himself up. "Just one more question, if you don't mind. Are you really nineteen?"

Josie stifled a groan. "Why does everybody doubt my age?"

"Well, truth is, you just don't look nineteen. Don't sound it, neither. Most men your age have deeper voices."

Josie decided not to dignify his comments with a response. She turned and started trudging up the hill.

"Sorry, Snipp," Howard called after her. "Didn't mean to offend."

She nodded without turning around, breathing deeply to keep her calm. How long could she keep up this charade? Long enough to make a difference for the Union? She hated deception, but what choice did she have? As long as the army forbade women to join, she would have to wear the disguise.

Lord, forgive me.

⌣

Levi returned to camp during afternoon drills. Rather than return Rosie to the livery, he directed her toward the hospital, where he planned to check on privates Morse and Hodgers, as well as a few others from Company B who had fallen ill enough to warrant hospitalization.

In front of the makeshift hospital, he reined in Rosie, nimbly flung his right leg over her neck and hopped down, then tied Rosie to the hitching post before approaching the big open door. Overhead, a barn owl perched in broad daylight on the roof peak. The sight was strange, if not eerie, and he hoped it wasn't a bad omen—not that he took much stock in such things.

Added to the usual barn smells were the odors of medicines, blood, human waste, and even death. Levi cringed at the assault to his nostrils, then quickly prayed for divine strength and unmatched compassion for each suffering soul.

There seemed to be fewer medics on duty now than on his last visit, and he presumed most of them had needed to report for drills. He did, however, spot Major Walden, who stood with his back to Levi as he tended a patient. Levi's gaze traveled to Walt Morse's cot. It was empty, and a pang of sorrow gripped Levi's heart. Morse must have passed in the night, and while it wasn't a great surprise, the realization still hit him with a hard, painful thud. Thankfully, he then spotted Jim Hodgers sitting up, his color improved. Two others from Company B—Private Stan Gray and Corporal Richard Fuller—lay on their backs in two cots not far from where he stood. They appeared to be sleeping, so he chose not to disturb them.

"Sergeant Albright?" Hodgers pushed himself straighter by propping his skimpy pillow behind himself.

Levi offered him a smile and strode across the room toward him. As he did, Major Walden turned and gave Levi a brief wave. "I'll be with you shortly," he said.

"No hurry," Levi assured him. "I'll just visit with Private Hodgers."

When he reached Morse's bedside, he smiled down at the patient. "You're looking better today."

"I'm feeling some improved, thanks. 'Course, I didn't have the same ailment as Walt Morse. He came down with pneumonia, on top of some other things. I s'pose Doc Walden could fill you in better than I. Fellow was sicker than a rabid dog."

Levi shook his head.

"He's better off now, though, I suppose."

"Indeed he is. As the apostle Paul writes in the book of Philippians, to live is Christ, but to die is gain. By that, he meant that as long as we are on this earth, we should seek to live each day to the fullest, allowing Jesus to do His work through us. In that way, we will find joy and satisfaction. But to die is far better, because then we shall dwell with Christ forever. In that way, dying is to our benefit. I'm sure that Private Morse is experiencing that reality firsthand."

Hodgers squinted his eyes in a quizzical expression. "I don't know much about the Bible, Sarge, but I sure hope Morse didn't pass through the pearly gates."

Levi arched his eyebrows. "You would wish the alternative on him?"

"'Course not. I'm just sayin', I hope he don't pass through 'em before his time."

"Before his time?" Levi frowned in confusion, then removed his hat and whisked his fingers through his scruffy hair. "I don't think I'm following you. Private Morse isn't in his cot. I presumed he—"

"Private Morse made a rapid recovery, Sergeant," came Major Walden's voice from behind Levi.

Levi pivoted his body and stared at the approaching doctor. "Are you serious? He certainly appeared to be on his...well, his last legs, as they say."

"I agree wholeheartedly, and in all my years as a physician, I've never seen such an inexplicable recovery. That man was coughing and breathing erratically one minute, not to mention wheezing like a barking seal; the next minute, his temperature started dropping back to normal, his heart rate slowed, and his color returned to its customary shade. He's not completely well, mind you. He's weak and still working to regain his appetite. But I told him he could go back to his quarters because, frankly, he wasn't sick enough to stay. Hodgers, here, will be next to get released. He's made a remarkable improvement, as well, although Morse was far sicker than he. I don't understand it, myself; but then, that's often the way of the human body. It decides for itself when it's going to give up, and I guess, in Morse's case, his body wasn't ready to kiss this old earth good-bye."

Levi couldn't help the grin that sprouted on his face. "Don't you remember saying to me that if I were a praying man, you'd suggest I send up a prayer on his behalf? That about the only thing left was to try to keep him comfortable?"

Major Walden pinched his brows together. "I suppose I vaguely remember saying something to that effect. But you surely don't expect me to believe God had anything to do with this."

"I certainly do."

"Why would God miraculously cure these men while allowing countless others to perish on the battlefield every day?"

Levi shook his head. "I could never hope to explain it, Major. I only know that God sometimes chooses to move in extraordinary ways on behalf of His children, sometimes not, just as we see in His holy Word. It is not for my limited mind to try to understand; rather, it is for me to believe. Experiences such as these are what help to build our feeble faith. Surely, you can open your mind at least a small amount to the possibility that God just may have had a hand in Morse's recovery."

"Hmm." The furrows deepened in the doctor's brow. "I guess I'll have to think on that. In the meantime, I must get back to work. How about you pray for the rest of these patients? Maybe God will choose to heal some of them, as well."

Levi chuckled. "Ah, then you do believe."

"I didn't say that, Sergeant. Don't go putting words in my mouth."

Levi's smile stayed put. When he glanced at Hodgers, he found him wearing a half grin.

11

As August gave way to September, the weeks started melding together, each day like the one before, albeit becoming cooler and less sunny. While fall hadn't officially arrived, the trees had started changing color, and with the cooler nights upon them, everyone knew that summer's door would soon shut tight. Yesterday evening, Josie had even dug out her poncho for some extra warmth as she'd sat outside and chomping on hardtack and talking to the Gower boys. She'd learned that Joseph, twenty-four, had a wife and two children back in Butler, Pennsylvania, and that Henry, twenty-two, had left behind a sweetheart he planned to marry if he made it home alive. "Of course, you'll make it home alive," Josie had told him. "Just keep your head down."

When Henry had asked her if she had a girlfriend back in Philly, she'd answered with a vague comment about how she wasn't serious about anyone in particular, though she had a number of close female friends. Her answer seemed to satisfy the men, who soon switched topics.

Later that night, after retiring to her own tent, she'd lain awake thinking about home and her church, and wondering what Allison had told any fellow parishioners who might have inquired as to why Josie had stopped attending the weekly service. No letters had arrived from Allison, even though Josie had penned two more since the first one she'd sent to her cousin. The weekly mail call had become a lonely experience, with Josie scurrying to the mail wagon when she overheard the shouts announcing its arrival, and then waiting with hope in her heart for the mailman to call out her name, only to walk back to her tent empty-handed. Had her letters even reached Allison? Perhaps Aunt Bessie had confiscated them, although such an act would be utterly out of character for her aunt. Bessie wasn't the most affectionate person, but neither was she malicious.

At least twice a week, Josie went hunting before breakfast—one of her few pleasures these days, not to mention an excellent means of escaping the drudgery of army life. Some days, she managed to steal away by herself; other times, one or both of the Gower brothers went along. She liked them fine, especially since they didn't tend to pry too much with questions about her background. Her hunting efforts had paid off; lately, droves of soldiers had been drawn to Harv Patterson's fire by the aromas of roast duck or venison stew. Harv had kept his word, cooking whatever the hunters caught, although he joked that he was going to start charging by the bowl. Joking aside, Josie knew that if they could somehow continue hunting into the winter months, the extra nourishment of what they caught would help them survive the harsh elements. Last year, two soldiers had died in a blizzard, or so she'd heard.

"Knock, knock!" said a familiar-sounding male outside her tent the next morning. "Anyone home?"

Her heart took a strange leap at the realization Levi had come to visit. She hurried to tidy up the space. "Yes, yes, come in." As always, she endeavored to keep her voice low and controlled.

As Levi ducked into her tiny abode, the tent seemed to shrink to about the size of a dollhouse. It wasn't big enough for even Josie to stand up in, and now it seemed smaller than a pea pod with his crushing presence. She had to work harder than usual to conduct herself with composure.

"What're you up to, kid? Want to walk over to the hospital with me? You mentioned you had an interest in helping with the sick and wounded, and I figured you might want to come along."

Excitement churned inside her at the prospect of spending time with him. "Sure, I'd like to, but what about drills?"

"We're not having any today. Truth be told, I think Grimms is giving us the day off because we're about to move on soon."

"Move on?"

"Word is we're headed to Culpeper, Virginia."

"Culpeper? Where's that?"

"Twenty-five or so miles northwest of here. It'll probably amount to a two-day hike. It's not official yet, but I spoke with Grimms earlier, and he said the orders came down from Bateman yesterday."

"Then what in the world did we accomplish by comin' here? I thought surely there'd be a battle."

"There've been picket lines all up and down the river. Just because we aren't actively involved doesn't mean others aren't."

"I haven't seen any action yet, other than the dreadful drills."

One of Levi's eyebrows shot up. "And that disappoints you?"

Josie shook her head quickly. "No, not that. I just want to know that there's more to the army than drills, drills, and more drills."

Levi smiled. "You do know drills serve an important purpose, don't you?"

"O' course, but...."

"Gordon, any day that we don't have to shoot at somebody is a good day. Mind you, it's no way to win a war, but I frankly prefer drills to actual battles."

"Well, I don't have a hankerin' to pull the trigger on anyone, but I will if it means helpin' to save the Union."

"You're a brave young soldier, Private Snipp, and I'm proud to know you. As far as why our superiors sent us to the north fork, they wanted us to watch for enemy invasions. We pushed the Rebs back after Gettysburg, and it's been our job to make sure they stay back."

Josie frowned. "I don't think I've helped much in those efforts."

"You've helped more than you realize. Our presence alone was enough to deter them."

"Well, I guess I'd like to think I'm accomplishin' *somethin'* for my country."

"Oh, you are, Gordon. Right here in Company B, you've lifted plenty of spirits. Now then, have you had your breakfast?"

"No, sir, and my stomach was just remindin' me I need to eat."

"Well then, come on. Let's grab a bite and then head over to the hospital. I'll show you around."

She tossed her Bible into her knapsack and carried it along, in case she had a chance to read Scripture to some of the patients.

En route to the hospital, Levi talked about his new position as chaplain. "I'll be holding my first service Sunday after next. Whatever the conditions at Culpeper, there will be a service. I'll see to it."

"You're really gonna preach?" Josie asked him.

"I sure am."

"You write your sermon already?"

"I did, with a lot of divine help. Still don't consider myself a preacher. I'm nothing but a simple Quaker."

"But you can do all things through Christ who gives you the strength, remember?"

Out of the corner of her eye, she saw his look of surprise. "Maybe I ought to have you deliver the sermon the Sunday after."

Josie laughed. "No, thanks. I sure am lookin' forward to hearin' your message, though. I'll invite everybody I talk to."

Levi grinned. "I think you'll be my number one supporter."

"I think I already am, sir."

⌣

When the usual odors greeted them at the door to the hospital, Levi watched for Gordon's reaction. To his surprise, the boy didn't so much as cover his nose. It was so good to see Morse's cot empty, even though several additional beds were now occupied. Morse's recovery had been nothing short of miraculous; and while it had taken Morse a week or more to fully regain his strength, Levi did not believe it could've happened outside of God's healing touch. Morse seemed to agree, and had turned himself into a modern-day apostle Paul, evangelizing constantly and driving some of the soldiers crazy in the process. He was not to be deterred, however. He had experienced a miracle, and he meant to give all the glory and honor to God.

Major Walden greeted Levi with his usual hurried wave from the bedside of a patient. As far as Levi knew, the fellow never took a break, unless it was a brief pause to answer nature's call.

"I brought a friend with me today, Doctor," Levi said. "You can feel free to put him to work. He assures me he's got the stomach for the job."

Major Walden came over to greet them. "What's your name, young man?"

"Snipp, sir. Gordon Snipp." Good private that he was, Gordon saluted the major.

"At ease. Nice to make your acquaintance. I'm happy to put you to work, though the tasks may be rather tedious."

"I'll be glad to do whatever you ask of me, sir."

The major glanced at Levi with raised eyebrows, then proceeded to assign Gordon the tasks of carrying in the boxes of medical supplies from the latest delivery, emptying them, and organizing the items in their designated places; filling medicine bottles with pills and then labeling the bottles; folding clean cloths and stacking them on shelves; and, finally, checking patient after patient for fever. While Gordon worked, Levi also moved about the hospital, asking the patients if there was anything he could do to ease their misery, and offering to lift them in prayer if they so desired. His job was not to force himself or God's Word on anyone, but simply to administer comfort as best he could, even simply by sitting in silent prayer beside a suffering soldier.

One soldier named Ray from Company F asked Levi to record a letter to his mother for him. Levi pulled up a wooden stool and sat next to Ray, paper and pencil in hand.

Ray had barely gotten out the last of his stop-and-start dictation before closing his eyes and dropping into a fitful sleep. Levi would have to ask him later where to send the letter, for Ray had failed to give him an address. Levi folded the missive and stuck it under a dish on the crate next to Ray's cot, then glanced around. Gordon was about to pass by him, carrying a bedpan. His face was beet red—whether from the heat of the day or from embarrassment, Levi couldn't say. Gordon disappeared outside and didn't return right off, so Levi went to check on him. He had walked to the well in the barnyard and was rinsing out the pan. When done, he set the pan on the ground, then bent and splashed water on his face. Poor kid wasn't accustomed to this sort of work.

"You've been toiling away in there, Private. Are you quite fed up with the job already?"

Gordon turned with a lurching movement. "Sergeant! I didn't hear you comin'."

"You all right?"

"Of course. I was just—just cleanin' out this pan, here." He pointed to the vessel.

Levi gave a half grin. "Good thing you have a strong stomach, Snipp."

Gordon returned the smile, albeit his seemed rather forced. "A little blood don't bother me none, and it's common enough to stand around while another man relieves himself; I just ain't accustomed to havin' to dispose of his bodily waste."

Levi laughed outright. "I doubt anybody enjoys that aspect of nursing. You're doing a fine job, from what I can tell. But if you're ready to be done for the day, we can head back to camp."

He stood and ran a hand down his wet, rosy-cheeked face. "I think I'll stay here awhile longer. The doctor said he appreciates the help."

Levi raised his eyebrows. Gordon Snipp kept surprising him, from his mettle in the midst of unfavorable work to his familiarity with Scripture. "Well then, keep up the good work. I'll see you later." He glanced around again. "Where is the major, anyway?"

"I don't know. He simply told me he had some quick errands to run and would return in short order."

"I see. Well, I'll catch up with you later, then. You keep up the good work."

"Yes, sir." He bent to retrieve the bedpan, then strode across the grass toward the barn.

⁓

He darted from tree to tree, checking from behind each thick trunk to ensure no one followed. He didn't like delivering messages in broad daylight, but this one couldn't wait. He had to get word to the Rebs that the 23rd was moving out tomorrow. Culpeper was their next destination. He'd heard Grimms exchanging words with Albright, and he had to act fast. The way he understood it, Union forces planned to attack the Confederates right near the Orange and Alexandria Railroad between the Rappahannock and Bristoe Stations. He quivered with excitement at the prospect of passing along that juicy bit of information. Perchance it would even reach the ears of General Lee, and wouldn't that put a feather in his cap?

"Hey! Who goes there?"

The imposing male voice brought him to a quick halt. He turned slowly and saw a Union soldier, his rifle resting in the curve of his shoulder, aimed straight at him. In the shadow of the towering oaks, he didn't recognize him. Separate companies camped so close together that they meshed, every unit sharing the responsibility of guarding enemy lines. "Private Hemlock from Company B," he called back. "Who are you?" He raised his arms in a show of surrender, his own rifle hanging off his shoulder.

The fellow stepped closer. "Company B, eh? What're you doing out here in these thick woods? You're off base. You have a pass?"

"I ain't got no pass. Didn't know I needed one. No cause for worry, though. I'm just doing a little exploring. I asked your name."

"Exploring?" The fellow lowered his rifle a notch. "Explore all you want, but in your own territory, soldier. You're a good two miles from your home camp. Go on back."

"I might consider doing that…after you give me your name."

The soldier issued him a partial smile, but it was a cold one. "Sergeant Thomas Loyal, Company D. Satisfied?"

"Not really. What's your problem?"

"I've got no problem, other than that I asked you to go back to your camp, and you haven't moved yet."

"You didn't ask me, you told me."

"Look, I'm just doing my job. You might be a Union soldier, but I don't like your attitude. Matter of fact, I don't much like you. Now, get going."

They stared intently at each other. "Ain't that a shame, you dislikin' me right off? I'm a real likable character once you get to know me."

"Uh-huh. Be on your way, now."

"You mind if I go behind that tree over there and lift a leg first?" He used his head to signal behind him.

The soldier ran a hand down his smudged face. "Yes, I mind. How about taking your sorry self back to where you came from and seeking comfort behind one of your own trees?"

Anger welled up inside him. Had this man no respect for his own comrade? Yanks were alike—hypocritical mules, all of them. He might be wearing the same uniform as this low-life, but the creep wasn't worth beans. He tried to tamp down his inner rage, but it was no use. "Seems to me you're the one with the attitude."

The soldier hefted his rifle back up, aiming squarely at him. "I'm not going to tell you again. Get back to your company. Everybody knows a soldier with any brains doesn't trudge off into the deep woods on his own unless he's got some ulterior motive. What'd you say your name was?"

Blast! He couldn't recall the name he'd blurted out earlier.

The soldier swallowed hard and adjusted his footing, also setting his finger on the trigger. "I swear, I'll report you to your commanding officer if you don't go back." He gritted his teeth, his eyes dark and challenging. "Now."

He had had about all he could take. In an instant, he kicked the rifle out of the Yank's grasp. The weapon flew through the air and landed on the ground several feet away.

"What in the—?" Shock washed across the Yank's expression as he stood there, frozen in place.

He grabbed the soldier by the collar and hefted him up. "How's it feel, Yank? Who's the bully now, huh?"

The soldier's eyes bulged, as he fussed and whined and tried with all his might to thrash out of his powerful grasp until he dropped the Yank like a sack of rocks, and the fellow scrambled for breath, crawling to get away. Dumb coward! The problem was, he could not allow his escape. The Yank knew too much. He'd seen his face, and he'd be able to identify him if they ever met again. He hefted his rifle and cocked it. The soldier rolled over on his back and stared up at him. "No, please. Don't," he whimpered. "I'll keep my mouth shut. I promise."

He gave a gravelly laugh. "You fool. You think I believe you?" He aimed his rifle at the soldier's head."

After it was over, he stared down at the motionless body, blood oozing from both ears. He debated whether to drag the corpse into a more remote area but then decided he'd already lost enough time. Better to get moving before anyone detected his absence, or that of the dead Yank. With nary a look back, he set off on a run.

12

Curled up on the hard ground in her tent, Josie covered herself with a wool blanket to ward off the odd chill that ran through her body on this mild, late September evening. She felt utterly exhausted. Sure, they'd marched three days to reach Culpeper, but it hadn't been nearly as grueling a trip as the one they'd taken from Warrenton Junction to the north fork of the Rappahannock. This one had been a bit more relaxed, and they'd even taken plenty of rest breaks, camping two nights instead of one, and arriving the day before yesterday. She'd managed to find a somewhat private spot to pitch her little tent, not too far from a thicket of bushes, and only a short walk to the creek bed. Another chill raced through her, and her body took to quivering.

She worried that she might be coming down with the same illness that had stricken several other soldiers—ones she'd helped nurse back to health. After all, she'd fed them, pressed cold cloths to their foreheads, handled their bedding, and even carried their waste to the camp outhouse. "Lord, help me," she prayed with chattering teeth. "You know I can't afford to be sick. I can't go to the doctor, because then he would discover my secret. Moreover, I can't return to the hospital to help the others if I'm sick, as I might infect those who are recovering from battle wounds. Please heal me, Lord." But even as she uttered the prayer, she wondered if the Lord would honor it, since she was knowingly practicing deceit. Her head spun with a mix of confusion and pain, and the light supper she'd eaten earlier now churned around inside her stomach, threatening to come back up. She swallowed down a hard, burning lump, then coughed.

"Hey, Snipp, you in there?"

She quickly sat up and fixed her cap squarely on her head, gulping down her nausea. "Come in."

Private Walt Morse pulled back the flap of her tent and poked his head inside. "You settlin' in for bed already? Sun just barely went down."

"I was thinkin' on it."

He tilted his head at her. "You feelin' okay? You don't look so good."

She sat straighter and forced a smile. "I'm fine. What can I do for you?" And then came a cough she couldn't control. The sound was unsettling.

"That don't sound good," he said, ignoring her question. "You might be gettin' what I had for a while, there. I swear, I would've died if God hadn't reached down and spared me."

Josie maintained a happy face. "That was a miracle, all right, the way you turned the corner so quick-like. I'm not as sick as you were. Fact is, I don't even know if I'm sick. Might be just tired." All this she spoke with chattering teeth, unable to control them.

"Uh-huh." He eyed her skeptically. "How 'bout I just go get the doc? I bet he'd come right over and give you a quick check. He's got some powerful medi—"

"No! I don't want to see Major Walden. I—I don't wish to be a problem to anyone. I'll be fine by tomorrow. You'll see."

Morse shrugged. "Well, all right, then. But I'm not promisin' I won't come back and check on you later. In the meantime, I got some mail for you."

That news instantly cheered her. "You do?" She hadn't even bothered walking down to the mail wagon the last couple of times it had come, lest she grow more discouraged at never receiving anything.

Morse nodded. "Three letters, in fact, all from one Allison Garlow." He reached in his pocket and extracted three letters. "You got somebody back home that's sweet on you, Snipp?"

She gaped at him for a moment, then feigned a casual laugh as she took the letters from him. "No. Allison Garlow's my cousin."

"Ah, that's nice. Only people who write to me are my sisters and my ma. I was married once, but my wife left me. She was a wild one."

Josie barely heard him, between her pounding head and the distraction of three letters she was desperately eager to read. "I'm sorry about your wife," she muttered.

"Oh, it was a long time ago. You enjoy those letters, now, hear? Me, I'm gonna read the Good Book by firelight. Like I said, I'll come back later to check on you. You still got water in your canteen?"

"Yes, thanks. And thank you for bringin' my mail."

Morse studied her for a moment more. "You're welcome, kid. You get some rest."

As soon as the tent flap shut, Josie reached over and tied the strings to secure its closure, then collapsed on her back to catch her breath. After a minute or so, her strength returned enough for her to open her letters and read them in chronological order.

August 11, 1863

My dear Cousin Gordon,

I hope this letter finds you in the finest of health. I thoroughly enjoyed your letter. Please keep writing, as I want to hear all about your experiences. Forgive me for my curiosity, but have you had to shoot a Rebel soldier yet? It cannot be easy living outside when you were so long accustomed to having a roof over your head.

My mother was not pleased to discover that you had run away, and she is even less pleased with me for my refusal to share any details with her—to the point I fear she may begin withholding my meals. Please let me know when I may share your address with her. I do not wish to break my word to you; although, looking back, I don't believe I actually promised not to share it. You simply told me not to.

As it is, I have hidden away your letters in a place I'm confident she will never find them, and I will wait to receive permission to tell her of your whereabouts.

My younger brothers and sisters miss you madly. They ask continually where you are, and my response has been that you went away for a short time but will return soon. I hope I haven't told them an untruth.

I am still attending school, according to Mother's wishes, although I don't know how it shall benefit me in the future if all I do is marry a farmer and raise a bushel of children. It would please me greatly to do a man's work, such as practicing law or medicine. Of course, those fields are out of my reach, as I have no money for such frivolous dreams.

Mother is calling me to the kitchen now, so I must conclude this letter. I will try to post it tomorrow, in hopes that you will receive it in a timely manner.

I pray nightly that our Lord and Savior will keep you in His loving care.

> *Yours sincerely,*
> *Allison*

Josie smiled, despite her queasy stomach and aching head, not to mention the cold chills still running through her. She'd struggled to hold the letter still for all her trembling, but it was a relief to finally hear from Allison. She quickly read the second letter and the third, which brought more news of home but nothing earth-shattering. Still, to read them all did her heart much good.

Tomorrow, she would write a reply and let her cousin know that she need not withhold her address from Aunt Bessie any longer, but she would also emphasize that no amount of begging or coercing on Aunt Bessie's part would convince her to come home. Especially not when she felt God was using her in the hospital to encourage the soldiers, share the message of His love, and facilitate the healing process.

She carefully folded the letters, then tucked them into the bottom of her rucksack. Next, she decided to walk down to the creek to rinse her face and also tend to her nighttime ablutions. Perhaps doing that would make her feel better.

⁓

Levi kicked a few stray embers back into the fire, staring at the flickering flames, not participating in the conversation being carried on by several other soldiers seated nearby. In his pocket, he carried three new letters from Mary. He'd hurriedly read them on his walk back from the mail wagon. She was something, his Mary. Strange that he should think of her as his girl, considering he hadn't once looked upon her face or heard the sound of her voice. Perchance he wouldn't even like her upon meeting her, although he doubted that. Her letters made him believe she was a woman of patience, kindness, and generosity. No doubt, she would make a fine wife someday.

"What do you think our mission will be here in Culpeper?" asked Corporal Frank Vonfleet, drawing Levi out of his private musings.

"I ain't heard nothin'," answered Mark Wilson. "I'm just a medic. I'm always the last t' know."

"I heard we was supposed t' start throwin' up breastworks tomorrow," said Private Hodgers. Like Morse, Hodgers had made a full recovery; the difference was, he didn't attribute his healing to divine intervention but rather to pure strength of will. "Hear we're preparin' to charge the Rebs any day now. We got swamp and gulley on either side, so it'll be a straight shot. They got nowhere to go but back."

"Where do y' get your information?" asked John Cridland.

"Oh, here and there," Hodgers replied. "I just hear stuff."

"Probably just a rumor," said John. "Everything's hearsay till Grimms gives the final word. You heard anything, Sarge?"

Silence fell on the group, and Levi realized that the question had been directed at him. "Hodgers is right," he answered quickly. "We're to start building breastworks tomorrow in preparation for a possible battle. Need to keep pushing the Confederates further south. I've no idea how many troops they have, but word is they're closing in. Grimms is plenty happy that Captain Bateman issued orders for us to join in the fighting. For a while, there, he was worried we were going to finish out the war guarding the supply wagons."

"I frankly prefer guardin' the supply wagons to fightin'," said Howard Adams. "I ain't too keen on dyin'."

"I feel the same, but I'll fight if I have to," said Mark Wilson.

"Well, 'course I'll fight if I have to," Adams added. "That *is* why we're all here. It's just that I'd sooner live than die."

"Don't we all wish for that?" said Levi.

"Not me," put in Hiram McQuade. "I'd sooner fight than waste away. You're all a bunch of cowards."

"Are not," said Chester Woolsley.

"And you're the biggest one of all," McQuade snarled at Woolsley.

"Lay off him, won't you?" said John Cridland.

"Why should I? He's always askin' for a fight."

"Am not," said Woolsley. "You're the one who's always pickin' 'em."

Walt Morse entered the scene then and plopped down next to McQuade, his Bible in hand.

McQuade's frown spread. "You plannin' t' read your Bible right here and now?"

Morse looked at McQuade once he'd situated himself. "Actually, yes, I am. I need the firelight. Do you object?"

"Sure do. We was carryin' on a conversation, here. Why can't you go build your own fire? This is the army, not Sunday school."

"I built the fire," said Willie Speer. "And it's no skin off my back if you want to read by my firelight."

"Well, thank you very much, Corporal." Morse surveyed the rest of the men around the fire. "Carry on. Don't let me disturb you." Then he crossed his legs, opened his Bible in his lap, and began to read in silence.

Levi admired his courage and his newfound commitment to the Word of God. "You've made me think I ought to go get my own Bible," he said.

"Same here," said Charlie Clute.

"Me, too!" said Louie Walker.

"Suffering catfish, you're all a bunch of religious half-wits." McQuade pushed himself up from the ground, scowling down at them. "I ain't hangin' around here another second. Don't need Morse's pious poo rubbin' off on me."

No one tried coaxing him to stay.

"That McQuade is a contrary ol' cuss," said John Cridland. "Not sure how he came to have venom runnin' through his veins."

⌣

He lay on the ground, staring up at the stars and wondering what Company D had said about their fallen comrade Sergeant Thomas Loyal. Had there been a regiment-wide investigation? Or had the captain simply chalked up his unfortunate death to a sneak attack by Rebel fire? He almost hoped there'd be an investigation so he could laugh behind their backs when they came questioning his unit. Not a soul from Company B had missed him that day.

He'd passed three Union soldiers sitting on stools and munching apples from a nearby orchard. So engrossed were they in lazy-mannered talk, their rifles all propped against a tree stump, they'd never even detected him slinking past behind a large cluster of overgrown brush. Dumb fools. And they were supposed to be guarding the regiment against enemy invasion? Once he'd delivered his message to one Captain Lars Peregrine, he'd skedaddled back across the lines, this time accompanied by the captain himself. After crossing into Union territory, he was on his own, but he'd relished the royal treatment he'd received while on Rebel land. He was making a difference in this war, even if by picking off one Union soldier at a time. He thought about his family, once again recalling their mangled, bloodied bodies murdered at the hands of Union forces, and knew he couldn't quit yet—not until the South won the war. Not till then would he lay down his weapon and find peace. Resting here in the dark, with several soldiers snoring around him, he promised himself he would continue the charade and remain above suspicion, always endeavoring to be the best friend any soldier could ask for, all the while hating every last one.

He drifted off to sleep with a smile on his face.

13

True to his word, Morse returned later to Josie's tent to check on her. When he poked his head inside, she was reeling with nausea and felt hotter than a chimney.

"I'm goin' for the doc," he told her.

"No! Please. I can work through this on my own. I'm strong," she argued in her firmest voice. The last thing she needed was for the doctor to give her a good checking over.

"You look *real* strong," he said, tilting his lantern to get a look at her face.

She frowned at him.

"All right, I won't summon Major Walden—yet. But if you take a turn for the worse tomorrow, there'll be no argument, you hear? Gimme your canteen."

With a shaky hand, she passed it over to him.

"I'll put some fresh water in there. Be sure to keep drinkin' throughout the night."

She nodded. "Yes, sir."

"Be back soon," he said, then disappeared.

Half an hour later, there had been no sign of Morse. Moaning with discomfort, Josie clutched her middle. Her stomach twisted crazily, and an instant later, the inevitable hit. She was going to be sick. Turning on her side, she grabbed for the pan she'd situated nearby and let go all of what she'd eaten at her last meal, which hadn't been much, thankfully. What a fine predicament! A groan of agony tumbled out of her. She waited a minute, retched again, and then sighed with relief when her stomach finally settled.

Approaching footsteps rattled the dry leaves outside her tent. "Hey, kid, it's me." Levi peeked inside. "How you doing? Walt told me you— oh, kid, you really are sick."

Anybody else would have quickly extracted himself from the situation, but Levi crawled inside, felt her forehead, and frowned. "You're burning up. You want me to fetch the doctor?"

"No."

He sighed. "I thought you might say that. Walt told me you were being mighty stubborn. I ran into him down at the creek and offered to bring back your canteen. I bet you'd appreciate your aunt about now."

"Not really. I do my best sufferin' on my own."

"Well, at least I can take care of this for you." He picked up the pan of vomit. "Here's your canteen. Morse filled it with fresh water."

His kindness touched her to her core. "Thanks, but...you shouldn't be comin' anywhere near me. I would hate to get anybody else sick."

He paused on his way out of the tent. "Don't worry about me. I've been exposed to a fair share of illness in the army, and I'm pretty sturdy." He was that, all right. Even illness couldn't keep her from admiring his sheer solidness.

He returned in less than five minutes. "Rinsed it down at the creek," he said, crawling inside the tent and setting the pan next to her. "All ready for your next, uh, you know."

She turned up her top lip. "Don't say it. I prefer to think there won't be a next time." She shivered, then pulled her wool blanket closer to her throat.

"You're shaking like a wet pup." He touched his cool hand to her forehead again, and she closed her eyes. How good it felt. "I'll go fetch another blanket from the supply wagon."

"No, please. You don't need t' do that."

"I know, I know. You prefer to suffer on your own. But let me tell you, if you get any sicker, the doctor will insist on admitting you. There's no suffering on your own once you go to the hospital."

She exhaled a shuddery sigh. He made a good point. "All right, but I don't wanna put you out."

He issued her a half smile. "I'm the chaplain, remember? It's my duty to tend to the sick and dying."

"Dyin'? Do I look as if I'm dyin'?"

"Not yet, kid, but we're not taking any chances. I want you well enough to come listen to my first sermon on Sunday, so you can tell me how to improve for next time."

Josie shook her head. "I'm sure you'll deliver the finest sermon ever, first time 'round."

He gave a light chuckle. "You haven't heard many sermons, then."

She closed her eyes to ward off the beginnings of a headache, and silently prayed God would administer a speedy healing so she could attend the Sunday service.

She must have drifted to sleep, for the next thing she knew, someone was tucking another blanket around her body. She relished the extra warmth. "Thank you," she mumbled without opening her eyes.

"Try to get some sleep, now. I'll check on you again later."

"Hmm," she managed to mutter.

The one benefit of falling ill was being excused from drilling and building breastworks—not that she enjoyed shirking responsibility, but she simply didn't have the strength or energy to help. During the days of her sickness, she'd heard men shuffling past her tent, sergeants shouting orders, and soldiers cussing loud enough to burn her ears clean off. Mingled in with all that were snippets of halfway decent conversation and the occasional spurt of laughter. When they weren't constructing breastworks, the men were doing drills, their guns firing while the drill sergeants screeched orders. She could always tell when they stopped for a break, as a blissful hush fell all around.

Sick or well, the hardest part of her day was sneaking away to take care of her personal hygiene and then freshening up at the stream. She didn't want anyone to notice or point out her preference for privacy, so she always tried to sneak away at night and in the early-morning hours. Fortunately, several other soldiers in the camp seemed as modest as she, which helped her not to stand out as much.

It was three days later when Josie started feeling human again. She still had a lingering cough that threatened to unravel her patience, but she was confident the worst was over, and thrilled also to realize she'd seemingly caught a milder form of the ailment than many of her fellow soldiers. Truly, God had been watching over her day and night.

"Hello? Anybody in there?" came a male voice outside her tent on her first day of feeling well enough to get up.

She hurried to cover herself. "Come in.".

Private Howard Adams poked his head inside the flap. "Brought you your wage."

Her heart lurched. "My—wage? You mean, money?"

He laughed. "You didn't think you were workin' for the government for free, did y'?"

"No, I s'pose not." She sat up and ignored the dizziness that engulfed her. It would take a few more days for her to regain her strength completely.

He studied her. "You're startin' to look a wee better, boy. I don't never want the ague. So far, I've managed to avoid it. You feelin' okay?"

"Much better, thanks." She was glad for a chance to tell the truth.

"I ain't gonna get sick if I come in contact with y', am I?"

"I don't know. You'd better stay clear o' me."

"Easily." He opened up his bag and produced a large money pouch. "As company recorder, I also got the job of distributin' men's pay. Comes in the form of notes, mind you, but they're good as gold at any bank. The sutler will trade with 'em, too." He reached inside and rifled around, then finally withdrew two ten-dollar notes and some coinage. "Here you go. Glad you're feelin' better."

"Thanks." She accepted the money, reveling in the way it felt in her hands—her very own payment for service to her country.

"The form here indicates y' got paid accordin' t' how many days you been in service. You should be gettin' your next money ration right around Thanksgiving. It'll be a full two months' worth then, you'll see. Anyway, y' earned every cent o' that money, soldier." Howard closed the pouch once more and dropped it into his sack.

A warm spot blossomed in her heart. "Thanks, Private. I appreciate that. I need to send at least half o' this back to my aunt. What's the best way to go about doin' that?"

"Oh, that's easy. You gotta sign up through the Allotment Commission. You can talk to Grimms about that. It's a pretty safe way to send money home, as long as you work through Grimms. It'll go straight to the post office where your family member will pick it up. Some soldiers don't trust the system an' hang on to their money till they can find what they consider a safer method. Me, I just spend it all at the sutler's wagon or in town whenever we get a day or night off."

"I see." Josie frowned. "Do we ever get a day off?"

Howard chuckled. "Not lately, but this winter, there'll be opportunities for breaking camp. Not much fightin' goes on in the dead o' winter."

"I've heard that."

"Hear we can expect to do some fightin' real soon, though. Guess you may have to stay back till you're feelin' better."

"I'll pull my weight no matter what," Josie told him. "I didn't join the army so I could lie around an' mope."

He slanted his head at her. "You're pretty brave for a young whippersnapper."

"No braver than any of the rest o' my comrades."

"If you say so. Well, I best be gettin' around to the rest of Company B. News will spread that the paymaster came in, and they'll all be wantin' their money."

She thanked him again, and he vanished through the tent opening, his boots making a rustling sound in the leaves as he departed.

All through that night, Josie battled further with her sickness. Every time she thought she was on the verge of recovery, the malady came back with such a vengeance that she wondered if wrestling a Reb might be less torturous. By morning, she felt no better, but she wouldn't let on if asked. She did not want anyone sending for the doctor.

Company B had met up with several other units to conduct a mock battle. With the continual musket fire and cannon blasts, she couldn't have slept for all the world. She'd figured she might as well try stretching her weak, shaky legs outside instead of lie inside and mope about her sorry state. The air was unusually brisk, even with the bright sun beaming down, and she ventured out with her blanket wrapped around her.

"Hey, Snipp. How you doin'?"

She turned and smiled at Chester Woolsley as he approached. The big fellow had a clumsy gait and a happy, childlike demeanor—unless Hiram McQuade was around. Did he truly understand the implications of war and the role he played in it? "Hello, Chester. I'm feeling a little stronger today. Thank you for askin'. Why aren't you out on the field today?"

Chester shrugged. "The lieutenant, he tol' me to stay back and keep watch."

"Keep watch? And what might you be lookin' for?"

"The Rebs, silly." He palmed the rifle tucked under his arm, and she wondered if it was fully loaded. "Ain't you always on the lookout?"

"Oh! Yes, indeed." Levi had told her in confidence that mock battles sometimes sent Woolsley into a nervous frenzy, and so the drill sergeant often excused him. Josie wondered why the army didn't just send him home. Levi had said Company B recognized his inability to reason like a normal adult, so his comrades looked after him—with the exception of McQuade, who looked out only for himself.

"Do you need anything?" he asked, coming up beside her.

"No, but thank you for askin'."

"I could fetch you some fresh water from the creek."

"My canteen's almost full, so that's not necessary."

"How about I go get ya somethin' from the sutler's wagon?"

"Right now, I'm not too hungry for anything, Chester. Anybody ever tell you you're a thoughtful guy?"

He beamed and stuck out his chest. "I get told that all the time. I like helpin' people."

"Well, you do a fine job of it."

By now, Josie's legs were threatening to give out, so she sat at the base of a tree just outside her tent. Once she'd plopped down, she waved her hand to invite Chester to join her. He sat on the ground, leaned back against the tree trunk, and crossed his legs at the ankles. "I sure do miss my mama," he mused aloud, a wistful smile on his face. "She sends me a letter every week." Then he scowled. "But Hiram McQuade, he's jealous o' my letters. That's why he's so mean to me."

"Does he get any mail?" Josie asked.

"Not that I've seen."

"I wonder if he has family."

"He don't talk about his family, but I know he gots some."

"How do you know?"

"I…I just know, that's all."

"Oh." She decided not to pry.

"His mama—well, never mind. My mama always tells me to stop runnin' off at the mouth, an' I oughtta mind what she says." He paused. "Someone tol' me you got no parents. Is that true?"

Josie nodded. "It's true, all right. My parents died when I was just a young g—kid." It shocked her that she'd almost let the word *girl* slip past her lips. How thankful she was that Chester evidently hadn't noticed her blunder.

"How old was y'?"

"I was eleven. My brother was nine. We went to live with my aunt and uncle and a slew o' cousins. My uncle passed into glory last year, and since then, times have been hard on Aunt Bessie. I joined the army so she would have one less mouth to feed. She's barely getting by as it is, with all her kids."

"That's nice. Sounds like fun. Livin' with all those cousins, I mean. It ain't fun losin' your parents. My papa died, y' know."

"I heard that, an' I'm sorry. But you have your mother and all her letters to hold on to."

Their conversation continued until Josie grew too tired to go on. "I think I best go lie down again, Chester," she said as she struggled to her feet, using the tree trunk for support.

"Okay. It was real nice talkin' to y'."

"Likewise." She turned toward her tent.

"You goin' t' church tomorrow?" he asked.

"Church?" She twisted around to look at Chester. "Is tomorrow Sunday?"

"It sure is. That's what Sergeant Albright tol' me. He says I should come to hear 'im preach."

Sickness had caused her to lose all track of time. "You bet I'm goin'."

He smiled, revealing a top row of yellow, crooked teeth. "Wanna go together? I'll come by your tent 'round seven o'clock."

"That'd be real nice, Chester. I'll see you in the mornin'."

14

On Sunday morning, Levi woke to rumbling thunder and heavy rain. He wondered if anyone would even bother showing up to the service, which he planned to hold beneath the towering oak tree just outside his tent. One major benefit about assuming the role of chaplain was that he'd inherited the former chaplain's living quarters. The tent was large enough to accommodate five or six people, so he supposed that if the attendance was low enough, they could just assemble inside, safe from the elements. Fortunately, he didn't have to carry the cumbersome tent; whenever they marched, he threw the bulky thing on the back of one of the supply wagons.

He slipped outside and hurried down to the creek to tend to his morning ablutions. It was barely dawn, so he had to pick his way downhill through the dark with care. Several others had gathered there, as well, but no one seemed in the mood for talking on such a gloomy morning. Levi went about his duties and had just started back up the hill when he saw Private Snipp coming down. The fellow didn't walk with his usual chipper gait, but he at least appeared on the mend from his troublesome bout with the ague.

Gordon spotted him and smiled. "Mornin', sir."

"Good morning to you, Gordon. How are you faring on this fine, wet day?"

"Better than yesterday, sir."

They paused to converse beneath the boughs of a tree, partly protected from the drizzle. "That's good news. You came through it without the doctor's assistance, after all. Good for you."

Gordon puffed out his narrow chest. "I told you I was strong."

Levi couldn't help chuckling. "That you did. Are you strong enough to come to Sunday service this morning?"

"Indeed. Chester and I plan on walkin' over together."

"So, Chester is coming, too, is he? Good. That's three of us, then."

"There'll be more. I'll see to it."

Levi swiped a sleeve across his rain-soaked face. "You do your best to rally up the men, Gordon. I don't mind saying I'm a trifle nervous."

"No need to be. I'll be prayin' for you. The Lord's gonna bless every word that comes outta your mouth. I just know it."

Lightning split the sky, followed by a thunderous boom, and the heavens opened up to release a gush of rain. It felt as if someone had tipped an entire kettle of water on their heads. With a hasty farewell, the two parted ways, Levi racing for his tent, and Gordon finishing his trek down the hill.

Levi could hardly believe it when close to 30 soldiers showed up for Sunday worship. Since there was no way to squeeze everyone into his tent, a couple of fellows strung up a big canvas tarp in a nearby copse of trees to create a crude yet effective shelter for the attendees. Of course, there wasn't a dry one among them, but no one minded. At this stage, most of them had grown accustomed to all manner of weather.

Once the men were gathered in the makeshift sanctuary, Levi quickly prayed in silence that the jitters he'd had ever since awaking would dissipate. Then he smiled and cleared his throat. "Good morning, everyone. Thank you for coming out to worship with us today."

"Our pleasure," Gordon piped up from his position smack in the middle of the front row. A couple of men echoed him with "You bet" and "Amen."

Levi shifted his weight from one foot to the other. He didn't know half the men in attendance, as they'd come from other companies. He pressed his Bible to his chest and said, "How about we open our service with prayer? Bow your heads with me." He offered up a simple prayer to invite God's presence into their service, and as he prayed, a wave of peace came over him.

Rain pelted the canvas roof, and continuous bolts of lightning and booms of thunder competed for the men's attention; Levi did his best to reel them in. They started by singing "Amazing Grace," albeit a bit out of tune. Next, Levi announced his plan to hold a service every Sunday, barring any unforeseen battles. He also encouraged the men to come find him at any time throughout the week if they wished to talk or pray.

After that, he went straight into his sermon, based on the passage Chaplain Morris had suggested: Philippians 4:13, "*I can do all things through Christ which strengtheneth me.*" He recognized how difficult it was to be away from loved ones, especially in the face of the dangers and hardships of war. He talked about the loneliness that plagued the soldiers, that feeling of total isolation, and even the fears that beset them when on the battlefield, such as wondering if they would wake up the next morning with all their body parts intact. He reminded them of their humanness and assured them that it was normal to think these thoughts, but he also emphasized that there is hope, even in the darkest of situations, for those who place their trust in Christ—the One who would lead them through the trials of war and never leave them.

He ended his message with a question: "Do you walk in confidence, knowing Jesus as your Savior?" Then they bowed their heads again for the closing prayer, after which Levi invited anyone who wished to speak with him afterward to come forward.

Although the drenching rain continued, it didn't affect anyone's spirit, as far as Levi could tell. He dismissed them, saying he hoped to see them all again next Sunday, and encouraging them to invite others. Several soldiers approached him to shake his hand and thank him for his encouraging message. No one sought him out for prayer, and that was fine. He was the new chaplain, and it would probably take them awhile to get to know him well enough to feel comfortable confiding in him.

Gordon Snipp was the last to approach him. He grinned. "You did real good. See? No need for nerves."

"Thanks," Levi said. "I'm not sure I got the message across in the most eloquent way, but I appreciate the encouragement, my friend."

"Oh, but you did. It's like you was born to speak behind a pulpit. Perhaps one day you'll be a minister in a church."

Levi tossed back his head and laughed. "Not in the Society of Friends, I'm afraid. We don't have any ordained reverends."

"Well, you could take a pulpit for another denomination, right?"

Something pricked at Levi's spirit. He had never entertained the notion of leaving the Society of Friends. "I…I suppose. I just don't see myself taking on such a role. I'm a farmer at heart."

"Couldn't you do both? Farm during the week, preach on Sunday?"

Levi chuckled. "I think there's a lot more to being a pastor than just preaching on Sundays."

"Hm. You're probably right. Besides, a person needs to feel the call of God before takin' on such an endeavor. I'm just thinkin' you'd be good at it. You're a real good encourager, you got wisdom, and you know the Bible."

"I appreciate your words, Gordon, but I don't think I have what it takes."

"Weren't you just preachin' about gettin' your strength from the Lord? When you don't feel up to a particular task, you call on God for strength."

Levi swept a hand through his hair and shook his head. "You got me good on that one. I did say that. I suppose I'd better put my own words into practice."

"That was a fine lecture, Chaplain," said an approaching soldier Levi recognized from past Sunday services but didn't know personally. He was unusually tall and looked to be in his thirties. "I daresay you deliver as good a sermon as Chaplain Morris used to do." The fellow extended his hand, and they shook. "Name's Terry Brady." He glanced down at Gordon. "Sorry, didn't mean to interrupt."

"Not at all," Gordon said, craning his neck to meet the fellow's eyes. "We was just makin' small talk. I'm Gordon Snipp." He shook hands with Brady, still gazing upward. "What's your unit?"

"Company D. We're the ones who lost a soldier to…strange circumstances. Sergeant Thomas Loyal. Did you hear about that?"

"Yes, I heard about that." Levi noticed the look of confusion on Gordon's face. "You missed the news when you were sick, kid," he explained. "Someone shot a Federal out in the woods." Then to Terry Brady, he added, "Has the investigation turned up any answers?"

"Last I heard, they concluded one or more Rebels must've snuck over the line an' shot him at close range. It's not clear whether there was a struggle, but it didn't appear so. Looks like they just picked him off."

"He must've been out there on his own, then, huh?" Levi said.

"I don't know the particulars, but I'm assuming so," Brady said.

"Nobody's safe." Jim Hodgers joined their circle. "I overheard you talkin' 'bout that soldier some Reb shot last week. What a rotten deal."

"Loyal was a pretty good guy, too." Brady sighed. "Well, I'd better return to my unit before I miss roll call. Nice talking to you all. See you next Sunday."

"And bring some friends," Levi told him.

"I'll do my best."

The morning trumpet sounded. "There's our signal for roll call," said Jim. He tipped the bill of his cap at Levi and Josie, then walked off. The sun decided to peek out from behind some clouds for a moment, but just enough to tease; as quickly as it had appeared, it disappeared behind another veil of gray. At least the rain had lessened.

"You feeling up to a full day today, Gordon?" Levi asked. "The drill sergeant has been running Company B into the ground this week."

"I'm gonna give it my all, sir. I'm feelin' much better today—especially after that sermon. I can do all things through Christ who gives me the strength."

"That's the spirit." Levi winked and gave Gordon a pat on the shoulder. "You're good for me, you know that? You always manage to make me smile."

Gordon gave a sheepish grin and looked at the ground. The toe of his boot made a little hole in the dirt. "Well, thanks, Sarge. You do the same for me."

Levi chuckled. "I'll see you at roll call."

~

So much for investigative skills. No one had discerned the fact that there'd been a tussle before the murder of Sergeant Loyal. It felt good to know he was doing his part for the Confederates, not to mention avenging the massacre of his family. It was his duty, and he would not quit until the Confederates had won the war.

He'd forced himself to go to the church meeting because he had to make sure he showed up whenever or wherever there might be a valuable exchange of information. He never knew when he might learn something vital to pass on to his Rebel comrades. Good thing he'd gone, too, because now he knew he was completely free of suspicion concerning Loyal's death. What a bunch of dumb Yanks.

~

The drills were especially rough that day, but Josie wasn't about to complain. She'd missed almost a week due to illness and simply needed to get back into the usual routine. She didn't want anyone thinking her slothful. By the time they broke for the noon meal, she was awash with sweat and about as weak as a newborn lamb. Keeping her eyes on the path, she followed her unit back to camp, anxious for a chance to rest a bit before returning to the fields for another mock battle. Her ears buzzed from the echo of cannon fire, and her mouth was parched. Some days, she wondered what on earth had possessed her to take on this role of soldier. Was she really making a difference for her country? In the end, would there even be a sense of true satisfaction? Her shoulders drooped with exhaustion as she shuffled toward her tent.

"Hey, boy, wait up," someone hollered from behind her.

She stopped and turned.

Howard Adams waved at her. With him were Jim Hodgers, John Cridland, and Willie Speer. Soon the four caught up with her.

"You feelin' better?" Howard asked.

"Yes, thanks."

"You don't look so chipper," said Willie. "You'd better stay back and rest after you've eaten."

"I'm fine." Josie waved him off. "Besides, I've already missed almost a week of drills. I need the practice."

"I heard the Rebels are movin' closer to the lines," said John. "You need all the practice you can get."

"Who told you they were movin' in?" asked Willie.

"Heard it from Vonfleet. He ought t' know, seein's as he's in good with Grimms."

"I wish he'd tell the rest of us," said Howard. "I hate those sneak attacks."

"You and me both," said Jim. "One o' these nights, we'll be sleepin' sound when a band o' Rebs comes in an' finishes us off."

"That's why I sleep with my gun," Willie confessed. "Got my trigger finger in place, too. Ain't no Reb gonna pull one over on me. No, sir!"

Josie listened to their banter but didn't join in. Listening was plenty enough to make her nerves turn inside out. What if the enemy did sneak in unawares? Would she be prepared? Moreover, if coming face-to-face with a Confederate, would she be able to look him in the eye and actually pull the trigger? That's what these drills were all about. She couldn't afford to miss any more practice. She pulled back her shoulders and took a deep breath. "Let's go get us some grub," she said, forcing strength into her tone.

They trooped off in the direction of Harv Patterson's camp. Harv had promised venison stew today, and the line would be long.

15

The first half of October was quiet. The 23rd Regiment had been posted at Culpeper for days, guarding the Orange and Alexandria Railroad, doing fatigue duty, picketing the lines, and drilling daily, but making little advances on the enemy. Soon, however, the peaceful atmosphere was shattered when news reached Company B that General Robert E. Lee had taken the Army of Northern Virginia across the Rapidan River in an attempt to outmaneuver General Meade's Union forces at Bristoe Station.

Lieutenant Grimms ordered Company B to make haste and ready itself for battle, saying they had exactly one hour to fill their haversacks with three days' rations, an extra set of clothing, blankets, and a full canteen. Levi was down at the creek with Gordon Snipp, Jim Hodgers, Willie Speer, and several others, washing their tin plates and cups after a rather skimpy noon meal, when the orders came in. Distant gunshots and cannon fire sputtered, and everywhere Levi looked, soldiers were donning their gear, gathering their bedrolls, assembling their rations, and readying their weapons—examining barrels, looking down sights, and checking their supply of ammunition. Suiting up for battle always brought on a mixture of emotions; everyone desired to do his part to end the war, yet also feared the consequences of coming face-to-face with the enemy.

As regiment chaplain, Levi had his mind centered more on his fellow soldiers than on the contesting Confederates. He would carry his weapon for self-defense only. Instinctively, he searched out Gordon but lost sight of him, hoping against all hope the boy would know what to do. He whispered a prayer for him and for the rest of Company B's newest recruits. As Levi headed in the direction of the livery to fetch his horse, Lieutenant Grimms came upon him on horseback, his spine as straight as a pin in the saddle, his chest puffed like a proud peacock. A few of his men rode along behind him, and they all pulled back on the reins when Grimms called his horse to a halt and leveled his gaze at Levi. "Finally got some decent orders, Sergeant." He gave a slanted half grin. "This is our chance to prove our worth. See to it that Company B follows your lead."

"My lead, sir? I'm the chaplain now, remember? It's Sergeant Clute who will lead them now."

"Clute's fine, but I trust your shrewd thinking. He'll appreciate your support. Word is that General A. P. Hill's Confederate corps tried to cut off what Hill thought was the rear guard of Meade's retreating army to Centreville. He was sadly mistaken, though, and it's costing him plenty in horses and soldiers. Trouble is, Union soldiers are dropping like flies, too, so we have to march up to Auburn, where the fighting is most severe, and lend a hand before moving on toward Bristoe Station. It's going to be a bloody mess, I'm afraid. You'll hear a drum roll in less than an hour. I expect you and Sergeant Clute to see to it that Company B is in tip-top shape and ready to fall in line with the rest of the Twenty-third. Another brigade is advancing from Washington. Between us, we'll whip them Rebs to shreds."

"I'm sure you're right, Lieutenant," Levi replied with a quick salute.

Grimms returned the gesture, then urged his horse forward, his solemn-faced men following.

Levi's heart thumped hard against his chest as he jogged off to the livery. At the stable wagon, he mounted Rosie, thankful that the liveryman had already saddled her up and was awaiting his arrival. He gave her a hard squeeze in the ribs with his feet, then headed toward his camp to pack up. "Lord, go with us," he whispered.

The drum sounded at one o'clock on the dot. There was a scurry of soldiers coming from every direction to form a line. One of Grimms's soldiers, Sergeant Tom Harold, sat tall on his horse, holding high the Union flag, his proud-looking shoulders pulled back. Grimms guided his own horse around and rode up and down the line, stern-faced, assessing each man. Drill sergeant Louie Walker and a few other appointed soldiers presented everyone with several boxes of ammunition and ordered them to fill their weapons to the extent of 100 rounds. Levi was thankful for Rosie's saddlebags to carry the weight, but he worried that some of the younger fellows—Gordon, in particular—would have a rough go of it, marching with all that extra weight. Levi searched out his young friend and finally spotted him halfway back, a determined expression on his flushed face. He'd recovered well from his bout with that awful ague, and the way he stood there now, body taut, shoulders firm, one wouldn't even guess he'd been sick. Pride welled up in Levi for the way he'd bounced back.

"All right, men, listen up!" shouted Grimms. "News came down that there is skirmishing up near Bristoe Station. General Hill marched his men into Union territory in an attempt to drive the Union further north. So far, our men are holding their own, but they need reinforcements, so that's why we're moving. See to it that you all push forward, stay strong, and put your rifles to good use. Keep your heads down. We don't want no heroes here, just brave soldiers working together."

"Yes, sir!" came a loud call in unison.

At the sound of tramping feet in the distance, Levi knew more units were on the move. There would be hundreds, if not thousands, descending on Auburn and Bristoe Station today. He hoped and prayed everyone from his squadron would remain safe, in spite of the likelihood that some would be lost.

"Sergeants Clute and Albright will give the orders as we pass them down," Grimms added. "Stay alert." Without further ado, he turned his horse and galloped to the front. "Forward, march!"

The soldiers tramped along single file, weapons propped on their firm shoulders. No one talked today. This was a ceremonial event, grave and solemn, and Levi knew the mind of every soldier had to be racing with all manner of thought. He prayed for the men as he gave Rosie a tender kick in both sides, coaxing her into a trot.

⟜⟝

Josie marched and prayed, marched and prayed. This was to be her first real battle, and she wasn't ashamed to admit her fear, at least to herself. At the same time, a sense of exhilaration welled up inside her. This was her chance to do her part, to carry out Andrew's passion and fight for the Union, to preserve her country. "Lord, help me. Give me strength and courage." She found herself repeating Deuteronomy 31:6 in a quiet voice as she trudged along: *Be strong and of a good courage, fear not, nor be afraid of them: for the LORD thy God, he it is that doth go with thee; he will not fail thee, nor forsake thee.*

"Say it a little louder," said Harv Patterson, whom she was following. She repeated the verse for his sake, and when she'd finished, someone behind her said, "Amen."

The sun shone brightly, but it didn't warm her as much as desired due to the brisk autumn wind nipping her nose and cheeks. They marched along the riverbank, and were it not for the dire circumstances under which they moved, she might have taken a moment to enjoy the sight. Later on, they passed deserted farms, dilapidated shacks, and broken fences. All around were the ravages of war. Josie adjusted the weight on her weary back and tried not to think about how weak she still was from having suffered that horrid illness. At the same time, she thanked the Lord for preserving her life. Surely, He had a special purpose in store for her.

They had traveled at least three miles when hundreds of Union soldiers started slogging past on the retreat, shoulders stooped, faces wearing dull expressions, as blood oozed down their faces. Able-bodied men carried stretchers conveying those who couldn't walk, and as they passed, a few of them made eye contact with Company B and muttered such comments as, "Turn back while you still have the chance." "Don't go out there. You're gonna catch the wrath of the devil if you do."

Josie could feel her eyes bulging, but she resolved to keep pace with her unit. Levi had been riding up and down the line, speaking words of encouragement not only to Company B, but also to the units in front and behind them.

If only she could climb up behind him in the saddle, wrap her arms around his middle, and bury her face in his strong back. She gave her head a shake at the silly notion, forcing her mind to return to the present—not a difficult transition, considering the constant roar of artillery and the splash of musketry up ahead, the earsplitting blasts becoming louder as her unit approached them. The dreadful load on her back made walking difficult, but she kept on because none of her comrades faltered.

Soon the regiment slowed almost to a stop, so Josie poked her head out from the line and saw that they'd come to a large field. Others craned their necks to see, as well. Slowly, they progressed forward until they came to a ravine, which they began to cross. When Josie was halfway to the opposite bank, a shower of bullets riddled the ranks, sending soldiers into a state of frenzy. Some were killed instantly; others squealed with pain from having been shot. Mass confusion ensued, with men gathering and scattering simultaneously. Sergeant Albright gave a loud shout to fall in, and those who heard, obeyed. "Forward!" he repeated. "Forward! Enemy at right flank!"

Most of Company B, and a few soldiers who'd been separated from their own units, followed Levi into a thickly wooded area, hoping for concealment from the enemy. Still, bullets could find them, Josie knew. She sagged under the weight of the load she carried, but she would not give in to fatigue. Besides, her mind and spirit were on full alert. Green as she was in battle, she was ready, with God's help, to fight for her country.

Charlie Clute rode into the area and quickly dismounted. "The Rebs lay in ambush at that far side of the field," he reported. Josie had seen the puffs of white smoke coming from the thickets and brush and every felled tree and log.

"All right, then what's the plan, Sarge?" Levi asked his friend. "You're in command here."

Everyone crushed close together, breathing hard and straining to hear over the rounds of gunfire blasting in the background. Clute heaved a loud breath, swallowed, and nodded. "Okay, men, we're going to spread out. If we move forward in one cluster, we're apt to be pummeled by the same Minié, and if that happens, we all go down. Better one than ten."

"I'm prone to agree," Levi said. "But some of us who are more experienced ought to pair up with a greenie. I'll take Private Snipp."

Josie refused to let her relief show; instead, she kept her lips pursed and gave a curt nod.

"I'll go with Hugh," said Howard. "Private Galloway, you can follow us."

"You three watch out for one another," Levi said.

Everyone quickly paired up with someone else, leaving Hiram McQuade and Chester Woolsley looking at each other.

Levi leveled Hiram with a steady, stern face. "You take care of him, hear?"

Hiram lifted the corner of his top lip. "I ain't gonna shoot 'im, if that's what you're gettin' at."

Levi turned his head a notch but kept his eyes firmly locked on Hiram. "I'll hold you to that."

"Do I hafta go with him?" Chester said with a low groan.

Bullets whistled through a clump of trees not ten feet from the outermost person in the huddle. "No time to argue," said Charlie. "When I give the order, I want you to go out shooting. Don't stop, whatever you do. There are breastworks out there, and plenty of trees and fallen logs. Run for cover, but keep shooting—and shoot straight." Everyone gave a solemn nod. "And remember this: we're going out as a team, but in the end…well, it's going to be every man for himself. You got that?" There were more nods and solemn grunts of agreement. "All right, then. May God go with you."

Once Charlie gave the order, it was pure pandemonium. For a moment, Josie froze in place, caught off guard by the hoots, cheers, and primal howls coming from the men around her as they cut loose with their weapons. The next thing she knew, Levi's big hand gripped hold of her arm and yanked her out of her stupor. "Come on, soldier boy. You can do this."

⌒

Levi dragged Gordon behind him, firing off continuous shots from his weapon in the direction of the enemy, but hardly able to see a thing for all the smoke and dust. When they came upon a felled log, he pulled Gordon down beside him. The poor kid already wore a shocked expression, and he'd barely seen anything yet, unless one counted the two dead bodies they'd had to jump over while running. "You okay, Gordon?"

"What?"

Levi gave him a little shake to awaken him from his dazed state. "A good way to get yourself killed is to run out in the line of fire without firing back. I'm a pacifist by nature, but even I am not going to run into battle unprepared. I swore that I wasn't going to use my gun today, but I've been forced to go back on my word. I want to live another day, and I want you to, as well."

Gordon's eyes rounded like big boulders. "I didn't realize it was gonna be so loud and so…."

"Terrifying?"

Gordon nodded. "But I'll be okay. I'm ready to defend myself and my country." He readied his rifle, adjusted his position on the ground so that he lay flat on his belly, and then propped his gun on the log, squinting through the sight. Levi grinned and lay next to him, his weapon aimed and ready.

"When do I fire?" Gordon asked.

"Now would be good."

"All I see's white smoke."

Bullets whizzed over their heads. Gordon's body jolted. He gave a whoop and a holler, then fired off three shots.

16

*J*osie squeezed shut her smarting eyes against the flying dust and smoke, and repositioned herself behind the fallen log. Bullets continued buzzing past, but fortunately, none of them found her. Levi had gone to tend to the wounded, leaving her with strict orders not to move but to continue firing in the direction of the enemy. Of their company, Lieutenant Grimms had taken a bullet to the leg and fallen from his horse. Private Stan Gray and Corporal Richard Fuller had also suffered wounds, but she couldn't tell from where she lay if they were dead or alive. "Oh, Lord, help us. Protect us," she muttered as she reloaded her rifle.

On the front lines, a soldier from another company manfully bore the Union flag. Heavy fire concentrated on him and the men nearby, and soon a number of them fell to the hard earth. She couldn't distinguish who they were, since all the companies were mixing together, and she could only tell the Rebs from the Union soldiers by the color of their uniforms. Rebels opened fire, using grape canister and shell and whatever other heavy manner of deadly missiles they had on hand, and the Union fired back with just as much vehemence. To Josie's untrained eye, it seemed the Confederates had an edge in the battle; but then she noted just as many Rebs sprawled out as Federals, so it was hard to tell. She mournfully wondered if any of her bullets had met their targets. Above the roar of gunfire were cheers and yips from both sides. Who was winning this awful skirmish? She continued firing, determined not to let down or disappoint her comrades, Levi most of all.

After several minutes, Levi's voice broke through the din of artillery: "Gordon, we're advancing." He waved an arm at her to follow, so she did, running through a thick cloud to get to him. "We're heading for that section of trees over there," he said, pointing. "Don't lose sight of me."

"I won't."

He took off running, and she hastened after him. A moment later, she tripped over something—a fallen soldier's leg, she soon realized—and fell to the ground, her upper and lower teeth clashing when her chin hit the hard earth. Someone grabbed hold of her arm with a pinching grip, and she went still as a dead dog. Lying beside her, a Rebel soldier glared at her with fierce eyes. Blood trickled from a terrible head wound. "Water," he rasped. "I…need…water." His breaths were short and labored. She thought of the biblical command "If thine enemy thirst, give him drink." Without a second's thought, she reached for her canteen, unscrewed the cap, and touched the rim to his open lips, then slowly poured the liquid in. It filled his mouth to overflowing, for he didn't swallow; he just let it run down the jaws of his grimy face. His steady gaze on her went dim until there was no life left in his eyes. She sat back, stunned and shaken, realizing she was the last person to have seen him alive—this man-boy who must've been close to her in age. Did he have a girl waiting for him back home? A mother fretting over him? Siblings who prayed for him every night?

She reached down and closed his eyes. No sooner did she do that than she felt another firm grip on her arm. "Gordon, come on. We've got to move." As gunfire sizzled overhead, she gave the poor Reb one last hurried glimpse, then let Levi yank her across the field, the two ducking and diving as they went.

Bullets filled the air, clipping every little bush and weed and blade of grass around them. Some men had their hats blown off, but better that than their heads. Peering through the clump of trees where several from Company B had escaped, Levi spotted overcoats, haversacks, and even a few weapons strewn about on the field, along with bodies too numerous to count. It was a frightful scene, but from what he could tell, most of Company B was still alive. Grimms had been shot in the leg and quickly taken away by stretcher, even though he'd grumbled all the while that he was fine and needed to stay with his unit. Private Stan Gray suffered a surface wound, and Corporal Fuller's shoulder had taken a shot. Fumes from burning gunpowder filled Levi's nostrils and burned his parched throat. Riderless horses thundered past, and cannonballs flew in all directions, cutting off huge tree limbs that fell to the ground in earth-shattering quakes.

Levi looked around for Charlie Clute but couldn't find him. "Anybody seen Charlie?"

"Not I," said Frank Vonfleet. "I think he fell in with another unit."

"Another unit? He's supposed to be issuing commands to us."

"Last I saw him, he was dancing over some bullets," said John Cridland.

"Well, I hope he's all right." Levi worried for his friend. "For now, we need to advance along with the rest of our regiment. If we stay focused, watch our backs, and stay alert, we'll push back the enemy to the point of retreat. That's our goal, anyway. Captain Bateman has issued orders to companies D and K to bring in the heavy artillery. When they arrive, be prepared to charge after the blast of the first cannons. We're assigned as relief. Understand?"

Everyone nodded his assent, including Gordon Snipp. The poor kid had seen more today than Levi hoped he'd see for the rest of his life, although something told him it was only the beginning. "Lord, go with us," he said aloud.

"Amen," the men returned in unison.

〜

Cannon fire exploded like the fiercest thunder and lightning, striking down each Rebel soldier advancing on their camp. It angered him to see such brutal treatment of his Southern brothers. The battle raged on for the possession of Bristoe Station, every man armed with nerves of steel and ice to do his utmost. Trouble was, the Union was winning, as the Rebs fell back like cowards. He wanted to scream at them not to give up the fight. Instead, when the clouds of smoke grew too thick and heavy to see through, he moved up behind the closest Federal he could find and fired his weapon into his back. The fellow fell to his death with a thud, and a tiny thread of satisfaction wove itself around his heart. He turned the blue-coated soldier over with a good shove of his boot, then narrowed his eyes as he assessed him to make sure he was dead. Satisfied, he moved on, enjoying a small taste of triumph in this bitter battle.

Hearing Sergeant Albright shout "Onward!" through the din, he moved further away from the fallen soldier and into line with his troop, rifle aimed and ready. He only hoped he wouldn't find himself in a position of being expected to kill a Reb. If he ever came face-to-face with one in battle, he would sooner surrender his weapon and let the Rebel take him, dead or alive, than kill a Southern brother.

〜

About the time the sun started setting, friend and foe alike put an end to the fearful slaughter, at least for the day. From what Levi could tell, and based on the news that had come down from their regiment officers, the Confederates had suffered a far greater loss of lives than the Union had, at a ratio of approximately three to one. The Confederates had, however, managed to take out a big section of the Orange and Alexandria Railroad. As soon as the Union succeeded in pushing the Rebs back far enough, repair work on the tracks would have to begin, as the railroad was a major means of transporting much-needed goods and supplies for the Union.

Levi was numb with exhaustion, but he had no time for feeling sorry for himself when so many sick, wounded, and even dying men needed him. Company B had fared well compared to those who'd led today's battle, namely, Battery F, under the command of Lieutenant Bruce Rickets. Levi had no idea of the total number dead, except that it was in the hundreds. And he was almost certain the fighting would resume in the morning.

After joining the others to wolf down a bite of supper, Levi made his way to the temporary medics' quarters. Everywhere, the smell of death lingered, and groans of pain resonated. Dusk was falling, so soldiers knew the urgency with which they had to act as they collected the corpses strewn across the field. Designated privates had already buried scores of soldiers, and the wounded had been laid out on makeshift beds in the open air. Horses, too, lay dead, their bodies already swelling. They would be the last to receive burial, if they were buried at all. Wolves and other wild animals would no doubt come to consume the carcasses. The whole landscape was a mass of ruination.

Gordon came up alongside Levi. "Mind if I join you?"

"I'd welcome that," Levi answered, not slowing his pace. "You did well today, Gordon."

"Thanks. Thought I was pretty much a coward for the first half or so."

Levi shook his head. "Don't talk that way. Nobody knows how he'll do in his first battle."

"Thanks for, you know, comin' to my aid. I might be dead right now if you hadn't been watchin' out for me."

Levi smiled. It was a relief to carry on a regular conversation after a day of such massive destruction. "You're a good soldier, and don't let anyone try to convince you otherwise."

Gordon pushed his mop of brown hair out of his eyes, then tucked a thick clump of it under the front of his cap. Every soldier could use a good bath, shave, and haircut. Well, most needed a shave, anyway, except for Gordon. Levi still believed the boy to be closer to the age of fourteen or fifteen—certainly not nineteen, as he claimed to be—but he wouldn't bother questioning him further, as it mattered little to him. The kid had his reasons for joining the army, and as long as he fulfilled his obligations, it was nobody's business but his own.

They soon reached the medic's wagon, where doctors and their assistants were doing their best to treat the wounded. A loud wail split the air, and Levi imagined someone waking while undergoing a grueling surgery. Dozens upon dozens of soldiers lay sprawled on mats, some still covered in blood because no one had found the time to assess their wounds. "I'll go see where the doctor can best use me," Gordon said.

"Sounds good. I'll talk to you later." Once the boy had gone, Levi approached the nearest patient and knelt down next to him. The fellow had fallen into a fitful sleep, so to avoid bothering him, he simply lifted up a prayer on his behalf, then moved on to the next soldier, and then the next, and the next. He found Lieutenant Grimms among the wounded just as the fellow was standing with the aid of a couple of other soldiers.

"What are you doing, Lieutenant?" Levi asked. "You shouldn't be up and around yet."

Grimms looked up and gave a flick of his wrist. "Pfff. I'm better off than most everyone else. I'm not staying here when I'm needed on the field. The major bandaged me up just fine. Says I was plenty lucky."

"Is that right? Well, you should at least take the remainder of the night to sleep. You'll be better off all around if you get some rest."

"No time." Then to one of his men, he said, "Get my horse, Corporal."

The young man nodded and hurried off.

Around ten o'clock, flashes of lightning lit the sky, and thick storm clouds opened up to dump torrents of rain on man and beast alike. Thunder rolled overhead, and in the ruckus, a few horses, some wounded and others simply wild with confusion, came running through the darkness, making for a gravely dangerous situation. After several minutes, someone managed to corral the runaways. As the night wore on, the rain let up, and word had it that reinforcements were moving in, disembarking by the boatloads. Soon, hundreds of soldiers slogged past, giving off whoops of encouragement. "Don't worry, boys," they shouted. "We'll whip them Rebs in the morrow." Even the sickest soldiers turned their heads at the sight of them and managed a tiny grin, Levi heaving great breaths of relief himself.

Throughout the night, Levi caught glimpses of the tireless Gordon Snipp tending to the wounded—lifting their weary heads and giving them drink, or changing bandages that covered gaping wounds. The boy was a wonder, the way he went from one man to the next, bending over him and sometimes doing nothing more than whispering in his ear before moving on. By four in the morning, Levi had managed to visit at least a hundred wounded soldiers who had suffered the gravest of injuries. Some of them were delirious with pain and unaware of his presence, and others clung to him for glimmers of hope in their dark reality, moaning in agony and begging for relief. Doctors and medics administered large doses of whiskey to temporarily put them out of their misery, knowing the process would have to be repeated every few hours.

Just before dawn, Levi plopped down at the base of a big tree, the cold, muddy earth soaking through to his skin. He'd been up since early dawn the day prior, and now, almost 24 hours later, he couldn't go another minute ignoring his deep need for rest.

As he lay down, trying to find a comfortable position, Gordon came along and dropped down beside him. "Think I'll do the same, Sarge. I'm whipped." His voice cracked from weariness.

"Make yourself at home, boy."

Gordon turned one way and then another, finally coming to rest on his side facing Levi. Levi lay on his back, staring at the overhead branches still heavy with leaves that were now orange and yellow. It wouldn't be long before they covered the earth in a blanket of varied hues. He felt Gordon's eyes on him, so he turned his head toward him. "You did good tonight, boy. You've got a noble heart."

"As do you, Sarge."

He studied the boy's face a bit. Something about the somewhat effeminate features bothered him, though he couldn't quite pinpoint it. He scrunched his brow and gave his head a little shake.

"What's the matter?" Gordon asked. "You look downright puzzled."

He didn't dare bring himself to tell Gordon that he looked a little like a girl. He'd embarrass the poor kid, surely hurt his feelings. "It's nothing. Get some rest."

"I will. Hope you can do the same." Gordon closed his eyes and lay back, and Levi considered his features once more. His eyelashes seemed unusually long for a young man. Levi frowned again, and then, because he didn't dare scrutinize another man for an excessive period of time, he flipped onto his side, putting his back to Gordon, and willed himself to think about Mary Foster. *Mary is so pretty*, his sister Frances had written in her last letter. *She is so eager to meet thee face-to-face. Truth be told, I think she is falling in love with thee. It would be to thy benefit to reciprocate her affections, brother, dear.* Within seconds, he drifted off, but his troubling thoughts kept him from deep slumber.

17

When Josie awakened, she opened her eyes and found herself lying on her side, nose to nose with a sleeping Levi. At some point, shivering in her damp clothes from the drenching rain, she must have unconsciously drawn closer to Levi to borrow his warmth. Good gracious, what would he think if he woke up and found her so near? His breaths came out soft and steady, and Josie lay there a moment, enjoying the feel of them wafting warmly across her cheeks. *Lord, but he is handsome. If only I could tell him the truth about my identity.*

She abruptly switched to her other side, inwardly scolding herself for entertaining such an alarming thought. Telling him would ruin everything. Their friendship would change, the teasing would stop, he would quit speaking to her, and, worst, he would hate her for deceiving him and all of Company B. Not only that, but he would report her to Lieutenant Grimms, who would immediately serve her discharge papers. If that happened, the Lord only knew where she'd go. She couldn't return to Aunt Bessie's, and she couldn't possibly make enough money on her own to support herself. She lacked the schooling for a professional job. Besides, she'd joined the army in honor of Andrew, determined to pick up where he left off. Deserting her duties now would only bring disgrace upon Andrew's memory, and she couldn't bear the thought of that.

Images of yesterday's long battle chased through her mind, and she felt her brow wrinkle with distaste at all she'd seen and done. Whether the shots she'd fired had hit any Rebels, she couldn't say, but the very thought of the prospect set her nerves to jumping. Would the 23rd have to endure yet another battle today once the sun rose, and both sides came to life? More soldiers had arrived in the night—it had sounded like hundreds or even thousands. Now, the noises she heard were the moans and groans of injured soldiers and the murmurs of medics offering assistance. She covered her ears with her hands in hopes of drowning out the pitiful cries, but it was no use. She couldn't lie there another minute. Ailing soldiers needed her. Rising, she brushed herself off, cast one last look at the slumbering Levi, then adjusted her hat and set off toward the medic's wagon.

The fighting continued for the remainder of the week, but after that first day, it dropped off dramatically as the Union forces succeeded in driving the Rebels further back, captured five guns of the Confederate battery, and dismantled several divisions. The aftermath was ugly, with almost 1,400 Confederate casualties to the Union's 540. It was a victory for the Union, but not as decisive as some would have liked.

On October 14, the 23rd rendezvoused at Centreville with the rest of the Army of the Potomac to await further orders. Once they were settled in Centreville, Josie worked with Major Walden and the staff of medics almost round the clock, taking her meals on the run and sleeping only when she could no longer hold her head up. Assisting the sick and injured fulfilled a need in her, perhaps in some small way assuaging the sting of Andrew's death and giving her a greater sense of purpose. Furthermore, it kept her body busy and her mind focused. She saw Levi daily, as he, too, tended to the sick and injured, the difference being that he ministered to their souls while she ministered to their physical needs. It was a good bond that they had formed, but her growing awareness of him, if not her physical attraction, made her ever conscious of the need to maintain her male façade.

The stench of death was everywhere. It had taken days to gather all the dead and wounded soldiers from the battlefield, and even when the Army of the Potomac advanced to Centreville, the remains of many Rebel soldiers still lay on the ground unclaimed, stiff and hollow-eyed. Some lay sprawled behind logs, their bodies dismembered, whereas others still gripped tightly to their guns, their bodies intact, as they lay on their stomachs as if taking an afternoon snooze, the only signs of death being the large bloodstains covering their jackets. On the march to Centreville, Josie had even spotted one Rebel leaning against a dry stump with a violin tightly grasped in his hand, no doubt having been killed instantly. Another poor fellow sat leaning against a tree. Frank Vonfleet had walked over to him and removed his hat, revealing that the Reb's complexion had turned a sickening grayish yellow. Frank then gave him a shove, and he toppled like a dead limb onto his side, his leg pointing to the sky. A few soldiers had chuckled, but Josie had grimaced. Never would she accustom herself to the sight of a corpse, even though many people would claim that war had a way of hardening the heart, of making a dead body appear no different from a fallen tree.

O Lord, keep my heart soft toward others and Thee, she'd prayed. *Please don't allow this war to change me to that extent.* It had already changed her, of course. Some days, she felt far older than nineteen. She had seen too much not to feel the impact; but instead of making her cynical, the sights, sounds, and smells had strengthened her resolve that she'd made the right decision in joining the army. It was the least she could do.

When the mail wagon rolled in on October 24, to Josie's delight, she received three missives—two from Allison and one from Aunt Bessie, all postmarked a few days apart. She fingered the letter from Aunt Bessie almost fearfully for several moments before finally lifting the seal and unfolding the feather-light paper. Settling on the ground and leaning back against a tree, Josie braced herself for the contents.

She gave a start at the greeting—"*My dear Josephine.*" At least her aunt had addressed the letter using Josie's pseudonym. Her heart thumped hard. She could only pray that no one had opened the paper ahead of her, although it did not appear to show any evidence of tampering. Besides, the seal had been intact. Josie would have to make it clear in her reply that her aunt must use her army name in future correspondence, yet somehow express it in a way that would not trigger suspicion, should anyone open her letter for purposes of inspection. She sighed deeply before reading on.

I was shocked to hear that you had left to join the army without so much as a good-bye to your cousins and me, and was further surprised, not to mention displeased, that you did not wish to share your mailing address with me. Of course, I understand that your intent was good, so I shall forgive you. I can only hope that you did not join because you felt pressured to leave your Philadelphia home. I never meant for you to feel unwelcome here. Yes, times are hard, but not so much that we cannot get by. Ever since you and Andrew came to live with us, I have tried to treat you as one of my own; but I suppose I wasn't always forthright in letting you know how much I cared. I miss your presence here, as do your cousins, and we will always miss dear Andrew.

I hope you are faring fine, staying healthy, and getting enough to eat, in spite of what I've heard: that the rations are slim and sickness is rampant. I pray the Lord will keep you safe. I can't bear to think that something might happen to you. I've already lost the rest of your family.

Several folks from Philadelphia Methodist have been asking about you on Sundays. They are determined to wheedle as much as they can out of Allison and me. Do not fear; we did not tell them you had joined the Union, as I feared they would go to the local newspaper. You never can tell what some people will do. Instead, I told them that you'd decided to make your own way in life. Perhaps you can let me know how to handle their questions in the future. Reverend Tisdel has also inquired, so I took him aside and told him the truth. I wish you could have seen how his eyes nearly popped out of his face. I swore him to secrecy, then felt foolish for it afterward. He is the minister, after all. If we can't trust him, whom can we trust?

Among our family, your cousins Arnold and Janice have inquired the most about your absence, likely since they are the most aware of it, given their age. They cannot understand why you left with nary a good-bye. Allison tells them nothing, except that you're fine. They are quite irritated that she knows something they do not. At least, everyone is busy with school activities, so that has proved a good distraction for all, including Allison.

As autumn is here, I trust you're staying warm at night. I cannot imagine your sleeping accommodations. I suppose it is for the best that I don't know all the details. It is enough for me that God knows. He will watch over you and, I trust, bring you safely home when the time is right.

Do take care of yourself. It is not necessary that you write back to me, as Allison has said she will share your forthcoming letters with me.

I shall hold you continually in my prayers, dear niece.
Aunt Bessie

PS: At my last visit to the post office, I received your bank note. My dear child, I must tell you how much I appreciate your generosity, but please do not send me any more of your hard-earned money. You must hold on to it for your own needs. We are faring well enough here on the sale of eggs and my handmade items. We had a good harvest this year and will survive the winter. The Lord is good to us.

Josie quickly folded the missive, planning to reread it later before turning in for the night. How good it felt to know Aunt Bessie held no animosity toward her for leaving so abruptly. Granted, she'd made it clear she didn't approve, but she also hadn't insisted Josie drop everything and return to Philadelphia. Josie sighed with relief at not having to reply to her. Perhaps this would be the one and only letter Aunt Bessie would send her, as well. She hoped so, for she couldn't take any chances with her using Josie's given name again—or referring to her as her niece.

Before reading her letters from Allison, she glanced about and spied several other soldiers sitting in the shade of a tree, engrossed in their own mail. Just then, her eyes connected with Levi's, and the two waved hurriedly to each other. He dropped his gaze first, so she watched him for a few more seconds as he unfolded a piece of paper, no doubt another letter from his beloved Mary Foster. A niggling irritation stung her at the core whenever she thought of his growing affection, perhaps even love, for this woman he had yet to lay eyes upon.

She gathered her belongings, deciding to return to her tent to read her other letters. An awful urge to cry had hit her unawares, and the last thing she needed was for another soldier to catch her in an emotional state, particularly the crude and rude Hiram McQuade, who was, even now, sauntering past wearing his usual sneer. He appeared to be heading in the direction of Chester Woolsley, probably to taunt the poor man about his thick stack of mail. Normally, Josie would have stuck around to defend Chester, but today, she didn't have it in her. Upon standing, she cast another glance at Levi, but he was too engrossed in his letter to look up.

Dry sticks crunched beneath her boots on her walk back to her tent. She was glad that the majority of Company B had gathered around the mail wagon. She would take advantage of her solitude to go in search of a private spot to switch out her soiled rag for a clean one. It was her wretched "time of the month."

⌒

He settled into a seat not far from Hodgers, Vonfleet, and Cridland, all absorbed in their own letters. He never got any mail. Why should anyone write him? Most didn't know where he was, and if they did, they didn't care. He had no relatives to speak of, not any longer.

He was still plenty perturbed by the outcome of the battle at Bristoe Station. Too many Rebs had lost their lives, mostly due to Lieutenant General A. P. Hill's misdirection. Oh, the Confederates had briefly secured a foothold—until the Union's II Corps came up from Auburn and staged an ambush, driving them back and capturing several of their big guns. To make matters worse, Colonel Mallon was killed in the fighting, weakening Confederate forces the more.

He'd heard little talk about the Union's next move, but as soon as he learned something, he'd notify the Rebel army. He wouldn't let them down. And if the 23rd was summoned to fight in the next battle, he'd do his part by picking off a few more of his Union "comrades." Perhaps he'd choose someone from his own company next time.

Through narrowed eyes, he studied that idiot Woolsley sifting through his letters from home. He'd make the easiest target for miles around. The big galoot couldn't hit a cow from five feet away. Then, there was Louie Walker, the drill sergeant. He wouldn't mind knocking him off. He could always aim for Private Gray, or maybe one of the medics, such as Sergeant Mark Wilson. He'd consider Sergeant Albright, but that fellow was fast and clever. He'd sooner concentrate on the weaker ones. There was always that sissy Snipp fellow. Kid insisted he was nineteen. He would believe that the day he saw a goat lay an egg.

Snipp would make a good target. Now to watch for the right opportunity.

⌒

My dear Levi,

Thee cannot know how much I cherish each word in thy letters. I must confess, I pore over each one and even try to read between the lines. I notice I tend to write five missives to thy one. I know thee leads a busy life, so I fully understand why it is so hard for thee to keep up with me.

My life here at Father and Mother's house has been somewhat dull of late. Mother and I have finished most of the preserving and drying, putting up such foods as potatoes, squash, carrots, and such for winter storage. My younger brother and sister are busy with schoolwork, and I have been helping Father in our store.

I have enjoyed getting to know thy parents and siblings at Meeting on First Day. I can only dream of dinners around thy family's table, *and the raucous laughter that is sure to fill thy house. Of course, wartime changes things, and since thee is fighting hard to help preserve the Union, I am sure the laughter in thy house, and in many other homes across this great land, has been reduced a great deal.*

Thy sister Rebecca and her sheriff husband paid a visit to Arch Street Meeting House this past First Day. I had met her only once before that. She is lovely, and her children are quite endearing and friendly. It appears thy sister and brother-in-law are devoted parents. I look forward to having a family of my own one day, hopefully a houseful of youngsters. Has thee ever considered how many children thee would like? But perhaps this is the sort of topic best discussed in person.

I must soon prepare for bed. The nights here are growing quite chilly indeed, and already I dread the frigid temperatures of winter. I pray that thee will be warm enough in that season, wherever it is that your unit may be settled. Perhaps one day soon, thee will decide thee has had enough of the army and will return to thy home on Sunset Ridge.

As always, I look forward to thy letters with great anticipation, such that my heart flutters whenever I see an envelope marked with thy fine penmanship. I pray I have not embarrassed thee too much with this silly admission. I don't normally speak so frankly. In fact, most people think of me as being somewhat shy. However, with thee, I seek to be as honest and open as possible. Perhaps one day, we shall be more than just friends.

With tender thoughts of thee and, of course, my heartfelt prayers,
Mary Foster

Levi exhaled a heavy breath while folding Mary's letter. It would seem the young lady was moving right along with her affections for him and not being shy at all about expressing them. He didn't know quite how to feel about that, as he had been much less forthright with her. He supposed his attraction to her was growing. She did seem like a lovely person and would probably make a fine wife someday, but was she the one God had chosen for him?

He broke the seal of his next letter, one from his mother. Hers would be far less doting, full of news from the farm—how much the family missed him, how unhappy she still was that he'd joined the army when she'd raised him to be a God-fearing pacifist, and how lovely it would be when he finally returned to Sunset Ridge to live in the little house he'd built on the family's property and resume his farm duties. He felt a tiny prick in his spirit as he recalled Gordon Snipp's suggestion that he consider the preaching profession, reminding Levi that there were plenty of denominations that hired preachers. That was true enough, but was Levi fit to stand behind a pulpit Sunday after Sunday to present God's holy Word? He was nothing but a common, ordinary fellow.

He removed his mother's letter from the envelope and read it, then chuckled to himself. It contained almost everything he'd anticipated. His mother was nothing if not predictable.

He read his few remaining pieces of mail, then refolded each one, returned it to its envelope, and stuffed everything into his sack before heading back to his tent. He had a Sunday sermon to prepare, the premise of which was already swirling around in his head.

18

As October drew to a close, the air had chilled to the point where snow seemed imminent. Josie stretched her legs out straight so that the fire's warmth would penetrate her boots, then pulled her cap down further, her freshly cut hair reminding her how heavily she'd always depended on her long locks to keep her ears warm. Several other soldiers had visited the traveling barber today, including Levi, who'd stood in line behind Josie, awaiting his own shave and haircut. They'd conversed while they waited their turns, he inquiring more than ever before about Andrew and the battle he'd so bravely fought at Drewry's Bluff. Josie had been happy to share every detail she was aware of.

When it was her turn to sit in the barber's chair, she noticed Levi watching her intently. She smiled up at him while the barber chopped away at her hair, cutting it close to the nape of her neck.

"No whiskers yet, eh, boy?" the barber had mused.

Josie hadn't replied, other than to give a forced chuckle. She was glad when the barber lathered up her face, anyway, and then rinsed it with cool water.

"Late bloomer," Levi had put in.

"A *real* late one," supplied Hiram McQuade in a snide tone, laughing sarcastically from his spot in the line.

Oh, how Josie loathed that character. Levi, on the other hand, had been slowly stealing her heart. She had never been in love, but the feelings she had for him were probably as close as it came. What a predicament! He would never know her true feelings, and now that he seemed to be scrutinizing her more closely than usual, she knew she ought to avoid spending time alone with him.

She sat with a group of soldiers around Harv Patterson's fire that night, gnawing on hardtack and jerky and sipping hot coffee. It had been a relatively slow day, in terms of labor. No one from Company B had been assigned to work on fortifications, and so they'd mostly taken advantage of their unexpected free time to catch up on writing letters, reading, playing cards, whittling, and even napping. Josie had volunteered at the medic's wagon, but even that hadn't been laborious; several patients had been shipped off to a bigger hospital, while others had recovered enough to return to camp.

Things seemed to have quieted down on the front lines, too, although skirmishes still happened, and battles raged in various parts of the country every day. In the past week alone, news had filtered in about fighting in Florida, southern Virginia, Arkansas, and Tennessee.

Soon Levi joined the group, and, sure enough, he sat next to Josie. At least they weren't alone this time. It couldn't hurt to make small talk with him. "I sure enjoyed your sermon last Sunday," she told him.

"Why thank you, Private," Levi said with a grin.

"So did I." Howard Adams kicked a small stick into the fire. "I never was much for church, growin' up, but now that you been preachin' every Sunday, I find myself not wantin' to miss."

"I never went t' church, neither, but I ain't about to start now," said Hiram McQuade. "No offense to you, Albright."

"None taken. Everyone's got his own opinion regarding the Lord Almighty. I just happen to believe He has a great love for His creation, and He'd like nothing more than for souls to come to Him in total surrender."

"What's that mean—total surrender?" asked Mark Wilson. "Like, we gotta lay down our lives an' let the enemy walk all over us? I ain't doin' that."

Levi chortled. "Not at all. Surrendering to God is a completely different thing. It means giving our lives wholeheartedly to God, through Jesus; it means seeking His forgiveness for our sins, being truly repentant for the wrongs we have done against Him and others, turning away from our sin, and starting a brand-new life with God. We're still human, so we'll make plenty of mistakes along the way. This world is far from perfect thanks to our earliest relatives, Adam and Eve."

"They's what started this whole big mess," put in Chester Woolsley.

A few of the men laughed out loud, including Levi, and not for the first time Josie thought how pleasant a voice he had. He was just the sort of man she wanted to marry someday—kind, generous, patient, likable, and having a strong faith. She quickly upbraided herself for such a thought. Good gracious, she had joined the army to serve her country and to honor Andrew's memory—not to fall in love with a man who took her for a boy.

"Whatcha preachin' on this Sunday?" asked Stan Gray, who had made a remarkable recovery from his battle wound.

Levi scratched his head. "Not sure yet, but I've no doubt the Lord will put an idea or two in my head. You planning to come?"

"I might." Stan shrugged. "Depends on how long Adams, here, keeps me up playin' cards." He winked at Howard. "He plays for blood."

"That ain't the kinda thing y' tell a preacher, fool," Howard snapped. "He'll condemn us all t' Hades."

Levi tossed back his head with a laugh. "Luckily, judging's not my job. I hand that responsibility over to Him," he said, pointing heavenward.

After a few minutes, the banter wound down. Josie yawned and stretched her arms. "I think I'll say g'night, fellas."

When she stood, Levi did the same. "I'll walk with you, kid."

The pronouncement both delighted and unnerved her. On the one hand, she loved walking and talking with him; on the other hand, she still thought it best to avoid being alone with him. Yet she couldn't very well tell him she didn't want his company. She gave a nonchalant nod. If anyone thought it odd that he'd offered to escort her back to her tent, he didn't let on. In fact, most of the others were getting to their feet, appearing ready to turn in for the night. Only Howard, Hiram, and Willie Speer remained seated.

"Major Walden told me he sure appreciates your volunteer work in the field hospital," Levi said, hands tucked in his pants' pockets as he strolled beside Josie. The cold ground and dead leaves crackled and crunched beneath their boots.

Josie made a point to keep enough distance between them so as not to brush against him. Lately, the slightest touch from him sent a quiver up her spine.

"Did he say that? Well, I enjoy helpin' as much as I can. It brings me pleasure to help make the soldiers comfortable." She concentrated on her voice and her gait, ever striving to sound and maneuver like a man. Her success was questionable, she knew, given how mercilessly Hiram McQuade pestered her. "I wonder what the future holds in terms o' battles. I'd hate to see more injuries like the ones our men suffered at Bristoe Station."

Though she kept her head down, she could feel his gaze on her. "Injuries are bound to happen, Gordon. This is war."

"I know that. Doesn't mean I accept it."

"You've got a soft heart."

His remark made her nervous. Was he beginning to see through her charade? "I...I guess I've always had a soft spot—for all livin' creatures."

"Yet you've spoken of your fondness for hunting animals."

"Well, that's different. A person's got to eat. Don't mean I want the poor critters to suffer. That's why I practice target shootin'. When I aim, I want that bullet to hit its mark on the first try."

"I've noticed you are a good shot."

What else had he noticed? Her heart thumped hard. She cleared her throat and hurried her steps.

"Gordon, I want to ask you something."

Her pulse jumped as she reached her tent. "Well, here we are," she announced. "I'll say good night, now." She gave him a brief upward glance, then turned and quickly bent down to lift the flap.

Levi grabbed her arm before she could crawl inside. She stood up once more but looked off into the distance, over his shoulder.

"Is there something you haven't told me?"

"What do you mean?" She kept her eyes averted.

"I mean, you've been acting strange lately."

She jerked her head back and dared to look at him. "That so? It wasn't intentional," she fibbed. "I think you're the one who's been actin' odd."

"Me?"

"You're always starin' at me, as if there's somethin' wrong with me."

"I'm not!"

"You are."

"Well then, maybe you've given me reason to."

"What's that supposed to mean?"

"I don't know, exactly. What I do know is that you don't...you don't...."

"Don't...what?" she probed, not truly wishing to know the answer.

Levi sighed. "Sometimes, I wonder who you really are."

"Well, if that ain't ridiculous."

"Right now, for example—your pitch is higher than usual. Some days, it's extremely low, and other times, you speak almost like a soprano."

"So, my voice is inconsistent. Does that really matter?"

"It does if, as McQuade has said, you're probably more like thirteen or maybe fourteen. Makes me wonder if you've been lying—and if that's the case, then what *else* haven't you told me?"

Josie's heart nearly pounded out of her chest. "What? That's crazy!"

"Everything all right between you two?" Of all people, not Lieutenant Grimms! He still walked with a bit of a limp from his gunshot wound, but the injury had proven to be largely superficial.

"Everything's fine, Lieutenant," she answered gruffly, giving a salute. How thankful she was for the dark so that neither man could see the blush on her face.

Levi stood at attention. "Yes, sir, just fine. We were just having a heated discussion."

"A heated discussion, eh? Sounded more like a major disagreement."

"It wasn't anything important, right, Gordon?" Levi elbowed her gently in the side.

"That's right. It was real trivial, in fact."

The lieutenant's gaze traveled from Levi to Josie and back again. "Well, I'm glad, because, Albright, you're just the man I was looking for. Meet me at my tent in five minutes."

"Five minutes, sir?"

"That's what I said." Grimms shook his head at both of them, then turned and walked off.

Levi heaved a loud breath as he gazed after the lieutenant. Josie swallowed hard, waiting to see if he planned to finish their squabble. She prayed not.

"We'll continue this another time," he muttered quietly. "See you later."

She didn't respond but quickly slipped into her tent, then peered out the slit to watch him vanish into the night.

⌒

As Levi trudged up the path to the lieutenant's quarters, he thought he heard footfalls behind him, but when he glanced over his shoulder and saw nothing, he continued on. Probably just a squirrel.

Gordon Snipp was getting on his last nerve—if that was even the kid's real name. Just the other day, Willie Speer had commented on Snipp's girlish mannerisms. "He's a good young soldier, though," he'd added. "He's bright, quick, eager to please, and conscientious about his duties. I'll defend him to the end if anyone even thinks of givin' him a hard time."

"You best start with McQuade, then," Howard Adams had said. "He calls him a sissy to his face. I'll be a bit more discreet, but I can't say I disagree."

"What makes you say that?" Speer had probed.

"He ain't got a beard, for one thing. Not even the start of a whisker."

"What difference does that make?" Speer had asked.

"Boys his age ought t' have at least a little fuzz, don't you think?" was Adams's reply.

Speer had snubbed the remark, and soon the subject had changed to other matters. It had gotten Levi to thinking, though. Over the past couple of days, he had studied the boy at closer range, and Adams was right. There wasn't so much as a trace of fuzz. Of course, the boy's face was always smudged with dirt and grime, so it was hard to tell for sure without getting closer—which he wasn't about to do.

Levi shook his head and walked on. He liked the kid, and it irked him that he was having these doubts.

Behind him, a twig snapped. He halted and turned. "Who's there?" No one answered. Standing there in the shadows, he studied his surroundings. Not ten feet away, a raccoon dashed across the path he'd just taken. Dumb critters were forever hanging around the fires, looking for food; sometimes, a soldier couldn't remember if he'd washed his own dishes down at the creek or if a raccoon's tongue had done the job for him. Levi heaved a sigh, then turned and hurried the rest of the way up the trail to Grimms's tent.

The lieutenant's lantern gave off a golden glow through the canvas. "Sir?" Levi said at the entrance to his tent.

"Come in, Albright."

He started to salute, but Grimms waved him off. "Sit." He pointed to the empty chair across the tiny square table from him. Levi lowered himself into the seat and removed his hat, setting it on the table.

"How're you adjusting to your responsibilities as regiment chaplain?"

"Very well, sir. I've learned a great deal, and it's been very rewarding."

"Good, good, glad to hear it. You been traveling to all the divisions?"

"I do my best. Some days, I spend more time at one company than the others. Much depends on the needs and on time constraints."

"Yes, yes, I can imagine. Well, at least you've more freedom to travel than you did when you had to participate in all the drills."

"That's true, although I still drill when time permits so I can remain sharp."

Grimms picked up a tin mug from the floor and filled it with black coffee from a pot fresh off the fire, then handed it to Levi.

Levi accepted the cup and took a sip. He nearly burned off the end of his tongue. Not only was the coffee hotter than coals, it was as bitter as death itself. It was all he could do not to cough it up. He somehow managed to keep his composure and set the mug on the table, taking a couple of painful, hard swallows. Paying no attention, Grimms filled his own cup, then took a drink, gulping it down as if nothing were amiss. Levi thought his throat and stomach must be lined with iron.

"Something's been on my mind lately, Albright."

"Oh?"

"Actually, captains Bateman and Birney brought it to my attention a week or so ago when we met over at Company F. It's got me to thinking long and hard. I wondered if perhaps, in your journeys from company to company, you might have come across something."

Confused, Levi shook his head. "I have no idea what you're talking about."

The lieutenant set his mug down, pulled at his beard, then slid his chair closer and leaned across the table. His action prompted Levi to scoot forward, himself. "There's been some thought"—Grimms lowered his voice to a mere croaky whisper—"that there may be a traitor among us."

"A *what?*" This Levi said louder than intended.

Grimms crimped his gray eyebrows in a deep frown.

Levi cleared his throat and whispered, "As in, a spy? Why would you think that?"

"For a number of reasons," Grimms said quietly. "I can't get into any details now. I'd rather talk about it later, when there's plenty of daylight. I'm merely telling you now because I want you to start keeping your eyes and ears peeled for any suspicious activity."

"Of course." Levi nodded. "Although I have no idea what sort of 'suspicious activity' I'm supposed to find."

"Be on the lookout for someone who seems to show up at every turn, somebody who frequently inquires as to what the army's next move might be. It could be someone friendly or otherwise...I don't know. It might be someone right here in our own company, or in another division. You move among all the companies. You talk to many of the men. I figured you might have heard something that, to look back on it, gives you pause."

"Nothing comes to mind, sir. The description you just gave could apply to just about anyone."

"What about that Snipp fellow? He seem odd to you at all?"

"What?" Levi's chest constricted. "No!"

"Why were you two fighting when I came upon you just now?"

"We weren't fighting. Not at all."

"You were having a loud exchange."

"It wasn't anything serious. The kid is young and innocent. He's no more capable of being a spy than I am of being a—a rabbit!" he sputtered.

"Shhh," Grimms hissed. "Keep your voice down."

"Well, sir, you've got my dander up. You suggest there may be a spy among us, but you haven't given me much to go on."

The lieutenant raised both hands. "All right, all right, calm down. Like I said, we'll talk more when it's daylight. Never can tell who may be slinking around."

The comment brought to Levi's mind the peculiar sense that someone had followed him here.

"For now, just keep an eye on Snipp. On everybody, for that matter. Trust no one."

"No one, sir? What about Sergeant Clute? Shouldn't you be discussing this with him instead of me?"

"As I said, trust no one."

"Clute is a fine Christian man, and he's been taking his responsibilities very seriously."

"Again, I remind you to keep your voice down. I will talk to Clute. I will. For now, this is just between you and me. Understood?"

"I—"

"Understood?"

"Yes, sir. Understood, sir."

"Good. Now go back to your site and get a good night's sleep. We'll talk later."

A good night's sleep? Tonight, Levi would have to pray sleep would come at all. First, his argument with Gordon had put him in a sour mood, and this unsettling news only exacerbated it. He snatched up his hat from the table, pushed back the wooden chair, and stood. He prepared to salute, but the lieutenant stopped him again with a sweep of his hand.

"At ease, Sergeant. Relax. You're looking too tense, and that's not like you."

Levi dropped his shoulders. "Good night, sir. I'll see you tomorrow."

"Indeed, indeed." The lieutenant remained seated and watched him go.

Outside, Levi glanced around. The sound of a snapping twig made him shiver. The lieutenant had gotten him in a regular tizzy. Now he would start looking at everyone through narrowed eyes, wondering if he really was who he claimed to be. He stomped back to his tent, determined not to let his mind run wild.

⌒

Well, this was a fine predicament. The entire conference between Grimms and Albright had been conducted in whispers. He stood in the deep shadows, watching Albright stride back to his site, feeling none the smarter and a whole lot of frustrated. What had prompted Grimms to muffle his words? What had he said to get Albright in such a feverish tangle?

Something told him he had to lie low for a while. No way could he take a chance on blowing his cover—no, not his cover but his *mission*. He was in this army for one reason, and one reason only: to rid the world of the enemy, one stinking Union soldier at a time.

A worthy mission it was, too, but he would willingly put it on hold till he uncovered further information.

Just then, the urge to cough came upon him without warning. He dived into the brush and scurried off faster than a jackrabbit.

19

Dear Allison (and Aunt Bessie),

I received your letters with much joy and gratitude. It is a soldier's delight to hear the mail wagon coming into camp, but an even bigger thrill when the delivery boy holds up a letter and calls you by name! Most of us snatch our missives from his hand faster than a dog steals a piece of bacon from the breakfast table.

These past days have been difficult. Our battalion recently joined with the rest of the 23rd and several other regiments at Bristoe Station. It was a certain Union victory but, in my estimation, not a happy one. For as much as I dislike war, I hate injustice, division, and slavery even more; and so, as I march into battle with my fellow comrades, I know I am doing the right thing for my country.

I am always happy to hear about the goings-on at the Garlow house. I miss you all, and I promise to return one day again, Lord willing. Here, there are no guarantees. I have seen blood, death, disease, and other things no one should have to witness, and yet I give no thought to abandoning my responsibilities. Please pray for me *and my fellow soldiers, that we may win this war for the cause of preserving the Union and bringing an end to slavery.*

Please continue sending news from home, and I will reply as hastily as possible. It isn't always easy to find time to write. Our drills keep us busy all day and tire us such that we retire early to bed. This morning, I awoke before the sunrise, so I am writing by lamplight.

Please tell the church folks hello, but I'll ask that you neither give them my address nor tell them I joined the army. I know they probably consider me a weakling, as do so many in my own camp, but I can assure you I am a STRONG BOY, and I am convinced I'm a good soldier who is more than capable of serving <u>his</u> country with enthusiasm and skill.

With my earnest love, I—your beloved nephew and cousin—do leave you with this final verse: "Be careful for nothing; but in every thing by prayer and supplication with thanksgiving let your requests be made known unto God" (Philippians 4:6).

Gordon Snipp

When she had finished writing, Josie reread the letter in full to check for errors. She wanted to emphasize in as subtle a way as possible how important it was that Aunt Bessie use her army name in any future correspondence.

She began to hear the slightest stirring outside her tiny canvas abode, soldiers building much-needed fires, talking to one another, or walking past on their way to the creek. She shivered as she went about removing her uniform and putting on a clean one. Every couple of weeks, she washed her extra uniform and hung it out to dry. Lately, her garments hadn't been drying as thoroughly due to the cold, damp air and the more frequent rains. Even now, distant thunder rumbled in the west, and she prayed the storm would take a course that wouldn't touch their camp. She did not relish the thought of her clean, warm uniform soaking clear through to her skin.

Once dressed, she shoved her hat on her head, rolled up her bedding, set her Bible on top of that, and extinguished her lantern flame. Outside, she saw a few men moving about—some sitting next to fires eating breakfasts from tin plates, others sipping coffee, and still others just coming up from the creek bed. First on her agenda was finding a private spot in the woods to take care of "business."

On her walk down the knoll, she came upon Levi, and the sight of him caused her pulse to quicken, as usual. She'd had a difficult time sleeping last night due to their spat.

When he spotted her, his expression looked almost sheepish. "Morning, Snipp. How'd you sleep?"

"Not well," she admitted.

"Neither did I. Sorry about last night."

Josie shook her head. "No need to apologize. I was equally to blame."

"Friends?" Levi extended his hand.

She looked at it briefly before placing her palm in his. His hand felt warm and callused. She feared hers hadn't hardened up quite enough yet, but if he noticed, he said nothing.

"Friends," she answered in a solemn voice.

He dropped her hand after what she considered to be an exaggerated span of time. "I hope you have a good day. I'll be out making calls after I pay one more visit to Grimms this morning."

"I hope there wasn't a problem. With Grimms, I mean."

"No, no problem at all."

Why did she get the notion that he wasn't being entirely truthful? "Well, after drills, I'll be offerin' my services at the hospital."

"Good for you." Levi tilted his head at her in the same fashion he had last night, scrutinizing. "Well, I'll be off now," he finally said. "Good day."

"Good day to you."

That was how they parted ways—as if they'd just met for the first time yesterday. Her mood fell flat to the bottoms of her muddied boots.

〜

Just as the morning drills began, Levi hurried to Lieutenant Grimms's tent, hoping to catch him before he left for parts unknown. He found him emptying his washbasin. The man was hanging a towel on a tree branch when he turned at the sound of Levi's approach.

"Ah, Albright. I expected to see you bright and early. Well, I guess it's not particularly bright. Feels like rain is in our future. Coffee?"

Levi thought immediately of the coffee Grimms had served him last night, and he declined with a simple shake of his head. He removed his hat but didn't bother saluting. He wanted information, and the sooner the better.

"If you don't mind, I believe we'll sit outside so we can be aware of our surroundings. I have my men on watch at the outer edges of camp."

Levi raised his eyebrows. "You've taken to assigning guards?"

"I'm suspicious someone's been sneaking around—and before you accuse me of being overly cautious, let me say I definitely heard footfalls last night after you left."

"I had the sense that someone had followed me here, and I also thought I heard something when I left. The raccoons are always out, though. Spotted one last night."

"Pesky critters. This was no raccoon, though. Far as I know, raccoons don't get coughing spells. I grabbed my gun when I heard the noise, but by the time I got out of my tent, the fellow had run off. He's a sneaky one. For all I know, the roach is right under my nose, and I'm too dumb to recognize him."

Uneasiness slithered through Levi's veins as he glanced around at several tidy bedrolls and a few tents. Everyone else had left for roll call and then drills. At least for now, he was satisfied no one lurked about.

Both men lowered themselves into a pair of rickety chairs that faced each other. When they sat, their knees nearly touched. "What precipitated these suspicions in the first place?" Levi inquired.

Grimms threaded the fingers of one hand through his gray beard, his brow furrowed in thought. "The captains say it's something they've been investigating since late spring—shortly after the Battle of Salem Church."

Levi thought back to that battle in early May. "That's where some of the Union fellows shot at their own men, thinking them to be Confederates. It was a foolish mistake."

"Foolish isn't the right word. It cost me my good standing in Bateman's eyes. I'm only now earning back a portion of his trust. At least he called us to participate in Bristoe Station, so I felt good about that. Thing is, the captains have not determined yet what caused that fracas at Salem's Church. They've been trying to determine who fired the first shots."

"Perhaps it was simultaneous. To my knowledge, Company B was mostly in reserve that day."

"Are you sure about that?"

"Well, it's not as if I took roll call out on the field. Everyone was accounted for before we marched, though."

"But did you keep your eye on every one of your men?"

"No, that would be impossible."

"Exactly. According to the record kept by Howard Adams, we had eighty-seven men on the books at the time. How could you be expected to watch them all at once? Someone easily could have slipped off, and you would've been none the wiser."

Levi frowned. "I suppose it's possible, but I trust my men. They are good at following orders—that is, to the best of my knowledge. If there were any who strayed, I was unaware of it."

Grimms scratched the side of his head, then leaned in closer. "Captain Birney believes he witnessed the first shot, and says it was fired by someone dressed in Company B attire and wearing a cap with our insignia. The day was foggy, so he says he can't be sure; and, of course, he didn't recognize him. He had to dodge gunfire to get to the man, and as he did so, his horse took a Minié shot in the shoulder. He went down with his horse and lost sight of the fellow. After it was over, he found a dead Union soldier lying right where he'd spotted him."

Levi shuddered to think of such a traitorous act, turning on one's fellow soldier. "Why am I just now hearing about this?"

"It's classified."

"Well, who would do such a thing? I know these men well."

"You think you do, anyway. Traitorous fellows are known for their cleverness. There is a spy among us, Levi. I'm convinced of it."

Levi wanted to believe the best about his men, but a vile seed of paranoia started taking root as names started rushing to the surface of his mind—Frank Vonfleet, Jim Hodgers, Walt Morse, Howard Adams, John Cridland, Willie Speer, Hiram McQuade, and even Chester Woolsley. What if the big fellow McQuade called a "stupid ox" had been playing dumb the entire time? Good grief, he could be smarter than the lot of them, for all Levi knew! "What else has led you to this conclusion?"

Grimms resumed stroking his beard contemplatively. "Well, there was the shooting of Sergeant Thomas Loyal from Company D. Captain Birney found that particularly odd, since there was little evidence of much of a tussle. It would be awful odd for a single Rebel to wander so far into Union territory. He would've had to cross the river. Birney seems to think it was an inside operation. Of course, all this information is confidential; but with your being the chaplain and all, I'm fairly certain I can trust you to keep your mouth shut."

"You've got my word on that, sir." Levi took in a long breath. "At least we can be quite sure that none of our newest soldiers is involved." He thought in particular of Gordon Snipp.

"We can't be certain of anything, Albright. For all we know, one of those fellows enlisted for the purpose of going undercover. He may be in cahoots with someone else."

Levi's stomach soured at that proclamation, and the last bit of hardtack he'd partially digested some 30 minutes ago threatened to come back up. He took a couple of hard swallows.

He was almost afraid to ask, but he said, "Anything else, sir?"

"One more thing, yes. It's rather mysterious that one of our Union soldiers, a fellow from another division, took a bullet wound from very close range at Bristoe Station. To our knowledge, we held the Rebels at bay throughout most of the fracas, shooting from a considerable distance. We lost some to cannon fire, of course, but one soldier in particular died from a bullet wound to the back of his head—a bullet fired from close range. He was then rolled over on his back, as if the shooter wanted assurance he'd completed his mission."

Levi closed his eyes, folded his hands in his lap, and prayed a silent prayer before opening his eyes. "What do you want me to do, Lieutenant?"

"For now, do as I said last night: Keep your eyes and ears open for anything out of the ordinary. Listen for conversations that might clue you in to any sort of covert activity. Be on guard at all times, and as you move from company to company, remain your personable self, striking up dialogues and looking for traces of peculiar behavior."

Levi gave his head a couple of fast shakes and looked Grimms in the eye. "I'm the chaplain, Lieutenant, not a detective."

Grimms gave a crooked smile. "Well, Sergeant, for the moment, you're both." At that, he straightened and was the first to salute, an unusual gesture. "Dismissed," he said curtly.

Levi returned the salute, then stood and walked away, his spine straight, his mind filled with an array of crazy thoughts.

20

*J*osie found the next several days to be nothing but repeats of the day before: eating adequate meals, doing drills, taking turns keeping watch for enemy raiders who might sneak up on the wagons, going back and forth from the regiment hospital to offer aid, and, when there was time, sitting by a fire wrapped in her poncho because of the uncommonly cold temperatures. Most nights, someone brought out his fiddle or harmonica and offered up tunes while other men played cards by lantern light and smoked hand-rolled cigarettes, compliments of the United States government, which rationed out pouches of tobacco and books of rolling paper. Many soldiers claimed that smoking tobacco helped to soothe their weary souls, but Josie saw the habit as smelly and disgusting.

Almost every morning, just as the sun crept over the horizon, Josie and a few men went hunting. They couldn't stock up on meat due to the dangers of spoilage, so when they reached their limit of animals, they carried them back to camp and cooked breakfast. Soldiers from other companies even wandered over in hopes of partaking of the meals.

Since Bristoe Station, things had quieted down, but news spread fast that very soon the 23rd would make its way to the Rappahannock.

Josie dreaded the hike, but at least the strenuous marching would keep her body active and warm. Her load would be lighter, too, as much of what she'd carried before in her rucksack she now wore in layers. She'd seen less of Levi recently as he had been traveling from camp to camp, visiting other regimental divisions. She'd seen him at church two days ago, but so many soldiers had gathered around him after the sermon that she hadn't gotten an opportunity to tell him how much she'd enjoyed it. Once the crowd had dispersed, she saw Levi engaged in what appeared to be a serious discussion with that tall fellow from Company D, Terry Brady.

If only she could confirm with Levi that things between them were still good. All she could think about was that awful squabble they'd been having when Grimms had interrupted; and while the two of them had talked briefly the following morning about putting the disagreement behind them, she needed a more concrete reconciliation. At the same time, she didn't wish for anything too intimate to transpire in the way of conversation, lest Levi ask one too many questions, and she cave in and spill the whole truth about herself. That would ruin everything.

Well, it was official: the 23rd was marching back to the Rappahannock, although he didn't know just why. Perhaps something was brewing that he'd not heard about, although he'd been diligent about spying outside Grimms's tent whenever he had a spare moment. He didn't have enough information worth reporting to his Southern brothers, so for now, he would keep a low profile, feign friendship while playing cards with other soldiers, converse by firelight, roll cigarettes, and take his turn at guard duty.

One night, he went on guard duty with Gordon Snipp. The kid took his job so seriously, he didn't wish to talk. In fact, he kept shushing him like some kind of bigwig, and that angered him to no end. He thought about picking him off right then, but he also knew how foolish a move that would be. Bratty kid! Well, he would find the perfect opportunity—the right time and place—maybe during a future battle, or the next time he found himself alone with him yet not on duty. He'd see to it no one had to put up with the likes of Gordon Snipp any longer. Everyone would be shocked, especially Albright, who took an unholy liking to the kid. He would have to plan carefully so as not to arouse any suspicion.

⌒

On November 10, the 23rd crossed the Rappahannock on a pontoon bridge. Along with several other companies from another regiment, Company B traveled at the tail end of the wagon train. Levi surmised there must have been at least 500 wagons ahead of them, so it wasn't till dark that they finally crossed the floating bridge.

Before they'd set off two days ago, there'd been a bit of a scuffle with the Rebs, but the 23rd had served only as reinforcements for the 122nd, who had done the charging. For the better part of a day, the 23rd did nothing but lie on the cold, hard ground, muskets aimed at an invisible enemy, just listening to the fighting and expecting orders at any time to advance the 300 or so yards it would take to get into the thick, dark woods.

Those orders never came, however, and after a long spell, there was a ceasefire. Soon couriers started riding up on horseback to announce that it was over; the 122nd had driven back the Rebels, taken 1,600 prisoners, and acquired several guns and three cannons. They said to set up camp and be prepared to head out again at four in the morning.

Now, having finally crossed the Rappahannock with an exhausted, sleep-deprived, hungry regiment, Levi could only hope they wouldn't be called into battle before the men had gotten a decent night's sleep and a good breakfast.

Nobody spoke as the men unrolled their beds, and so, aside from the hoot of a distant owl and the occasional cough, the camp was dead quiet. Not even a single fiddler broke the stillness. While setting up his camp, Levi glanced across the moonlit expanse and spotted Gordon some 40 feet away, erecting his pathetic little tent. He'd purposely avoided the boy this week, but doggone if he didn't miss conversing with him. He'd spent long hours mulling over this whole notion of a traitorous soldier among them, having scoured the other divisions, listened in on numerous conversations, and searched for clues that might point him toward the same conclusion that had been drawn by the captains and lieutenants; but all for naught. In his eyes, nothing was out of the ordinary.

Levi dropped his bedroll, stood up, and brushed his hands on his pants' legs, then strolled over toward Snipp's tent. He had to make peace with the kid, as well as with himself. Time to stop doubting the boy and to simply accept that, while Gordon Snipp was different from the other men, he was a decent human being doing the best he could to serve his country, and he didn't deserve Levi's cold shoulder one more day.

"How's it going, Snipp?"

Gordon turned abruptly.

"Didn't mean to startle you."

"Not at all," Gordon reassured him. "Everything's goin' well, sir."

"That's good. Mind if I sit?"

Nobody in the surrounding area seemed to pay him any mind, which made him glad. He didn't wish to draw any attention to himself.

"Make yourself comfortable. I'm just securin' this last stake."

Levi watched him finish the chore he'd been doing nightly for almost three months now, and noticed how he accomplished it with hardly any effort. He'd come a long way in a short time, this boy soldier.

Levi lowered himself to the ground, as there was no nearby stump or fallen log on which to sit, then crossed his legs at the ankles and leaned back, his flat palms pressed into the cold, hard earth. With no cloud cover above, the air held an extra chill. A fire would be nice, but he didn't intend to stay long enough to make it worth his while to build one. "You as exhausted as everybody else?"

The boy stood up and stuffed his hands in his pockets. "Sure am, and a little hungry. What I wouldn't give for my aunt Bessie's chicken and mashed potatoes and gravy right about now."

Levi chortled. "I could go for a good home-cooked meal, myself."

The boy visibly relaxed. He sat down, as well, facing Levi, with his back to his tent. He wore a heavy poncho over his uniform. "With all the kids in your family, I s'pose your mama has to be a good cook."

Levi grinned. "The best. My sisters help in the kitchen, too, so there was always bread coming out of the oven, homegrown vegetables at the table, creamy onion or potato soup simmering on the stove, coffee percolating, and plenty of fruit pies, cakes, and cookies to go around. As members of the Society of Friends, we don't eat meat, so there's no partaking of chicken, pork, beef, and the like. Still, I never felt deprived. My mother knows how to season food in such a way that one never gives a second though to eating any sort of meat."

"Wait." Gordon held up his hand and crimped his brow. "You don't eat any meat? But I thought...."

Levi ducked his head and chewed on his lip. "I'll admit I haven't been a very good Quaker since joining the army. As a matter of fact, I've come to enjoy a tender piece of duck or a bowl of venison or rabbit stew just the way Harv Patterson cooks it. Boiled squirrel's not so bad, either, although it isn't my favorite. I have a hunch my mother would be chasing after me with a switch if she learned how much I've wandered from my roots. She's probably on her knees this very minute, praying I won't fall into sin.

"Anyway, we Friends treasure all life, including that of animals. Here's the thing, though—my father raises hogs and sells them at the city market. It's a little inconsistent with our views, I know, but Mother learned long ago not to question my father on certain issues, particularly when it comes to matters of money. They raised eight of us, so every penny counted. Papa never kills the hogs, mind you. He just hands them off to his customers. I recall asking him about it as a young kid one time as I rode with him back from the city. I said, 'Papa, how come thee sells the hogs if thee knows someone is going to slaughter them and serve them on their dinner table?' He considered my question for a while, then finally said, 'Well, how do I know what they're plannin' to do with the hogs once they get 'em? Maybe they'll keep 'em as pets. I never ask.'" Levi chuckled. "I recall thinking it was a roundabout way of saying that what a person doesn't know won't hurt him."

Gordon's laugh was more of a giggle—a girlish one, at that. Levi averted his eyes, reminding himself of his vow to quit doubting the boy's mannerisms and behavior. He was who he was; and if his comportment sometimes bordered on effeminate, then so be it. It didn't change their friendship. Levi supposed his own brothers acted a bit girlish from time to time. As an adolescent, he'd often teased them till they cried, and then he'd make matters worse by telling them to stop crying like a girl.

It's just that Gordon claimed to be nineteen.

"Well"—the boy sobered—"you may have strayed a bit from your Quaker upbringin', but you're a darned good preacher, so your dear mama shouldn't worry over your salvation any. I'm sure she'd be proud if you ended up as a reverend, even for a diff'rent denomination."

Levi shook his head. "As always, I appreciate your confidence. I just can't say I'm so confident my mother would approve. Or that I feel up for answering the call, even if she did."

"*Yet.* You should'a said '*yet.*' Sometimes, the Lord calls His children down pathways they never envisioned themselves walkin'. You just gotta keep your ears open for His voice so you'll know which road to take when you come to a fork."

He slanted the boy a glance. "You're awfully perceptive. Are you speaking from experience? Have you felt God tugging on your heart about some certain direction for your life?"

Gordon shrugged. "Maybe in some ways. Mostly, for me, it's just been lookin' back over my life and seein' God's hand in all the workings."

"How do you mean?"

"Well, I never expected both my parents to die when I was a young kid. I never pictured my brother and me bein' orphans. I had no idea we'd have to go live with my aunt and uncle, although I'm eternally grateful they welcomed us in. Then, to lose my brother last year—well, all those experiences helped mold me into the person I am today, sort of forced me to grow up, and I thank God for it all, now."

Levi raised his eyebrows. "You thank Him for the hard life you've had to live?"

"Sure. I believe I'm stronger inside and out because of how it's made me lean on the Lord."

"Some people would be bitter, you know, but you chose the other road. You came to that fork you mentioned, and had to decide: either take this road and trust God with my life, or take the other one and be sour and ornery."

"I guess you're right. You think that's what happened to Hiram McQuade? He's a mighty bad-tempered soul."

"I don't know his story, kid, but I'd like to learn it someday." Levi thought about how Grimms had told him to be mindful of everyone's deeds and actions. Just what was McQuade's story, anyway? Why was he so hateful? Was he the spy in their midst?

"You look awful deep in thought," Gordon remarked.

"Do I?" Levi blinked and smiled. "It's nothing." He studied Gordon. No way did he have a bad bone in him. He was good, through and through—and a fine Christian, too. "Well." He pushed himself to his feet. "I guess I'll go finish unrolling my bedding. You have a good night, Private."

"You, too, Sarge. Oh, and by the way—fine sermon last Sunday. I'm lookin' forward to the next one."

Levi grinned. "Thanks. I'm always thinking and praying about my next topic."

"Listen for God's voice. He'll tell you."

Levi gave his head a little nod, then started off, his smile still in place. Things were back to normal between Gordon and him.

21

On November 12, word spread that several regiments, including the 23rd, were headed to Brandy Station to spend the winter; but rumor had it that the information had come from a mule driver, so it didn't exactly qualify as official. Josie had learned early on that you shouldn't believe anything you heard until it actually happened. Everybody always wanted to know where his unit was going and why, but, more times than not, such information was privy only to the officers. If a soldier learned anything, it was to mind his business and follow orders. Period.

And so, Company B marched that entire day—marched; pushed stuck wagons out of knee-deep mud; marched, not knowing exactly when or where they would stop; pushed wagons; and marched some more. As dusk drew nigh, every member of the 23rd Pennsylvania Volunteers was a pathetic, muddy sight, and Josie doubted any of the other regiments looked much better. Orders came for them to make camp, but no one knew for how long.

Besides those who were still healing from wounds incurred at Bristoe Station, several soldiers continued battling disease, running high fevers and dealing with bouts of vomiting, diarrhea, and rashes.

After setting up her tent, Josie walked over to the medic wagons to see what she could do to help Major Walden. She found him in the third wagon, and upon climbing inside, she also spotted Levi ministering to men who had grown so weak from travel and lack of nourishment that they could barely lift their heads. Several soldiers had actually died on the trail that day, so a few privates had stayed back to bury their bodies, planning on catching up with their companies later. It was a grievous situation, and Josie mourned for the soldiers' families, remembering well how she'd felt when she'd learned of Andrew's death.

When the doctor saw her, he sighed with relief, then asked her to fill a bucket at the stream and bring it back to press a cool cloth to a series of feverish foreheads. As she went to retrieve an empty bucket, she walked past Levi, and the two exchanged nods and smiles. Then she climbed down from the wagon and headed for the steep hill sloping down to the fast-moving creek, navigating each step with care because of all the twigs and fallen branches in her path, and nearly falling a couple of times.

He spotted the boy just as he disappeared behind some trees on his way down the hill, a bucket in hand. Fortunately, many had made their way to the sutler's wagon or were busy elsewhere, so he seized his opportunity and set off after the boy. Oh, how he savored the thought of putting his whole company on edge by doing him in. How he would enjoy that sense of power, that supreme satisfaction of knowing something no one else knew. The question was, how to do it without drawing immediate notice? Perhaps he should strangle the kid, then toss him in the stream. Wild animals would do away with his remains, and everyone would assume the boy had drowned when he failed to return to camp by nightfall. In the morning, they would discover his bucket on the riverbank, but there'd be no sign of him. Maybe they would assume he'd deserted, like so many others had done since enlisting. Stupid cowards.

He picked his way through the trees before starting down the hill. Because of its steep grade, he had to take the hill sideways, one step at a time. The boy made it safely to the stream and bent down to dip the bucket in the water.

He stepped on a dead branch, which caused it to snap, and Snipp turned around. "Oh," he said. "You startled me. What're you doin' down here?" Turning his back to him, the boy continued to hold the pail in the water.

He didn't answer him right away, just watched, considering how best to catch him off guard so he could grab his neck with both hands and squeeze until he dropped his pail to the ground and breathed his last. There would be a struggle, for sure, but the kid was shorter than he by a long shot and wouldn't stand a chance of surviving.

Snipp finished filling the bucket, then set it on the bank and stood with his hands on his hips. "What are y' doin' down here?" he repeated.

He smiled. "Came down to do some business."

"Oh. Well then, I'll give you your privacy." Snipp bent to pick up the bucket, but before he could place his fingers fully around the handle, he snagged him hard around the forearm and drew him back up.

"What are you—? Ouch! Let go."

"You still down there, Gordon?" It was Albright!

He dropped the boy's arm and whirled around to see the sergeant making his way down the hill, a bucket in hand. "Major Walden thought he could do with one more pail of water, so I volunteered to get it."

Trying to hide his fury with Albright for foiling his scheme, he swallowed a cuss, then looked at the kid, who was rubbing the place where he'd gripped him. "Sorry, Snipp. It looked like you were losin' your balance, and I wanted to keep you from fallin' in the creek. I didn't hurt you, did I?"

Snipp scrunched his brow in a suspicious expression. "No, 'course not. I'm fine." He continued rubbing the spot. "Why'd y' have to grab so hard?"

"I told you, I thought you were fallin' in."

"Well, I wasn't."

"Good, that's good."

Albright reached the bottom of the hill. He smiled at Snipp, then turned his gaze on him. "Didn't expect to see you down here."

"Well, I come down to do my business and found Snipp. I'll be off now." He tipped his hat, then hurried away before his anger could get the better of him and cause him to take out the both of them.

⌒

Levi couldn't sleep. Exhausted and sore from marching, weary of ministering to the sick and wounded, and distracted by the surprisingly sweet letter he'd received from Mary Foster that day, he couldn't catch a single wink. Uncommonly cold wind blew around his tent and found its way inside, nipping his nose and cheeks till he'd lost all feeling in them; and no matter how much he fluffed up his coat for a pillow or pulled his wool blanket up close to his chin, he couldn't get comfortable.

Before turning in for the night, he had glanced around and seen that everyone else seemed to have found someone to bunk with. The men were huddled in threes and fours under wagons, beneath trees, inside trenches they had dug, or in tents. In the army, men had no compunctions when it came to survival. They did what they had to do, even if it meant lying close to another soldier to sleep.

Well, everyone but Gordon Snipp, that is. That fellow refused all nighttime company, no matter that the temperature had dropped well below freezing. Tomorrow, a train would arrive with fresh supplies for building stockade tents—sturdy wooden structures with pork-barrel-topped chimneys of stick and stone, and a heavy canvas roof to keep out the rain and snow—and then the boy would have to submit to sharing his space with other soldiers. Meanwhile, the tents they had been using—Levi's included—would be rolled up and stored for the winter.

Levi looked forward to helping to build the stockade tents. He was skilled and efficient with his hands, having helped his father on many occasions in his woodworking business. Perhaps he'd convince Gordon Snipp and Charlie Clute to bunk up with him for the winter. They ought to make a good trio.

The sounds of yelling and cursing awakened him in the night. He pushed off his blanket, jumped out of bed, turned up the wick of his lantern, then untied his tent opening and set out in the direction from which the noise came. Several other soldiers were already headed that way, and as Levi passed Gordon's tent, Gordon poked his head out the flap. "What's goin' on, Sarge?"

"I don't know, but I intend to find out."

Gordon and several others fell in step with him, and they all walked with purpose in the direction of the squawking and screeching. They found Hiram McQuade straddling a bawling Chester Woolsley, Hiram's fist drawn back and poised to strike Chester in the face.

"McQuade!" Levi shouted. "Stop right there!"

Ignoring Levi's order, Hiram delivered the punch, and Woolsley's squealing escalated as blood poured down his face. "My nose! You broke my nose!"

Levi and several others stepped forward and hauled Hiram up by the arms. He had a bloody nose, himself, so it appeared Chester had given him a good punch, as well—or perchance he'd started the whole thing, for all Levi knew.

"What are you two doing, fighting in the middle of the night?" Levi demanded. "You woke the whole camp, and probably the next company over!"

"He won't leave me alone!" Chester yelled.

"Liar!" Hiram shouted. "*You* came to *my* camp, remember? You just had to show me your mommy's latest letter!"

"What letter?" Levi asked.

"My mama tol' me to tell Hiram to leave me alone," Chester explained, "so I comed over t' tell him what Mama said, and he got all in a huff."

Levi sighed. "It couldn't have waited till daylight, Chester?"

Chester blinked at him. "He told me to let him read the next letter I got from my mama. I was just doin' what he said."

"What do you care if he gets letters from his mother, McQuade? And why would you want to read them, anyway?" Howard Adams asked from the back of the huddle.

"None o' your stinkin' business," Hiram spat. "This ain't nobody's business. Clear outta here, all of you. Get!"

All the soldiers gladly returned to their own camps until Levi was left alone with the two combatants.

"All right, McQuade. What was this really about?" Levi asked.

"He just told y'," said Hiram. "He wanted to rub his mama's letter in my face."

"Did not," whined Chester, his nose still bleeding. "You said yourself that you—"

"Shut up!" Hiram hissed.

"He hates my whole family!" spouted Chester.

"I told you to shut up." Hiram's bloodied up nose didn't look any better than Chester's.

"Don't have to!"

Levi shook his head, disbelieving that all this talk was coming from two grown men. Then he looked from one to the other. "All right. How about we all have a little talk?"

"I ain't havin' no little talk," said Hiram.

"Yes, you are. You woke me up, and I'm not about to go back to bed until we've settled this. I'm sick of all your bickering, and so is the rest of Company B. It's been going on from the first day you joined us. What gives? Did you know each other before you joined?"

"'Course we know each other!" Hiram blasted back. "He's my rotten little cousin."

That news caught Levi by surprise. "I had no idea."

"I ain't rotten, and I ain't little!" Chester protested.

"You might not be little in height, but your brain's the size of a pea," Hiram sneered.

"Is not!"

Their bloody noses were about three inches apart as they glared at each other.

"Stop it, both of you. People are exhausted and trying to get some rest. Let's walk over to my tent." Levi pointed in that direction, and the three of them set off, Hiram mumbling curses under his breath about not wanting to go anywhere, Chester crying, and both men using their sleeves to wipe their noses.

Inside his tent, Levi hung his lantern, then motioned with his hand for them to sit with him on the ground. "All right, now. Who wants to start?"

No one volunteered.

"Okay, I'll start by firing off some questions, and you'll start answering."

The way the two sulked put Levi in mind of a couple of ten-year-olds. He swallowed and took a deep breath before forging ahead. "If you two are cousins, why all the hatred between you?"

"I don't 'zactly hate him," Chester began, "but he sure hates me. It wasn't my fault, but he still wants to blame me."

Levi frowned. "What wasn't your fault?"

"Shut up, buzzard breath," Hiram muttered. "Albright don't need t' hear about our sorry family's history."

"No, *you* shut up," Chester whined. "You been shuttin' me up since I was a little kid. It's my turn t' talk."

Levi's eyebrows shot up almost of their own accord. He'd never known Chester to be so forceful.

Hiram threw up his arms. "All right. If you wanna make a fool o' yourself, go ahead."

For the stretch of a minute or two, no one spoke, and Levi figured Hiram had bullied Chester into silence yet again. He didn't really want to pry into private family matters, but he'd had enough of their constant fighting. Next thing he knew, one of them would seriously hurt the other. He kept quiet, but it was all he could do not to speak.

"Our mamas is sisters," Chester finally shared.

Levi nodded. "And…?"

Chester lowered his head and mumbled just loudly enough for Levi to discern, "An' Hiram's daddy chased after my mama."

Hiram glared at Chester. "Your mama did all the chasin', stinkweed. She drove my mother straight to the grave with her carousin'. Broke her heart clear in two. And then, after Aunt Vesta finished with my pa—'cause she never stuck with no man much more 'n a few months— she went straight to somebody else, and then somebody else after that. Everybody knew she was a man chaser. And you was the result of one o' her affairs. The man that was married to your ma before he died was never your real daddy. My mother told me so before she passed."

"I already knowed that," Chester said. "My mama tol' me the truth after she asked God t' forgive her for her sins."

"Pfff." Hiram spat on the ground right next to Levi's boot. "Not even God can forgive her."

"All right, all right. I think I've heard enough." Levi's mind was spinning. Why did Hiram blame his simpleminded cousin for the sins Chester's mother had committed? Wasn't Hiram's father equally to blame for falling under this woman's spell? Perhaps Chester was a painful reminder of all he'd had to endure as a kid. Levi didn't know. He wasn't trained to understand the complexities of how the mind worked.

"I'm sorry that both your parents betrayed your trust, but you two have to learn to put this behind you," he began. "You two must reach some sort of agreement whereby you will cease with all your ridiculous fighting. If you can't do that, then I'll have to speak to Grimms about transferring one of you to another company." Levi already knew Hiram would be the one to go. Chester wouldn't survive being uprooted. Nobody else in the army would put up with his slow-wittedness.

"Why don't you just send him home to his mama, where he belongs?" Hiram spat. "The army don't need the likes o' him. Dumb fool don't even know how to shoot his gun proper-like."

"Do so. Want me to show you? I'll go get it." Chester started to rise.

Levi hauled him back down again. "Stop it, Chester. I used to think Hiram was the bigger cause of the spats between you two, but now I see that you're also to blame. Maybe I will speak to Grimms about sending you home."

"No!" he bawled. "I don't wanna go home. Company B needs me." Real tears formed in his eyes, glistening in the glow of the lantern.

Hiram clicked his tongue. "What a baby."

"Shh," Levi said, tired of the whole fiasco. "You're both grown men. It's time you started acting the part." That remark silenced them. "Now then, let me ask you a question, Hiram. Why would you blame Chester for the sins of your father and his mother?"

Hiram had nothing to say, for a change.

Levi turned his gaze on Chester, who also remained quiet.

"I have a theory that may or may not be right, but I'll toss it out there. Hiram, I think you relive the injustices done to you as a kid through Chester, when, really, he had nothing to do with any of them. Furthermore, you seem to think his mother is beyond forgiveness when, in truth, nothing in God's eyes is unforgivable. Each of us has sinned, but none of us is ever outside of God's grace and pardon."

"Sure," Hiram replied sarcastically. "So you say."

"I'm not the one saying it. God is. The Bible says in the book of Romans that all have sinned and fall short of the glory of God, and that we're justified freely through the redemption that is in Christ Jesus."

"You don't have to preach at me, Chaplain. I know the Bible."

"You do?" Levi arched one of his eyebrows. "And how did that come about?"

Hiram gave a short-lived, icy smile. "My father, one of *his* mother's lovers"—he threw another hateful glance at Chester—"was also a preacher of God's Word." He laughed sardonically. "Now can you see why I can't abide your preachin' at me? It's all fake, every last word. My father's burnin' in the halls o' Hades right now. He was no more a Christian than this glob o' dirt, here." Wearing a fierce scowl, he gathered up a fistful of black clay, then tossed it to the earth again. "What've you got to say to that?"

"I stand by my word," Levi told him resolutely. "No one is beyond saving. God says it, and I believe it."

"Then you're the real fool among us, I guess." Hiram stood. "I'm done here. I still have a few hours o' sleep comin'." To Chester he said,

"And you best not wake me up again, or you might not live to talk about it the next day, hear?"

Chester gave a slow, quiet nod, and Hiram disappeared into the starry night.

22

On November 23, Captain Bateman called on Lieutenant Grimms; and everyone knew it, because when Bateman rode in with several of his men, the whole of Company B was chopping down trees not far from the lieutenant's tent to clear space for winter housing. The newcomers entered his tent, where they stayed for a full three quarters of an hour before Grimms stuck his head out and called for Sergeant Clute to join them. He also asked for Sergeant Albright, but Levi had been summoned to Company K to minister to a dying soldier.

"What d' you suppose they're talkin' 'bout?" Josie asked of Howard Adams and Willie Speer, who had been working alongside her for the better part of the day.

"They're probably plottin' our next move," said Willie.

"But I thought we were spendin' the winter here in Brandy Station."

"If there's one thing you gotta get through your head, kid, it's that this is war, and you can't count on anything good lastin' too long," Howard told her.

"I think we'll hole up for the winter somewhere in this area, but my guess is, we'll settle closer to the Potomac just so we'll have a good water source," Willie mused aloud.

"So, we're clearin' all this land for nothin'?" asked Josie.

Willie laughed. "Could be. Or could be, we're clearin' this land for another regiment. They never tell us why, kid. They just give orders, and we follow them. At any rate, no matter where we finally land, we're bound to have to leave from time to time. We can only wait and see. Don't bother worryin' about it."

"I ain't worried, just curious." Still, even as Josie voiced the words, her nerves went into a tizzy. Her mind often replayed the gruesome scenes of Bristoe Station, the battle when the reality of war had truly sunken in.

Josie still couldn't help but wonder what the army officials' discourse entailed. To keep her mind busy, she worked harder and faster than ever, sweating like a horse as she labored. Today, she'd fight anybody who dared call her a sissy, including McQuade.

Shortly after supper, while Josie sat at Harv Patterson's crackling fire with Walt Morse, Chester Woolsley, Willie Speer, Howard Adams, Louie Walker, Levi Albright, and several others, who should saunter into their midst but Lieutenant Grimms and his men? "Gather everyone together with your bugle, Speer," Grimms ordered. "We're to have a quick meeting."

Willie jumped to attention. "Yes, sir!" He returned in short order and sounded the piercing instrument. Within seconds, the whole of Company B, except for those still battling sickness, assembled around Harv's fire. The last Josie had heard, Company B consisted of 83 men. A typical company had 100, but it wasn't unusual for numbers to fluctuate, as men either deserted, were transferred to another unit, or, God forbid, died.

"I'll not beat around any bush," Grimms began. "I've called you here to inform you there'll be some sort of surprise action soon, and Captain Bateman wants B Company to be a part of his front command. I don't have much in the way of information; I know only that we'll be leaving in a couple of days to be close to the Mine Run River. Now, listen here, men: we have a good chance to prove ourselves to Captain Bateman.

After that debacle at Salem Church, Bateman has not had much confidence in us."

"We showed him what we were made of at Bristoe Station," John Cridland chimed in. "Don't that count for somethin'?"

A few others muttered their agreement.

Josie kept quiet, shooting a stealthy glance at Levi. Since he didn't appear ruffled, she allowed herself to relax. If she could just remain in his shadow on any battlefield, she'd stay safe. She'd convinced herself of that. Her only challenge was to keep him in sight at all times.

"Which is why he wants us to participate," Grimms went on. "I want this company to be the best in the Twenty-third. Is that understood?"

There was a swishing sound as the soldiers raised their arms in a stiff salute. A hearty "Yes, sir!" echoed through the air.

"Adams. Where is Private Adams?" Grimms asked.

Howard moved out from behind a couple of other fellows, stood straight and tall, and kept his salute in place. "Sir!"

"See to it that you keep an accurate account," Grimms said. "And bring your book to my tent later. I haven't reviewed it for some time."

"Yes, sir!" Howard beamed. If anyone took his job seriously, it was Howard Adams. That fellow was forever taking notes in his little book. Josie would like the chance to snatch it out of his possession sometime and read what he'd written about her. To her knowledge, she'd never given him reason to doubt her.

Lieutenant Grimms rotated, as did his men, and started to walk away; but then he made an abrupt stop and pivoted to face the soldiers once more. "Oh, and one more thing. As most of you will recall, last month, President Lincoln stated that our country, divided as it is, ought to set aside a day of thanks-giving. He suggested the fourth Thursday of November. In looking at my calendar, I see that tomorrow marks that particular day. Therefore, a wagon from Washington will arrive in the early morrow with sweets, meats, and other such foods. We will partake of the meal around two o'clock and then ready ourselves for marching, perhaps as early as Friday morning. Sergeant Clute will advise you."

So, they were to move close to the Mine Run River. He had no idea what that meant, other than that they were mobilizing. If he had more information, he would get the word to his Southern brothers, but he figured they probably already knew as much as he did. The 23rd would not be the only regiment involved, and the Confederates would be ready and waiting. He could only hope they would be stronger in future battles than at Bristoe Station. Otherwise, he would again be forced to help them with their efforts.

Since failing at his first attempt to rid the world of Gordon Snipp, he'd had a couple of more opportunities, but none of them had come to fruition. There was always someone else nearby. He figured he would recognize the right time, as everything would fall perfectly into place. Until then, he'd keep his nose clean and stay out of the limelight. The less other folks singled him out, the better. He wasn't one who thrived on attention, like so many others he knew. If he could fade into the background, never to be seen again, it would be all right by him. So far, he'd done a fine job of disappearing unnoticed on important missions, and he intended to keep it that way.

His heart pumped with excitement for what lay ahead, whatever that might be.

Like clockwork, a food wagon arrived in the morning hours, just as Grimms had said it would, and not a single soldier from Company B had to lift a finger in preparing the meal for this first official day of thanks-giving. Levi wondered if President Lincoln's intent to continue the tradition year after year would stick.

That afternoon, when Willie Speer sounded his bugle, a long line formed at the food wagon, each man carrying his plate in hand and his eating utensils in his pocket. The meal consisted of boiled eggs; fresh, soft bread; butter that, for once, was not more than a few days old; beef stew with potatoes; dried peaches; and coffee with sugar.

Several soldiers jokingly wondered aloud whether they'd died and gone to heaven, but Grimms assured them they weren't that lucky. He wore a grin for all to see as he stood next to the wagon, watching as the men walked away carrying plates brimming with food. He even slapped a few on the back and offered an encouraging word. Levi figured his good mood came from the fact that Bateman had invited his unit to march into the front lines of battle. It didn't matter to Grimms that he'd taken a bullet in his upper thigh just weeks ago; he wanted to dive into the fray, no matter what it might cost him. He was a fine soldier, if not a bit overzealous.

After the meal, Grimms brought out several bottles of whiskey, which had to have cost the army a pretty penny. The only whiskey Levi had seen at camp in the past months was kept for medicinal purposes and stored in a locked box under Major Walden's cot. Were it not for the occasional doses the doctor doled out for the purpose of dulling patients' pain, some soldiers probably would have lost their minds. Grimms walked through camp, topping off the men's coffees with a healthy share of the stuff. When he came to Levi, Levi lifted a hand to decline, and noticed a few others doing the same: Gordon, then Willie Speer, Hugh Fowler, and Charlie Clute. It mattered little to Levi who chose to imbibe, as long as the lieutenant knew where to draw the line. The last thing his company needed was a bunch of dumb drunks marching into battle tomorrow—if tomorrow proved to be their next marching day.

That night, most of the men were more conversational than usual, perhaps because the whiskey had loosened their tongues. They talked of home—the loved ones they missed, the jobs they'd left behind, their farms, their workshops, their general stores, and so on. It put Levi in a mood as he set to thinking about his parents and all his brothers and sisters. He wondered how the harvest had gone. Mother had mentioned only how much he'd been missed. In fact, this year marked his third missed harvest, and he wondered whether he would be present for the next one. Would the war still rage on, with him still in the thick of it? Or would the generals on both sides have signed a peace treaty by then? Levi prayed for peace, but not at the expense of tearing apart the Union.

He was due to be mustered out in about 10 months, but if the Lord nudged him to reenlist, he would heed the call.

He'd received another letter from Mary today, filled with news from home. His letters to her seemed repetitive and boring in comparison. Never did he wish to disclose many details about the ravages of war, so he tried to keep the topics light, commenting on the weather or a favorite meal, retelling one of Willie Speer's pathetic jokes, or sharing a favorite Bible verse. He even told her about Gordon Snipp, describing the boy as a rather odd duck who claimed to be nineteen but couldn't be much older than fourteen, considering his lack of a single whisker. Levi usually had trouble filling even one page to Mary's typical three. He often imagined meeting Mary in person, somehow fearing that he'd so built her up in his mind—or she had him—that when they met at last, they wouldn't feel the tiniest spark for each other.

Around another nearby fire, a few boys sang a familiar tune, accompanied by another fellow on his fiddle. Across a clearing and in another cluster of trees, yet another group sat around their fire, talking and laughing. It was a night of merriment, to be sure, one of those rare times when the soldiers let down their guard and pretended there wasn't a war storming around them.

"I got some fresh jokes, if anyone is of a mind to chuckle," said Willie Speer.

Several men moaned in protest, but Gordon, seated next to Willie, said, "I'm game. You'd better make me laugh, though." He gave the fire a good poke with the long stick in his hand.

"We're all ears," said Hiram. "Try to get a grin out of us."

For a change, nothing contrary had come out of Hiram today—even now, with Chester seated in his midst—and Levi couldn't help but wonder if he'd thought some about the talk they'd had in his tent. One could hope so.

"Well, I ain't makin' any promises," Willie cautioned. "After all, my audience ain't the brightest, you know. Plus, these came in a letter from my younger sister, so you can blame her if they ain't any good. Here's the first one: 'How do you cure a bachelor of his achin' heart?'"

"How?" asked Frank Vonfleet.

"You carry to him eleven yards of silk…with a woman in it."

Growls droned through the air. "That was bad, Willie," said Levi. "Please tell us your next one is better."

"I'm startin' out slow, working up, y' know. Major Walden ought to appreciate this one." His mouth turned up at the corners as he cast Walden a glance over the fire.

"Try me," said the major.

"It was said that a doctor told his friend, 'I saw a man the other day with somethin' awful on his arm. Unfortunately, he will have to live with it.' 'Really? What was it?'" his friend asked. The doctor frowned. 'Why, it was his wife.'"

That one produced a few chuckles, and even Levi felt a grin pop out on his face. "That was a notch above the first," he told Willie.

"Not bad," said Walden. "I almost smiled."

Willie lifted one eyebrow. "All right, I'll give it one more try. If this don't work, I give up."

"Promise?" asked Walt Morse.

Ignoring him, Willie said, "A rather seedy-lookin' fellow walks into a New York City restaurant. He asks of the proprietor, 'What do you charge for a nicely cooked beefsteak, well done, with onions?' The proprietor looks at him and replies, 'Sir, I charge twenty-five cents.' 'Twenty-five cents,' says the man. 'That ain't bad. How much for the bread?' The proprietor replies, 'We throw in the bread.' The man nods his head in approval. 'That's mighty nice of y'. What about the gravy?' 'Well, we throw that in, as well.' 'Really?' says the man. 'I've changed my mind on the beefsteak. I'll just have the free bread and gravy.'"

There were a few chortles mixed with some more groans. "I can hardly wait for your sister to send another batch o' jokes," said John Cridland.

"Some free bread and gravy sounds good about now," said Charlie Clute.

"What?" Gordon looked at him. "Ain't you still feelin' as stuffed as a goose after that meal we had earlier?"

"My stomach hasn't felt fully satisfied since I left my wife's cooking behind," said Frank Vonfleet. "Although I'll admit today was worth writing home about."

That comment set the men to talking about their earlier meal, and then about Grimms's rare friendly mood. Levi listened closely to the exchange, examining each man seated around the fire and trying to picture him as a spy. Maybe he was overlooking something, he couldn't imagine how any of these men could be a traitor.

Gordon was the first in the group to expel a loud yawn. He stood and brushed the dirt off the seat of his pants. Everyone was in dire need of a good bath, but at least Gordon didn't smell as bad as the rest. More than once, Levi had observed the boy carrying a pail of river water into his tent, no doubt to use for sponging off the dirt and grime. Personally, Levi preferred stripping down to his undergarments in the river to wash off—hence the rarity of baths in wintertime. He was also far less modest than Gordon, thanks to his years in the army. His Quaker upbringing had instilled in him a sort of quiet reserve, but the war had stripped him clean of proper decorum. It wasn't that he'd lost his sense of decency, but few things embarrassed him anymore. Clearly, Snipp hadn't reached that point, but his youthful spirit probably kept him from it.

The boy yawned once more. "I don't know about the rest o' you, but that moon overhead tells me it's time for bed."

"I'm with you, boy," said Levi, standing. "Never know what tomorrow might bring. Besides, I've got some letters to write."

"To your sweetheart back home, I suspect." Mark Wilson grinned in the glow of the fire.

Levi merely shrugged.

A few others stood, as well, stretching their backs and announcing they, too, were turning in. Those who remained seated around the fire nodded good night to them.

Levi had to jog to catch up with Gordon, who was walking at a fast clip. "What's the hurry?"

Gordon shivered. "Oh, I'm just cold, that's all."

"You think this is cold?" Levi laughed. "Wait till next month. And then January. That's when the frigid temperatures really set in."

"Can't say I look forward to it, but I'm sure I'll accustom myself."

"You'll sleep a lot better once we're settled in our stockade tents. They held together pretty well last winter, even in the bitter winds. You'll bunk up with Charlie and me."

That remark brought the kid to an abrupt halt. "I ain't bunkin' up with no one."

Levi chuckled. "Of course, you are. Nobody gets a whole tent to himself."

"I'll just continue sleepin' in my own little tent, and I'll manage fine," Gordon insisted, and resumed walking.

Levi followed after him. "Sorry, kid, but I don't think your tent will keep you alive through the season. I thought I was doing you a favor, reserving a place for you. Most everybody, excepting McQuade and a couple of others, have already chosen their bunk mates. Would you rather share a tent with Hiram?"

Gordon slowed his gait. "No...."

"I didn't think so. Don't worry so much. You've got to dismiss some of that modesty. This is war."

"I know it is," Gordon huffed. "I been in the thick of it since August, remember?"

Levi had no idea what had put the boy in such a sour mood, but he wouldn't try to inquire tonight. He wanted to pay a call on Grimms yet this evening. When they reached Gordon's tent, the boy muttered a curt "Good night" before crawling inside with nary a backward glance.

Levi could see the tent moving as Gordon tied the flap shut from inside. He grinned and shook his head. "See you in the mornin', kid." Then he hurried to Lieutenant Grimms's quarters.

When he arrived, he found the tent empty. A note was posted in the entryway. Levi squinted in the moonlight to make out the words. "Off to visit Lieutenant Martin at Company K. Back late."

With a sigh, Levi sauntered off toward his own tent. Tomorrow was plenty early enough to tell Grimms that his search for a traitor in the camp had yielded no results, and that, frankly, he thought this whole spy matter a bunch of blather.

23

Even before the sun's first glimmer of light, Willie Speer blew his bugle, producing the loudest, most discordant screech Josie had ever heard. Instinctively, she pushed off the wool covers and jumped to her feet without a second thought.

"Prepare to march in twenty minutes!" someone barked.

Twenty minutes? That hardly gave her enough time to button her coat, throw on her cap, jump into her boots, roll up her bedding, fill her rucksack with the food rations she had on hand, and dismantle her tent. Of course, she'd completed the routine with such frequency that she could do it with her eyes closed. But in twenty minutes? She had a strong urge to seek out a thick bush, but there wouldn't be time for that until they started marching and she could fall out of line, do the deed, and then jump back in. If she'd learned anything since enlisting, it was that she could move as quick as lightning to answer the call of nature.

They crossed the Rapidan River just north of the Mine Run River around ten o'clock that morning. Josie was tired and hungry, but she wasn't about to complain. Doing so only made matters worse, for herself and for those around her. No sooner did they cross the river than the Rebels greeted them with a rush of flying Minié balls. Thankfully,

Company K was marching in front and ably shooed them back while the rest of the army marched on. It wasn't anything too perilous, but it certainly served to wake everybody up. Josie, for one, went on high alert, her pulse quickening at the close call, and her hand supporting the butt of her rifle in preparation for snapping it into position, if necessary.

Not more than fifteen minutes later, they received the order to advance. The command came just after Josie had mistakenly thought all was well. *Foolish girl*, she chided herself. *When will you ever learn that things are never well in war?* More Minié balls whizzed past, and she instinctively searched for Levi but failed to spot him. "Lord, please don't leave my side," she whispered.

They traveled through dense woods and thick underbrush, the foliage forcing soldiers to fall out of line in order to move forward. Crouching low, Josie darted from tree to tree, doing whatever it took to avoid the hot metal coming at her, as smoke clouded her vision, and sounds of cannon fire split the air. A bullet whistled past, but from behind, and for an instant, she sat frozen next to a tree, feeling vulnerable and exposed, her breaths coming out jagged and uneven. It wasn't until she caught sight of Levi up ahead that she was able to start moving again. It also helped that Louie Walker came up behind her and gave her a nudge in the back as he passed her. "Keep movin', boy. Sittin' still makes you an easier target."

She hadn't thought of that. Now her brain kicked in, and her breathing evened out. With her rifle aimed and ready, she advanced to another tree, then stopped to catch her breath. She glanced behind her, and it was then she caught sight of something, or someone, out of the corner of her eye—someone standing a hundred or so feet back from her, also hiding behind a tree. She could have sworn the tip of his rifle was pointed straight at her, but because the smoke was so thick, she couldn't be certain. She couldn't even be sure if he was a Reb or a Yank, but she pointed her musket at the tree behind which he stood, squinting as she tried to make out her target. It looked like…no, it couldn't be. Why would a Federal be aiming his rifle at her? She shook her head and peered once more at the figure. If she had the slightest doubt that he was a Federal, she wouldn't shoot. She knew that was the origin of the fiasco at Salem Church, and she certainly didn't want to be responsible for starting a similar incident. But he sure looked like a Yank, and he was staring daggers at her.

"What are you doing?" she yelled. "I'm Federal, just like you."

He stepped out from behind the tree, but his hat was pulled so low over his face that she couldn't recognize him. "Sorry, kid."

Steady, she told herself. *Don't fire unless fired upon*. The thought occurred to her that hesitating could be the difference between life and death. She held her musket in perfect position, her finger resting on the trigger, and cleared her throat. Her heart pulsed loud in her ears. Suddenly, she heard a louder crack than any of the others sounding all around. She ducked, but it was too late. A burning sensation ripped through her left shoulder, the impact jerking her body into a spiraling motion and sending her cap sailing right off her head. The whole thing so startled her that for a second, she just stood there, then plopped down on her bottom, too dazed and shocked to move. Had a Union soldier actually shot her? She turned her head in the direction from whence the shot had come, but no one was there. Surely, her eyes had deceived her, and the shooter had been a Reb. But if that was the case, what was he doing in Yankee territory?

"You okay?" Levi's voice sounded distant and muffled, but when she turned her head again, she found him hunkered down right next to her. Gunshots and cannon fire flew all around them. "Gordon, you all right?" he screamed in her ear.

She gathered her wits and nodded.

"Well, come on, then." He thrust her hat into her grasp. "You can't just sit here. We've got to move. Quick." He grabbed her by the arm—her good one, thankfully—and hauled her up. "Captain Bateman has ordered a bayonet charge, and we're lagging."

She nodded numbly, feeling as if she had somehow slipped out of her body and was now looking down on all the action from above. In rote fashion, she put her hat on again, then set off at a run behind Levi, musket in hand, rucksack still riding high on her back. She stumbled a couple of times, hardly able to see where she was going, and was thankful for Levi's firm grip on her arm. They plunged through a tangled web of dead leaves and twisted branches. Up ahead, Grimms shouted, "Come on, boys, come on! This way!" Her legs picked up speed in order to match Levi's long strides, and soon they got close enough to the others for her to make out a few familiar faces. Their company had blended with several others, but that didn't matter, considering they all were fighting the same enemy.

The Rebs kept firing, and the Yanks fired back. Everywhere—overhead, beside, in front, and behind—lead hissed past. Just then, a man from B Company went down. "Stay here," Levi told her, leaving her behind a tree as he set off after the fallen comrade. He turned him over, closed his eyes in a mournful expression, and then darted back to her. "It's Stan Gray."

"Is he...is he...?" She couldn't put it into words.

"He's dead." Levi grimaced. "Come on. We've got to keep moving. See that cluster of trees up ahead?"

She gave a quick nod as several other soldiers raced past.

"We'll head there. Ready?"

"Ready."

"All right. Go!"

Levi darted out, and she chased after him, determined to keep up. As they ran, the woods began to crackle like heaping kettles of popped corn, and then the air vibrated and whirred as Miniés flew over their heads. "Hurry!" Levi yelled.

"I'm coming," she screamed in return.

Smoke from all the volleying rolled out to meet them, and the thought occurred to Josie that the enemy could be lurking on the other side of that black curtain, muskets and bayonets in hand, just waiting for them to break through the cloud. She and Levi reached the band of trees and squatted side by side behind a thick trunk, their backs pressed against the rough bark. They both breathed heavily, desperate for air amid the smoke. Slowly, Levi peeked around from behind the tree, then faced forward again. "I don't see a thing."

"Sounds like the fightin' has moved in that direction," Josie said, pointing.

"It seems to have gone southward," Levi agreed. "I came back because I didn't see you and wondered what had happened. What were you doing, sitting on the ground like a stunned bird?"

Josie had almost forgotten about having been shot. She put her right hand to her left shoulder and felt a large pool of wetness. When she drew her hand back to look at her palm, it was covered in blood.

"What in the name of all things eternal? You've been hit!" Levi looked more alarmed than she'd ever seen him. "Here, get this off so I can have a look."

He immediately went to work tearing off her thick wool coat. The wound had bled straight through the fabric. Dizziness overtook her at the realization, but he pushed her to the ground, which kept her from losing consciousness. "Let's get your arm through this sleeve." He started to unbutton her shirt.

"No!" she squealed. "No." She pushed his hand away and tried to sit up. "You can't."

"What do you mean, I can't? You're hit, kid." He gawked only briefly before tearing open the top two buttons of her shirt. "Can you move your arm?"

"Stop," she said. "You…you can't…look at me."

"What are you talking about? You're wounded."

"I'm…I can't let you look, because I…I'm not who you think I am."

He clamped his mouth shut and stared at her, blank-faced. After a moment, he removed his hat, scratched his head, and then plopped it back in place, his brow crinkled in confusion. "What's that supposed to mean, exactly?" He rocked back on his heels, still crouching on the ground.

"I'm…a woman." There. She'd finally said it, and it felt oddly freeing.

"A woman." It wasn't a question but a stunned statement. "A woman," he repeated.

"Don't hate me."

"Hate you." He shook his head but never shifted his eyes away from her. Nor did he speak.

She wished she could read his thoughts, but they were lost to her, and maybe even to him. "Say something," she pleaded. She gritted her teeth and gripped her left arm, not wanting to waste a second thinking about her wound but also not able to ignore the searing pain. She tried to sit up, but queasiness kept her from doing so.

"You're shaking."

"I'm so cold."

"We'll have to go back to my horse so I can get you to the medic's wagon."

"The medic's wagon?" She shook her head. "No, I can't go there."

"You have to. Can you stand?"

"Yes, of course, but I can't—. I don't want anyone to know—"

"What in the world were you thinking, Gordon—or...or whoever you are?" He put both hands on his head, as if to hold it in place, then closed his eyes. "I knew it. I just knew it. I could tell something was different, but I didn't want to let myself believe it. It's enough...it's enough to make a preacher swear." He exhaled a loud sigh. "What's your real name?"

⌒

Levi gave the surroundings a quick survey, not wanting anyone to sneak up on them. Good stinking grief, Gordon wasn't Gordon. "He" wasn't even a *he*, for crying out loud. "What's your real name?" Levi repeated. She was bleeding, but she wasn't dying, and he wasn't about to take her to see the doctor until he got a few answers.

Her long lashes fluttered and glimmered with tears as her eyelids shut. He should have known. It all made complete sense now—the girlish gait, the effeminate mannerisms, the unevenly pitched voice. The utter lack of facial hair. He'd told himself that Gordon was just different. Now he knew better, and he felt like the biggest idiot this side of the Mississippi.

"Josephine Winters," she finally answered. "My family always calls me Josie. Aside from my identity, I've always been truthful. I told you why I joined the army. All my reasons remain the same."

"Always truthful?" Levi scoffed. "You've been a walking lie." That comment was harsh, he knew; but, for some reason he couldn't define, he was as angry as a bear. Maybe it was because he'd liked Gordon Snipp, the innocent young boy who reminded him of his kid brother. Now, he had to face the fact that "Gordon" was actually Josephine Winters. He tried to make sense of it, but his head couldn't wrap itself around the truth.

She grabbed her shoulder, and blood oozed through her fingers.

Levi snapped to attention. "All right, let's get you back to Major Walden."

"But he'll find out. He'll report me to Lieutenant Grimms."

"And *I* won't? You can't stay in the army, Gord—er, whatever your name is. You're a woman, and women aren't allowed."

Now that he considered her with her coat off, wearing just a shirt, it was clearer than ever that "he" was a she. No wonder she'd always kept her coat on, even in that drenching August heat, and worn clothes two sizes too big. How could he have been so blind? Furthermore, why hadn't any of the others caught on? Were they just as thickskulled as he?

"That isn't fair," she stated.

He snapped back to attention. "I don't make the rules."

"Please don't tell, Levi," she said, her pleading tone already sounding very different from how Gordon Snipp would speak. "You're my friend, aren't you? Can't you respect my wishes? I joined so I could carry on where my brother left off. I'm doing this for him, to honor his memory. Can't you please help keep my identity a secret?"

Her eyes were big and as brown as chocolate. He'd never noticed them before, but now that he did, he couldn't help but admire their entrancing sheen, their perfect oval shape.

Good glory, what was he doing? Now was no time to focus on her womanly features. "Your identity is a pretty big deal, Josephine—"

"Please, call me Josie."

More anger boiled inside him, and he didn't think it was of the righteous sort. "What in the blue fire do you want me to do, *Josie*—lie for you?" He extended his hand to her. "Get up." The gruffness in his tone sounded foreign to even him, but he was downright mad, and there wasn't much point in trying to hide it.

She sat up slowly. Because she'd lost some blood, she was about as white as a dove. Her pallor only emphasized the fact that her skin was as clear as a mountain stream.

He shook his head to rid it of the distraction.

When she stood, she started to topple, so he reached out to steady her. "You all right?"

She didn't answer, just gave a little moan as her eyes rolled to the back of her head. He managed to catch her fainting figure in his arms. She weighed about as much as two duck feathers. At least he wouldn't have any trouble carrying her the mile or so back to the tree where he'd tied Rosie.

What a fine pickle this was. To the south, the fighting continued.

And in his heart, a different battle raged.

24

*J*osie awoke to the familiar sounds of groaning patients, only to discover that she herself was a patient, lying prone on a hard cot in a covered wagon. She turned her head and fought off a wave of dizziness. Her mind was a befuddled mess. What had happened, and why was she here? Upon further investigation, she noticed the large bandage on her left arm that extended up to her shoulder, and then discovered that her arm was secured in some sort of cloth sling tied around her neck. When she tried to sit up—because she wanted nothing more than to escape—a wave of nausea overcame her.

"Ah, Gordon. I see you're waking up."

A terrible memory surfaced about being shot in the shoulder and then, worse, having Levi discover that she wasn't a man named Gordon Snipp but a woman. She thrashed around, trying to make out her surroundings—which wagon she was in, whether she recognized any of the patients, and the identity of the man who'd just spoken to her.

"Lie still," the voice repeated. She couldn't quite make him out, as she seemed to be seeing two of him.

"My eyes…I can't see right." She tried her best to sound manly.

"It's the medication I gave you—a combination of morphine sulfate—and then, of course, the chloroform. I had to do something for your pain."

"What pain? I'm fine."

"You're fine now, but you weren't before. You've also lost a fair amount of blood, so that's why I'm keeping you here for a couple of days, to rest and recover.

She started to panic. "Who are you?"

"Shh. It's me, Major Walden."

"Who?"

"Dr. Walden. You know me, Gordon."

"Oh." He spoke in such a soothing tone that her heart rate slowed a bit, and she started to relax. Of course, she knew Major Walden. What was wrong with her? She lifted her hand to feel where the sling kept her shoulder in place.

"You took a gunshot wound, but you'll be fine. It was a clean shot. Went straight through, so I didn't have to remove the bullet."

"Bullet?"

"Yes, bullet. Fired at close range, from my assessment. Did you happen to see who shot you?"

She had a faint recollection of seeing someone standing by a tree, but that was all she could remember for now. She gave her head a slow shake. "No."

"All right. Well, Lieutenant Grimms thinks it's odd that a Confederate would have wandered so deep into Federal territory."

She squinted, still seeing two of him. He had four eyes. "I…I don't understand."

"He's worried that maybe it wasn't a Reb who shot you but one of your own comrades."

"What?" A dreadful memory resurfaced of having seen a Union soldier step out from behind a tree. She winced. This was too much to think about. Did Major Walden know her to be a woman? Surely, he did. After all, he'd worked on her injured shoulder. She lifted her right hand and weakly snagged the front of his shirt. "Do you...do you know...about...me?"

He nodded and gave her a smile. Two smiles, actually, since he had two mouths. Then he leaned so close that she could see the whiskers of his two scraggly beards, not to mention the hairs in his four nostrils. "Yes, I know, um, *Gordon*," he whispered. "Your secret is safe with me."

"Thank you," she answered, still using her Gordon Snipp voice, lest another patient overhear. "Where is Levi?"

"He went back."

"Back?"

"To the field."

She looked away and saw two medicine bottles on a table. "He hates me."

"He doesn't hate you."

She heard cannon fire in the distance, but the blasts were spaced far apart. "The battle seems to be slowing down," Major Walden said, as if sensing her worry. "We were able to push the Confederates back. Levi will be in soon, I'm sure, to check on the patients. There were only a few casualties, thankfully. I'm afraid we did lose Stan Gray."

She burst into tears, which was bewildering. She seldom cried. Not only that, she didn't even know Stan Gray. Yes, he'd been a part of Company B, but she'd failed to get to know him. His family would be heartbroken. "I'm sorry to hear that." She cried some more.

The doctor dabbed at her eyes with the corner of her bedsheet. "There, there. Things will look brighter when you're back to yourself." He came closer again and whispered, "You do know you won't be able to stay in the army, Gordon. Or shall I call you Josie?"

"But I—I'm a good soldier. And you promised not to tell anyone."

"You are a good soldier. One of the best. And I always keep my promises."

More tears came. She was so tired. "But...."

"Never mind all that now. It's time you got some rest." He patted her right shoulder, then straightened. "Close your eyes, now."

She did as told. *I will stay in the army.* That was her final thought before she drifted to sleep.

⌒

Curse this tremor in his hand! His first shot at the kid had bounced off a tree; the second had hit its mark, but not at the spot where he'd intended. He'd been aiming for the heart, not the shoulder! Was he losing his touch? Worse, was he losing his mind? To make matters worse, the kid had yelled out to him, which meant he'd spotted him standing behind that blasted tree. Now he worried Snipp might have recognized him, even though the smoke had been thick.

He cussed under his breath as he trudged back toward camp with the rest of the Federals, glad in some respects that the Confederates had given up the fight, at least for now. He wanted to go drown his sorrows in a bottle of whiskey, if he could just get his hands on some. Grimms had been liberal in dispensing the liquid yesterday. Perchance he could talk him into sharing a few more swigs. He needed a good dose so he'd be able to sleep.

"What you so all fired up about?" asked Corporal Richard Fuller, who walked beside him. "We're heading back. It's another victory for the Yanks."

A few whoops and hollers rose up around them, and many of the men joined together in a victory chant. The sound only augmented his fury. As cold as it was outside, he broke into a fiery sweat. He wiped his brow with the back of his hand and said nothing in response to Fuller's remarks.

"Anybody hear how Snipp's doing?" asked a soldier somewhere behind him.

His stomach lurched.

"I heard he was shot, but I don't know much more than that," someone else answered.

"He'll be fine," said a voice he recognized. *Albright.* "He took a bullet to the shoulder. Dr. Walden said he'll need a few days' rest to recover from losing so much blood."

He ought to turn around and shoot Albright in the face. If Albright hadn't come to the kid's rescue, he might have been able to move in closer and finish the job. He swore that the next time anybody got in his way, he'd fix that man for good. He'd had about enough of these fool-hardy Yanks. He ought to just give up his uniform, desert, and join his Southern brothers. But, no, he was right where he needed to be, picking off one useless Yank at a time. This is where he could do the most good for his countrymen.

"Too bad about Stan Gray," said Frank Vonfleet. "He was a quiet sort. Never did get to know him very well."

Several others murmured their regrets at the loss of another good soldier.

He kicked a big stick out of his way, and the thing flew up in the air, accidentally striking Hiram McQuade in the back.

"Hey!" he growled. "What's wrong with you?" He jumped out of line and pulled back his arm, preparing to swing at him.

He gritted his teeth, balled his fists, and readied himself for a good fight; but Albright jumped in and put himself between them. "Cool down, both of you. This isn't a war between our fellow comrades."

McQuade fingered a large cut on his face, probably one he acquired in the woods. "Well, the least you can do is apologize."

"Sorry," he sneered, then sped off to get away from all the accusing stares.

"What's wrong with him?" someone asked.

"Who knows? War does strange things to people."

"Just leave 'im alone. He'll cool off," said another.

He focused his eyes on the two-track path ahead, eager to reach camp. He had so much hatred festering inside him, he felt on the verge of exploding.

Whiskey, he thought. *I need whiskey.*

⌒

Levi couldn't concentrate. In his latest letter to Mary, he'd written exactly ten words so far.

Dear Mary,

Today has been another day on the battlefield.

Beyond that, he couldn't think what to say. He couldn't tell her about all the bloodshed he'd seen or how blasted loud the cannon fire was, or about the loss of one of the men in his company, or that he'd discovered his young friend Gordon Snipp was actually a woman named Josephine Winters. No, he especially couldn't tell her that.

He supposed he could tell her about the army's day of thanks-giving, and ask if she'd observed the new holiday. But with everything that had happened since that day—only yesterday—it seemed like old news.

He tossed the paper aside and lay down to stare at the canvas roof. A steady rain had started falling an hour ago, and it didn't sound as though it planned to let up any time soon. Streaks of lightning created short bursts of illumination in his otherwise dark tent. He pulled his two wool blankets closer to his chin and thanked the Lord for the cot that kept him off the ground, so that the dampness couldn't seep through his clothes. He would be glad for a day without any fighting so the soldiers could focus on building their semi-permanent housing structures for the winter months. With a little luck, they'd march back to their winter location soon.

His mind wandered to Gordon, now Josie. He still had to retrain his mind to think of her as a woman. He regretted that she'd lost so much blood. He hadn't realized the severity of her wound until Major Walden had ripped off her shirt and revealed the hole in her left shoulder.

The major had taken the news of her gender in stride, almost as if he'd suspected it. Being a doctor, he'd probably seen just about every-thing. As far as going straight to Lieutenant Grimms, though, he'd said it wasn't his place to do so; it was her news to share, not his.

Levi couldn't decide how to proceed. Josie had begged him not to tell anyone, but how could he not? Wasn't it his duty? He could be held for treason if he kept such a secret. Was he willing to take that risk?

Based on the doctor's assessment of the wound, Grimms believed she'd been shot at close range, and that Josie very well could have seen the shooter's face. Moreover, he was suspicious it had been a Union soldier who'd shot her. The thought put a terrible taste in Levi's mouth, especially after he'd canvassed all of Company B for potential spies and deemed the notion unlikely.

He stood and turned up the wick on his lantern. Time to read his Bible before going to bed. He prayed that God would somehow enlighten him as to what to do about Josie and also give him clarity in regard to the possibility of a spy in their midst—who he might be, or even whether he existed.

But when Levi turned down the wick and put his head to the pillow, he felt no closer to answers and even further from peace. Between the rain pelting the roof and the pictures of Josie that filled his mind—her pleasant face; her plump lips; her chocolate eyes with those long, dark lashes; and her endearing smile—he had little hope of sleeping well.

25

On December 4, the 23rd Pennsylvania Volunteers arrived at a spot about 30 miles east of Brandy Station and not far from the banks of the Potomac. To everyone's great relief, Grimms announced that the fighting was most likely finished for the year, and the men set to work on their winter structures.

Josie could do very little to help, since her left arm remained in a sling, and lifting and carrying heavy logs required two strong arms. But she felt useless simply sitting there watching the others labor, so she spent her time gathering sticks and small branches for firewood with her right hand, then stacking them for later use. It was tedious and slow going, but at least it kept her body busy and her mind occupied. She also helped Harv Patterson with the meals, doing what she could with one arm, which amounted to stirring pots; feeding the fire; cutting up pieces of venison, rabbit, or squirrel meat to put in a stew; and carrying buckets of water from the creek for washing utensils and pots and pans. She'd also continued assisting Major Walden, her chores limited for now to counting pills, delivering cups of water to the patients, reading letters to them, and also writing down the replies they dictated.

Major Walden said she'd been fortunate that the bullet had whizzed right through her arm, missing major arteries and doing only minor damage to the surrounding tissue. When he'd bandaged the wound, he'd issued strict orders that she return daily so he could change the dressing and keep a close watch on the entrance and exit areas of the bullet, to ensure no infection set in. As of yesterday, he'd told her everything was healing nicely, but he warned her that the pain surrounding the two areas would no doubt persist for weeks to come. She was to avoid excessive strain so as not to delay the healing. As for her strength and energy, neither one had returned in full, which only made her feel more useless. More than once, she wondered if she oughtn't to go to Lieutenant Grimms and spill the truth about her identity. But doing so would bring an abrupt end to her admittedly brief career, and she still believed God had a purpose for her serving in the army, even if it was just to encourage or be a friend to someone.

There was no denying that Levi had been avoiding her. He'd always gone out of his way to be friendly to Gordon Snipp, but now that he knew her as Josephine Winters, he'd made a point of keeping his distance. She didn't blame him, of course. He was angry with her, and rightfully so. But, looking back, what could she have done differently? The army didn't accept female soldiers, so she'd had to disguise herself in order to answer what she believed to be a God-given call to serve. Couldn't he see that? She'd told him countless times that she wished to finish what Andrew had started, that she considered it an honorable gesture, and that her brother would be proud of her efforts. What difference should it make to him that she was a woman and not the boy he'd befriended? At least he'd kept the matter a secret—so far.

Her shoulder injury had complicated matters even further, for it was believed that a Union soldier had shot her. She had wracked her brain to bring to mind the face of the man she'd spotted behind the tree, but his countenance eluded her like a misty fog. Who among her company, or in the whole of the 23rd, would wish to kill her? To her knowledge, she'd done nothing to offend anyone, and couldn't imagine why someone would pick her as a target. None of it made any sense, and her befuddlement had been making a good night's sleep impossible. When she managed to slumber, her head filled with dreams about running full force either *at* or *away from* the enemy, screaming, as muskets flashed in her direction, and dead soldiers—always dead soldiers—lay on the ground, sometimes in heaps, their eyes wide open, staring holes into her soul.

Most times, she dreaded nightfall for all the dreams that were sure to haunt her. More than once, she'd awakened shouting the name of Jesus. She'd always drawn comfort from saying His name, and it was her only hope for finding peace and a refuge from her nightmares. She prayed for His presence to prevail, but right now, her fear was overwhelming.

Once the winter structures were built, Levi decided he had avoided Josie long enough. He had to go and remind her she was to bunk up with Charlie Clute and him. She didn't have a choice, really. He already knew her to be a woman, and he'd broken the news to Charlie that very morning. His friend had been surprised, at first, but then he'd admitted, "I always did think him a little too girlish for his good." At any rate, between them, they would keep her safe. If she bunked with anyone else, her secret wouldn't keep long, and that could present even bigger problems. She would probably argue—again—that she would be fine in her scrawny little tent, but Levi had already endured two winters in the army, and he knew all too well that her chances of survival were far slimmer on her own. Last winter, a few men had frozen to death.

He still hoped she might go to Grimms and confess her shenanigans, but there was another part of him that hoped she would stick out this bitter war. The truth was, he'd missed talking to her. Actually, he'd missed talking to Gordon Snipp, but that was another story. If he'd learned one thing in his recent study of the Bible, it was that he wasn't to judge others for their actions. That was for the Lord to do. Levi's priorities were to be prayer, compassion, and encouragement. So far, he'd done a lousy job concerning Josephine Winters.

He found her as she was hauling a bucket up the hill from the creek. "Need any help with that?"

She paused, clearly out of breath, and looked up at him. "No, thanks. I'm doing just fine."

"You're obviously not." He tried to take the bucket from her, but she pulled her arm away, the motion causing some of the water to spill.

"Don't," she hissed. "Someone might see."

"So?"

"They would think it odd that you were helping Gordon Snipp."

He sniffed and shifted his weight. "I guess you're right, *Gordon*."

"I haven't seen you in a few days."

"I've been making a lot of calls." That much was true. Since the recent Mine Run Campaign, he'd paid many a call on injured men throughout the regiment. Thankfully, the casualties had been relatively few. "And working on our winter shelter. Charlie and I finished it today."

"I see. I thought you might be avoiding me."

"Why would I do that?"

She resumed walking up the hill, so he turned and climbed alongside her.

"Because you're angry."

"I've gotten over that."

She didn't reply.

Now that he knew her to be a woman, he did notice her movements a little more than might be proper. He forced his eyes to look over her cap. "What was your hair like before...you know?"

At the top of the hill, she stopped and turned t him. "Shh. You shouldn't ask me that sort of question. Someone might overhear." She lowered the bucket to the ground and straightened, wincing a little.

"There's no one nearby." He spread his arms out wide. "Look. It's just us."

She glanced about, seeming satisfied to see that everyone was busy working on the winter housing. "If you must know, my hair came down to here." She touched her right arm to her lower back.

Levi tried to imagine how that would have looked, and found himself wishing he could see for himself. "Do you miss it? Or do you like playing the part of man-boy? You're quite convincing, by the way. You had me fooled. Well, for the most part. I was starting to have my doubts."

"Yes, I miss my hair, and I shall grow it out again someday—after I've completed my mission for Andrew. If you'll recall, that is why I joined—to honor him. I hope you haven't told anyone else."

"I told Charlie."

"What?" She gaped at him. "But he'll go and tell—"

"He won't say anything to anyone. He had to know, since you're bunking up with him and me for the winter."

She frowned. "I already told you, I'm not—"

"And I already told you, no one stays alone."

"But...but I am a"—she leaned forward—"woman."

He gave her a half grin. "Nothing unseemly is going to happen, if that's what you're worried about."

"Well, I wasn't—I didn't mean *that*." She quickly bent to retrieve the bucket. There was an unmistakable blush on her pale cheeks that strangely made him feel something for which he wasn't prepared.

"We'll see to it that you have your privacy," he assured her, as they resumed walking.

"And how do you propose to do that?" She kept her gaze pointed forward.

"I don't know, but we'll think of something. Some sort of...partition, maybe. Charlie and I will figure it out."

She exhaled what sounded like a sigh of relief.

"I hear that Grimms paid you a visit in the medic's wagon."

"Yes. He thinks a Union soldier tried to kill me."

Soon they reached Harv Patterson's site. A big fire was going, and a steaming kettle hung over it, the aroma of its contents wafting through the air and making Levi's stomach growl. Harv was nowhere to be seen, however. Levi leaned forward to peek inside the pot.

"Rabbit stew," Josie informed him as she set down the bucket.

"Hmm. Smells good." He stepped back from the fire and studied her expression. "So, I hear they suspect it was a Union soldier who shot you."

She shivered, then nodded somberly. "It might have been a Federal, I'm just not a hundred percent certain. All I know is, I was somebody's target."

He cast a glance around, then took her by the arm and led her to a couple of tree stumps situated by the fire. "Sit down. I want to talk to you."

"All right." She sat and gave him her full attention, the sparkling glimmer of her dark brown eyes disarming him.

"Grimms thinks there may be a traitor among us."

Her body gave a little jolt. "A traitor? What makes him think that?"

"You're not a spy, are you?" He didn't truly suspect her, but he had to ask the question.

"Of course, I'm not a spy. Are you crazy?"

"Shh. No point in getting riled. Right now, everyone's a suspect."

"So, you think I shot myself to mislead everyone?"

"No."

"Well, I'm glad we straightened that out," she hissed. "I'm Union, through and through."

He grinned at her spunk. "I believe you."

Her lower lip went into a pout. "Are you sure?"

"Yes, I'm sure."

Since the pout stayed put, he leaned closer to her and whispered, "You're using your womanly wiles on me, Miss Winters."

"I am?" She looked genuinely alarmed.

"Most men don't stick out their bottom lip like that. You'd best watch yourself if you want to keep up that masquerade of yours."

She corrected her facial expression, then slouched on her seat, extending her legs in front of her.

He chuckled. "There. That's much better."

She began digging in the dirt with the toe of one boot. "So, if there were a spy in our midst, why would he go after me? What did I do?"

"Maybe he doesn't have a reason, other than he just hates Yanks. Lieutenant Grimms, along with captains Bateman and Birney, believe that a few of the deaths earlier associated with Rebel fire may have actually been caused by a Federal."

She raised her eyebrows. "That's a crazy thought."

"War makes people crazy."

"Who's crazy?" asked Harv Patterson as he joined them, picking up a long-handled wooden spoon from a nearby table.

"No one in particular," said Levi.

"That's right; this unit's full of crazies—'specially that Gordon Snipp fella." Harv winked at Josie. "Never can tell when he'll go a little berserk."

"That's the truth," said Levi, giving Josie a playful shove in the side.

"Hey," Josie protested. "When have I ever acted crazy?"

"Just jokin' with you, Snipp. You're probably the most even-tempered of us all." Harv dipped the spoon in the kettle and set to stirring.

26

The very last thing Josie wanted to do was share a tent with two men. But here she was, lying on a halfway decent cot, wrapped in two wool blankets, and staring at the peaked ceiling. She was thankful that Levi and Charlie had rigged up a partition of left-over canvas to separate her from them, giving her about one-third of the structure to call her own. It didn't serve as a noise barrier, though, and every time one of them cleared his throat, turned over, whispered to the other, or sniffed, she heard it—which made her realize they heard every tiny sound she made, as well. Oh, how she longed for more privacy. She would've insisted on remaining in her own little tent through the winter, but the news that a couple of soldiers in another unit had frozen to death last year was enough to dissuade her.

"How you doing over there?" Levi asked.

"Oh, fine, just fine," she answered. "Happy as a pig in mud."

She could almost hear the grin on his face.

"You're not gonna start snortin' like one, are you?" asked Charlie.

She snorted twice. The men both laughed, and she couldn't help but do the same.

After a few moments of silence, she said, "Thanks for providing me with a place for the winter. I appreciate it."

"Our pleasure," said Charlie. "I admire you, you know."

"You do?"

"Sure. Levi told me about your brother. I'm sure he would be proud of you."

"Thanks."

More silence.

"How much longer do you think this war will go on?" she asked.

"That's a good question, kid," said Levi. "The Union is gaining ground, no question about that, but the South doesn't seem anywhere near ready to surrender."

It warmed her heart to hear him call her "kid" again. And she knew without question that she felt more affection for him than was proper. In fact, if she were honest, she'd have to admit she loved him. Would she ever have the chance to tell him? Or would that truth remain forever buried?

Within minutes, both men had drifted off to sleep; she could hear Levi's snores and Charlie's rhythmic breathing. She, however, could not sleep, still haunted by images of flashing musket fire. She recalled her initial ride to camp, when she'd spotted that dead Reb boy lying on the ground. She hoped someone had found him shortly thereafter and given him a proper burial.

Oh, the things she thought about when the darkness closed in.

Sometime in the night, Josie awoke to a scuffling sound outside the tent. She sat straight up, pushed the covers off herself, and stood. No doubt, it was a raccoon or some other critter scavenging for food; but, to be certain, she slipped her boots onto her feet, threw her coat over her shoulders, and headed outside to investigate. Neither Charlie nor Levi stirred as she stealthily ducked through the slit in the makeshift curtain and tiptoed past them, then pushed through the canvas doorway and stepped outside. The icy air caused her breath to come out in cloud-like puffs. Wrapping her arms around herself for warmth, she sneaked around the tent and a soldier in Union uniform bent down, fanning a flame at the base of the structure.

"What're you doin'?" she demanded, trying her best not to squeal like a girl.

Startled, he leaped up and took off in the opposite direction.

"Hey!" she hollered, then turned and began stomping on the flames that were already crawling up the sides of the tent. "Help!" she shouted. "Fire!" In minutes, a dozen or more other soldiers, including Levi and Charlie, emerged and began beating the flames with blankets, coats, and anything else they could find, until, at last, the fire went out.

"How'd this happen?" asked Mark Wilson.

"Somebody ran past our tent into the woods a few minutes ago," said Louie Walker. "Didn't get a good look at 'im, though."

"You mean, someone set the fire on purpose?" Charlie asked, standing back to assess the charred portion of the tent.

"I'm afraid so," Josie said. "I heard a noise and came out to investigate. That's when I saw a soldier—at least, he was dressed like one—fannin' the flames."

"Did you get a good look at him?" asked Levi.

"Just a glimpse, really."

"Not enough to recognize him?"

"Sorry, no."

"How did a Reb get past the guards?" Mark asked.

Josie swallowed hard. "He was wearin' Union colors."

"You're sayin' a Union soldier tried to burn down your tent?" asked Willie Speer. By now, even more fellows had gathered around them.

"Who'd wanna do that?" asked Louie.

"Good question," said Levi.

Charlie gestured to the tattered canvas, and beneath it Josie's cot, still smoldering. "Looks like somebody wants Snipp gone," he said.

"One of our own, you mean?" asked Louie. "But who'd wanna hurt Snipp?"

Silence settled as the men eyed one another with looks of suspicion.

Finally, Charlie exhaled a heavy breath. "I'd better go wake Lieutenant Grimms."

"Yes, he needs to know." Levi shoved his hands in his pockets and looked around at the gathering crowd. "Men, it appears we are living with a traitor in our midst. If anybody sees or hears anything suspicious, he is to report it immediately."

He cursed under his breath and punched his pillow. Could he do nothing right? In the shadows, he held up his hand and couldn't deny the tremor he saw. What was wrong with him? His nerves were shot. That dumb kid had seen him, probably even recognized him. Come morning, they would hang him from the gallows—if not sooner. He should make a run for it while he had the chance. His stomach churned with queasiness. Everything had turned sour on him. He'd meant to do right by his Southern brothers, but he'd failed miserably. He rolled onto his back and pulled his covers up over his face.

John Cridland, his roommate for the winter, pulled back the canvas door and slipped inside. In the flicker of their dimly lit lantern, he stood there, staring down at him. "You awake?" he asked.

Here it came. The moment when John would tell him his deceitful game was over.

"Yes," he muttered.

"Where were you?"

"What do you mean?"

"Didn't you hear all the commotion?"

"What commotion?"

"Some fellow just tried to burn down Albright's tent, with him, Clute, and Snipp inside. They all might've died, but Snipp heard a noise and went outside to check. Says he found a Union soldier fannin' a fire at the base of their tent. The fellow took off runnin' when he saw Snipp, who yelled "Fire!" A bunch of us ran over there to help put it out. I'm surprised you didn't hear the rumpus."

"Me, too. Who'd wanna burn down their tent?"

John stood over him, staring. "I got no idea. You?"

He didn't care for John's accusing tone. "What are you gettin' at, Cridland?"

"Where were you when I left the tent?"

"I was out waterin' the ground."

John scrutinized him with piercing eyes. "Where'd you go?"

"Down the hill. Why all the questions?"

John sat on his cot and pulled off his boots. "Just wonderin', is all. Weren't you curious why I wasn't in my bed when you came back?"

"I didn't even look. I ain't your keeper," he grumbled, turning on his side to face the wall. "Did the kid get a good look at the soldier?"

"He saw him, all right, but not his face. Or maybe he just doesn't want to name him. He said it was a Union soldier, though."

"Really?" He gritted his teeth and clutched his blanket with a tight fist, hardly daring to breathe. "Seems he'd just come out with it if he knew 'im."

"Maybe he's afraid."

He said nothing in return, and soon heard John crawling back into his cot. At last, John's breathing slowed as he fell back asleep.

Meanwhile, he lay there plotting how to do away with that dumb kid before he talked.

⟡

Willie blew his bugle at five, well before sunrise. It had been a restless night, with the attempted arson and now a gaping hole on Josie's side of the tent. Levi had insisted she take his cot for the remaining hours of night, and he'd slept on the ground. Levi hated to think what might have happened, had Josie not awakened and gone to investigate the sound she heard outside. She could have gotten severely burned, and might even have died. Who knows what would have befallen Charlie and himself.

He and Charlie would repair the tent today, but even more important was catching the person responsible for the damage. No longer was it somebody's wild notion that a spy lurked in their midst. It was a fact, and Levi meant to find the culprit before he did any more harm.

At roll call, every man was present but three: Tim Anderson, George Marley, and Chester Woolsley. It was said that Tim and George had gone to the medic's wagon due to illness, but no one knew where Chester was until midway through the meeting, when he sauntered onto the scene, looking confused.

"Nice that you could join us, Woolsley," Grimms said. "Where you been?"

"I…I didn't know we was havin' no meetin', sir. I didn't hear no bugle, and nobody waked me up."

"You're responsible for waking yourself. Let this be a lesson."

"Yes, sir!"

"Now then, as I was saying…after last night's fire, it's clear to me there is a traitor in our camp."

"What fire, sir?" asked Chester.

Grimms scowled. "Somebody catch Woolsley up later. No more interruptions, Soldier."

"Yes, sir. I mean, no, sir. No more." Chester put his hands behind his back and tried to straighten his hunched shoulders. The poor guy shifted his weight from one leg to the other, obviously rattled by Grimm's lack of patience.

"I've suspected it for some time, as have sergeants Clute and Albright," Grimms continued. "And now the rest of you know. Rest assured, we are going to catch this treacherous individual; and, when we do, he will pay for his wrongful deeds. Colonel Hughes does not look mercifully on turncoats." His dark gaze roved vigilantly about the crowd, and no one made a sound, except for a few who cleared their throats uneasily. "Anyone here aware of any covert activities?"

Next to Levi, Josie stood as stiff as a tree trunk. What was she thinking? Levi knew she hadn't slept much the rest of the night; he'd heard her tossing and turning continually on his cot.

"As you know, the penalty for treason is death, so you'd best not hold anything back," Grimms added.

All was quiet while Grimms continued his examination of the company—a sorry sight of bleary-eyed, bewildered men. Levi studied their expressions in turn, searching for signs of guilt. He also silently prayed for God's intervention.

"Sir," said Henry Gower, from his position in the middle of the huddle.

"Yes, Private?"

"What if one of us has a suspicion about someone in particular?"

"Then you should come and tell me about it."

Henry nodded. "Yes, sir."

"Or you can just say it out loud for the rest of us to hear," Howard Adams put in. "Shouldn't we all be aware of who he's accusin'?" He directed the question at Grimms.

Josie flitted Levi a nervous glance.

"Sure, go on and say it out loud," said Hiram McQuade. "We should all be aware."

"Oh, I don't have anyone in mind," Henry said quickly. "I was just asking."

Grimms lifted his hands to quiet the men. "Captain Bateman and Colonel Hughes are joining me later this morning, when we'll begin conducting private interviews with each of you. There is no need to talk among yourselves, although I'm sure you'll do it, regardless. Be aware that two Union Intelligence Service agents are also riding in today to start an investigation of their own. I expect full cooperation from everyone. Sergeant Clute will set up your appointment. See to it you're punctual.

"In the meantime, we'll go about our day as usual, building furniture for the stockade tents, unloading supplies from the delivery wagons, clearing a section of brush to make way for the new sutler, who's bringing fresh provisions, and, if there's time, doing some drills. Colonel Hughes assures us we are in for a quiet winter, but we must be prepared. I also received word that the paymaster is due sometime today or tomorrow. Private Adams, see to it that you meet up with him so you can disperse the monies."

"Yes, sir."

Grimms straightened and saluted. "That concludes my agenda." As the soldiers mirrored the gesture, he made an about-face and headed back toward his quarters, his usual entourage of subordinates following.

~

Well, this was a fine fix—interviews with the lieutenant and Union Intelligence Officers, scrutiny on every side, and suspicious glances from his tent mate that morning. He didn't think that little weasel Snipp had seen his face last night, but he couldn't take any chances. He had to do something about him.

That would prove even harder now, with everybody on the lookout for a spy, questioning the slightest vagary in his comrades' behavior. Why did he have to be such a clumsy ox in the most crucial of moments? The tremor in his hand seemed to be getting worse, and his brain was a mess of mixed-up thoughts. Sometimes, he wondered if he wasn't losing his mind.

He kept to himself that day, awaiting his 4:30 appointment with Grimms and Clute. He tried to tell himself not to worry. Nobody had any real evidence on him. And even if Snipp named him, who was going to believe the youngster?

He kept an eye on Clute and Albright as they repaired their damaged tent, with Snipp doing what he could with his good arm. He wasn't wearing the sling anymore, but he still hadn't recovered full use of his left arm.

A string of curses came out of his mouth, albeit whispered. That kid should've been buried six feet under by now.

Someone he didn't recognize approached Albright and Clute, and he watched their exchange, frustrated that he couldn't read their lips to know what they said.

After a while, Albright threw down the tool he'd been using and went off with Clute. Simultaneously, Snipp headed down the trail leading to the medic's station, a ramshackle shed that Major Walden and his assistants had transformed into a makeshift hospital.

He decided to follow at a good distance. Perhaps this would be his opportunity to corner the kid, once and for all.

27

I'm pleased with the way your shoulder is healing, Gordon." Major Walden smiled. "How are you doing without that sling? Are you putting your arm to use as I suggested?"

Josie nodded. "Yes, sir, as much as possible."

"I don't expect you to do anything too strenuous, but it's important you regain the muscle you've lost, so start small and increase gradually." He proceeded to clean the remains of the wound. "I heard about the fire last night." He shook his head. "A fine stroke of luck you awakened in time."

"I'm not sure it was luck as much as divine intervention," Josie said. "I'm grateful every day for the times God has spared me."

He made no further comment but motioned with his hand for her to step down from the table. Still moving gingerly with her left arm, she picked up her shirt and put it back on, buttoned it, and tucked it into her pants, thankful for the curtain that had protected her privacy during the doctor's examination of her shoulder.

"Any idea who tried to burn down your tent?"

"No, sir. I got a tiny glimpse of him, nothing more."

The doctor fingered his beard. "Do you suppose the arsonist is the same fellow who shot you?"

"I'd assume so, Major."

"Well, you be very careful out there. You're a fine soldier, Private Snipp." Leaning closer, he added, "Braver than a lot of *men* I know."

She felt the warmth of a tiny blush on her face. "I appreciate your confidence. How can I help you today?"

"Well, I'm clean out of bandages, but I don't want you walking down to the river by yourself to wash them out. How about you refill my medicine bottles? You'll find everything you need on the table by the west wall."

"Of course." She gripped the curtain enclosure, prepared to pull it open, then stopped and looked back at him. "Thank you for all you've done for me."

He flicked his wrist. "I'm the one who's thankful."

She stepped into the room full of sick and wounded soldiers and approached the table Major Walden had indicated. She saw plenty of empty medicine containers but couldn't locate the medicine powder she was to measure out and put into each bottle. Glancing around, she saw the doctor busy with a patient. Then she spotted a pile of soiled bandage cloths and, next to it, a box of soap. Despite the doctor's hesitation, she decided to walk down to the river and do the wash. What could go wrong in broad daylight? Besides, she never went anywhere without her weapon. She would make quick work of the cloths, then carry them back up the hill and drape them over the line to dry. She picked up the cloths and tossed them into a wooden crate, which she then hefted up with her right hand and carried toward the exit.

A few patients groaned as she passed their cots. Washing bloody bandages was the least she could do for these poor men.

She picked her way down the trail to the river below, taking intermittent glances behind her to ensure that no one was following. Today, the water flowed steadily, bits of debris and branches moving on the surface, which dazzled like diamonds in the bright sun. Once at the river's edge, she crouched down, laid her rifle on the ground, and began to wash the bloody bandages one by one in the icy water, glancing over her shoulder periodically to confirm that she was alone.

She was wringing out the last cloth when she was startled by a noise from behind her. Gasping, she dropped the cloth in the water and stood, somewhat relieved to see it was only Howard Adams. "You sure startled me," she said, hiding a nervous giggle.

"Did I, now?" He stepped closer.

"This is the second time you've followed me down to the river."

He laughed. "So it is."

She'd heard him laugh before, but never with such an eerie overtone. Her chest constricted uneasily, and she tried to put some distance between them, knowing that just one step backward would land her in the icy waters of the Potomac. It was *he*. It had to be. "What did I ever do to you, Howard? We're fellow soldiers. You're a Federal, just like me."

"Don't call me that," he clipped. "I may be wearin' the uniform"—he gave his chest a couple of emphatic jabs—"but I'm a Confederate, clear to my dark soul!" And then he produced his gun.

Her heart throbbed so hard, it pained her ribs. If only her own rifle were handy. She knew she wouldn't be able to reach it in time to save herself. Better to try to keep him talking, to somehow distract him, so she could make a run for it.

Lord, help me, she silently prayed. *If ever You're going to command Your angels concerning my safety, please do it now.*

Josie had said she was going to see Major Walden, so the medic's station is where Levi ran, Clute following close behind. She could be in danger, or not, but he wasn't taking any chances. After Grimms had shared with him and Clute the private diary of Howard Adams, it was clear they had their spy. Now it was a matter of catching him before he did further harm.

After the assembly that morning, John Cridland had told Grimms that he'd found some spent matches on the ground by his cot. Suspicious, Cridland had done some digging through Howard's belongings and discovered a diary. He was Company B's recorder, yes; but besides keeping a record of every man in the unit, he also kept a detailed account of his own life, and the picture was gruesome. In it, he told how his family had been brutally murdered, and how he believed it to be his duty to seek justice for them, namely by fighting for the Confederate cause from the opposite side of the line. He spelled out exactly how he'd killed the first Union soldier at Salem Church, resulting in additional Yankee soldiers being shot by their own men. He also explained how he'd come upon a Union soldier from Company D by the name of Thomas Loyal in the woods. He described the satisfaction of killing on behalf of his "Southern brothers."

His writings took a turn after that, growing increasingly disjointed, while his penmanship became less and less legible. He detailed his plan to start picking soldiers to eliminate from his own company. Without explanation, he identified Gordon Snipp as his first intended victim, soon lamenting his botched attempts to do him in. He despaired of the mess he'd made, trying to right all the wrongs done to his family and him. "Life isn't fair," he lamented. "No one should have the privilege of breathing air." After that, his words ran into one another; there was a series of short, incomplete sentences, followed by a list of names—soldiers' names.

Levi was out of breath when he reached the hospital. He found Major Walden inside, tending to a patient. The doctor turned abruptly when Levi entered. Clute stood in the doorway, panting.

"Have you seen Josie—er, Gordon Snipp?" Levi asked.

"Yes, in fact. He's right over…wait. I had some medicine bottles in need of filling. I—"

"I saw him walk out the door with some cloths in his hands," said one of the patients.

The doctor's mouth gaped. "The river. He went down to the river."

Levi left without another word, Clute right behind him.

⌐

His forefinger rested right where it should, although there came that odd tremor again. He swallowed and lifted his upper lip to show his distaste for the boy.

"I thought we were friends," Snipp said.

"Well then, I fooled you good, didn't I? I ain't nobody's friend."

"You shot me, didn't you?" The kid rubbed his injured shoulder.

"'Course I did, but my aim wasn't true. This time'll be different."

"And the fire…?"

He grinned at him, positioning his rifle so the butt rested nicely against his shoulder. His nerves jumped, so he took a few deep breaths to try to relax.

"You've got lots o' friends, Howard. All of Company B likes you."

"Well, too bad for them. They ain't my brothers. The Rebs are."

"But you're a Yankee, Howard."

"Weren't you listenin'?" he growled. "I told you, I'm a Confederate at heart."

The kid's eyes rounded like little beads, as if he were trying to figure him out. "You don't want to do this, Howard," Snipp said, his voice strangely higher than usual. In fact, he sounded downright feminine. "Let me tell you something."

He shifted positions and adjusted his rifle. "This ain't no time for talkin'." Closing one eye, he used the other to look down his scope and target the boy's narrow chest. Sweat dripped down his brow and blurred his vision.

"I'm not who you think I am."

"Shut your trap."

"I'm not Gordon Snipp."

"Stop talkin' like an idiot."

"I'm a woman, Howard. A woman. My name's Josephine Winters."

He lowered his rifle a tad and let his eyes wander up and down the boy's figure. "No, it ain't."

"It's true. See, you and I have more in common than you might think." Snipp spread his—her—arms wide. "You've been living a lie, and so have I. In some ways, we're both running. I don't know your story,

I imagine you're trying to assuage some deep, unfathomable pain. You think that disguising yourself as a Union soldier and killing off your own comrades will somehow settle a score, but it won't. Only God can help you with that."

"God?" he sneered. "There ain't no God."

"God loves you."

His brain buzzed. "Shut up!"

"Confederates killed my little brother, Howard. Both sides of this ugly war think they're right. I joined the Union army to honor the memory of my brother, to finish the work he started. What are you running from, Howard? Whatever it is, God can help you."

He shook even more now, his whole body trembling fiercely, and his head hummed like a million killer bees. "I know what you're doin', kid. You're tryin' to make time stop. Well, it ain't gonna work. You're still gonna die. Got it?" But even as he spoke the words, he asked himself whether he could kill a woman. *Of course, you can. Those ugly Union soldiers didn't think nothin' of killing your mama.* It made no difference to him that Gordon Snipp wasn't who he'd thought him to be. This was his duty, perhaps even his *dying* duty.

He regained his focus and reset the rifle in position, his finger back on the trigger.

"Adams! Stop right there!"

He gave a hurried glance behind him. Albright and several others were wending their way down the hill. When he turned his head back around, he saw Gordon trying to escape, so he lurched forward and gave the kid a giant push. He stumbled backward and landed with a splash on his back in the glacial waters of the Potomac. *Good.* Maybe the boy—girl—would drown. In his mind, that would be just as satisfying as if he were to kill her himself.

"Gordon!" Albright raced downhill toward Howard, who now aimed his weapon at him.

"Put down the gun!" shouted Sergeant Clute.

Howard ignored the order, and pretended there wasn't a host of other soldiers with their own weapons trained on him.

"If you know what's good for you, you'll drop it, Adams. The game is over. We know all about what you've been up to, thanks to the details in your diary. Drop your gun, now!"

His *diary?* How dare they intrude on his private business? He froze in place, his rifle sight shifting from Albright to the men trooping down the hill. Where to aim was the question.

Albright jogged right past him without a word. "Josie!" he yelled.

Howard supposed it was true, then. The kid was indeed a girl. Well, who cared about that, anyway?

"Throw down your gun, Private, or I will be forced to shoot you," ordered a man he didn't recognize. "I'm an Intelligence Officer hired by Allan Pinkerton and appointed by President Lincoln himself, and I have the authority to drop you right where you stand."

He swallowed, and a newfound resolve grew strong and mighty within him. He gritted his teeth and let loose a low growl. He would not bow to these wretched, pitiful men in blue. Didn't they know he wasn't a quitter? Weren't they aware he had a mission to accomplish? Without any further thought, he grunted once more and pulled the trigger, the sound thundering in his ears. He never saw where the bullet went, though, because a searing pain jabbed him in the side, and another vicious stab went straight to his chest. Dizziness assailed him, and he dropped his weapon as he clutched his chest. He looked down at his hand and saw rose-red blood seeping through his fingers. Slowly, he lifted his head to the blurry figures running down the hill. He teetered backward, trying to regain his balance, but to no avail. With a hard, painful thud, he crashed to the ground, his final thought being that he hoped the last bullet he'd fired had done some good.

⌒

"Josie, swim to me. It's not far to shore. Come on, girl, you can do it," Levi shouted from the riverbank. She seemed to be paddling for all she was worth, but she made no progress. Her head went under the water, then bobbed back up.

"I—I can't—"

The current wasn't terribly strong, so what was the problem? In a flash, he realized: She couldn't swim. Seconds later, he'd stepped out of his boots, thrown off his jacket, and jumped into the river. The grade was extremely steep, so there was no touching the bottom with his feet. The near-freezing water sent a wave of shock through his body, but he recovered quickly and swam to Josie. When he reached her, he tried to flip her on her back so he could support her head with his shoulder as he swam to shore. But it seemed she was stuck, as if her clothing had attached itself to something, and she couldn't kick free.

"Josie, look at me." He came within inches of her ashen face. She huffed and puffed from exhaustion. "Hang in there. Keep treading water." She said not a word, just gazed at him with dull eyes. "Do you hear me?"

"Hurry," she squeaked out.

He took for granted that others could swim, when the reality was that many couldn't. He thanked the Lord he'd learned the skill early on in the old swimming hole at Sunset Ridge, where he'd grown up. Gathering a deep breath, he dove under the surface and opened his eyes wide, trying to see through the murky waters. At last, he spotted a bulky piece of wood jutting up from the ground, perhaps from an old bridge built years before. A protruding nail had ripped a hole in the pocket of her pants' leg, trapping her in place. Levi yanked at the fabric, praying that he would manage to free her before having to swim to the surface to snatch a breath of air. He glanced upward and saw her head come close to his, her eyes wide with terror. He pushed her back to the surface, and up they went, each gasping for air. "Breathe!" he yelled. "Breathe."

She coughed, then took a breath.

"I'm going back down. Put your feet on my shoulders. Do you hear me? Stand on my shoulders!" He went under again and clenched her foot with one hand, securing it in place. With the other hand, he pulled and twisted at the heavy fabric, and with one final, hard tug, he ripped it loose, freeing her.

He swam to the surface, gulped a huge breath of air, then wrapped an arm around Josie's side and dragged her to the shore. When they reached the river's edge, Clute and a couple of others were there to pull them out. Clute hauled Josie onto the shore, where she lay like a wilted flower, her breaths coming out as big puffs of cloud-like steam. She turned on her side and coughed out a bit of water. She could have drowned, probably would have, if Levi hadn't reached her in time. When she started shaking, Clute hollered, "Someone grab some blankets. Fast. Major Walden will have some on hand."

By now, a dozen or more soldiers had heard the commotion and raced down to the river. One of the intelligence agents lent a hand to Levi, who crawled to shore and collapsed in a heap next to Josie. Even though he shivered from the cold, his first thought was to cover Josie. So far, besides himself, only Dr. Walden and Charlie Clute knew her true identity, and he didn't want her wet clothing to reveal any suspicious curves. He reached for his coat that lay on the ground next to him, then threw it over her. That would do until the blankets arrived. He hadn't been in the water as long as she, and so he had no concerns for himself—only Josie. *Lord, protect her. Don't let any further harm come to her.* In that moment, lying beside her on the cold, hard ground, watching her shiver almost uncontrollably, he realized what losing her would have done to him. She had come to mean a lot to him. Oh, bull—he cared for her, perhaps more deeply than was right or proper. He averted his gaze to the sky above as other soldiers gathered around and spoke in low whispers. Were they discussing how much "Gordon" looked like a girl?

Someone returned with the blankets a minute or so later, and Major Walden also arrived to assist Josie, helping her to stand and then wrapping her in a blanket. With one arm around her for support, he started up the hill. "I'll keep an eye on Gordon tonight," he announced, looking over his shoulder at Levi.

Levi stood, took the blanket that was handed to him, and tossed it over his shoulders. "Good idea, Doctor."

"Yes, yes, do what you can to make the boy comfortable," said Lieutenant Grimms. "He was a true hero today, standing up to Adams as he did, stalling him with conversation. Mighty brave move on his part."

Big and gentle Chester Woolsley came alongside Josie to take her other arm. Halfway up the hill, she stumbled, but the doctor and Chester managed to steady her.

"Where's Adams?" Levi asked of the soldiers standing nearby.

"Gone," said Walt Morse. "Dead as that tree over there. Those Union Intelligence agents shot him. Two fellas already carried him up the hill and are preparin' to dig his grave this very minute. Though he really dug his own, so to speak, lyin' to us the way he did, and then killin' Union soldiers. I heard he made a list of all the men in our unit he planned to kill, and wrote in that diary o' his the order in which he intended to do it. Major Walden was to have been his next victim."

A cold shiver ran through Levi. He'd read the diary and had seen the list. His name had appeared just beneath Walden's.

He gathered the wool blanket more tightly around himself. "Lord, what has this war done to us?" he murmured.

28

*A*fter taking a nap and then consuming a bowl of stew and a piece of bread, Josie felt well enough to sit up, walk around, and maybe even return to her tent. However, Major Walden insisted she spend the night in the hospital, where he could keep an eye on her. He said he wanted to ensure her lungs remained clear of pneumonia before he released her.

She'd agreed to his terms, albeit reluctantly. It was thoughtful of him to set her up on a cot in a remote corner, even hanging a curtain to afford her some privacy. She appreciated the special treatment but felt unworthy of it.

"I never finished washing the cloth bandages," she told the doctor when he came to offer her a drink of water. She sat up and laid aside the old newspaper she'd been perusing.

"I told you not to go down to the river, young lady," he said in a stern yet quiet tone.

"I guess I don't take orders too well." She sipped the water and thought aloud. "I feel bad for Private Adams. Is that wrong of me? I know he killed Union soldiers, but he was such a lost soul. I heard about the faction of Union soldiers who slaughtered his family. I hope they paid for their crime."

The major rubbed his beard and nodded. "I hope so, as well. And, no, I don't think it's bad for you to feel as you do. You have a soft heart... almost too soft for the army." He lifted one eyebrow, and she knew exactly what he implied. She ought to confess to Grimms and leave as soon as possible.

"I told Howard the truth, you know," she whispered. "I had hoped the information would make him think twice about trying to kill me. I'm just glad no one else was harmed. I would feel so terrible if that had been the case."

"None of what happened was your fault," the doctor told her.

Someone across the room called for Walden, so he smiled and started to turn. "I'd best see to that soldier."

"When do you sleep, Major?"

He looked back at her and grinned, his sunken brown eyes warm yet somehow distant. She realized she knew very little about him—his family, his wife, where he'd lived before the war. Was he even married? "I catch my winks whenever possible, and I manage fine. Speaking of sleep, you get yourself some rest, now."

Once he had gone, Josie lay back down, drawing the covers up close to her chin to keep herself warm in the drafty space. She stared at the beamed ceiling and prayed for each sick soul with whom she shared the room, then asked God what He would have her do. "Should I go to Sergeant Grimms and confess my deceit?" she whispered. "If I leave after so short a time serving in the army, will I have fulfilled my purpose for joining?" While she lay there listening for an answer, a familiar voice just outside the curtain around her cot said, "Knock, knock."

Her heart did a giant leap. "Come in!" One thing was certain: Had she not joined the army, she never would have fallen in love.

Levi poked his head inside and grinned, the twinkle in his eyes making her heart spring to life. He pulled up a wooden stool and sat down, close enough that she could see the tiny smile wrinkles at the corners of both eyes. She studied his face, clean-shaven now, and thought she'd never seen, or even known, a man more handsome than he.

Levi took off his hat and set it on the floor. "How are you feeling?"

"Perfectly fine. I told Major Walden I could leave the hospital tonight, but he said no. Something about wanting to make sure I don't get pneumonia."

Levi nodded. "He knows what's best. I'm glad you're feeling better. I was worried about you earlier. You were as pale as fresh-fallen snow."

"I was pretty frozen, I'll admit."

They stared at each other, neither one speaking for a full half a minute.

"Thank you for saving me," Josie finally said. "I...didn't get a chance to say that earlier. You risked your life for me."

"I didn't exactly risk my life." Levi's voice was a husky whisper. With his hands folded between his spread knees, he leaned even closer, and his grin became more of a crooked slant. It made her melt a little inside, despite the chill in the air. "I was more worried about you than myself. How's your shoulder?"

"It hurts a bit more right now from overuse, but the doctor did say it would take a while for it to heal fully. How are you feeling?"

"Me? I'm fine. If you're fine, I'm fine."

She gave a little giggle, and he laughed quietly.

Their conversation seemed stilted. She was suddenly so aware of him, so cognizant of her feelings for him. It frightened her that the dynamics between them might change if she didn't get a grip on herself. She wanted to revert to being Gordon again, but Gordon seemed so far removed from her. On a whim, she asked, "Do you miss him? Do you miss Gordon?"

His brown eyes popped, and he sat back a bit on his stool, then combed a hand through his thick, dark hair. She'd caught him off guard. "Do I miss him?"

She sat up higher, yanking the blanket snugly around her waist. "Yes. He used to be a good friend of yours."

"We're still friends...aren't we?"

"I…I don't know. I mean, I'm not exactly sure how you feel about everything. I hated living a lie and making you believe I was somebody else. There were days I wanted to tell you the truth, but I just couldn't find the right opportunity; and I thought that if I did, you'd hate me, and…I don't know if I'm making any sense."

"You are." He reached out and touched her arm, which made her nerves tingle. *Lord, help me, but I love him.*

He cleared his throat. "Okay, at first, I was frustrated. Maybe a little angry. Nobody likes being deceived. I didn't think it was fair that you knew everything about me, while I'd believed for so long that you were a boy. Well, a feminine boy," he added, with that crooked grin. He retracted his hand.

"Everything else about me is true, I swear." She lowered her voice even more. "The details about my parents' dying when Andrew and I were young kids, and our having to live with our aunt and uncle and cousins; the little church I told you about, and the small farm, and then my uncle's passing last year—all of that's true. The only difference is, I'm a girl."

He shot her a half grin, and his eyes roved downward from her face to where the blanket hugged her stomach. "You're a little more than a *girl*."

"Oh!" She raised her knees to her chest and stayed huddled beneath the blanket. Had he truly just alluded to her womanly aspects? *My, but he had a way of setting her pulse to spinning with just a simple glance. How was she ever going to stay in the army?*

There came another awkward silence. Josie kept her gaze lowered, knowing his eyes were locked on her face. "I'm sorry, Levi. I'm sorry for everything."

"No, don't be. It's over and done."

She rested her chin on her knees, wrapped her arms around her legs, and studied the movement of her toes wiggling beneath the blanket. "Do you know that ever since I joined the army, you've been saving me, time after time?"

"Have I?" He chuckled a little. "I don't think that's the case."

"Oh, but it is. From that first day, you made sure the men treated me right; you looked after me at every turn, making sure I had enough to eat, that I marched in formation, that I stayed safe. You helped nurse me back to health when I got sick. On the battlefield, you made me stay near you; when I was shot, you were right there. You insisted I winter with you and Charlie. Then, today, you had to dive in freezing water to save me from drowning." She lifted her head to look at him. "When you think about it, I'm a terrible soldier."

"You're not."

"Yes, I am." Still keeping her voice down, she blurted out, "Everybody keeps telling me I'm a good soldier. I even heard Lieutenant Grimms say it earlier, though I wasn't fully conscious at the time. But now that I think on it, I believe they say it because, in everyone's eyes, I'm just a young kid, and they think I need bolstering." Of all things, tears emerged from her eyes. She blinked them back and sniffed.

Levi rose from the stool and situated himself on the cot next to her, making the canvas screech when he sat. She lowered her knees and tucked them under her to give him room. He lifted his hand to dab at one tear with the pad of his thumb, and then he leaned over and lightly kissed her cheek. She told herself it was just a friendly gesture, perhaps even brotherly, but the shock of his soft lips did something very strange to her insides. Next, he cupped her cheek with his hand, turning her face toward his. She tried to stop the stream of tears, but it continued coming. Levi's dark eyes bore into her, and for a moment, she thought she might melt under their scrutiny.

"Don't cry," he murmured, his large hand gently caressing her cheek. He moved in closer and touched his lips to hers in a feather-light kiss. *Oh, my*, she thought. *Oh, my!* He paused there for a magnificent moment, his breath melding with hers, and she could only hope her erratic pulse wouldn't make her heart burst through her chest. *God, help me*, her soul cried.

He pressed in even closer now, his lips fully covering hers, and all she could think was, *How simply divine, how absolutely delightful, how achingly beautiful.* The kiss went on, and she felt herself giving in to it.

Being that this was her first, she had no idea how to react or what to do, but it seemed instinctive to encircle his back with her arms. He did the same to her, hugging her against him while he tasted, and then she tasted; while he tested, and then she tested.

When he withdrew for a moment and brushed his lips across her forehead, she held her breath, too afraid to move. After lightly kissing both her cheeks and even teasing one of her earlobes, he at last recaptured her lips, this time with a bit more fervor than before, and the sensation transported her into a dreamlike state. His hands caressed the small of her back as his kisses turned sweeter, and her mind swam through a haze of feelings and desires she never knew existed.

A shuffle on the other side of the curtain finally ended the series of kisses. Levi sat back and dropped his hands to his sides, but he didn't avert his gaze, so she kept her eyes fastened on him, as well, even though she had to swallow hard and bite back the urge to shout to the rafters that she loved him. She dared not utter such dangerous words for fear of the ramifications. She simply needed to take a moment to realign her tangled thoughts and get her heart to start pumping at a normal rate. Clasping her hands tightly, she waited for him to say something.

He gave a light sniff, and she cleared her throat.

He rubbed his nose, and she licked her lips.

"I guess…I should go."

Wait. I want to know why you did that! Her mind formulated the words, but her mouth refused to utter them. "Yes, probably so," she said instead. She dropped her gaze to her blanket and found a tiny ball of lint to roll around between her thumb and forefinger.

Wasn't it for him to give an explanation? Suddenly, everything felt awkward and odd.

He stood, brushed his hands together, and took a step toward the curtain. Then he made an abrupt turn and looked at her. "I…I'm not sure we should've done that."

"No, you're right. We shouldn't have." She kept her voice strong and clear of emotion, even though a sense of heaviness settled in her chest. He regretted kissing her.

"I mean, as long as you're going to conceal your true identity, we should, you know, not ever—"

"Of course," she cut in. "No need to speak about it. Or even give it another thought."

His expression clouded with uneasiness. "We're...just friends. Right? I mean, it's the only way to make things...I mean, it's just... awkward."

"Stop. Please." She raised her hand. "It's fine, Levi. I understand."

"You do?"

"Yes." *Just friends.* This time, she held her tears at bay. Tears made her vulnerable, and they were decidedly *un*soldier-like. No, sir, she would not reveal her raw emotions. "Absolutely." She raised her chin. "Well, thank you for the visit."

"You're welcome. I hope you continue feeling better."

"I'll be fine by tomorrow."

"Back to your old self." This he said in a tone that implied she had better return to being just Gordon Snipp, so that this kissing business wouldn't happen again. "We've got a new cot in the tent for you."

"Oh. Thank you." She had a feeling she wouldn't be using it.

He scooped up his hat off the floor and slapped it back on his head. "Well, I'll see you later, then." He ducked out the curtain and disappeared, the sound of his footsteps quickly fading. As far as she knew, he hadn't stopped to speak to any of the other patients or said good-bye to the major. She picked up a damp rag from the tiny table next to her, wadded it up, and threw it at the curtain. It hit its mark before landing on the floor. Then she plopped back on the cot and stared hard at the rafters while tears burned her eyes. "Just friends," she muttered. "That is all we will ever be, and don't you forget it, Josephine Winters."

After a few minutes, Major Walden peered inside the curtain. "You and the sergeant have a nice visit?"

"It was fair," she mumbled. Thankfully, she'd dried her eyes and could only hope he didn't detect any puffiness.

"Ah." He stepped fully inside now and took a seat on the stool Levi had vacated. Sitting was something she rarely caught the doctor doing.

"Now that he knows you to be a woman, I presume the feelings between you two have changed. Am I right in my assumption?"

With discouragement surging in her veins, she gave a slow nod. "At least they have changed on my part. I'm not sure how he feels, exactly." She would not tell the doctor about their kisses, although he was a perceptive man.

He patted her arm in a fatherly fashion. "What are you going to do?"

"What do you think I should do?"

A low chuckle escaped his throat. "Do you truly want my advice?"

"I do."

"If you wish to remain true to yourself—and the army—and desire to make things less complicated all around, then you should probably pay a visit to Lieutenant Grimms and disclose who you are."

She sighed. "I've been thinking the same. I'm committed to this army and its cause, but…well, it would be better, like you said."

"Something else to consider is that by revealing your identity to a few, you have put them at risk. Anyone who withholds vital information is subject to a possible court-martial. I'm not worried for myself, because they need me; but Captain Bateman or even Lieutenant Grimms could just as easily dismiss Sergeant Albright or, worse, imprison him until the war ends."

Josie gasped. "I never thought that far."

"Not that they would do that. He is regiment chaplain, after all."

"But I don't wish to mar his reputation."

The doctor nodded. "I would miss you greatly, of course. You've been a fine soldier and a wonderful help."

There it was again. *You're a fine soldier.* In a single flash, it occurred to her that she'd been nothing but selfish. In hoping to honor Andrew's memory, she'd joined the army, but, really, what was honorable about the way she'd gone about doing it? She'd based her life as a soldier on deception.

"Thank you, Doctor."

He smiled. "For what?"

"You've opened my eyes. I now know what I have to do." She sat up, preparing to leave, but he gently pressed her back down.

"Not so fast, Private. You'll make no decisions until tomorrow, is that clear? You need a good night's sleep."

She lay there, staring up at him. He was a pristine man, despite all the sickness he dealt with on a daily basis, not to mention the lack of adequate rest. Never had she seen him start his day without a neatly trimmed beard and a clean uniform. Since he'd been so forthright with her, she dared to ask him something personal. "Where is home for you, Major? And do you have family waiting for you?"

"Home for me?" He glanced past her, his eyes locking on the wall. "I hail from Pittsburgh. Indeed, I have a lovely wife, and she has been more than patient in awaiting my return. I left behind an active medical practice, which, after the war, I shall start up again. I felt strongly about doing my part in the war. It's been a difficult time, but also rewarding in many ways. I believe the North is winning, and if we stay faithful to the cause, the conflict shouldn't drag on much longer."

She enjoyed listening to him talk. "I hope you're right. Do you have children?"

Sadness washed over his countenance. "My wife suffered multiple miscarriages, so, no, we've never had children."

Moistness gathered in Josie's eyes. "I'm sorry."

"No need to be. Life has been good to us, in spite of the bumpy ride."

She wished to ask him if he had a relationship with Jesus, but the question stuck in her throat.

He stood and gave her a kindly smile. "You get some rest, now. You've had a very traumatic last couple of days. You'll need a clear head for tomorrow."

She bit her lower lip and nodded. She would need a clear head, yes; but the truth was, she'd already made up her mind about what she had to do. She'd served her time, such as it was. After tomorrow, her future would rest in the hands of Lieutenant Grimms. In some ways, a huge burden had been lifted from her shoulders, but in other ways, she'd inherited a deep grief.

She wished she had her Bible nearby, but it was back in her tent. She closed her eyes and called to memory every comforting verse of Scripture she could, and soon drifted into a fitful sleep.

29

The next morning, a Sunday, Levi and Charlie rose before dawn. While Charlie was seeing to his ablutions, Levi dressed in a clean uniform, one he'd boiled and dried three days ago. The uniform he'd worn yesterday, when he'd dived in the river to save Josie, hung to dry on a tree branch. Later today, he would boil that suit, as well, so he'd have a spare clean one on hand.

He'd endured a restless night of sleep, half of it spent with his eyes wide open as he pondered his feelings for Josie and asked himself just what he planned to do about them. Not for anything could he get the memory of those delicious kisses out of his head, nor could he forgive himself for initiating them. In an instant, life had gone from casual to complex, from routine to convoluted. To top matters off, he'd received exactly four letters from Mary Foster this past week, and had answered none of them. As the weeks had gone by, it had become increasingly clear that she had developed much stronger feelings for him than he had for her, and somehow he had to put into words a gentle exhortation for her to slow down. They hadn't even met, and she had already started hinting at the idea of spending the rest of their lives together.

He ran a hand down his face and, feeling whiskers, snagged his straight-edge razor from his rucksack, along with a towel and a bar of soap, and left the tent. It was a frigid morning, and he had a sermon to deliver—if anyone bothered braving the cold to show up. As he made his way along the frosty ground toward the river, the earth crunching beneath his boots, he wondered if Josie would feel well enough to come to church, or even if she dared face him after yesterday. How were they to act around each other, now that they'd both let down their guards? He couldn't risk telling her he loved her, lest the declaration spark a change in her behavior that would arouse suspicion from the other soldiers. Yet he had to somehow let her know that he'd been foolish to insist they were just friends. There had to be a way of going about it, a simple agreement made between them that would ease matters, allowing them to express their feelings while at the same time enabling them to maintain a healthy distance.

To his surprise, a number of men showed up for the service that morning in the clearing behind the sutler's wagon, including John Cridland, who arrived early to build a fire; Charles Woolsley; Richard Fuller; Walt Morse; Jim Hodgers; Willie Speer; Charlie Clute; and, of all people, Hiram McQuade. Terry Brady brought with him three of his comrades from D Company. It was odd not to see Howard Adams. Levi now realized the man had come to Sunday meetings only as a means of covering his deception. How thoroughly he had fooled his fellow soldiers.

Levi thought about Josie, and how she, too, had managed to deceive her comrades. The difference was, she meant no harm. Her intentions were good, whereas Adams had been bent on death and destruction.

To Levi's disappointment, Josie did not come to church. He hoped she wasn't feeling poorly. Since he'd started preaching, she'd not missed a single service. More likely, she had decided it best not to face him after what had happened yesterday. Well, he would make things right with her, and see to it that neither of them had to suffer another minute of awkwardness going forward.

After the service, several fellows hung around to talk, and a popular topic of conversation was what had transpired yesterday with Howard Adams. Terry Brady wanted to know all the particulars so he could report them to his company, and, of course, everyone had his own opinion about just what had caused the man's mind to snap. Most of them didn't know the details of his personal diary—and they didn't necessarily need to know them.

Harv Patterson announced that all were welcome to come to his tent that day after drills for some rabbit stew. Apparently, the Gower brothers had gone out hunting at break of dawn and brought back a bountiful supply of hares.

Levi considered stopping by the hospital to check on Josie, but Frank Vonfleet informed him that Lieutenant Grimms wished to see him before roll call. A visit would have to wait.

Levi found Grimms standing outside his tent, sipping coffee. He turned to Levi, solemn-faced, and told him to come inside, neglecting to acknowledge his salute with even the slightest nod. Grimms never had been an amiable man, but this particular morning, he seemed ornerier than ever. A sense of anxiety rose in Levi's stomach. Something wasn't right.

"Sit," Grimms barked.

Levi lowered himself quickly into a chair. "What is it, sir?"

"It seems we've had more than one counterfeit in our midst."

Levi's gut turned over several times. The lieutenant had found out about Josie. Who had told him? Had Major Walden reported her? Surely, Charlie wouldn't have done so. "What are you talking about?"

"Don't play dumb, Albright. Certainly, you knew, but you didn't consider the information important enough to disclose. I could hold you responsible, you know." The lieutenant rubbed his trim beard and studied him through eyes that were narrowed to mere slits.

He maintained his composure as best he could. "I assume you're referring to Gordon Snipp."

"Don't you mean Josephine Winters? *Miss* Josephine Winters?" The lieutenant leaned over him with a penetrating stare. "Well, she's gone now. Let's hope there aren't any more surprises up anybody's sleeve. If there are, you best find out what they are, and reveal them by day's end, Sergeant."

Gone? Josie *gone*? He couldn't quite digest the notion. "What do you mean, 'gone'? And who turned her in?"

"Yes, she's gone; and, if you must know, she came to me this morning, early, before anyone had even roused. I myself was just waking when she rattled my door. You can imagine my surprise when Private Snipp greeted me, holding a lantern to my face, while I was dressed in my night robe. I invited him in—her, rather *her*—and she confessed her deceit."

Levi's heart banged against his chest. "Where did she go?"

"I escorted her to the tent she was sharing with you so she could collect her belongings. You and Sergeant Clute were both out at the time. I put her on a wagon, and Private Hermanson drove her to Fredericksburg, where she's to catch a train. I settled things with her, money-wise, although I should have withheld her final pay, seeing as she wasn't even legal."

"You sent her away without giving her a chance to say good-bye to anyone?"

"I didn't think I owed her that privilege, Sergeant."

Ire had Levi rising to his feet. He leveled his superior with a stern gaze. "You have to admit she was a good soldier. You said so, yourself."

"She may well have been, but that doesn't change the fact that she joined the Union under false pretenses. Women aren't allowed, and for good reason."

"You still haven't told me where she went."

"That is because I have no idea of her destination. She had enough money to buy a train ticket to most anywhere."

"But…you didn't even ask her what sort of plans she might have?"

"I didn't think it necessary. The woman is lucky I didn't send her off to prison."

Despair overwhelmed him. She was gone, and he hadn't gotten a chance to speak to her about his feelings. What had prompted her to confess to Grimms? And why today? Had his kisses so affected her that she felt she had no choice but to flee? Couldn't she at least have told him her intentions? Or did she wish to leave before their relationship grew more complicated? Was it possible she didn't feel as strongly toward him as he did toward her? Was her confession mixed with a need to escape from any further romantic intentions on his part? Or perhaps it was the opposite: She believed her feelings for him went deeper than his for her. He had, after all, made that thoughtless remark about their being *just friends*. His head ached with confusion and bewilderment.

"Is that all, sir?" he finally asked.

Without a trace of emotion, Grimms nodded. "That's all, Sergeant. You're dismissed."

Levi marched off without even saluting, feeling nearly choked by anger and frustration.

⌒

Josie folded the letter she'd penned to Levi and held it in her lap, then glanced out the window to watch the passing scenery from the train window. It was late Sunday afternoon, and everything about the day had been surreal, starting the minute she'd told Grimms the truth. Her aunt and cousins in Philadelphia would be surprised to see her, as she'd no opportunity to forewarn them of her coming. She hoped Aunt Bessie would welcome her, at least for a few days' stay, until she could make further plans. She'd given much thought to her next steps and had decided to go to Washington, where she hoped to sign up to volunteer in an army hospital. In retrospect, perhaps she should have done that from the beginning, but then she wouldn't have earned any wages—not that her pay from the army had amounted to anything exceptional. Besides, she'd wanted nothing more than to follow in Andrew's footsteps. Oh, what a mess she'd made of things.

At the train station in Fredericksburg, she'd seen a poster indicating a need for trained nurses. Surely, the work she had done under Major Walden's tutelage would qualify her.

She fingered the letter in her lap, then unfolded it to read through once more.

Dear Levi,

By now, you have learned of my departure from the army. I hope all of Company B, and especially you, will find it in their hearts to forgive me for my deception. I joined with only the best of intentions, but as I lay in bed last night, it occurred to me that my reasons were more selfish than anything. The army would've been better served had I chosen to stay home and stitch blankets and wool socks for the Union soldiers. I'm sorry I was not able to bid you farewell, as Lt. Grimms insisted I leave immediately. In fact, he escorted me to a horse-drawn wagon and watched me ride away. I suppose he didn't fully trust me to leave on my own.

Gordon Snipp wishes to thank you for all you did for him during his time with Company B. You were most helpful. I, Josephine Winters, wish also to thank you. It was never my desire to complicate our friendship. I hope you understand and believe that. Even though we did share a few kisses last night, I understood what you meant by qualifying our relationship as friendship. That being said, I felt it necessary to visit Lt. Grimms at break of dawn. I do not wish to clog your mind with thoughts of me when you could very well have a happy future in store for you with Mary Foster. Besides, you have more time to serve in the army, and it is my desire that you keep a clear head. I am sorry if I have caused any problems for you. I pray that you will not be court-martialed. If you are, it will be my fault.

Please do stay well, do not get in the way of any flying bullets, and continue on your godly path of teaching others about the ways of our loving heavenly Father. You are indeed a fine example for all.

May God forever keep you safe.
Josephine Winters

She dabbed at a few stray tears, then refolded the letter and, this time, put it in her rucksack holding the scanty collection of her personal effects. At the earliest opportunity, she would post the letter, and hope it would reach Levi in a timely fashion.

It was nearing eight o'clock when the driver slowed his two-horse team to a stop in front of the Garlows' rambling farmhouse. Josie's heart tripped at the sight of it. Lights glowed inside, indicating the family was still up and about. She shivered, more from excitement than from the cold, then leaned forward to pay the driver his fee, and finally picked up her bag and stepped down from the rig. Had she not appeared to be a man, the driver certainly would've helped her out. As it was, once her feet touched the ground, he urged his team forward, driving away before Josie even reached the bottom porch step.

She gave a light knock on the front door and peeked through the sheer curtains. Her heart thrilled at the sight of Allison's approach. The girl drew back the shades for a peek, then quickly opened the door. The girls stood there gaping at each other for a moment, until Allison gave a whoop of joy and swept Josie into her arms.

Around the corner from the kitchen came Aunt Bessie, thirteen-year-old Arnold, ten-year-old Janice, and eight-year-old Hazel, all of them hustling. My, but it was a welcome reunion, everyone hugging, kissing, and asking all manner of questions. Josie could not have been more relieved by the warmth of their reception.

They conversed well into the night, with the exception of Janice and Hazel, whom Aunt Bessie sent to bed; four-year-old Corinne had gone to sleep before Josie's arrival. Josie shared liberally about her experiences in the army but skirted the subject of her feelings for Levi. That would come out later, when she and Allison had a chance to chat in private.

"You're welcome to stay as long as you wish, dear," Aunt Bessie said when there came a lull in the conversation. Josie had told about her intentions to travel to Washington to see about offering her services at an army hospital.

"Thank you, Auntie, but I shall be here for a week, at most. I must look through my wardrobe to see what needs mending and ironing, perhaps sew a couple of new dresses, and then begin the process of repacking. Frankly, I shall be happy to return to being Josephine Winters."

"Your hair is quite short, though," Aunt Bessie reminded her. "You'd best wear a bonnet."

"Yes, I'm hopeful it will soon grow long enough for me to pin up, for a comelier look."

"Give it a few months," her aunt said. "You're a beauty, either way."

Aunt Bessie's comment warmed her, especially since she wasn't one to readily shower others with compliments.

They talked a bit longer, Arnold having gone to bed an hour or more ago. He'd wanted to hear everything she had to say about the war, but when the discussion had turned to womanly matters, he bade everyone good night.

Later, lying next to Allison and staring into the blackness, Josie tearfully told her about her love for Levi and how she'd left without even saying good-bye. Even her cousin shed tears at the telling, and promised to pray that she and Levi would reunite someday.

30

Mid-December brought enough snow to cover the ground, and the stuff didn't look close to melting. Snow this early in the season was unusual for these parts, and it was accompanied by a brisk wind that forced the men to double up on their clothing layers during drills and various chores. At least the fresh-fallen snow did a good job of concealing certain undesirable parts of the camp, such as the trench latrine.

One afternoon, companies B and D staged a snowball battle, with B Company playing the role of the Rebs. About the time it looked like B was losing the fight, somebody landed a good one at a poor soul on the other side, and the clash continued with a good deal of amusement. That tall character, Terry Brady from D Company, had a good arm and just as good an aim, and he took down Hiram McQuade with a solid blow to the eye. A whole lot of cursing sailed out of McQuade's mouth, but then he joined in the combat, forming a decent-sized ice ball that he hurled back—albeit missing his target and hitting someone else instead. It wasn't long before several soldiers from other companies who had heard about the snow skirmish made their way over. Levi guessed that before the fight was over, there had to have been at least 600 soldiers doing "battle."

Since Josie's departure, Levi's spirits had been in the dumps, although he did his best not to show it. He still had duties to perform: sermons to prepare, soldiers to tend to, and men who needed his prayer support and faithful visits. He had to stay strong, but underneath that façade of strength, he *missed* her, and her absence only amplified the fact that he also *loved* her. He'd loved Gordon Snipp like a brother, and when he discovered his "little brother" to be a pretty little woman, it hadn't taken much for him to tumble off the cliff.

Of course, no one suspected it—except for Charlie, to whom he'd outright confessed about the kisses he'd stolen from her the night before her departure. If he could figure out where she'd gone, he could at least write to her, but she hadn't told Grimms, and the lieutenant hadn't thought to ask. Grimms had her aunt's address buried somewhere, he'd told Levi, but he hadn't the time to go looking for it. "Besides," he'd said, "private addresses are classified, and that little counterfeit doesn't deserve mail, anyway." Levi figured the lieutenant would calm down in time and eventually give in, if Levi only remained patient. If he had to guess, he'd say Grimms was resentful of Josie's having informed Levi of the truth before going to her lieutenant. Captain Bateman had gotten wind of the news, and now Grimms had another demerit to his name for failing to detect her true identity.

The fellows had taken the news about Josie just about as hard as Grimms, some of them angry over her deceit; some disheartened by it, if not humiliated; and others, just plain shocked. It came as no surprise to Levi when Hiram McQuade claimed to have known all along. "Anybody could see she wasn't a real man, the way she carried herself and bent over backward to look the part. I'm surprised the rest o' you didn't see it," he announced to those seated with him around a fire one night.

"Well, I thought Gordon acted a little girlish; but then, so do you, McQuade, so I didn't think nothin' of it," jested Charlie.

"Hey!" Hiram said, putting on a mean face. But soon he joined in the good-hearted laughter of his comrades.

Levi could be wrong, but he thought he detected a bit of softening in the chump. He and Chester seemed to be getting along a bit better. At least, Levi hadn't had to break up any fights lately. And he'd noticed Hiram's attendance at the past several Sunday services, though Hiram always departed before Levi had a chance to speak with him about the message.

For the past week, the regiment had busied itself chopping wood, drilling, chopping more wood, and drilling some more. One night after a supper of stew and hardtack, the mail wagon rumbled into camp. Everyone gathered around it in hopes of snatching a letter or two from the mail boy. Not surprisingly, Levi received three letters from Mary Foster. He felt a ping of guilt for not having responded to her previous four missives. Just as he was turning to leave, letters in hand, the boy called his name again, then tossed him two additional letters: one from his mother, and the other with no return address, and handwriting he didn't recognize. It had a feminine flair to it, though, which made his heart flip at the notion it could be from Josie. While he was eager enough to rip it open, he decided to wait till later that evening, when he would read his letters by the light of his lantern.

He passed Charlie sitting with a few other soldiers by someone's fire, so it pleased him to have the tent to himself. He turned up the wick on the lantern, pulled off his gloves, and tore into the mystery letter. He read the signature line first. *Josephine Winters.* So formal, he thought. In fact, he found the whole letter stiff and to the point, making him wonder if he'd placed more importance on their kisses than she had. He ached to see her, but she'd failed to give him an address. How was he supposed to tell her that his feelings went beyond friendship if he couldn't contact her? He read the letter again, thinking maybe he'd overlooked something, but no luck. The missive was little more than an amiable note wishing him and the rest of Company B well, telling him to be safe, and encouraging him to continue his ministry to others.

With little enthusiasm, he breezed through the other letters, and then, like a sulking boy, stretched out on his cot, folded his arms over his chest, and stared at the shadowy ceiling.

Working at the army hospital was anything but boring. In fact, Josie found herself so caught up in administering aid to the sick and wounded, hardly knowing where to turn next, or which patient needed her the most, that she barely had time to think about her own aching, lonesome heart. She yearned not only for Levi but also for her aunt and cousins. After leaving the army, she'd stayed with the Garlows exactly eight days, and while the reunion had been sweet, it had been busy, too, as she prepared for her move to Washington.

Early on, she'd felt strongly about picking up where Andrew had left off. But now she believed she had to finish what she herself had started—this time, with true conviction that God had led her to this point. No more deception about her identity or what she wished to accomplish. No, sir. This time, she had gone straight to the Superintendent of Army Nurses, Miss Dix, to inquire as to where her services could be put to the best use. From her seat behind her desk, the woman had studied Josie from top to bottom, then asked in a forthright manner just what her intentions were.

"I'll be honest with you, ma'am," Josie had said, squaring her shoulders. "I joined the Union Army disguised as a man. Due to a variety of circumstances, notwithstanding my conscience getting in the way, I confessed to the lieutenant in charge of my unit that I was a woman, and he immediately discharged me and personally escorted me out of camp. I served four months, ma'am, out of a duty to my brother, who was killed at the Battle of Drewry's Bluff last year. But now that my obligations there have met an end, I wish to continue serving in a different capacity. I assisted in the Twenty-third Regiment's hospital under the tutelage of one Major John Walden, and I feel that I can at least carry out minor medical duties in order to allow those with more training to meet the urgent needs of patients. I saw a poster in Fredericksburg that made a plea for hospital help, and so…well…here I am, ready and eager to avail myself." She intentionally left out the part about her shoulder injury. The wound still pained her considerably, but not so much as to impair her mobility, and she didn't want to give Miss Dix any reason for rejecting her offer to volunteer.

After listening to her overlong explanation, Miss Dix had said nothing for a time. She'd arched her right eyebrow, tilted her head one way and then another, and given Josie one more full-body assessment. At last, she'd sucked in a long breath, exhaled slowly, and said, "Well, I think you'll do fine. I wondered about your short hair. Your saying you joined the army as a man explains it. I'll have Andrew Blackmore, one of my aids, take you over to Mansion House Hospital."

"Mansion House?"

"It's a former hotel in Alexandria. Union occupied now, of course, with some six hundred beds." She'd risen to her feet, so Josie had done likewise. Miss Dix had taken a pen from an inkwell and set to scribbling something on a piece of paper. "I'm writing a letter of recommendation. When you arrive, seek out Dr. Edwards and give him this letter. He'll put you to work."

Josie hadn't been able to help the smile of excitement that had quickly popped out on her face. "Thank you, ma'am."

Miss Dix had reciprocated the smile, though hers was guarded. "No, thank *you*, Miss Winters. Oh, and don't be surprised if I'm about the only one to give you a word of thanks. Unfortunately, some of the doctors you'll encounter—Dr. Edwards included, I'm afraid—aren't too fond of women helping in the hospitals." She'd clicked her tongue and given a shake of her head. "It's plain ridiculous, if you ask me. Ungrateful brutes. Just ignore them as much as you can and carry out your duties without complaint. They'll soon come to appreciate you. And based on your time in the army, you shouldn't have any trouble adjusting to the doctors' customary curtness. Just the same, if you should encounter any issues or come across someone who simply refuses to work with you"—she put on a guileful expression—"send for me. I'll take care of the matter."

Josie had no doubt she would.

"Oh, and keep that tidbit about your army disguise a secret. Some of the doctors might not take too kindly to knowing you were a soldier.

They might view you as dishonest." With a somewhat sly smile, she'd added, "I, however, quite admire you."

Mansion House was a big hospital, and crowded, each room holding as many as six or seven cots; and, from what Josie had observed, there were not nearly enough doctors or nurses to provide adequate care. Even so, new patients arrived on a daily basis, reminding everyone that the brutality of war seemed to be swallowing everyone up, soldiers and citizens alike. It also seemed to have erased any cause for celebration. Though it was nearing Christmas, the only signs of the holiday's approach were the brutal winds and the icy air. No greenery or festive ornaments graced the windows.

One afternoon, several ambulances arrived at the hospital. Thankfully, the head nurse received advance notice and had worked tirelessly, assigning her staff various duties in order to provide for the incoming patients. Many suffering soldiers had to be shifted to different locations, and those less grievous cases were released to an outside tent that housed a number of patients in various stages of recovery. Much moaning and groaning took place in the transition, and it pained Josie to have to cause anyone any undue misery.

She thought of Major Walden and the rest of the 23rd, and wondered how they fared. Since the fighting had slowed down, doctors were dealing with fewer wounds than with dehydration, bloody diarrhea, severe cases of influenza, and, in some instances, infectious diseases that required quarantine. No one wanted to work in the quarantine unit, but since Josie had willfully devoted and dedicated her work to the Lord, she didn't hesitate to volunteer when the need arose.

Among this latest batch of arrivals were nine cases of typhoid fever, and during an afternoon staff meeting, Josie stepped forward to offer her help. So did two others: a former slave named Adam and an older woman named Sarah. Dr. Morton would oversee the patients' care, his claim to have survived typhoid two years prior making him a logical choice.

The quarantine unit was a tent located in a large yard beside the hospital. While the weather was indeed brutally cold, this tent was one of the few boasting a central woodstove that vented through a smokestack in the roof. The patients were also given extra blankets, but Josie soon learned that a typhoid patient raging with fever and delirium generally threw off his blankets, in many cases precipitating a terrible case of the shakes.

Most of these men were infested with lice, so the first rule of business was ridding them of the terrible critters, a difficult job unto itself. Josie and the other nurses would mix together a solution of kerosene and various oils, which they smeared the men's scalps until the lice literally drowned in the substance.

One night, when all her patients had been taken care of, at least to the best of her abilities, an exhausted and hungry Josie curled up in a dark corner on a spare cot specifically designated for volunteers. Desperate for a nap, she squeezed her eyes shut, but that only prompted a flood of tears—tears she'd long held back and refused to shed. Now they flowed like a river, and while she wished for the luxury of screaming out in agony and frustration, she held her sobs at bay. The image of Levi's face dashed across her mind, and her tears fell the harder. She dabbed at her eyes with the corner of the scratchy wool blanket she'd draped over herself, but nothing could stop the flood. She longed to write another letter to Levi and tell him what she was doing, perhaps even share her address; but what good would come of it? He'd made it clear they were no more than friends, despite the intimate moment they'd shared—and the more she dwelled on those kisses, the more convinced she became that they had meant far more to her than to him. Why else would he have felt a need to qualify their relationship? The kisses simply shouldn't have happened.

Josie cried some more until she drained the well and, before she knew it, drifted off for a much-needed slumber.

31

For the 23rd Regiment, Christmas came and went with very little fanfare, excepting the package Levi received from his mother two days before Christmas: a box full of homemade goodies such as biscuits, small cakes, muffins, miniature loaves of bread, apples, cookies, and an assortment of candies. When Levi unwrapped the crate, it seemed the whole of Company B descended upon him, mouths watering, eyes bulging. Even Hiram McQuade squeezed in to look over everyone's shoulders, a wide grin on his face at the sight of such marvelous pickings.

Sharing was inevitable, and even joyful, as much as Levi would have loved to hoard just a few of the delicacies for himself. By the next day, not a crumb remained. Most of the men received something special in the mail during the week leading up to Christmas, but in his letter home to thank his mother for the package, Levi said he was certain his box of treats far surpassed anyone else's.

On Christmas Eve, most of the soldiers gathered in groups around their fires, playing games, singing carols, or playing an instrument. The night was cold, but no fresh flakes had fallen since that first snow a few weeks earlier. And Christmas morning, as on that first day of

Thanks-giving, the government delivered a few extra rations so that the soldiers could enjoy a somewhat decent meal.

Sickness spread through the 23rd and other nearby companies, filling the hospital beds as never before, such that Major Walden sent an urgent request to Captain Bateman for additional doctors. Three arrived a few days later, giving the major some reprieve. So far, Levi had managed to stay healthy, aside from some token sniffles, chills, passing headaches, and bothersome coughs. He figured his time spent in the army had conditioned his body to fight off the most common diseases, and his reading of newspaper articles on cleanliness and sanitation had him making a conscious effort to make frequent use of the lye soap provided by the army, washing his hands before eating and also bathing as often as possible. Major Walden seemed on board with the new theory that cleanliness and proper sanitation could help stop the spread of disease, and Levi figured it couldn't hurt to abide by the doctor's exhortations, especially since his duties as chaplain brought him into regular, and close, contact with ailing men who needed to hear an encouraging word, a prayer, or some Scripture.

Never did Levi wish to push religion on anyone, but he certainly wanted the soldiers to know that salvation was available, so he looked for subtle ways to communicate that message. One thing war had taught him about humankind was that when people were down, discouraged, and diseased, they received the Word of God more readily. Thus, when the opportunity arose, he seized it.

Such was the case when Hiram McQuade suddenly took ill with a raging fever and a severe headache, and he was brought to the hospital. A couple of times, he even suffered delirium.

"What is it he has, Doctor?" Levi had asked, standing over Hiram one evening around midnight.

"Could be a case of typhoid, but there's no way to know for sure."

"Typhoid is terribly contagious, isn't it?"

"It certainly can be. That's why I'm trying to isolate him from the others as much as possible."

Hiram seemed confused as to his whereabouts. He cried out several times, claiming to see spiders and snakes alike crawling up and down the walls and coming closer to his bed. "Get them away from me!" he screamed, waving his arms about. "Get them away!" No amount of comforting or assurance could convince him that there were no bugs or slithering creatures present.

Levi pulled up a stool and sat next to him, rested his hand on his arm, and began reciting the Twenty-third Psalm, then prayed aloud for him in a quiet monotone. Miraculously, Hiram stilled for the first time in days, and finally fell asleep.

When news reached Levi the next morning that Hiram needed him, he fully expected to find him on the verge of death. He hurried to the medic's station, and almost as soon as he walked through the door, Hiram lifted a weak hand to wave him over. Relieved, Levi sat down with a smile. "You look improved, Hiram. How are you feeling?"

"Better, but I wanna know what sorta magic you performed to send that angel to visit me. There were these hideous creatures, real scary-like, screamin' and scatterin' when he showed up." His voice came off cracked and husky. "Doc Walden says you was here prayin' for me when it all happened, and I wanna know what you did."

Levi's smile broadened, and he said a silent prayer of thanksgiving to the God who delivers His children from demons. "I don't perform magic, Hiram. I pray to the one true God. It is for Him to decide who lives and who dies. I don't pretend to understand the workings of the Holy Spirit, except that He ministers to those in need, and He visits us in our most desperate times. I believe an angel drew near to you to reveal just how great are God's love and healing mercies. Jesus loves you and would like nothing more than for you to invite Him into your heart. You've seen how great are His works. Now, all you have to do is ask Him to take charge of your life so that you can live out the rest of your days with the joy of knowing you will see Him when you pass into glory and will spend eternity in His glorious presence."

Hiram lay there, obviously weak and worn, his face beaded with large droplets of sweat, his body reeking. "I don't…see how a body could be happy in the middle o' war."

Levi could sense the effort it took for him to speak. He leaned forward and placed a hand on Hiram's damp chest. "I didn't mention happiness. I'm talking about joy. There's a difference. Happiness is an outward show of emotions, but joy comes from a deep place in the heart. One could say it is accompanied by peace. In other words, you can be filled with peace but not necessarily be happy. That's where I am right now, if you want the truth. War is not a happy place to be, but I'm still experiencing peace in my heart."

"Hmm." Hiram closed his eyes and took in a deep breath. "I…I'm tired o' hatin'," he murmured.

Levi nodded. "Hate has a way of devouring a person's spirit."

Hiram didn't respond, and as the silence stretched on, Levi took out his Bible, preparing to sit there and read while the fellow slept.

He had read a full chapter when Hiram stirred, opened his eyes, and turned his face toward Levi. "So, how…how do I go about it?" he rasped.

Levi's heart soared. *Oh, God, give me wisdom.* "Well, it's really quite simple. I'll pray a prayer aloud, and you can repeat it, either out loud or in your heart. Does that sound like something you'd like to do?"

Wonder of wonders, Hiram gave his head a slight nod. The whole room seemed to have gone quiet; Levi heard not even a single patient coughing. He wasn't about to turn and gawk, but even Major Walden seemed to have stilled. Was everyone listening? Levi took a cavernous breath before proceeding, loudly enough for all to hear. "Lord, I come to Thee, asking for the forgiveness of my sins. I confess that Jesus is the Son of God, and that He died on the cross, that I might be forgiven and have eternal life in heaven. I believe that Jesus rose from the dead, and I ask Thee, Lord, to come into my life and be my personal Lord and Savior. I turn from my sins and promise to worship Thee all the days of my life. I now confess that I am Thy child, and I have been born again and cleaned by the blood of Jesus. In Jesus' name I pray, amen." He swallowed hard and opened his eyes, then hurriedly glanced down at Hiram. In all his days, Levi didn't think he'd ever seen a brighter smile, certainly not on the face of someone as grumpy as Hiram McQuade. He wanted to rise to his feet and shout, "Glory!" but instead, he kept his composure and gave the man a pat on the arm. "Congratulations, Hiram. You are now officially born into the kingdom of God."

"I am?"

"Indeed."

"Well, jumpin' butter beans. Ain't that somethin'?" He breathed deeply and closed his eyes. "Thank you, Preacher."

Levi's chest constricted. It was the first time anyone had ever referred to him as "Preacher," and it humbled him straight to his center.

Later, on his walk back to camp, something stirred inside him, something real and vivid. *I want you to dedicate your life to Me.*

"Yes, Lord," he murmured into the cold air, his breath rising like mist into the air.

I want you to dedicate your life to preaching My Word.

Preaching? He stopped dead in his tracks and stared straight ahead. Had he heard right, or was his imagination taking off on him?

"You okay, Preacher—er, Chaplain?"

He glanced up at Chester Woolsley, who met him on the muddy trail. "What—what did you call me?"

"Huh?" Chester looked as surprised as Levi felt. "I jus' asked if you was okay."

"I know, but what did you call me?"

Confusion washed over his face. "I think I called you 'Chaplain.' You are the chaplain, ain't ya?"

"Yes, but…but I thought you called me 'Preacher.'"

"Oh. Well, yeah, I guess I did. You ain't mad, are you?"

"No, no, of course not. Where are you headed, Chester?"

"T' see Hiram. I'm a little scared, but I got to settle things up with him."

"You do?"

"We've been treatin' each other so bad, I'm plain tired of it. An', well, now that he's sick, I figure it's as good a time as any t' talk to 'im. Maybe he won't have the strength to haul off an' slug me."

Levi gave a half chuckle. "I'm sure it'll be fine, Chester."

"It ain't neither of our faults, what our parents done did."

Levi smiled. "You're absolutely right, Chester. I'm sure Hiram will be…well, I think he'll be glad to see you."

"You think?"

"I do. Just keep your distance, as Major Walden fears he has typhoid. It's contagious."

"He ain't gonna die, is he?"

"I don't think so."

They nodded at each other before going their separate ways.

He kicked at some sticks in his path as he strolled along, pondering what he'd perceived to be God's voice. Was it real, or had he imagined it? For some reason, a picture of his mother's face came to mind. How would she react if he told her he'd received an audible call from God? Even if he believed in the deepest parts of his heart that God had called him to a higher purpose, would she consider it a betrayal of his Quaker roots? The Friends Society did not believe one man should assume the authority given to preachers. Friends were to gather their knowledge from God Himself, from His written Word, and from the occasional teachings of the elders, who spoke only when they detected a strong pull from the Holy Spirit. Would God truly call Levi into such a position? Remarkably, the next face that came to mind was that of Josephine Winters. He recalled the comment she'd made—well, Gordon Snipp had made—about the possibility of his serving as a minister someday. When he'd told her he wasn't qualified, she'd paraphrased a verse of Scripture, reminding him that he could do all things through Christ who strengthens him. *Lord, I'd want her at my side. Is there any way You could make that happen if You are indeed calling me to preach?*

He pulled back the flap on his tent and stepped inside, but no sooner did he enter its warmth than he heard the voice of Jim Hodgers shout, "Sarge! Lieutenant Grimms is lookin' for you."

With a deep sigh, he looked heavenward, shrugged his shoulders, and headed off for the lieutenant's quarters.

He found Grimms, and a large number of other soldiers of varying ranks, standing outside his tent. When Grimms saw him coming, he waved him over.

After a few exchanged pleasantries, Grimms cleared his throat. "I'll get right to the point, men. I called you to this gathering because orders just came down early this morning from Lieutenant General Caldwell. Anyone entering the army on or before September tenth of eighteen sixty-one is due for furlough. You fellas are dismissed until February eleventh. And let me add, you're all very deserving of a little leisure time."

His announcement came as a shock to Levi. Apparently, the rest of them felt the same, for they all stood around gape-mouthed, glancing at one another.

"Well, say something," Grimms demanded.

"Is—is this real?" sputtered Sergeant Green.

"Of course, it's real. Now, am I going to have to chase you out of here, or are you going to leave of your own accord?"

In an instant, all manner of chaos broke out as the news began sinking in. Someone tossed his hat in the air, followed by another and then another. They started laughing, shaking hands, and punching each other in the shoulder.

A sort of numb bewilderment settled in Levi's head. He scratched under his ear and squinted his eyes.

"What's the matter, Albright?" asked Grimms.

"I—I don't know what to say, sir."

"Well, 'Good-bye, see you on February eleventh' would be good for starters," he teased. Lieutenant Grimms had never been one for teasing.

"But—I have a lot of responsibilities here. Men who need me."

"They will survive." This he said with a tone Levi would almost describe as warm.

He grinned and rubbed the back of his neck. He was going home? The mere notion gave his stomach a case of the flutters.

"Oh, before you go...." Grimms reached deep into his pocket. "Take this."

Levi stared down at the folded piece of paper the man handed him.

"It's her aunt's address."

Levi's stomach pitched again.

"I can't say that's where she went, or if you'll find her there, but at least it's a start."

His jaw dropped as he took the paper, unfolded it, and studied the Philadelphia address of one Gordon Snipp. Then he looked into Grimms' eyes and, for the first time, recognized a glimmer of kinship there.

Grimms slapped him on the shoulder. "Now, get on with you, before I change my mind and make you stay here till September eleventh, which is the day you muster out."

Levi closed his mouth and gave his head a little shake. Then he clicked the heels of his muddy boots, drew back his shoulders, looked Grimms in the eye, and gave him a proper salute. "Yes, sir. Thank you, sir."

Lo and behold, Grimms returned the gesture—and with a smile.

32

"Miss Winters, I need you in the surgical room," spoke the gruff voice of Dr. Edwards. "I'm about to amputate a leg, and I'll need your assistance holding down the patient. Two of my aids have ridden out to help bring in three wounded soldiers, so I'm down to one assistant."

"Sir?" She looked up from the sick man to whom she'd been administering medicine.

"Hurry along, now."

She, Adam, and Sarah had been working tirelessly for days alongside Dr. Morton in the quarantine tent. One of the nine patients had died, but the others were hanging on, and they needed constant care.

Josie glanced at Dr. Morton, who waved her toward the door. She snatched her coat off the back of a chair, put it on, and hurried after Dr. Edwards across the yard to the hospital. Walking to the back, she entered the surgical room. The whole place smelled of sickness mixed with odorous medicines, perspiration, soiled clothing, and urine. "Lord, help me," she muttered under her breath. She'd witnessed and even assisted in a couple of surgical procedures, but never an amputation. She had no idea what to expect, or why Dr. Edwards would consider her qualified to help. Surely, he knew her to be a volunteer aid, not a true practicing nurse. Once in the room, she said to the doctor, "I've never taken part in this sort of procedure, sir."

"Well then, prepare yourself, miss," was all he said.

The patient lay half awake, the smell of whiskey rancid on his breath. Next to the bed was a table with a variety of instruments lying on a stained towel, but Josie barely noticed anything except the hand saw used to cut through bone and the long, thin knife used to cut through ligaments. These she'd learned about upon first coming to the hospital, when one of the nurses had taken her on a hurried tour of the facility. She had seen similar instruments in Major Walden's possession, of course, and she'd heard he'd had to perform a few amputations, himself. She'd just never witnessed any of them. She'd shuddered at the thought of having one's limb cut off, and now she literally trembled.

In the room was another nurse wearing a bloodstained apron. She glanced up when Josie entered the room and ordered, "Come, stand here—at the patient's head."

Josie moved none too fast and stepped into place.

"See this basin of water? You'll take the cloth and wring it out, using it to dab the patient's forehead while the doctor works. When he begins the procedure, grab ahold of the soldier's head on both sides to keep him from thrashing too much. You'll see we've tied down his arms. If need be, rinse out the cloth in this basin of cold water a couple of times. The doctor will administer the chloroform, but in some cases, it doesn't put the fellow entirely under."

Josie nodded, then positioned herself and then waited for the doctor to begin. He took up a small vial of liquid, broke it open at the top, and then poured the contents onto a handkerchief. "This is going to help make you sleepy, Soldier," he said. "Don't be surprised if you still feel something, though. I'm going to cut through the bone just below your knee. If we don't do it now, you'll lose your whole leg. Gangrene is already setting in. You understand?" The soldier groaned in agony but managed a small nod. "All right, then, we'll get started." Dr. Edwards placed the handkerchief over the moaning soldier's nose and mouth, and held it there until the fellow closed his eyes and slept. "All right, let's get this done," he said. "Hand me that scalpel, Nurse Meyer."

The nurse wordlessly followed his first order, and then the next one, and the next. Throughout the procedure, the fellow kept releasing torturous moans, and Josie worked to keep him as calm as possible, taking up the cold, wet cloth, wringing it out a couple of times, and continually patting the soldier's forehead while also doing her best to hold him still. By focusing on his comfort rather than the gruesome procedure, she somehow made it through without retching.

In all, the process couldn't have lasted more than ten minutes. Finally, the doctor tied up the end of the stump with a piece of white, gauzy fabric, secured it with a knot, and then nodded at Nurse Meyer and Josie in a curt manner. "One down, two more to go."

"T-two more?" Josie stammered.

Dr. Edwards ignored her query and directed his gaze at the patient. "Give him some more whiskey, Nurse, then release his arms. I'll check on him later."

"Yes, sir." Nurse Meyer picked up a tall bottle from a nearby table. Glancing at Josie, she said, "Help me lift his head so I can pour this down his throat." Josie gave a dull nod, dropped the cloth back in the basin, and did as told. The patient took several swigs of the liquid, then fell back against the cot, exhausted. The nurse untied one of his arms, while Josie did the other.

"He'll sleep awhile," the doctor stated in monotone. Then he swiveled his body around. "Who's next, Nurse?"

"Over there, sir." Nurse Meyer pointed at another groaning soldier across the room. "It's his left arm."

With a nod, he picked up the small wooden table that held the bloodied instruments he'd just used, and carried it across the room, the nurse following behind. Not for anything could Josie get her feet to work. She glanced down at the sleeping soldier.

"Come on, Miss Winters," the nurse snapped impatiently. "We don't have all day."

"But…but I thought I was to work in the quarantine tent."

"Around here, your duties change from minute to minute. Hurry up, now. The doctor has work to do."

Lord, give me strength, she prayed, as she left her post and moved to the next one.

⌁

Levi's chest tightened with anticipation at the sight of the Garlows' farmhouse. Positioned at the base of a hill, the two-story structure, with its several outbuildings, was not nearly as big as his family's farm on Sunset Ridge, but was a pleasant little place nonetheless. Granted, it could use a few repairs, with its sagging roof, broken porch railing, and crooked shutters. Levi imagined a blooming garden in summer and grapes on the trellis where now everything lay brown and dormant. A dog came charging out of the barn, greeting him with a friendly bark. He dismounted his horse, Stony, hitched him to a post next to an outbuilding, and made the trek toward the house, his pulse pounding in his head at the prospect of seeing Josie within minutes. He'd dressed in his best attire and hoped to pass muster with her. *Please, God, let her be here. I've so much to say to her.*

He climbed the creaky porch steps, gave a couple of raps on the front door, and waited. No one came. In fact, now that he thought about it, the whole place was quiet, save for the dog, and the chickens and two nanny goats roaming about. He leaned forward and peered through the window, but all was still—not normal for a household with kids. He recalled the ruckus he'd caused at Sunset Ridge when the driver had dropped him off at the Albright farm, and how all his family members had come running from every direction.

He'd arrived yesterday, a Sunday—First Day, as the Quakers referred to it—and he hadn't been able to get a word in edgewise for the first five or so minutes, between his mother crying, his littlest sister holding him tightly around the waist, his brothers doing a happy jig, his father chucking him in the arm and then giving him a giant bear hug, his two brothers-in-law nearly shaking his arm off with their firm grips, his two married sisters beaming with wide smiles and giddy giggles. It was pure circumstance that his married sisters were there, as they lived a distance away. The only one who hadn't been present was Lydia, who lived in Boston. Still unmarried, she enjoyed her position as a schoolteacher, as far as he knew. My, what a hubbub of laughter, shouts of glee, and loud commotion they'd all made.

No, this was not normal, and his spirits sank as he took another peek inside the house. He would simply ride back here tomorrow, and the next day, and the next—until he found someone at home. They all must have piled into a wagon and set off for the city, which couldn't be more than a mile or two away. They all would be here tomorrow. They *had* to be.

With heavy heart, he descended the porch steps, mounted Stony, and started for his next destination—one he didn't look forward to with nearly as much enthusiasm. He'd sent word to Mary Foster that he was coming home for a brief time, and that he would enjoy the pleasure of meeting her face-to-face on Monday. She'd sent a reply to the Albrights, saying she would be free the afternoon of Second Day. Levi's sisters were beyond thrilled at the prospect of his meeting her for the first time, and they'd instructed him on how to dress and carry himself—and cautioned him not to forget to use the plain pronouns. He couldn't count how many times he'd neglected to use plain speech since returning home.

Not surprisingly, his mother had accused him of backsliding because his comportment wasn't quite up to Quaker standards. He'd laughed in response. "Mother, if you heard the way my comrades speak, you would probably fall into a dead faint," he'd told her. And it wasn't until his mother had tilted her head at him in a scolding manner, with lips pursed, that he realized he'd failed, even then, to use plain pronouns. "Forgive me, Mother," he'd said with a sheepish smile. "I shall try to be better. Will thee forgive me?" She'd given him a playful slap and tried, without success, to hide her grin. "I shall think about it, but thee must be careful not to let it happen again." This, he knew, would require great concentration.

The directions he'd received for getting to Mary's home were easy enough. The Fosters lived on the outskirts of the city, Mary's father being a merchant rather than a farmer. He ran a small general store, and he did a fair business, according to Levi's parents. Of course, the Fosters were good Quakers, Papa had said—faithful attendees at Arch Street Meeting House, and good stewards of their finances, meaning they contributed their share to the Society to keep it operating.

Levi had said nothing to his family about Josie, nor had he mentioned the recent experience in which he'd felt the call of God upon his heart to consider the preaching profession. He would eventually talk to them, of course—to his parents, in particular—and, at some point, if all went according to plan, he would bring up the matter of Josephine Winters, aka Gordon Snipp. He knew he'd mentioned Gordon a couple of times in his correspondence, but that was before he'd discovered the truth about Gordon's identity. Levi trusted God to cause everything to fall into its proper place when the time was right. For now, he knew he must at least give this young lady, Mary Foster, a fair chance—even though he already knew he couldn't possibly offer her his heart. It already belonged to another, no matter that Josie had no idea she held his heart captive. He nearly shuddered when considering how his mother would react once he finally worked up the nerve to tell her he'd fallen in love with a girl who'd joined the army disguised as a man. Once again, he would simply have to trust God and watch how things played out.

He steered Stony up the dirt drive leading to the Foster home. It was a two-story redbrick foursquare with a third-story dormer in the middle, nicely detailed with a large covered front porch and four big pillars. He climbed down and wrapped Stony's reins around a post out front. The porch swing hung silent and vacant, swaying ever so slightly in the gentle breeze. He climbed the steps, finding them much sturdier than the ones at Josie's aunt's farmhouse. He raised his hand, but the door opened before he had the chance to knock. There in the doorway stood an attractive young lady wearing a full-skirted, long-sleeved beige dress gathered at the waist and buttoned to her throat. Atop her tight blonde bun of hair was a white prayer cap. With both hands hanging at her sides, she gave the slightest curtsy. "Hello, there. Thee must be Levi Albright."

"Yes, and you—er, *thee* must be Mary."

She smiled broadly, revealing a slight gap between her two top teeth. Charming. "Please, come in." She stepped to one side to allow for his passage.

He entered and removed his hat and coat, which she quickly took from him and hung on a coat tree. Then she gestured with her arm to usher him into the family's formal gathering room. It was nothing like the farmhouse on Sunset Ridge, but it was welcoming nonetheless. A large fireplace occupied one wall, and the mantel above it held a number of framed tintypes, some knickknacks, and a tall vase of dried flowers. A quick glance around revealed that these Quakers enjoyed the finer things of life. Although Mary dressed plainly, Levi couldn't see a single plain thing about the way they dressed their home.

"I'm sorry to say my parents are not currently home," Mary said. "My father is over at our store on Markland Street, and Mother left a while ago to take my little brother and sister to our cousins' house for a visit."

"I see. How nice." A secret wave of gratitude surged through Levi, knowing he wouldn't have to meet them for now.

She directed him to a maroon velvet divan. "Please, may I serve thee a cup of coffee? Mother and I also made corn muffins this morning. Might I interest thee in a buttered muffin?"

He wasn't the least bit hungry after the feast his mother had prepared for the noon meal, but he also didn't wish to offend Mary. He turned his hat in his hands. "Uh...sure. I mean, that would be nice. Thank you—*thee*. I'm sorry. Please forgive me for being unaccustomed to plain speech. I've grown a little lax over the past couple of years."

She frowned. "The war...it must be dreadful. And to have to mix with all those filthy men.... I'm sure thee is just as anxious as the rest of us for this war to end. I pray daily that Meade will convince Lee to surrender."

"Yes." He could think of little else to say.

"Please, sit."

He did as told, then watched as she floated off to the kitchen. Sitting there, he listened to her move about, heard the tinkling of china cups and saucers, the rattling of utensils. It had been so long since he'd held a fine teacup in his big, bulky hands, he feared he would spill the whole thing on his freshly pressed trousers. It wasn't that she made him nervous. Quite the opposite, actually. It was that she was a perfectly nice young woman, and he didn't wish to hurt her feelings by his lack of personal interest. How to go about letting her know that he had no plans to pursue her, or that it would be futile for her to send him any further letters? All he could think about was Josephine Winters and how disappointed he'd been not to find her at her aunt's.

Mary returned to the room with a small silver tray on which she carried a teapot, two dainty cups, and a small plate of three muffins.

Levi abruptly stood. After more than two years in the army, he had to force himself to remember the basics of chivalry.

Mary carefully set the tray down on the table in front of the sofa, then lowered herself to the divan and started to pour the steaming contents of the teapot into the cups. At least two feet separated her from Levi, which suited him fine.

"Would thee care for any cream or sugar with thy coffee?"

"Neither, thank thee."

"I do hope coffee meets with thy liking rather than tea. Mother had already prepared it on the stove an hour or so ago, so it's piping hot."

"That'll be just fine. Thank thee."

Soon, they both were sipping quietly, sitting with spines straight. "Well," they said in unison. Awkward laughter pealed out of them.

"You first," Levi said.

Mary nodded. "I was going to ask thee about the war. How terrible is it? Does thee see an end in sight?"

He set his cup on the sofa table, thankful that he'd managed not to spill any coffee thus far, and pondered his answer. "It's not ending any time soon, as far as I can tell, although the Union has managed, on several occasions, to push back the South. After Gettysburg, it's clear they'll never attempt Pennsylvania again. I believe their troops are dwindling. Then again, we don't always hear the most current news. I think the chief officers withhold the worst of it. In the army, one learns to follow orders and ask few questions."

"I see." A crease appeared on Mary's flawless brow. "I…I guess I don't quite understand why thee joined, considering the war goes against thy religious standards of pacifism. Thee has never endeavored to offer an explanation in thy correspondence. I know we are each entitled to our innermost convictions, but it is something I often contemplate. Has thee…well, has thee ever had to…to *kill* someone?" She winced when saying the word, and he winced at the thought of answering. She was so delicately proper, the complete opposite of Josie.

"I have had to aim and fire, but I have no idea if any of my bullets ever hit a target. I don't like to think about it. I have yet to do any face-to-face combat, and I hope it won't come to that. I don't operate the cannons, but I've seen the damage they do to large numbers of soldiers on both sides."

Mary gave him a disconcerted frown. "I had rather hoped thee would soon return to thy roots."

Levi bristled a bit. "Does thee suggest I've wandered from God?"

"No, not at all, but I do question whether thee is certain thee is accomplishing God's best purposes for thy life. It would seem thee could serve thy country in a different capacity."

"I told thee in a letter that I assumed the role of chaplain."

"Yes, but thee also said thee still carries a gun."

Levi shrugged. "Well, it's war, so, yes, I haven't hung up my weapon yet. I know of others from our Society who are fighting for the Union. I even know of a couple Quakers who sacrificed their lives for the cause."

"And they would be alive today, had they chosen to stay home."

"Well, that is true, but perhaps they would wonder all the rest of their days if they could have done more to help preserve the Union, or to save just one more Negro from having to live in slavery. I know I would have wondered." Levi sighed. "I simply don't think pacifism is black-and-white." He could see they'd already built a wall, of sorts, that kept them at odds.

"How does thee think thee will be received back into the Society after the war?"

"Actually...." He paused before answering, wanting to choose his words carefully. He hadn't even told his parents yet what he was thinking about. "I'm considering the call to preach."

Mary's eyes widened. "But surely thee knows that the Society does not believe any man to be worthy of such a calling. It is for each of us to instruct one another and to rely solely upon the Inner Light of the Holy Spirit for guidance. We all are on equal ground, in God's eyes."

"Well, I wouldn't preach for the Society. I would serve in a denomination that fully embraces the gospel of Jesus Christ."

"Oh." She hastily lifted her teacup to her lips, her eyes focused downward. She had lovely eyelashes, he noted, but they didn't compare to Josie's. Nothing about her compared to Josie. She lowered her cup to her lap, gripping it with both her tiny hands. "I thought thee would return to thy family's farm. Thee already has a nice homestead at Sunset Ridge. What of that?"

"Well, of course, my home will stay in the family. Perhaps one of my brothers or my brothers-in-law would wish to purchase it someday. That is all incidental for now, as I haven't even fully made up my mind. All I know is, I have received what I consider to be a genuine call on my heart from God, and if He continues to lead me in that direction, I shall certainly obey."

He could almost see the battle raging in her mind. Apparently, she'd envisioned herself living in his finely constructed home on Albright property, and he'd dashed her hopes with his pronouncement of his plan to follow God's call into the ministry.

"Well, I suppose this changes things a bit between us," she said, after sucking in a deep breath. "Mother and Father would be deeply disappointed if I were ever to leave the Society."

Deep in his chest, Levi wanted to release a great gasp of relief. Instead, he held his calm. "And I fully understand thy thinking, Mary. Thee wouldn't wish to disappoint thy parents."

They both took several sips of coffee, eyeing each other over the rims of their cups. After a few moments, Levi set down his drink. "Well, I should probably be going. I promised my brothers I would help them in the barn today."

Mary stood, and he quickly followed suit. She pressed the wrinkles out of her skirt with her dainty hands. What sort of farmer's wife would she make, anyway? He could scarcely imagine her digging in the dirt. The thought almost made him burst into a hearty chuckle.

"I'll see thee to the door."

"It was lovely finally meeting you—*thee*," he corrected himself as he followed her to the entryway.

She turned the knob, opened the door, and stepped aside. "Yes, it was lovely meeting thee, as well. I hope thee stays safe and healthy." She issued him a smile, albeit a reserved one.

Still, it was best for her to find out now that they weren't a good match. Levi put on his coat, placed his hat back on his head, and tipped the brim at her before crossing the threshold. After untying the reins of his patient horse, he glanced up and saw Mary standing in the doorway, leaning against the frame. "Perhaps we'll meet again sometime," he said.

"Yes, perhaps so."

He didn't plan to hold his breath. He mounted Stony, turned him around, and headed toward Sunset Ridge, the winter sun warming his shoulders, the tiniest hint of a smile lining his lips.

33

*J*osie could barely keep her eyes open. So much sickness, heartache, and hopelessness—and hardly any time to breathe, let alone eat and sleep. Daily, the hospital beds filled with new patients, sick and injured alike. In many parts of the country, the war had all but ceased due to inclement weather; in other parts, however, it raged on. Would the savagery never end? Josie longed to talk to Levi, but because of her hectic, yet oddly rewarding, schedule, those days spent with Levi and the rest of Company B had somehow found a place to hide in the distant recesses of her mind—a defense, of sorts, to shield her from further pain.

She'd written exactly two letters—one to Aunt Bessie and one to Allison—but in neither had she been able to expound upon the details of her work before being interrupted by either a suffering patient's summons, a doctor's urgent request for aid, or an assignment to a different location. Miss Dix had certainly been right in saying Josie would receive little to no thanks from the personnel for her willingness to volunteer. No one had time for such pleasantries when even the doctors worked without taking any breaks to eat or sleep. Many volunteers came and went, due to the demanding nature of the work required of them, but

Josie determined to stay the course until the Lord called her to serve in some other capacity.

While she did not earn a single cent for her efforts, the army had provided her with a small room on the third floor of the hospital in which to sleep, and food enough to keep her satisfied—when she found the time to eat. She had no real need for money, unless it was for purchasing an assortment of personal items, which she bought using the salary she'd accumulated from the army, minus what she'd sent to Aunt Bessie. If necessary, she would find another job to supplement her needs, but she was committed to continue working as a medical volunteer. Sick soldiers needed her, and she would not let them down.

She spent the majority of her time in the quarantine tent, tending to those suffering from typhoid, and thanked her Maker that she'd managed to avoid contracting the dread disease. Dr. Morton had told her that if she hadn't got it yet, she probably wouldn't, so she could do little but trust his word and pray for God's protection. She also took every possible precaution, including the practice of continually washing her hands, as both doctors Walden and Morton had taught her.

That afternoon, when her fatigue was truly wearing on her, a Union soldier entered the tent and announced that he required her services.

She turned, water basin in hand, and stared at him. He was a tall, lanky man with a dark shadow of whisker growth. "My services? But—"

"Dr. Edwards said you was to come with me. Out to the field."

"The field, sir?"

He nodded. "There was a minor skirmish, and there's some soldiers lyin' out there in need of assistance. We're takin' a wagon out to bring in the bodies."

"But—but I'm not a nurse." She threw a desperate glance at Dr. Morton.

"You'll do fine, Miss Winters," the doctor assured her. "I've watched you these past weeks, and you're catching on very fast."

"Wouldn't it be better if you were to go?" she asked him.

"My services are in greater demand here at the hospital."

"You ain't the only nurse goin', miss," said the soldier. "Plus, there's a doctor who specifically requested you. Come on, now. The wagon's waitin'."

Someone had requested her? She hesitated only briefly before taking a deep breath and quickly donning her long, woolen coat and warm bonnet. At least she wasn't leaving Dr. Morton entirely on his own. Adam and Sarah were there to assist him.

On her way to the door, the doctor intercepted her. "Here." He stretched out his arm and handed her his trusty black doctor bag. "You might need this."

They locked eyes for a brief moment. Then Josie took the bag, picked up the hem of her long dress, and hurried out the door.

She rode for at least seven miles on a hay-filled wagon with two other nurses—Genevieve and Hannah—and a young doctor named Martin Baylor, who seemed particularly interested in carrying on a conversation with Josie. She had seen him in the hospital on several occasions, but only in passing. Certainly, they'd never conversed. The four of them hugged their coats closed in an attempt to stay warm. It was an especially frigid day. Snowflakes drifted down, though they weren't enough to cover the ground. Josie's stomach clenched with anxiety over what they might find, as the memories of battle cluttered her thoughts.

"Don't look so worried," Dr. Baylor told her. "You'll do fine. I've heard good things about your nursing skills."

"You have? But I'm not truly a nurse."

"Ah, but you have grit, determination, and skill, not to mention compassion. All qualities that make for a good nurse."

"Thank you, sir."

He leaned closer. "Please, call me Martin."

She ignored his comment and gazed out over the barren terrain, wishing the driver would move a little faster.

"If I may be so bold, I've noticed your hair is a bit shorter than the style nowadays," Dr. Baylor remarked.

Josie pulled her bonnet a little lower on her head. "I decided to try a slightly different style, but I'm growing it back," she said. So far, she'd managed to keep hidden the fact that she'd served in the army.

The bumpy dirt path caused the wagon to pitch and sway. "Whoa!" the driver finally called, drawing his four-horse team to a halt.

Three armed, bloody soldiers approached the wagon. "Battle ended 'bout two hours ago," one reported. "The Rebs moved south and out of sight, but that don't mean they won't come back. We got men standin' guard to hold them at bay, so you might hear firin'. Try not to be alarmed."

"We're accustomed to hearing gunfire, soldier," said Dr. Baylor. "Where are the wounded?"

"Scattered about," another soldier answered. "We thank y' for comin'."

"Let's see what we have here," the doctor said. He jumped down first, and he and one of the soldiers assisted Josie and the other two women out of the wagon. When Dr. Baylor took Josie's hand, he gave it an extra squeeze. She avoided looking at him.

"This way," one of the soldiers said. "You'll find 'em easy enough. Just listen for their cries."

Single file, the team walked through the thick brush. Josie held tight to Dr. Morton's black bag.

"Over here," someone called.

Everyone turned at the sound. Soon, another soldier let out a loud yelp, and then another. It was clear to Josie that they would be busy for the next several hours tending to the wounded, doing what they could until the soldiers were able to be transported to the hospital.

While Genevieve and Hannah ran in two different directions, Dr. Baylor took Josie by the elbow and led her to a soldier lying on the ground, surrounded by twigs and brush. The poor man writhed in pain. "Help me. It's my leg."

Dr. Baylor knelt down beside the soldier, whose pant leg was saturated in blood, his arms and face a mass of cuts and scrapes. Josie crouched down on his other side and opened Dr. Morton's bag. Baylor removed a knife from his pocket and cut the man's pant leg up the middle. A severed bone protruded out of a deep gash, and the soldier screamed in pain when the doctor touched the wound around it. In the bag, Josie found a cloth and some salve, with which she started tending the several cuts and scrapes covering the man's face and neck.

"Do you want me to try to save your leg or cut it off, Soldier?" asked Dr. Baylor. "Either way, it's going to hurt like fire. I can try to reset the bone, but it's broken clean in half, and I don't think the rest of it is even intact. It will be a miserable ordeal, and I can't guarantee the tissue around the area will heal. Or, I can amputate, since it's already half gone. Whatever you choose, I'm afraid you'll never walk normally again."

The man gave a loud shriek of pain. "Am I gonna die?"

"Not if I can help it."

"Just…do what you gotta do."

Josie and the doctor exchanged looks.

"I think it's best I amputate," Dr. Baylor said." What do you think, Nurse?"

"Me? I—I can't say for sure. I'd say it's up to the soldier."

"He's in no condition to make a decision."

"Well, if you say that some of the bone is missing, then it's probably best to amputate, yes."

Dr. Baylor opened his bag and withdrew a flask of chloroform and a cone-shaped cloth, which he used to put the soldier to sleep. And then he proceeded with the amputation.

All told, it took three hours to do what they could for each soldier. While they tended to the wounded, several soldiers dug holes to bury the dead, marking each grave with a wooden cross. At last, every single body, dead or alive, was accounted for, and Josie and the others started the long trek back to Alexandria, exhausted and drained.

Josie leaned back against the side rail of the wagon.

Dr. Baylor dropped down next to her. "You did a fine job out there, Nurse."

She opened her heavy eyes. Overhead, a trillion stars twinkled in a black sky. "I told you, I'm not a nurse."

"You were today. You're very good at what you do. Where did you learn your skills?"

"Here and there." She wasn't about to tell him she'd tended to many wounded soldiers in the Pennsylvania 23rd Regiment.

"Did you study under anyone in particular?"

"In the weeks since I've been here, Dr. Morton has taught me a lot."

"Hm, you're a quick study, I'll say that. Where are you from?"

"Philadelphia. What about yourself?"

"Lima, New York, not far from Rochester. You got a sweetheart somewhere?"

She wished. If only she'd given Levi an address at which to contact her. But she hadn't wished to be a distraction to him. Besides, they were just friends—no matter the kisses. *The kisses.* Would she ever forget them?

"Well?" he asked, elbowing her in the side.

"Um, not really."

"Not really. What sort of an answer is that? Either you do or you don't. You're awfully pretty, you know. I've had my eye on you these past few weeks."

"Is that so?" She endeavored to hide her discomfort at his remark.

"Might I accompany you on a walk through Alexandria some evening?"

"Oh, I…." Great saints above. The very notion of his interest in her set her nerves on edge. Yes, she'd worked alongside him all afternoon and into the evening, but she'd paid little attention to him and his generous remarks, thinking him just overly sociable. "I couldn't possibly. There's so little time for frivolities."

When she glanced up at him, the moonlight revealed one arched eyebrow. "Walking through town is a frivolity?"

"I've no time to get away, Doctor."

"You are volunteering your services without pay, are you not?"

"Yes."

"Well then, you have every right to take a walk whenever you choose. How's tomorrow, say, after supper? Or, better yet, how about I treat you to dinner at a restaurant?"

"Oh, that would be far too extravagant. I couldn't."

"Yes, you could. Say yes."

The wagon hit a bump, and several of the wounded soldiers moaned. "I'll go check on the men," she said quickly.

Dr. Baylor snagged her by the arm. "Won't you please allow me to take you out to dinner?"

"Oh, I—I suppose. But just this once." And only because the notion of eating in a restaurant made her mouth water.

She moved away from him, but even as she knelt next to a soldier, she felt the doctor's eyes on her.

34

Day after day, Levi rode out to the Garlow place, but each time he went home disappointed. He'd grown weary of dressing in a suit and sprucing himself up on the chance he'd find Josie at the residence, so today, he simply wore a pair of trousers and a decent shirt. He hadn't even bothered to shave. What was the use? She wouldn't be here.

However, when he rounded the bend that brought the family farmhouse into view, he saw a man out front tending to a horse's shoe. His heart lurched, and he pressed his heels into Stony's sides, urging him into a trot. The man suddenly turned and grabbed a rifle from his saddlebag. "Stop right there, mister," he hollered, aiming at Levi.

Levi reined in Stony and raised his hands. "I mean no harm, sir. I'm just looking for someone. I'm Levi Albright. You may have heard of Edward Albright. That's my pa."

The fellow promptly lowered his rifle, and Levi relaxed. "Why, 'course, I heard o' him. Builds mighty fine furniture. Fine family, the Albrights."

"Yes, sir."

"Well, if you're lookin' for Mrs. Garlow, she won't be back till sometime next week. Her former husband's brother passed on, and she took a long journey by train to stay a spell with the relatives. I just been comin' over every day at odd times to see to what livestock she's got an' t' feed the dogs and goats an' chickens."

"Oh." Levi's heart took a little dive. "Well, I was actually looking for her niece, a Miss Josephine Winters."

The man shook his head and pulled on his scruffy beard. "Don't know nothin' 'bout no niece. She jes' has that whole passel o' kids."

"And they all went with her to visit the relatives?"

"Oh, no, sir. They went to stay with some friends. No, Mrs. Garlow couldn't afford to buy coach tickets for all them kids. 'Sides, she didn't want them missin' school. They're over…hmm, let me think, now." He took off his hat and scratched the back of his head. "The Tuckers. Yep, that's where they went."

"The Tuckers? Might you tell me where they live, sir?"

"Why, sure. Y' just follow that road you was just on, oh, a good mile or so north, till you come to a fork. Veer right, then go a fair piece, maybe another couple o' miles. You'll come to another crossroad. Let me see, here…I believe you'll go left. Farm's about a quarter mile up that road. You get lost, y' just stop an' ask anyone y' see. They'll be able t' tell ya. Most everyone knows the Tuckers."

Levi repeated the directions aloud to the fellow, who nodded a couple of times. "You'll find it, no problem."

Levi should have known he wouldn't find the place, "no problem." After stopping at two houses that were not the Tucker residence, he finally reached what he hoped would be his final destination. Despite the chill in the air, there was a whole herd of kids playing out front and in the backyard of the rambling two-story brick farmhouse. A young boy came running up to greet him. "I'm Harold. Who are you?" he asked, as boldly as could be. He couldn't have been more than three or four years old.

"Is this the Tucker farm?" Levi asked.

The boy shrugged. "I don't know."

Another boy came along, a bit older. "Hello, there," he said. "You lookin' for somebody?"

"Yes, actually. Is this the Tucker farm?"

"Sure is. You want to see my ma?"

"No. Well, maybe. I'm just...are all the Garlow kids here?"

He nodded. "They been stayin' with us. Why?"

He breathed a sigh of relief. "And what about...what about a young lady named Josephine Winters?"

"Who?" the boy asked, squinting up at him. A cloud of steam came out of his mouth with every breath.

"Who you talkin' to, boy?" came a woman's voice. "Help y'?" she asked, stepping down from the porch. Like the fellow Levi had encountered at the Garlow farm, she was armed, her rifle hefted high. She looked like she knew how to use it, too. Levi supposed wartime set folks on edge, no matter how far removed they might be from the battlefield.

"I mean no harm, ma'am. I'm looking for Josephine Winters. She's Mrs. Garlow's niece."

The woman lowered her rifle. "Josephine's not here. What's your name, Mister?"

"Levi Albright."

"Albright. Don't sound familiar."

"Levi Albright?" A young girl came up behind the woman on the porch. "Are you really Levi Albright?"

"Yes, and you are?"

"I'm Allison."

"You know him?" the woman asked.

"Yes! Well, no, not actually, but Josie does. Please, Mrs. Tucker, might we invite him inside? He's quite harmless, I promise you."

Mrs. Tucker didn't look entirely convinced. She narrowed her eyes at Levi. "I ain't accustomed to invitin' strangers into my house, but I s'pose if she says it's all right, then we're safe."

Levi grinned. "I'm about as dangerous as a dead mosquito, ma'am."

"Well then, you come right in."

⌒

All the next day, Josie deliberated over how to get out of the proposed supper date with Dr. Baylor. She could feign a headache, but that would be an outright lie. She could say Dr. Edwards required her assistance, but he had said nothing of the sort; in fact, there had been no new cases of typhoid in three days, so activity had slowed in the quarantine tent. She could simply tell him she was too tired, which would be the truth; but then he would probably argue that she required sustenance to rejuvenate her body. Or...she could just go with him. The thought of a good restaurant meal did make her mouth water.

Around five o'clock, she went upstairs to her closet-sized room with a basin of warm water, a bar of lye soap, and a clean cloth, intending to give herself a sponge bath. She wasn't about to go overboard prettying herself up, but she looked forward to getting out of her soiled clothing and dressing in something halfway decent. It would be nice to look like a real lady for a change.

Dr. Baylor met her promptly at 6:30 in the hospital foyer. He told her she looked lovely, then gave her his arm. She took it, and as they stepped outside, she couldn't help but think that anyone who saw them would assume they were a couple. Dusk was upon them, and across the street, a lamplighter carried his torch from one light to the next, bringing illumination to the road.

"I've procured a carriage for our little excursion," he told her. "It should be along most any minute. I thought we'd eat at a fine little place by the river. I've gone there a few times and have found the food to be quite superb."

"That sounds lovely," Josie said, "but, really, I don't expect any special treatment."

He leaned closer. "Ah, but you are a lovely lady who deserves some special treatment. I told you I've been watching you closely."

She felt the warmth of a blush on her cheeks. "I don't know what to say."

"Say nothing, my dear. Just accept that you're someone worthy of notice."

"Well, thank you."

He was a fine-looking man—not as handsome as Levi, of course, but attractive. She knew she should be flattered by his attention, but, for the life of her, she couldn't drum up much enthusiasm for him. The only thing that truly interested her was his mention of superb food. Even now, her stomach rumbled from hunger. The biting wind made her anxious for the arrival of the carriage, and she found herself leaning closer to him simply for warmth.

"Mid-January, and still no snow on the ground," he mused. "Do you suppose we'll escape it this year?"

Josie shrugged. "It would be nice, although it's certainly cold enough for snow. We may as well have some to cover up all this mud."

"That's true enough. Ah, I believe our ride has come." A two-wheeled, covered carriage led by one horse pulled in front of the hospital. "Thank you, Driver," Dr. Baylor said to the man seated in front. "Please deliver us to Grady's Restaurant at Fifteen Cameron Street."

"Certainly, sir."

Dr. Baylor opened the carriage door, offered Josie a hand up, and then climbed in behind her. Once he closed the door, the driver set off. It took only a few minutes to reach their destination, and once there, Dr. Baylor stepped down first, paid the driver, and instructed him to return in 90 minutes, then lent Josie a hand down. It was all so proper and slightly awkward. Never having been formally courted before, she had no idea how to act. With Levi, everything had always been so carefree and easy; but with Dr. Baylor, she felt an obligation to act a particular way. He gave off an air of importance, as if he had been raised around wealth and prestige. Perhaps he would enlighten her tonight as to the details of his upbringing and background.

He offered her his arm again, so she took it once more, and he laid a warm hand over hers as he led her to the wooden sidewalk and helped her onto it. The clip-clop of horses' hooves on the road mingled with the sound of their own boots traversing the planks.

One could tell by the broken windows on the storefronts, the streets full of armed soldiers in blue, and the muddy, worn roads, that war had ravaged the now Union-occupied city of Alexandria. On the boarded-up door of the building next to Grady's Restaurant were printed the words "Birch & Price, Slave Dealers." If the war had accomplished anything, it was freeing some three million enslaved people.

The doctor opened the restaurant door, and a wonderful wave of welcome heat and enticing aromas wafted out to greet them. "Shall we?"

Josie smiled and eagerly proceeded inside.

35

*L*evi rubbed a circle in the frost covering the train window to peer out at Alexandria. Thanks to Allison Garlow, he'd learned that Josie had come here to work at Mansion House Hospital. His heart thumped hard against his chest at the thought that he could be just minutes away from laying eyes on her. *Finally.* The past several days had sped by, and in just a few weeks, he would report for duty. He hoped and prayed for an opportunity to let Josie know how he felt about her.

Last night, he'd lingered at the big house after supper with the family and had a very long talk with his parents in which he'd told them about his call into the ministry and also shared that he'd fallen in love with a young woman named Josephine Winters. The three of them had gathered in the living room around the warm fireplace after his siblings went to bed. Levi had been staying in his own house, a mile away.

Of course, his mother had approved of neither his "calling" or "the girl," as she referred to her. "Thee would pass up thy chances with Mary Foster when she is such a good match for thee?" Mother had asked. "She's devout and humble, not to mention pretty."

Levi had smiled. "Yes, Mother, I know all that. I met her, remember? I don't deny she is quite lovely, and we had a nice chat. We just…we didn't quite connect, and it wasn't just me. It was both of us."

His mother had pursed her lips while clenching a handkerchief as tightly as if she were trying to wring the life out of it. "Quakers do not accept pastorate calls, Levi."

"Which is precisely why I would not be preaching in the Friends' Society."

"What?" The way she'd lurched forward, he'd thought her dainty little prayer cap would fly right off her head. "Thee would go to another denomination? But...but thee has always been a Quaker."

"Quakers are not the only Christian denomination, Mother."

"No, I suppose not...but does thee really wish to leave thy roots behind?"

"Thee isn't planning to disown me, I hope."

"Well, of course not." She'd wrinkled her brow and given him a pained expression. "I'm not so straitlaced as to do that, but I shan't pretend to like it, either."

His father had cleared his throat and straightened his shoulders. "I'm proud of thee, Son. A bit disappointed that thee won't be taking over the family farm, as I have long dreamed, but it is always best to go the way the Lord leads if thee hopes to find true peace and joy."

Levi could always count on his father to calm the waters. He had a special knack for speaking the voice of reason to his wife and in somehow convincing her to compromise.

"Had thee decided to resume the livelihood of farming, thee might have wondered all thy life if there was something different thee should have done. I do not wish—nor does thy mother—for thee to choose thy life's pathway based upon our desires. Rather, we want thee to go the way the Lord leads." He'd nudged his wife in the side. "Isn't that right, Mother?"

She'd come to attention. "Well, of course, thy father speaks the truth. But that doesn't mean I have to be happy about it."

At that, Levi had given a low chortle. "I thank thee both for thy support."

"As to this *girl*—this disdainful woman who disguised herself as a boy to join the Union—how could thee possibly have been taken in by her? She committed a deceitful act and shows little promise as a godly preacher's wife."

Levi had smiled. "She is quite lovely, actually, and she has a deep faith and love for the Lord. Thee shall see it for thyself when thee meets her."

"And when will that be?" she'd asked, her tone a little snarly.

Levi had sighed. "I don't know. I finally located her, and now it's just a matter of meeting up with her so we can talk."

"Humph. Well, keep us informed," his mother had said, sounding none too impressed.

His father, on the other hand, had issued him a half smile and an approving nod. Levi had grinned back.

Now, as the train came to a huffing, puffing stop, Levi took another gander out the frosty window. A few people roamed the streets, but the area wasn't what one would call "bustling"—probably due to all the Union soldiers standing guard, rifles in hand. Whenever the army came in and occupied a town, there were always certain repercussions, including hard feelings coming from all sides. In some ways, Levi could sympathize with the South. After all, the government had moved in and uprooted their very livelihood, seizing what they considered to be their property, and claiming ownership of something it hadn't worked to build. No wonder the sense of bitterness ran so deep.

He stood to his feet, his body stiff from the ride, his nerves as taut as a new rope. When the train door opened with a loud rumble, a blast of glacial air poured into the car, curling around his ankles. He buttoned his coat close to his throat, situated his hat on his head, picked up his satchel, and stepped into the aisle to make his way to the door. "Lord, help me find her yet tonight," he whispered under his breath.

Outside, he approached a couple of fellows on a street corner and asked for directions to Mansion House Hospital.

"Ah, yes, the old Green's Hotel. It's about a mile up the road. Y' take this here street, King, several blocks thataway, then turn left at Fairfax and walk another block or so. If you come to the Potomac, you best turn around, 'cause you went too far. You can walk it in about twenty minutes, or you can hail yourself a horse-drawn cab."

"Thanks." Levi decided the walk would do him good and give him time to sort out his thoughts. The frigid air pummeled him as he walked toward the river, his steps fervent and purposeful, his mind filled with anxiety and eagerness alike. He could hardly wait to see Josie's face, the glimmer in her eyes and the glow of her cheeks. All he could do was pray it would go well.

Because he'd turned what could have been a stroll into a near jog, he reached his destination in just under fifteen minutes. Night had fallen, so a series of streetlamps lit the way, and the hospital windows themselves glowed with lamplight. When the hospital came into view, he paused across the street to survey the four-story structure. Was Josie tending to injured soldiers even now? Or might she be asleep? It was an odd time of day to pay someone a call, and yet, after traveling this far, he doubted he'd be able to sleep without at least saying hello to her. His heart jumped with anticipation. He swallowed a hard lump, gathered his wits, and set off across the muddy road. The street itself was lifeless, save for the occasional horse and buggy passing by. A few men stood on the sidewalk in front of the building next door, smoking cigarettes as they conversed.

Levi opened the big door of the converted hotel and stepped inside the hospital. A few nurses walked past, entering rooms on either side of him or ascending the wide staircase just ahead. They paid him no heed. He finally caught the attention of an older woman wearing a rather severe expression. "Excuse me, ma'am," he said.

She paused, a basin in hand, and scanned him from top to bottom. "Yes?"

"I'm looking for someone—a Miss Winters."

"Don't know 'er."

"She's a nurse here."

"As are most of the women here. Might be we work different shifts. Sorry, can't help you."

She left him standing in the middle of the foyer feeling helpless. He peeked into a large room to his right. Almost every inch of it seemed to be taken up with soldiers lying on cots, some sleeping, others crying out, and some simply staring into space, their expressions lifeless. The chaplain in him sought to comfort them, but he had to lay aside that urge and seek out Josie instead. Another nurse walked past, and he tried to grab her attention, but she was too busy to notice him.

Finally, someone had the courtesy to approach him. "You're looking a little lost, Mister. Can I help you?"

"Thanks. I'm trying to locate a nurse named Josephine Winters."

"Josephine Winters. Hmm. I can't say I know—"

"Josephine Winters?" a female voice cut in from behind Levi. "I know her."

The first nurse departed, and the second pushed a lock of white hair out of her eyes. "I believe she's out for the evening." She lifted her chin and studied him through her spectacles. "Who are you, might I ask?"

"My name's Levi Albright, ma'am. Might she have gone to a hotel room or something?"

She tossed back her head and laughed. "Hotel room? Mr. Albright, the nurses here are quite fortunate to find a vacant corner in which to lie. Just the same, I believe I overheard someone say she'd stepped out with Dr. Baylor."

"Dr. Baylor?"

She leaned in closer and winked. "I'm quite certain he has his eye on her, and I can't say I blame him. She's a fine nurse, works herself to the bone and cares deeply about what she does. She's a pretty thing, too." She stuffed her hands into her apron pockets, then eyed him as though it had only now occurred to her that she may have said too much. "Here I am, running off at the mouth. Forgive me. I would imagine she'll be back before too long. You could probably make yourself at home on that bench over there." She nodded to the side. "It's better than standing outside, isn't that right?"

Numbness settled around his chest. How quickly she'd forgotten his kisses, to have a beau already. No doubt, she'd wanted to forget Levi, or she would have given him her address. What had made him think otherwise?

"Are you all right, sir?" the nurse asked. She touched his arm. "You know, I just blurted out all that information without giving it one thought. I'm sorry if I've touched a nerve. I didn't mean—"

"No, that's fine. Really." Of course, it wasn't, but he smiled in order to hide his downcast mood.

Someone called for her, so while she excused herself, he moved to the bench she'd indicated, and plunked himself down upon it. He would sit here just long enough to warm up, and then...well, he wasn't quite sure what he'd do next. After a few minutes, he stood and made his way back to the door. Maybe he'd wait across the road and watch for Josie's return. If he could just get a glimpse of her, it might help him decide how to proceed.

Outside in the chilly wind once more, he set his hat firmly on his head, looked both ways, and hurried across the road to avoid being struck by the two-wheeled carriage that was slowing to a stop in front of the hospital. Seeking shelter in a covered doorway of a business that was closed for the night, he leaned against the wall, prepared to wait out Josie's return.

A couple disembarked the carriage. The fellow paid the driver, and as soon as the carriage pulled away, the man led the woman toward the hospital. Instead of opening the door for her, though, he directed her to the side of the building, and the two of them huddled close together. He placed his hands on her shoulders and bent low to whisper something in her ear, and she bubbled forth a flutter of laughter. Levi squinted in an effort to see better. He couldn't say for sure, given the distance and the long coat the woman wore, but her height and form certainly resembled that of Josie. The fellow spoke again, prompting another peal of laughter, this time loud enough for Levi to recognize the familiar tone of Josephine Winter's giggle. The fellow brought his face close to hers, and the next thing Levi witnessed was the two of them kissing. Josie even lifted her arms to encircle the man's back.

Levi huffed as a mixture of anger and resentment surged through him, followed by a huge wave of jealousy. Just over a month ago, he'd been kissing her; and now, here she was, fawning over someone else. Was she truly that fickle, or was he simply stupid and naïve? It took all his strength and willpower not to march across the street and give her a piece of his mind—and the fellow, a hard fist to the face. He'd spent days tracking her down, only to finally find her—in someone's else's arms. Frustration nearly strangled him. When the kiss ended, the fellow gave her one last embrace, which she readily fell into, and then he led her to the hospital door and followed her inside.

Levi stood there, staring and blinking, blinking and staring, his mind and body overwhelmed by shock. He deliberated between walking back across the road to seek her out and turning around to go back to the train station. He stood there, praying for an answer, but nothing came to mind that gave him any clarity, perhaps because he'd been so caught off guard that he couldn't think straight.

If he were a cussing man, a whole string of unsavory words probably would've rolled out of him; but, since he wasn't, he just stood there, trying to figure out his next move, asking God for a forgiving spirit. His heart hurt, his body trembled, and his head ached. The cold didn't help. He could hardly spend the next half hour simply standing here, so he made the sudden decision to return to the train station. Maybe he'd send her a letter once he got back home, and tell her what he'd witnessed—or maybe he wouldn't. Maybe he'd give the whole matter some time, and then see if he had the courage to come back and try again. Or maybe, just maybe, he'd try to put her out of his mind.

❧

Josie pulled her nightgown out of her small trunk, sputtering to herself the entire time. Why on earth had she allowed Martin Baylor to kiss her—and on their first date? Truth be told, she hadn't enjoyed one thing about the wet kiss, forget that she'd pretended she did by enfolding him in her arms. Now he would surely expect a second date from her, and then a third, and so forth. She supposed he'd been affable enough, but the restaurant meal was what had impressed her the most. In fact, she'd devoured it like a starved urchin—baked chicken, mashed potatoes and gravy, fresh bread, and, for dessert, a good-sized piece of apple pie, still warm, to boot. In all, the food had tasted almost as good as Aunt Bessie's cooking. Perhaps she'd kissed him out of a sense of obligation. But how to explain that to him? *Thank you for your kindness in treating me to a restaurant meal. My full-fledged kiss was merely a way of expressing my gratitude.*

She grumbled to herself while yanking off her clothes and then pulling the nightgown over her head. Why did she have to be so inexperienced when it came to men? She didn't know the first way to act around them—unless she was sitting around a campfire with a slew of them, pretending to be one, herself. She did know, after spending an evening with Dr. Baylor, that she was no longer impressed by the man. He'd talked mostly about himself and his own accomplishments, inquiring very little about her life, not that she would have divulged many details.

A slight rap sounded on her door. She jolted with surprise. "Yes?"

"Open, please," said a woman's voice.

She moved to the door and opened it a tiny slice. There stood Nurse Browning, of all people. The older woman gave her a sheepish grin. "Sorry to be a bother, miss, but a man came to inquire after you while you were out with Dr. Baylor this evening."

She opened the door an inch further. "A man? Did you get his name?"

"A Mr. Albright, miss."

"A Mr. Al—what?" she screeched, probably loud enough to have wakened every patient on the third floor.

"Forgive me, but I didn't ask him any questions. After he left, I got to thinking that perhaps I should have. He didn't offer any details, so I didn't inquire. Now I'm wondering if perhaps he meant something to you. I don't know. I told him you were out with Dr. Baylor. Was I remiss in doing that?"

"Where did he go?" Josie demanded, ignoring the question. She could hardly stop the fluttering of her pulse. "Did he say what he wanted? Is he still here? Did he—"

"Miss." Nurse Browning stuck her hand through the opening in the door and touched Josie's arm. "He told me nothing. Absolutely nothing. And I didn't want to appear nosey. As for whether he is still here, the answer would be no. He did sit on the bench down in the main area for a short while, but the next time I looked, he had disappeared. I even looked outside, but I didn't see him. Sorry. He didn't give me any indication if he was coming back. I just thought you should know." She started to turn, then stopped and looked at Josie again. "Did you have a nice evening with Dr. Baylor?"

"Oh, yes, it was fine, thank you," Josie answered distractedly.

"Well, that's good. I'll be going now."

Josie just stood there, dumbfounded, as Nurse Browning rounded the corner and disappeared. Levi had come to Mansion House Hospital—to see her? But, why? Wasn't he supposed to be with Company B? She closed the door, then leaned back against it, brought her clasped hands just beneath her chin, and closed her eyes. She had to find him. She wouldn't sleep a wink until she did.

She tore off her nightgown and jumped back into her clothes, then dashed down three flights of stairs to the main level. She ran to the door, wearing nothing but her dress and boots, and peered outside. It was still and cold, with nary a soul in sight. Where had he gone? Would he return? Had he perhaps found a nearby hotel to spend the night? There had to be several in Alexandria, but she could hardly walk from one to the next to inquire after him. *Oh, Lord, where is he? What made him come here, and how did he know where to find me in the first place?*

The cold air forced her back inside. With a long sigh, she took a few steps, pausing to peek in the rooms on her left and right. Most of the patients were sleeping, albeit fitfully. A few nighttime nurses walked from one bed to another, checking on the sick and wounded. Sorrowfully, Josie made for the stairs, and started her ascent. She wouldn't find him tonight, so she would do the next best thing: write him a letter and post it first thing in the morning.

36

*L*evi caught the eleven o'clock train, which had him arriving in Philadelphia around three in the morning. He was exhausted, but he determined to sleep in his own bed for the remainder of the night, so he searched out a driver to return him to his little farmhouse on Sunset Ridge. When he arrived back home, at a quarter to four, he didn't even take the time to undress; he just fell into bed, half dead. It had been an emotional night. He'd even had to swipe at a stupid tear or two while gazing out the frosty train window. He'd been a fool, and a lovesick one, at that. Well, later today, he would buck up, go out in the fields with his brothers, maybe chop some wood, muck some stalls, and work himself to the bone. That would help what ailed him. That, and prayer. Lots of prayer.

He awoke at nine and threw off the covers. He couldn't remember the last time he'd slept so late. Of course, he didn't usually go to bed at four a.m., except on the rare occasion that he stayed up all night tending to the sick and wounded, praying over them and reading the Scriptures. He wasn't due to report till February 11. That would give him plenty of time to study his Bible and listen for the Holy Spirit's still, small voice.

As he stood at the cook stove, making a pot of coffee, the sound of an approaching wagon had him pulling aside a curtain to look out the window. With long strides, Levi hastened to the door and opened it. "Papa, what on earth brings thee here at this hour? I haven't even stoked my fire yet, so it's plenty cold."

His father grinned while climbing down from his rig. "That's all right. I was planning a trip into Philly today and saw a bit of movement in thy kitchen, so I thought I'd stop by to say good morning." He walked with a limp, due to a serious fall he'd taken several years ago. Funny how Levi had never once heard him complain about his leg, though it must have pained him. "I thought thee had gone to Alexandria to seek out that young woman named Josephine."

"'Tis true, I did. But...well...things didn't quite turn out as I'd hoped they would."

"No? Care to tag along to the city with me and talk about it?"

Levi tossed out every other plan he'd made for the day. What could possibly be better than a father-son talk? "Give me a few minutes to shave and change into something different, and I'll be right with you!"

Despite the bite in the January air, Edward Albright never once hurried his two-horse team along the main thoroughfare to Philadelphia. If anything, the horses lagged, their giant nostrils huffing puffy clouds of steam with every breath, Papa holding loosely to their reins and allowing them to choose their own pace.

During the journey, Levi talked about the war, about his friends, and about the bloody battles, telling his father things he never dreamed of telling anyone—things he wouldn't think of sharing with his sisters, his mother, or even his younger brothers. His father asked many questions, and as Levi answered each one, his father didn't bat an eye; he just listened calmly, keeping his gaze trained on the road ahead.

"Thee has seen far more than most should see in a lifetime, Son—certainly far more than I—but I want thee to know that my pride for thee borders on sinful," Papa commented with a grin. Then he sobered to add, "Thee has sacrificed a great deal, and, believe it or not, I thank thee for taking a stand, even going against thy mother's wishes—yes, even that. Don't think for a minute that she isn't just as proud of thee as I. She may not voice it as readily, but believe it."

With a choked voice, Levi replied, "I thank thee for that, Papa."

They rode along in silence for a time, each one digesting the conversation they'd had till that point. After a bit, Papa heaved a sigh that was louder than usual. "All right, we've skirted the issue long enough. It's time thee told me what happened with this woman named Josephine. Did you both decide it wasn't going to work? Did she ask thee to leave?"

It was Levi's turn to sigh. "Not exactly, no. I...I didn't actually talk to her at all. I saw her in the embrace of another man, and so I left. That's pretty much the end of the story."

His father's lips formed a frown. "That's it? Thee saw her having an intimate moment with another man, and so thee turned around and left?"

"Well, yes. The sight didn't exactly sit well with me."

"I shouldn't imagine it would have, particularly since thee declared thy love for her—and she betrayed thy trust."

Levi winced just slightly.

"I would do the same—*if* I'd declared my love to thy mother before I married her and caught her kissing another man. Good chance I wouldn't give her a second to explain herself, either."

A bitter lump formed at the back of Levi's throat.

"Thee *did* declare thy love to her, correct?"

Levi hung his head. "Not...exactly."

"Well, does thee expect her to stay true to thee if she is ignorant of thy intentions?"

He felt like an utter dunce, but still, he wasn't sure what would have been a better response. "What was I supposed to do?" he asked. "Stand there and watch them fawn over each other?"

"How about fight for her?" His father drew the team of horses to a halt right there in the middle of the road, then turned his body to face Levi. "Son, does thee know nothing about women?"

"I...no, I must admit I don't." It was true. Never in his life had he loved a woman. Until now.

"Well...." His father stroked his beard. "One thing thee must learn is this: If thee loves someone, thee doesn't just give up without a struggle. How did I fail to set thy mind straight on at least that one point?" He shook his head. "Thee must return to Alexandria, and without delay."

As if he'd just been stuck in the rear end with a needle, Levi jerked to life, his spine going as straight as a steel rod. "Papa!" he shouted. "Get me to the train station!"

The horses hardly knew what hit them when his father snapped them into a fast gait. Into the cold wind, he gave a hearty laugh, then yelled to his team, "Onward, beasts! We've no time to dawdle."

⌒

The next morning, finding a break in her hospital routine, Josie hurried up the street to the post office. In her letter to Levi, she'd expressed how sorry she was that she'd missed his visit; that she had wanted nothing more than to see him, and that, if he chose to return, she would heartily welcome him. She did not speak of love, for she didn't feel she had that right; but she hoped with all her might he would read between the lines.

She still wondered what had brought him to Alexandria. Had he come on special business for the army? And if that were the case, how would he have learned of her assignment at Mansion House? Moreover, once he had located her and asked for her whereabouts, what had gone through his mind when Nurse Browning had informed him she'd gone out with another man? Had it bothered him at all, or did he still consider her as a mere friend? The questions swirled in her head like so many snowflakes—the ones she still waited to see in Virginia, to no avail.

It was another brisk, winter morning, but at least a splendid sun warmed her shoulders as she walked. She passed a few armed soldiers keeping watch; several men standing on a street corner, jawing about the war; a couple of horse-drawn wagons parked in front of a general store; and several deserted buildings with broken windows. How many citizens of Alexandria had fled to parts unknown to avoid the conflict?

She couldn't help but feel sorry for the displaced people who had played no active role in slavery and had no argument with the government, but had still ended up victims of the war. Every day, she prayed for the end to come; every day, the war raged on, with no indication from General Lee of a willingness to concede. How many more would have to die?

After posting her letter, Josie did not feel ready to return to the hospital. She'd informed the head nurse on duty, Mrs. Probst, that she had a few errands to run, never indicating a specific time she expected to return. She decided to walk down to the riverbank and watch the ships come and go. It would be a welcome respite from the physically and emotionally demanding task of tending to soldiers, both Union and Confederate. Yes, Mansion House was a Union hospital, but in the event Confederate soldiers needed care, there was usually one doctor or another who agreed to treat them, even if begrudgingly. Several nurses who were sympathetic to the South volunteered their help, as well; and so, in the midst of battle, both sides found some common ground and forced themselves to work together.

The waters of the Potomac were smooth today. Absently, Josie thought back to her near drowning, and how Levi had not thought twice about jumping in to rescue her. That brought to mind Howard Adams and her final words to him, trying to convince him that God loved him. She shook her head and sighed.

She found a deserted bench along the bank to sit and watch the ships pass—some carrying cargo, others bearing passengers; some were fishing vessels, while still others were army ships bearing Union emblems and American flags. As she sat there, pondering, an uncommon sense of peace came over her. It wasn't something easily described, just a feeling of well-being in the midst of turmoil. Even that awful kiss she'd allowed from Dr. Baylor last night could not crowd out the sweet presence that suddenly surrounded her.

Her hands had grown cold, since she'd forgotten her gloves in her room, so she stuffed them into her pockets. When she did, her right fist brushed against a folded piece of paper she now recalled having put there for safekeeping, a paper on which she'd copied some special verses from Psalm 46 while staying at Aunt Bessie's. She withdrew the paper, carefully unfolded it, and started reading aloud: "*God is our refuge and strength, a very present help in trouble. Therefore will not we fear, though the earth be removed, and though the mountains be carried into the midst of the sea; though the waters thereof roar and be troubled, though the mountains shake with the swelling thereof. There is a river, the streams whereof shall make glad the city of God, the holy place of the tabernacles of the most High. God is in the midst of her; she shall not be moved: God shall help her, and that right early.*'"

She stared at the verses momentarily, not fully grasping their meaning, yet still taking comfort in them. "God is with me," she whispered with upturned face, as the brisk air curled around her cheeks. "I have nothing to fear because even though turmoil surrounds me, God is in my midst, and He will help me through these troubled times." The simple revelation made her smile from ear to ear. She reverently refolded the paper and put it back in her pocket, then stood, raised her face to the sky, and whispered, "I thank You, Father, for always finding a way to make Your presence known to me."

That sense of deep, settled peace followed her all the way back to Mansion House, but she might have known it wouldn't linger after she passed through the hospital doors. Commotion of every kind swirled around her, with doctors blaring orders and nurses scurrying about, the arrival of several patients having created quite a stir. The newcomers lay on stretchers in the main hallway, awaiting beds. The hospital held several hundred beds, most of which were occupied. It was a matter of determining who, among the new patients, stood in direst need of care.

"Where have you been?" the breathy whisper of Dr. Baylor sounded in her ear.

She turned with a smile that was half forced. "Good morning, Doctor. I had a few errands to take care of. I had no idea the ambulances were coming, or I would have hurried back."

"No need to worry. Old Edwards will whip this ship into order in no time. And don't you think it's time you called me Martin?" he added with a wink.

She sucked in a breath. "Oh, I don't think that would be proper."

He chucked her chin with his thumb and forefinger. "Nonsense. We're an item now. I understand there's been some talk about us."

Her head jerked back almost involuntarily. "There has? What sort of talk?"

He arched his eyebrows. "Let's just say news of our kiss has gotten out. Apparently, one of the nurses happened to be walking up the street at the time of our return from dinner. Women do love to talk, you know. And who doesn't desire a little romance in the middle of a war?" He grinned, then leaned closer to whisper, "Would you be so kind as to accompany me to Grady's Restaurant again tonight? Perhaps we might steal away afterward to a less public place."

"Not tonight, Doctor, and probably not again. I'm sorry. It's nothing personal against you. I simply don't wish to—"

"Dr. Baylor, you're wanted—now." The stern interruption by Dr. Edwards was quite welcome to Josie, even if the older doctor cast her a harsh, disapproving glance. "See to that injured patient at the end of the hall." He gestured with a bob of his head. "He could be dying, for all we know, and you're here dillydallying with a volunteer nurse."

"We'll talk about it later." Dr. Baylor drew closer and whispered, "We've only just begun, Josie. Do not tell me you are already quitting."

She took a step backward and straightened her spine. "We should not have kissed."

He raised his eyebrows in a sly expression. "I thought you enjoyed it."

"You thought wrong. I was not prepared, and thus I reacted in an improper manner."

"Dr. Baylor. Now." Dr. Edwards's firm voice sounded like a drill sergeant's directive.

Dr. Baylor turned to go, but then he stopped, narrowed his eyes on Josie, and presented her with an impish grin. "I'm not convinced. Women don't normally turn me down."

"Well, this one does."

He shook his head and stepped closer one more. "Like I said, we'll talk later." Then he hurried off, leaving Josie irritated to no end.

Dr. Edwards shot her a searing glare. To avoid his gaze, Josie picked up her skirts and hastened to find Nurse Probst to determine whether she was to work in the quarantine tent for yet another day.

⌒

The train's piercing whistle sounded at precisely 3:10 p.m., and a glistening sun shone through Levi's train window as he peered through the glass at Alexandria. He could hardly wait to see Josie, and this time, he vowed not to return to Sunset Ridge without at least speaking to her. He'd been plain foolish last night, running off like a tempestuous child when he witnessed Josie kissing that doctor. Well, not this time. Even if she had fallen under the spell of another man, he would tell her his true feelings. As his father had exhorted him on the way to the train station, "If thee loves someone, thee doesn't just give up without a fight." He would not give up so easily this time. He loved Josephine Winters, and if his profession of love was the last statement he ever uttered to her, at least he would have the satisfaction of having made it known.

He disembarked, this time having no satchel or even a change of clothing. He easily could have walked to Mansion House, but he wanted to reach the hospital as soon as possible, so he decided to hail a cab. Spying a Negro driver standing next to his horse, Levi started toward him.

"Where to, Mister?" the man asked.

"Mansion Street Hospital, please—on Fairfax."

"Certainly, suh. No luggage?"

Levi shook his head. "I left in somewhat of a hurry."

"Well then, please make y'rself at home." He gestured at the open carriage. "You can use that there blanket on the seat for some extra warmth, if y' want."

Levi's heart beat with such a rapid rhythm that it warmed him enough from within. "I think I'll be fine, but thank you, anyway." He stepped up, pushed the blanket aside, and plunked himself on the hard leather seat. Then the driver climbed up and, with a light crack of his whip, directed his horse east on King Street.

Levi remembered the route. He sat back, sniffing in the brisk air, and tried to plan out what he would say upon seeing Josie. *I love you, Josie. I want to marry you.* No, that was too direct. He needed to work his way into it. *I've come to make something clear to you, because I don't think I did a sufficient job of it before Grimms sent you on your way.* No, that wouldn't do. It sounded too cold. *Lord, give me the right words,* he prayed instead. *Because, if You don't, I'm afraid I'll make a royal idiot of myself.*

Once at the hospital, he pulled a few coins from his pocket and handed them up to the driver. The fellow gazed at them with wide eyes. "Thank you, suh!" Apparently, he hadn't expected such a generous tip. "You wantin' me t' wait for y', suh?"

Levi thought for a moment. "No, you be on your way. I'll hail another driver if I need one later. Thank you again."

After climbing out, he stood on the wooden sidewalk and watched the man drive away, his chest a mix of anticipation and jumping, frantic nerves. Gathering a deep breath for fortitude, he walked up to the hospital door, pulled it open, and stepped inside. It felt very much like the night before, with people hurrying in every direction; only, today was busier, and there were patients laid out on stretchers in the hallway. Men and women scurried past him, some in medical garb, others not. It was difficult to know whom to consult about finding Josie.

"Mister! Help me, mister." A soldier lying on a stretcher called out to him, his head lifted just high enough as to make eye contact with Levi.

Levi hastened to him, noting the Confederate uniform he wore. It was caked with blood.

"Are you a doctor?"

"No, sir, I'm sorry I'm not. But I am a chaplain. Might I pray for you?" Confederate or not, the man was a child of God, and Levi determined to show him respect.

The fellow reached up, grabbed the front of Levi's shirt, and pulled him closer. His rancid breath nearly knocked Levi over, although he should have grown used to the smell by now. Few soldiers were as fortunate as Levi, whose mother had, from the war's onset, kept him well stocked with tooth powder and brushes.

"I need a doctor, not a preacher. I'm shot. Can you tell somebody I need care?"

"I—I just arrived, Soldier, but try not to worry. I'm sure they know you're waiting." He touched the fellow's arm in a show of reassurance, then bowed his head over him, praying silently.

"Who are you?" The harsh male voice from behind drew him up short.

Levi pulled himself straight and turned around. "Sergeant Levi Albright, Twenty-third Pennsylvania Volunteers, Company B. The regiment's chaplain, sir."

The man—a doctor, if his bloodied apron were any indication—looked down his nose at him. "What in the world brings you here?"

"I'm on furlough until February eleventh."

"Fine, but that didn't answer my question."

"I'm looking for someone, sir. Might I ask who you are?"

"Edwards. Dr. James Edwards. I run this place."

"Ah, Dr. Edwards. Pleasure to meet you."

"Who're you looking for?"

"A volunteer nurse who goes by the name of Josephine Winters."

"Ah, the much-admired Miss Winters. Ever since her arrival at Mansion House, Dr. Baylor has had his eye on her—and his head in the clouds, shall we say. She's created a distraction, and once again, the fool man has disappeared on me. You're a chaplain, you say?"

"Yes, sir."

"Well, I hope your duties haven't called you here to perform a marriage ceremony between the two. If so, I'll be requesting from his captain that he give him an immediate transfer elsewhere. I don't have time for romances in my hospital."

"Um, no, I can assure you no one called me to perform such a task. In fact, it is my wish to steal her out from under the good doctor."

This time, Edwards's facial reaction was a bit different from his first. He lifted his chin a notch higher and rocked back on his heels. "Is that so? Well, I must say, I wish you the best. You'll find her out in the quarantine tent, assisting Dr. Morton. You go back out those front doors and turn right. At the side of the hospital, you might've noticed a stockade fence with an arched entryway. The tent's back there, along with a lot of vagrants and misplaced freedmen holing up. I'd advise against going in there, though. There's all manner of disease, worst of all typhoid."

"Sir, I've been in the army since eighteen sixty-one and dealt with my share of sickness. I've prayed with some typhus patients and haven't caught it yet. I trust I'm not about to catch it now."

"Well, just the same, you would be taking a risk by going in there."

"No more of a risk than Miss Winters is taking."

The doctor scratched his temple. "I suppose that's true enough. She is a good nurse—if she can just keep that pretty little head of hers turned in the opposite direction of Dr. Baylor."

Levi grinned. "I'll see what I can do to remedy that."

The Confederate soldier groaned again, and Levi looked down at him. "Are you going to be seeing to this soldier's needs, Doctor?"

Dr. Edwards frowned. "He's not dying. I've bandaged his wound, and I'll have a nurse administer another dose of pain medicine. As you can see, we're a bit swamped. There was a skirmish just south of here, but nothing for the books, as I understand it." He cleared his throat. "Now then, you go see what you can do to win over that nurse. Surely, being a gentleman of the cloth, you have the Man Upstairs on your side."

Levi smiled. The fellow wasn't nearly as gruff as he'd first thought. "I've certainly been praying to that end."

They nodded at each other before parting ways. Levi stepped out into the brisk air, glad for the sunshine, and plopped his hat back on his head. Horse and foot traffic were heavy today, with citizens and military members alike traversing the sidewalks. Levi looked to his right, located the stockade fence the doctor had mentioned, and made his way to it.

On the other side, he saw debris everywhere, and a host of makeshift tents and homemade wooden structures meant to provide a bit of shelter for the homeless. A number of small fires burned, over which were hung kettles of either food cooking or boiling water being used for washing laundry. Clotheslines were suspended between trees, strung with raggedy-looking pairs of pants, shirts, dresses, and skirts. His heart went out to each misplaced soul, black and white alike.

Finally, his gaze fell on a large tent with a smokestack. In front of it was a large sign blocking the doorway. It read, in large bold letters, "ISOLATION—DO NOT ENTER." His very soul clenched at the notion that the woman he loved was still risking her life, now to help the unfortunate soldiers stricken with typhoid. He wondered if she would even come with him if he asked, or if she'd so devoted herself to her calling that she wouldn't dream of deserting. Worse, had she already yielded to Dr. Baylor's charm? He took in a deep breath, then strode to the tent, his mind awash with all sorts of scenarios as he imagined how things might play out. *Please, Lord, let me not make a complete bungle of everything.*

37

*A*bout tonight, Josie: I know you said you did not wish to go out with me, but how about I promise to be good?" Dr. Baylor chuckled. "We could return to Grady's Restaurant, then take a buggy ride through town." He raised both arms. "It will be hands off, I promise."

Josie was growing plain irritated by the man's presence. She didn't even turn around to speak to him, only continued with her task of filling a pitcher with water. "Dr. Baylor, you should not be in here. If Dr. Morton were to discover you, he'd be most unhappy."

He stepped toward her. "But you haven't answered my question about tonight." His warm breath tickled the hairs on her neck in a most unpleasant way.

Josie huffed a loud breath and cleared her throat. "But I have, Dr. Baylor. I told you that I don't wish to accompany you this evening, and that answer still stands. It is really quite simple."

"You are a tease, Josephine Winters."

"Dr. Baylor? I believe Dr. Edwards is on the hunt for you."

Josie gasped and nearly fainted at the sound of Levi's voice. She whirled around, her skirts flaring, and found him standing just inside the tent's doorway, looking handsomer than any man she'd ever laid eyes upon. How different he looked out of uniform, with his well-tailored black wool coat and nicely pressed trousers. Her mouth hung open, and all she could think to do was cover it with her splayed hand. She couldn't find a single word. Not even his name rolled off her tongue.

"And who might you be?" Dr. Baylor demanded.

"Sergeant Levi Albright, of the Twenty-third Pennsylvania Volunteers, Company B."

Josie still hadn't removed her hand from her mouth, nor had she taken her eyes off Levi's tall, muscular frame. He'd taken off his hat and held it in both hands. Her mouth went as dry as sand, so that she couldn't even swallow.

Dr. Baylor looked from him to her and then back at Levi. "Pennsylvania Volunteers? Why are you dressed in plainclothes? And, more important, how do you know me?" Then he jerked his head around and looked at Josie. "Do you know this man?"

At least she had sense enough to bob her head up and down.

"Well, say something, Josephine. Who is he to you?"

She dropped her hand to her side. "He's someone—from my past."

"Your not-so-distant past," Levi put in.

"What…are you doing here?" she managed, with choked voice.

"I'm on furlough till February eleventh. I had thought to go in search of you, since I had time on my hands. You didn't make it easy on me, though, since you included no return address with your letter."

"You never mentioned this man," Dr. Baylor told her accusingly.

She straightened her spine, raised her head, and found her voice at last. "You did most of the talking on our one and only outing, Dr. Baylor, so I'm not sure when you expected me to tell you about him—or about anything pertaining to my past. If you had given me a chance, perhaps you would have discovered that I served, in disguise, with the Twenty-third Pennsylvania Volunteers."

"What?" He took a step back and fairly gawked at her, his eyes wide with shock. "I find that most distasteful, Josephine. Is that why your hair—oh, never mind. I find myself quite appalled."

"She made a fine soldier, Baylor."

The doctor shook his head. "What she did was against the law." He now gazed down at her as if she were no better than the dogs on the street that sniffed the ground in search of some tiny morsel. "Good day, Josephine Winters. Oh, and you can forget about that invitation to supper tonight."

"I already declined it!" Josie retorted as he brushed past without a reply.

Now she stood with Levi, in the midst of a half dozen typhus patients needing her care. Dr. Morton would return most any minute and wonder why she hadn't finished refilling the patients' water glasses, feeding them their cups of steaming broth, applying salve to their rashes, and changing out the cool cloths on their blistering foreheads.

"Go see...your soldier, Miss," mumbled the patient nearest her. "Y' been tendin' us...real good. We can wait."

She smiled down at him. "I shall return promptly."

Levi strode over to meet her. "Hello, Josie."

"You must go back outside. Let me get my coat and come with you."

"No, I'll stay. Have you forgotten my role? Perhaps I can lend a hand. After we've finished here, we can talk."

"But, you're not— You don't—" She rubbed her temples and shook her head, still trying to believe she was in the same room with Levi, and still so full of questions. "I'm so confused."

"Shh." He pressed a cool finger to her lips, and she nearly perished at the featherlight touch. "I said we'll talk later. Trust me," he whispered. She stared into his dark eyes for a moment, until he broke the spell by shucking his coat, tossing it into a nearby wooden chair, and brushing his hands together. "Now then, put me to work," he said, as matter-of-factly as if they'd been laboring side by side for months. And then, she remembered that they had done just that, only under very different circumstances.

"Well," she said with a shaky voice, "you should first go wash up in that pan of water over there. You'll find some lye soap and some fresh cloths to dry your hands." As he headed in the direction she indicated, she added, "Put on a clean apron, as well. You'll find one in the stack on the table next to the basin. We'll start by filling the men's glasses with fresh water. They must drink fluids continually, lest the fever causes them dehydration. Most of these men have been here for about ten days and are recovering nicely, although they still have a ways to go."

"Is there no one else here to help you?" Levi asked, his back to her while he washed up.

"There are a couple of other nurses, but Nurse Probst gave them other assignments for today. They should return tomorrow."

She could barely believe she was talking to him, with so many questions snaking around in her head. Was she dreaming?

Levi draped the laundered yet eternally stained apron garment over himself, and tied it at the back. "How do I look?"

She paused before replying and gave her head a couple of slow shakes. "Wonderful."

Dr. Morton returned just as Levi and Josie were finishing feeding broth to the last of their patients, his extended absence having given Josie a chance to adjust to Levi's presence in the tent. When the doctor cast Levi a quizzical glance, Josie quickly introduced the pair, explaining that Levi's position as chaplain of the 23rd Pennsylvania Regiment had given him much experience working with the injured and ill.

Dr. Morton pumped Levi's hand. "Nice to make your acquaintance, Chaplain. Thank you for your kind assistance in my absence. I was needed in the hospital to assist with a procedure that took longer than anticipated. Why don't you two take a break now? It looks like things are well in order here. I'll keep an eye on things."

"Really?" Josie asked.

"Of course. Go. Take as long as you need. Looks like you two have some catching up to do." He leaned forward and lowered his voice to say, "You should know that Dr. Baylor wasted no time in telling a few nurses that you were enrolled in the army as a man. The news is traveling fast."

Josie sucked in a breath.

"Don't worry, though," he hastened to add. "My hat's off to you, young lady, and Edwards told me he's about to contact Baylor's captain and request a transfer for the fellow. At any rate, you two go on, now."

They bundled up and set off along Fairfax Street, then turned down the next side street and headed for the river, strolling next to each other but not touching, their arms swinging at their sides. The air was still brisk, with a strong breeze, but the sun still shone brightly, and Josie's heart was warmed by a mixture of delight and excitement.

"How's the shoulder been?" Levi asked, breaking the silence.

"I barely think about it," she answered, which was true. "It bothers me from time to time if I happen to lift something heavy, but for the most part, it's healed nicely. There's not even much of a scar."

"Excellent. I prayed for you, you know, that it would go well—the healing."

"Thank you." She stuffed her gloved hands into her pockets.

As they neared Cameron Street, Levi said, "Let's go inside where it's warm. What about that place over there—Grady's Restaurant?"

"Uh...."

"No? What's wrong?"

"I—I dined there with Dr. Baylor."

"Is the food bad?"

She laughed. "No, it was quite lovely."

With a hand to her back, he urged her across the muddy road. "Well, come on, then. Let's go eat some lovely food."

⌒

They found a table at the back behind the potbelly stove, which gave them privacy, and talked as they sipped steaming coffee and slurped hot chicken soup. Josie first asked how Levi had found her, which set him off on a long and detailed account.

When he'd finished, Josie wrapped both hands around her coffee mug to warm them and, keeping her eyes averted from him, said, "You went through a lot of trouble to find me. I knew my aunt had gone to visit relatives and that my cousins were staying with friends, but it never occurred to me to tell anyone about it, least of all you. I'm quite impressed by your diligence. I thought...I thought perhaps you would want to seek out your Mary Foster."

He smiled. "She's not *my* Mary Foster. I met her, yes, because I felt I owed her that much, but I quickly realized we are not a good match. We parted on good terms, though."

Now, she raised her head, and he swore he saw a hopeful glint in her expression. "Really? That's too bad. I'm sorry."

"Are you?"

"Well, I mean, yes. You did correspond with her a great deal. You must've been somewhat disappointed."

"Writing letters to someone, and then meeting that person face-to-face, are two vastly different experiences. She had it in her head that I should've come to my senses and realized my 'folly' in joining the Union, considering my pacifistic upbringing, and that maybe I'd decide to come home early. I assured her I had no such plans." He braced himself for Josie's reaction to what he intended to say next. "She also wasn't at all happy about my notion to leave the Society of Friends to go into the preaching ministry."

Now her eyes lit like two bright candles, and her mouth curled into a big smile. "You're really going to do it, Levi?" She set down her coffee and leaned closer. "You're going to be a real preacher? That's wonderful! I'm so happy to hear it. You're truly gifted, you know. I believe it's exactly what God would have you do. Didn't I tell you a while back that you ought to consider it?"

He laughed. "I can't tell if I'm talking to Gordon Snipp or Josie Winters. You've suddenly come to life, and I like it!"

She lowered her chin but kept her eyes on him, her smile somewhat dimmed. "Would you rather I were still Gordon Snipp?"

He couldn't help it; he reached across the table and grabbed her folded hands in both of his. "Was that question asked in earnest?" he whispered. "Gordon Snipp was like a brother to me; I could tell him anything. Josephine Winters...well, she's a woman who truly intrigues me—and I care very much for her." He watched her intently, his eyes fairly soaking up her face, as he waited to see if she'd pull her hands out of his clasp. She didn't.

"But you told me, before I left, that you wanted to make it clear we were just friends. I had a distinct feeling you regretted even kissing me."

Levi shook his head. "That was plain dumb of me. In retrospect, I think what I meant to say, and should have said, was that if you were going to remain in Company B, then we had to be careful in the future—and play the *part* of friends. My words didn't come out the way I wanted them to. The day you left, I was in the process of looking for you so I could clear up what I'd said to you, and let you know how I really felt about you, but it was too late. When I got that note from you a few weeks later, with no return address, well, I started thinking maybe you weren't as interested in me as I was in you, and"—he kept a firm grip on her hands, thankful she still didn't pull away—"the truth is, I *did* wonder, especially when I finally tracked you down, only to catch you kissing Dr. Baylor."

"What? You saw that?" Now she did try to retract her hands, but he just clung to them the tighter.

"I was so infuriated, I left without trying to talk to you. It was my father who talked me into coming back today to at least give you a chance to explain yourself. You have to admit, that was some kiss the two of you shared."

"Oh, goodness, Levi, I'm so embarrassed you witnessed that. If it's any consolation, I didn't enjoy a single second of it—even though it may have looked as if I did. I…I don't know what to say, other than…well, I had no idea where I stood with *you*, and I didn't know how to behave when he started kissing me, and…I'm just not very experienced when it comes to interacting with men…as a woman, that is." She grinned.

Without taking one moment to consider that they were in a public place, albeit at the back of the room with only a few other patrons about, he pushed back his chair, stood just enough to reach his body over the table, cupped her face with both his hands, and planted a light kiss on her lips. She kissed him back, and even though it was a brief exchange, it was soft and perfect and tender, and exactly what he'd needed to do. He pulled back but didn't sit quite yet, just kept his face within inches of hers. "Where you stand with me, sweetheart, goes like this: I love you, and I will be the last man who ever kisses you. Understood?"

Her eyes went as round as globes, then moistened around the edges. "Levi…" she whispered.

"Yes?" He dared not move until she finished what she'd started.

"I love you, too." Her voice shook when she uttered the words, but they came off as sweet as any melody he'd ever heard. "I love you," she repeated, as if testing the declaration for her own ears. "I've never said those words to anyone but my own family members."

"Nor have I." He kissed her once more, and would have let the kiss go on forever, were it not for the fact that he sensed someone standing nearby. He pulled away and sat back down.

The waitress stood there holding a coffeepot and wearing a little smile on her face. "Sorry to break things up, but thought I'd check t' see if you wanted more coffee."

Levi knew his face had turned a nice shade of crimson. He glanced across the table at Josie, who gave her head a quick shake. Her cheeks had a rosy glow of their own.

What a pair they made. "Uh, I think we're fine, ma'am," Levi managed.

The waitress giggled. "Oh, you two look a little more than fine. You stay here as long as you want to, you hear? I won't be bothering you again."

"Thanks."

They stayed for another hour, holding hands and staring into each other's eyes. Josie asked him all about the fellows in Company B, wanting to know how they had reacted to her departure. He told her that they'd been surprised—well, except for Hiram McQuade, who'd claimed to have known the truth all along. They both laughed at that. He went on to tell her about Hiram's own bout with typhoid, and then his conversion to Christ, at which she gave a little shout of gladness.

They discussed Josie's desire to continue assisting in the war effort by volunteering at the hospital, and how rewarding yet challenging the job had been. Even when the topic turned serious, Josie seemed to wear a perpetual smile, and Levi found himself unable to keep his eyes off her. Oh, how good it felt to have things out in the open, and to finally know where they stood with each other. He grew impatient to ask her to be his bride, but hadn't yet decided how or when to do it.

"Well, I hate for this time to end, but I should probably be getting back to the hospital," Josie finally said with a sigh. "Dr. Morton will be needing me soon."

"Uh-huh." They were going back to the hospital, all right, but not to stay. His insides churned with excitement over the idea that had just formed in Levi's mind.

He helped Josie with her coat, then donned his own before tossing a few coins on the table. Seeing their waitress watching them, he waved to her, and she returned the gesture with a smile. "Have a nice evening," she called to them.

Outside, Levi hailed a cab driver who had parked nearby. From high in his seat, the fellow nodded, promptly directing his horse to where they waited on the sidewalk. Levi helped Josie aboard, and they took the seat directly behind the driver. "Take us to Mansion House Hospital, if you don't mind," Levi said.

"Yes, sir. Right away."

Levi put his arm around Josie as soon as they'd situated themselves. She snuggled close, so he took advantage of the opportunity by turning her chin and brushing a gentle kiss across her forehead before moving to her mouth. "I love you," he whispered.

"I believe I love you more," she said between kisses.

"Impossible."

38

When the cab stopped outside the hospital, Levi instructed Josie to go inside, pack all her belongings, and return to him.

She could hardly believe her ears. "What? I can't do that. I'm needed here."

"I know." He kissed her soundly once more, then set her back from him. "Trust me. Just do as I say, and leave the rest to me."

She was so in love that she dared not argue. Once her feet touched the ground, she traipsed up to the hospital, threw wide the door, walked inside, and nimbly climbed the three flights of stairs, thankful not to have passed a single colleague on the way to her tiny room. She had very few belongings, so it took no longer than a few moments to put everything into her small trunk. When done, she glanced around the dimly lit space, illuminated by only the hallway lantern, and caught a glimpse of her reflection in the wall mirror. She frowned. What did a handsome man like Levi see in such a plain-looking girl as she? Under her bonnet was a head of dark hair that just barely reached her shoulders. Her eyes, while a nice brown, had always seemed too large for her face. In her estimation, she'd have done better with a larger nose, and her lips seemed a bit too plump. Yet Levi said he loved her. What had she done to deserve his affections? Taking one last glance in the mirror, she shrugged, then lifted her satchel, walked out of the room, and closed the door behind her.

Outside the hospital once more, she approached the waiting cab, Levi standing beside it. Levi motioned her aboard with a sweep of his hand. "After you, madam."

She took the hand he offered her, and stepped up. "What are we doing, Levi? Please tell me. I don't want to abandon my post."

He smiled. "Don't worry, you're not abandoning your post. You'll be back. I know how dedicated you are to serving ailing soldiers, and I admire that. Just trust me, alright? You'll know the details soon enough." Then he climbed up and seated himself next to her.

They settled in, their sides nuzzled close together. The horses set off with a light snap of the driver's whip, and Josie twisted around for one last look at the hospital before it disappeared from view. "Dr. Morton will think I'm never coming back."

"Oh, I assured him you'd be back—after my furlough."

She gawked at Levi, her mouth hanging open. "Wh-what do you mean?"

He grinned. "You're coming with me to Sunset Ridge."

"I am?" The whole of her insides flipped over. "But—but I'm a terrible sight."

His eyes were soft and tender as his bare hand touched her cold cheek and lightly caressed it. "You are a sight, all right—a sight more beautiful than any I've ever seen." He dipped his head under her bonnet and kissed the tip of her nose. "Don't worry, honey. They will love you."

The train arrived in Philadelphia at a late hour, so they had a driver take them to a hotel, where Levi got them two separate rooms. It was *not* a shabby establishment, and all Josie could do while waiting for Levi to acquire the keys from the gentleman behind the counter was stand and gawk at all the ornate details of the lobby. She told herself she must surely look like a beggar girl in comparison to all the loveliness surrounding her.

"Only the best for one so fine," Levi said, as if reading her mind. He took the keys from the clerk, then clasped her by the hand and led her to the carpeted staircase. "We're on the second floor," he said while they climbed, her dirty, worn boots sinking into the plush carpet.

They walked down a corridor until Levi stopped at a door. "You'll stay in here," he said as he unlocked it. "I'll be right next door. In the morning, we'll go buy you a new gown, some undergarments, and some new shoes. Would you like that?"

Again, her mouth dropped open. "But I've never—"

He took her cheeks in both his hands and kissed her square on the mouth. It was delightfully delicious and ended all too quickly. "You look as charming as a flower in my eyes, but I know you aren't feeling very confident about meeting my family, even though they're as plain as peddlers. Besides…." He unbuttoned her coat, opened it, and gave her dress a good perusal. "Even though you wear an apron, your dress is blood-stained. I'd say you need a new one."

She had to agree with his assessment—but a new dress? "I've never owned a store-bought dress, Levi."

He chuckled. "Nor has any of my sisters. Mother sewed all their clothes until they grew old enough to stitch their own. Quakers dress in plain clothing."

"Then I shall wear something equally plain. I do not wish to outshine anyone, nor offend."

He put a finger under her chin. "You are not to worry, you hear? Be yourself, and everyone will love you."

"But—"

"Shh. After we purchase your dress and some new stockings and shoes, there'll be one more little surprise before we head to Sunset Ridge by carriage."

She pressed her palms together, feeling much like a spoiled child—a princess, even. "What do you have up your sleeve, Levi Albright?"

He laughed. "Did you not hear the word 'surprise'?"

She sighed. "I've never been so excited—or so pampered."

"And I've never been so happy."

Early the next morning, Levi rapped on Josie's door. She swung it open immediately, as if she'd been standing there waiting for hours. She looked as fresh as a new daisy, despite her stained dress, and he could see she'd primped. "I took a bath!" she announced.

He tossed back his head and laughed. "As did I. Don your coat, my dear. We are going on an adventure."

They started with a leisurely breakfast in a nice little restaurant downtown. From there, they walked to a department store to shop for a dress. With the help of a very friendly clerk, Josie tried on no fewer than ten before finally finding one she liked. She refused to wear a bustle or a hoop. She'd never worn either accessory in her life, and she had no intention of starting now. Actually, she'd narrowed her dress options down to two favorites, both of them simple blouses with floral patterns, lacy cuffs, and collars, but in different colors. So Levi told the clerk they'd take both of them. Josie gasped in shock and tried to protest, but the clerk smiled and advised Josie never to argue with a generous man. When the woman began wrapping the dresses in brown paper, Levi told her to wrap just one, since Josie would wear the other one. When Josie disappeared into the dressing room once more, the clerk leaned over the counter and whispered, "I believe your young lady would do well to allow me to primp her hair a bit. I could trim the edges with a pair of shears to give it a bit of shape, and then find her the perfect bonnet to accent her dress and outerwear. After that, I would be happy to assist her in finding some underthings, as well as stockings and just the right pair of high-tops…something practical, mind you, but also fashionable."

Levi nodded gratefully. "You, madam, are a fine saleswoman."

She offered him a demure smile. "I do my best."

Amused, he replied, "And while you're working your magic, I'll run over to that jewelry store across the street."

"Oh, but where shall I tell her you've gone?"

He paused. "Just remind her that I said I had one more surprise up my sleeve."

"Ooh!" The woman clapped with glee. "It will be my pleasure."

Levi slipped off to the jewelry store and, with a bit of assistance, picked out a lovely engagement broach—a stunning ruby set in gold and encircled by a rim of tiny diamonds. His mother would frown on such extravagance, but he wasn't in love with his mother. He hid the broach in his pocket and returned to retrieve his wife-to-be. At first glance, he barely recognized her. She was lovely before, but now, he could barely look elsewhere. He paid the clerk the remaining balance, thanked her for her help, picked up the package she'd wrapped in brown paper, and then took Josie by the hand, leading her to the door. Outside, they headed up the street to the village square to procure a covered carriage for transport to Sunset Ridge.

Later, all situated in the fancy contraption, they both let out loud sighs of relief and contentment. "Oh, Levi, I haven't even the words. I've never known such treatment." Josie removed her new bonnet and nuzzled his shoulder. "I love you."

He kissed the top of her head. "You look beautiful."

She leaned back and looked into his eyes. "Thank you."

"Oh, before I forget." He set her back from him, then reached into his pocket and pulled out the velvet box holding the broach. "I got you one more thing to go with that pretty new dress."

"Levi! You've already done far too much."

"Never."

Her eyes feasted on the box, and he savored her little shriek of delight when he slowly lifted the lid. "What—? Levi, it's beautiful, but—"

"Hush now, and listen to me." He turned his body toward her, and while her eyes had filled with tears, she kept them fastened on his every move. "I knew the moment I met you, even masquerading as Gordon Snipp, that you were someone special. I often said you reminded me of my little brother—not in looks but in actions. I think I perceived, even then, how perfectly you would fit into my family. The true blessing came when I discovered you were not Gordon at all, but Josephine Winters, a lovely woman to whom I could fully give my heart."

"I knew when I was Gordon Snipp that I loved you," she inserted with a smile.

He leaned over and kissed one cheek and then the other. Then, taking both her hands in his, he continued, "I love you, Josie, and I would like nothing more than to introduce you to my parents and siblings as my fiancée."

Now the tears were coursing down her cheeks. "Really, Levi?"

"I love you, honey. How would you feel about being a preacher's wife?"

"I can't think of a greater honor, my love."

To seal the deal, he drew her into the circle of his arms, bulky coats and all, and kissed her again, this time truly drinking in her closeness, her sweetness, her softness, and her utter purity. After a time, he fastened the broach over the top button of her dress, then sat back to admire it. She put her hand to the piece and stroked it reverently. "I will cherish it forever, Levi—almost as much as I shall cherish and love you."

As Levi had assured her, his family fawned over Josie's unexpected visit. His mother seemed a bit on the cautious side until Levi announced his plan to marry her. At that, she jumped to immediate attention, issuing orders that put him in mind of Grimms. "We must send a telegram to Lydia. Samuel, thee must ride into the city and take care of that. Milton, I wish for thee to round up thy sisters Frances and Rebecca and pass the word that I shall expect them and their families this evening for a celebratory supper. Tell them to arrive as early as possible, and that we have big news. Don't tell them what it is, though. I want them to arrive with hearts full of anticipation." To Chrystal, ten, she gave the order to polish the silver.

"What should I do?" asked Henry, twelve, obviously feeling left out as the only one left without a chore.

Mother furrowed her brow and cupped her chin as she thought for a moment. "Thee, my boy, will wash the windows."

"Oh." His shoulders slumped. "Didn't I just do that a couple of weeks ago?"

"Ah, but they must sparkle, my son."

"May I help in the kitchen?" Josie asked.

Mother tilted her face at Josie for a moment, then lit up. "A fine idea, young lady. We shall use this time to get acquainted."

Mother took her by the arm, and off they went toward the kitchen, Josie casting Levi one hurried backward glance.

"Go easy on her, Mother." Even as he said the words, though, he remembered how well Gordon Snipp had handled himself in the army. He had no doubt Josephine Winters could carry her own where Laura Albright was concerned.

～

Levi's family was by far the bounciest, liveliest, most energetic that Josie had ever met. They made a houseful, when counting all Levi's darling nieces and nephews, not to mention his siblings and the husbands of his older sisters, Rebecca and Frances. Everyone spoke in plain pronouns, with the exception of Rebecca's husband, who was a sheriff in a nearby town. Even Levi slipped back into the speech with ease, most likely to please his mother, and Josie almost wondered if she oughtn't to give it a try herself; but when she did, she used the wrong pronoun, and everyone laughed, Levi included. "Do not trouble thyself, dear," his mother told her. "'Tis only Quakers who speak it, and I must say my own children do it only in my presence."

"Amen to that," Samuel chimed in. "I can't speak it in the city when doing business at the markets because the men don't understand me."

"I'm a Friend, Ma," said Clay, the husband of Rebecca. "But, not having been raised in the Society, I still can't adjust to it. Thank goodness my wife accepts me, heathen that I am."

"Thee is no heathen," Rebecca said. "Unless thee hammers thy thumb instead of the nail, such as thee did a few days ago. Then thee turns into someone I do not know." That comment brought on a raucous round of laughter, and Josie began to relax.

She ought to be accustomed to the chaos, considering the time she'd spent living with Aunt Bessie's passel of kids, but this family was much more demonstrative, and they also had a better sense of humor. She found herself warming to the unique personality of each member, individually. Everyone, from the littlest on up, enjoyed life—something that surprised her, in light of her former impressions of the religion to which they held so tightly. For some reason, she'd gotten it in her head that Quakers were a stiff and staunch bunch. Not so the Albrights—well, unless she counted Mrs. Albright. Of all the family, she was the most rigid and ceremonial, but even *she* loosened up, particularly when her sons-in-law and Levi and the other boys bantered back and forth, bringing up memories and delighting Josie with all manner of stories.

At the end of the evening, it was determined that Josie would stay in the big house in one of the girls' old rooms, and Levi would go back to his own home a mile out. This would remain the case for the duration of her stay until mid-February. They had discussed it and decided that once Levi's furlough came to a close and he went back to the field, Josie would resume her volunteer work at Mansion House Hospital. They would not marry until after Levi completed his term, and she would return on occasional weekends in preparation for the wedding. After a round of hugs, well-wishes, and promises to return, she and Levi lingered together on the porch for a few moments, kissing and saying good night. When he rode away, she watched until he disappeared from sight, then went up to her room. She found Mrs. Albright fluffing her pillows and making sure the blankets were turned back.

"I don't wish to be a burden, ma'am—er, Mrs. Albright," she said quietly.

The plumpish woman turned, her stained apron still tied around her waist, and her prayer cap still neatly pinned, not a hair out of place. She issued Josie her first truly warm smile. "Come, child. Let's sit on thy bed and have a chat." She patted the space next to her.

Josie crossed the room and settled in beside Levi's mother.

"First, thee is no burden. Let us settle that matter once and for all. Second, thee has made my son exceedingly happy. I see it in his eyes. It is something I've never before witnessed, and so I thank thee for putting such joy in his heart. Third, I am convinced that thee will make him a lovely companion, a supportive partner, and, yes, even a fine preacher's wife." She folded her hands in her lap and studied them. "Thee probably has heard that, in the Society of Friends, we do not recognize official preachers. However, we also realize that we are not the only Christian assemblage, and so we do not frown upon denominations that see the need for such a role.

"Now, I'm certain that Levi has told thee what a cantankerous woman I can be, and how I am hopelessly set in my ways, but do not let his words entirely persuade thee." She cleared her throat and lay a warm hand atop Josie's, then lowered her voice to add, "Sometimes, I will admit to putting on an act because I know what wonderful results it fetches, but, shhh. That shall remain our secret, hm?"

Josie giggled, her heart full of instant love for her future mother-in-law.

Mrs. Albright sobered. "Levi has told me how you and your brother lost your own parents at a young age. How hard that must have been."

Josie nodded. "My aunt and uncle generously took us in, but they had a houseful of their own children, and while they made us as comfortable as they could, I don't think I ever quite thought of their residence as home. Something about this house, though—well, let me say I have felt most welcome here, and I wish to thank you, Mrs. Albright."

The woman gave her a light squeeze, which surprised her, for Levi had warned her that his mother, for all her boundless love, had never been one to show much affection. "Thee is more than welcome in this family, dear. And let us do away with this 'Mrs. Albright' business, shall we? Call me Laura for now. Once thee marries my son, thee may call me Mother, if thee chooses, or Ma, as my son-in-law refers to me, even though he knows how much I loathe it. He likes to get my goat."

They shared a laugh, and Josie's spirits jangled with joy. Oh, how far the Lord had brought her in these past five months. Who would have imagined that joining the Union Army to honor her brother's memory—disguised as a man, no less—would result in her meeting the one man she thought existed only in the loveliest of fairy tales?

Only God could write so perfect a love story.

EPILOGUE

September 1864 · Philadelphia

It was a warm and sunny September afternoon, perfect for the wedding of any woman's dreams. Levi had mustered out of the army on September 11, and exactly one week later, here they were, Levi Edward Albright and Josephine Alice Winters, standing side by side before the altar of the Philadelphia Methodist Church, ready to be married by Josie's pastor, Reverend Mark Tisdel. They were flanked on either side by their witnesses: Josie's best friend, her cousin Allison; and Levi's brother Samuel, nearest him in age. The congregation comprised the entire Albright family, select members of Company B, a few choice friends, and Aunt Bessie and all Josie's cousins.

Josie was a vision in the fitted white dress Aunt Bessie had made, an exact replica of a dress Josie had spied in a downtown Philadelphia department store window while the two women were shopping on one of Josie's weekend trips home to plan the wedding. Her aunt had assured her that she could duplicate the design for a mere fraction of the cost, and had proceeded to stand there in the hot sun and sketch the lovely creation down to its last detail: the long sleeves, lace overlay, scoop neckline accented with delicate beads, and the 18 satin buttons going down the back. They'd proceeded straight to a mercantile, where, armed with the record she'd already made of Josie's measurements, Aunt Bessie had told the clerk precisely what she required in terms of yards of silk and lace, spools of white thread, and dainty buttons.

The woman was a wonder. When Josie returned a few weeks later to be fitted, the gown needed not even an inch of tailoring. Josie had deemed it finer than the one they'd seen in the display window, and upon seeing her reflection in the mirror, she'd been brought to tears. Instinctively she'd hastened to hug her aunt. Much like Laura Albright, Aunt Bessie wasn't one for showing affection, but this time she had welcomed the embrace, even prolonging it.

Josie could hardly contain her excitement as she stood beside Levi, who looked handsomer than ever in his standard black suit and starched white shirt. She trembled so with nervous energy that the small bouquet of roses in her hands rustled gently, and Levi fumbled with a loose thread at the hem of his suit coat. All along, she had been more enthusiastic than he about the pomp and splendor of the ceremony, but now she was as eager as she knew he was to say "I do" and to get to the kiss that would make her fully his.

⌒

"Levi and Josephine, please face each other and hold hands," said Reverend Tisdel.

Levi jumped to life, his back going as straight as a pin. He turned to face his lovely bride and took her hands in his, wondering anew how it could be that one so beautiful could love someone as plain as he. Saints and stars, but she was something. Her hair had grown over the past months, and she wore it now in a wavy coiffure with some kind of flowery creation topping it, and a light, frothy veil covering her face. He longed to lift that veil and claim her mouth. *Patience, man, patience.*

"Levi Edward Albright, do you take Josephine Alice Winters to be your wedded wife, to live together in marriage? Do you promise to love her, comfort her, honor and keep her, for better, for worse; for richer, for poorer; in sickness and in health; and, forsaking all others, to be faithful only to her, for as long as you both shall live?"

Levi sucked in a chest full of air, slowly let it back out, and beamed at his bride. "I do," he said, for everyone to hear.

Reverend Tisdel led Josie in the same vow to Levi, which she concluded with an equally decisive "I do."

The next moments flew by, and before Levi knew it, the reverend was inviting him to kiss his bride.

"It would be my pleasure," he said, prompting a collective wistful sigh from the female members of the congregation. He'd long anticipated this moment, had even dreamed of it, and now that it was here, he meant to make it count. He carefully lifted the gauzy veil off her face, smiling all the while. Next, he took her soft cheeks in his large, rough hands, and tenderly raised her head, and for a living, breathing instant, all the pair did was stare into each other's eyes. Then, at last, he lowered his face until their lips met like a whisper, and they both quivered at the sweetness.

They savored the kiss for as long as was proper, at which point Levi ended it. Another gentle sigh rippled through the church, followed by a whistle that could only have come from one of the guys in Company B—Willie Speer, if Levi had to guess.

The reverend then instructed them to face the congregation, after which he introduced the new Mr. and Mrs. Levi Albright. Levi held tight to his bride's hand, and together they rushed down the center aisle to the sounds of happy applause and an energetic piano piece, their attendants following close behind.

Josie found it impossible to contain her joy. Not only did she have a husband, she'd also gained sisters, brothers, a new mother and father, and what seemed like a whole herd of nieces and nephews. Her cousins blended right in, and before she knew it, children of varying ages had formed a game of tag and were racing all around the churchyard, while many of the ladies, including Laura Albright and Aunt Bessie, carried food to the tables, and the men stood in huddles, talking and laughing.

Allison snuck up behind Josie and wrapped her in an embrace. "Are you happy, Josie?"

"Oh, my sweet cousin, you cannot imagine my joy."

Allison rolled her eyes dreamily and clasped her hands together. "If only I could hope to be so happy someday."

"All in good time, dear girl. You must never rush love. It will come when the time is right." They chatted for a bit until one of Allison's church friends caught her attention, and off she went.

"Welcome to our family, Josie," said Levi's sister Lydia, who'd arrived home from Boston two weeks ago. Josie had enjoyed getting to know her. She was a lovely young woman with glistening brown hair and snappy green eyes. The two embraced, and then Lydia held Josie at arm's length, assessing her with a warm, wide smile. "You are the perfect match for my big brother. I used to tell him he would never find a wife if all he ever did was stand behind a team of horses and drive a plow. 'Patience, Lyddie,' he would say. 'If God wants me to marry, he'll bring the perfect woman to me.' I thought he'd truly blown his chances when he joined the army. I guess I didn't think it possible he would marry a fellow soldier." Her gentle laughter rippled through the air. "Look at you, so pretty in your dress."

"Thank you, Lydia. You'll be a beautiful bride, as well."

Lydia flicked her wrist. "I'm trying Levi's tactic, waiting for God to bring a spouse to me, but so far, I've seen neither hide nor hair of him. Of course, Mother wants me to marry the first eligible Quaker who crosses my path." She lowered her voice to add, "Don't tell Mother, but I've been attending a community church in Boston." She held a finger to her lips. "Shh."

Josie smiled. "Your secret is safe with me."

"I've not backslidden, mind you, but Mother would think otherwise. On the contrary, my faith is as strong as ever. In fact, I've been thinking about joining a missionary organization."

"Really? You would leave your teaching job?"

"Not immediately. There is much to ponder and pray about. For now, I covet your prayers."

"Then you shall have them."

"Lydia!" called a friend from across the yard. Lydia leaned over and kissed Josie's cheek. "I love you already."

"And I you." Josie watched her sister-in-law dash across the yard, her plain dress flowing around her legs, her bonnet strings flapping in the breeze.

Levi joined her then, putting his arm around her and drawing her to his side. "I saw you and Lyddie talking. I'm glad you two have had a chance to get acquainted."

"I love her so. She's sweet and funny."

He nibbled her ear. "Like someone else I know." His playfulness distracted her.

"Mind if I kiss your bride?"

Both turned at the voice of Harv Patterson.

"As long as you make it quick," Levi chided. "She belongs to me."

"Sure, sure." Harv wrapped Josie in a bear hug, then kissed her cheek. "The guys and I decided you make a much more convincin' woman than man. Lots prettier, too."

Just then, they were surrounded by the rest of the fellows in attendance from Company B: Charlie Clute, Louie Walker, Willie Speer, and John Cridland. The group had a good, long chat, laughing and bantering back and forth. It pleased Josie that their comrades had made the effort to join them for their day of celebration. Others had wanted to come, but the battles continued in Virginia, and Grimms had been able to release only five men for the day.

After continuing her volunteer efforts at Mansion House Hospital, it was with deep regret that Josie had given Nurse Probst her notice and said her good-byes, with promises to pray for all the staff. While she'd been passionate about her efforts at the hospital, her heart now belonged to Levi, and just thinking about the places God would take them as a married couple filled her with such excitement, especially when she considered Levi's call to a preaching ministry. Thankfully, Dr. Edwards had transferred the pesky Dr. Baylor to another army hospital shortly after

Josie's engagement, and without a bit of fanfare. Josie had wanted to say "Good riddance," but her Christian witness had prohibited her.

Toward the latter part of the afternoon, after the meal had been served and the guests had started leaving, Reverend Tisdel approached the couple, giving Josie a fatherly hug and then shaking Levi's hand. "You couldn't have found a lovelier bride, young man. I've known this pretty girl since she was eleven, and, I must say, she's going to make you one fine preacher's wife."

"I won't disagree with you, sir."

"Speaking of your future profession, have you made any decisions as to a college or seminary?"

Josie and Levi had talked plenty about his call to the ministry and how they would continually seek God's guidance and leadership in the weeks and months to come. While waiting on Him, they would reside at Levi's house on Sunset Ridge, Levi working the farm during the day and studying God's Word by night, and both being committed to pray daily. Now Josie would focus her efforts on being a wife, a housekeeper, a gardener, and, somewhere down the road, a mother. For now, though, things hinged upon Levi's call to the ministry.

"I've not made any decisions yet, but I've been doing a bit of research into the best schools," Levi told the reverend.

"I see. Well, I have some good contacts at a number of reputable seminaries that are seeking bright young men such as yourself. I'll be happy to assist you with the application process when the time is right." His words were another affirmation that God's plans for them went beyond their imaginings.

"I truly appreciate that, sir. I'm certain I'll be calling on you."

⌒

At the end of the festivities, Levi assisted Josie into the backseat of their waiting carriage, their hearts brimming and their spirits and futures as bright as the plentiful sunshine overhead. They poked their heads out the open windows and waved at the crowd of friends and family who had gathered to see them off. Of course, there'd been hugs all around before they'd departed, so there wasn't an ounce of regret at having to say good-bye for now.

As the carriage pulled away, Levi sat back and gathered Josie against him, and they took a deep, collective breath.

"At last, it's just the two of us," he said, letting out a long sigh of contentment. "I shall love you forever, you know."

Josie smiled. "And I shall love you one day longer than that."

"Hm. One day longer than forever?"

"Indeed."

He kissed the top of her head, then rested his chin there and gazed out the window at the scenery they passed on their way to the same hotel where they'd spent the night on their first trip together to Philadelphia. This time, though, they would share a room, and he would see to it that she'd never want to leave it.

How good the Lord had been to them. "What are you thinking?" he asked.

"About all of our tomorrows," she said.

"Hm. And the blessings to be reaped."

"And the plans God has in store."

"Too many to count just now."

They closed their eyes and let the dreams begin.

Questions for Book Club Discussion

1. How did you experience the book as a whole? Did it catch your attention immediately, or did it take you awhile to "get into it"?

2. Did you find Josie's reasons for joining the Union army disguised as a male justifiable? Did you admire her or disapprove of her actions?

3. Did you have difficulty aligning Josie's Christian faith with her obvious deceit? Did God bless her despite her having to conceal her identity? Explain.

4. How did you feel about Levi's abandonment of his long-held pacifistic persuasions? Did it remind you of a time you perhaps cast off a long-held conviction about something that no longer held the same significance for you? Do you care to expound?

5. Did you view the story as a page-turner—or did it drag in places?

6. Did you consider the novel to be more plot- or character-driven? Or did you find it to have a good balance of both? Were the characters believable? What specific themes stood out to you?

7. How did you feel about the spiritual element? Did it make sense, feel contrived, or leave you questioning?

8. Did any specific passages strike you as insightful, inspirational, or even profound? That is, did you pause to consider them or perhaps even highlight them so that you could go back later for further reflection?

9. Did this story change or inspire you in any way? Did you learn something new about the Civil War that gave you a new perspective?

10. Did the story reach a satisfying conclusion? Is there anything you would have changed?

Do you have specific questions for the author? Feel free to check out her website at: www.sharlenemaclaren.com or send her an email at sharlenemaclaren@yahoo.com.

Look for Sharlene at Facebook, Twitter, and Instagram.

Request to join her Facebook "Sharlene MacLaren & Friends" group! You'll find her group at:
https://www.facebook.com/search/top/?q=sharlene%20maclaren%20%26%20friends!

About the Author

Born and raised in west Michigan, Sharlene attended Spring Arbor University. Upon graduating in 1971 with an education degree, she taught second grade for two years, then accepted an invitation to travel internationally with a singing ensemble for one year. In 1975, she came home, returned to her teaching job, and married her childhood sweetheart. Together, they raised two lovely daughters, both of whom are now happily married and enjoying families of their own. Retired in 2003 after thirty-one years of teaching, "Shar" loves to read, sing, travel, and spend time with her family—in particular, her adorable grandchildren!

A Christian for over fifty years, and a lover of the English language, Shar always enjoyed dabbling in writing. She remembers well the short stories she wrote in high school, and watching them circulate from girl to girl during government and civics classes. "Psst," someone would whisper from two rows over, always when the teacher's back was turned, "pass me the next page."

In the early 2000s, Shar felt God's call upon her heart to take her writing pleasures a step further, and in 2006, she signed a contract for her first faith-based novel, *Through Every Storm*, thereby launching her writing career. With more than sixteen published novels now gracing store shelves and being sold online, she daily gives God all the glory.

Shar has done numerous countrywide book signings and made several television appearances and radio interviews. She loves speaking for community organizations, libraries, church groups, and women's conferences. In her church, she is active in women's ministries, regularly facilitating Bible studies and other events. She and her husband, Cecil, live in Spring Lake, Michigan, with their beautiful white collie, Peyton, and their ragdoll cat, Blue.

Shar loves hearing from her readers. If you wish to contact her as a potential speaker for a church function or would simply like to chat with her, please feel free to send her an e-mail at sharlenemaclaren@ yahoo.com. She will do her best to answer in a timely manner. You may also find her on Facebook!